GW00382739

Finding
Arthur

by John McClintock

Published in 2018 by Shanway Press,
15 Crumlin Road, Belfast BT14 6AA

Cover design: DavidLee Badger

ISBN: 978-1-910044-18-6

With thanks to Stan,
who gave me the push;
And to Vince,
who provided
an almighty shove.

ONE

On what might have been the last day of his life Arthur Williams awoke with an erection. This was not an unusual occurrence. Indeed, the mornings when he awoke in a flaccid state were few and far between. Ignorant of the evidence that suggests a full bladder stimulating erectile function, he blamed his dreams.

He kept his eyes closed, listening to his wife's breathing beside him in the swelling stillness of the room. The soft, warm memory of the dream was still upon him, intense with longing and fulfilled acceptance. Desperately he tried to cling to it, to wriggle back into its cocoon; but it fragmented with his growing wakefulness and soon it was gone. Reluctantly he opened his eyes.

A chink of lamplight from the street cracked the ceiling. His nostrils filled with the dusty upholstery smell of the carpet and the thick velvet curtains. A sudden itch tickled his nose and he smothered an urge to sneeze. Linda stirred, moaned a little and turned on her side, away from him. As he watched the outline of her body settling under the quilt, he felt his heart rate increase as if propelled by the sound of the early morning train to Belfast chugging out of the station, gathering momentum, finally hurtling into the distance.

The delicious warmth of his dream was a fast retreating memory, slipping into the blank void of the past. But he recalled what she had said, whispered to him, just before he woke. 'If you sow the seeds of loneliness, you will reap only sorrow.' Jeez, heavy stuff. Food for thought. It was no more than a dream, but where did they come from, those words spoken in the shadowland of the subconscious? And yes, at times he did feel utterly alone, a solitaire in the landscape of what had become his life.

Was it of his own making? Had he always been a loner? A loner? Who said he was a loner, apart from Linda? And if he was a loner, was it by choice or was it some form of social ineptitude? Was it normal to feel generally awkward and uncomfortable with other people, people he didn't know, new people who always seemed to be sizing him up, plumbing his depths (shallow, shallow), ruthlessly assessing his negligible likeability? He was often irritated with himself in unfamiliar social situations, with his feeling of vulnerability, with how he receded and drew into himself like a snail.

It was never like that when he was working, meeting people he was to interview, knowing he had to make them feel comfortable, at ease with him, willing to open up and talk. Knowing what he needed to find out, confident he had his questions prepared, feeling secure because he had his 'script'. Yes, he knew who he was in his work, secure in his professional role. But who was he privately, in his emotional life, lying there naked with his innermost thoughts, a sentient soul feeling his way, searching for closeness, groping in the dark after his human identity? Besieged by these questions, he shivered in the coolness of the room. It was lighter now. The day was coming to meet him.

As the light filtered in through the curtains he looked around the bedroom, from the inherited mahogany wardrobe to the velvet-curtained window, and he remembered coming to the house that first time, getting off the train from Belfast and tramping up the hill in an airy April shower, a buzz of expectancy whirring in his head as he searched for the estate agent's sign. In his mind's eye he could still see the house as it was then, five years ago.

It had come into view gradually as they came round a bend in the road, and he had stopped to look up at it: an old red-brick house built before the war, rising among the trees at the end of Carnalea Road, wreathed in a garden of enveloping shrubbery, the grey tiled roof flanked by gables and gutters in a mouldy shade of green, the window sills flaked in the same mossy colour under window frames that had once been white. It was a house that spoke of nooks and crannies, of empty rooms breathing dust-speckled light, of spaces to be filled and a life to be lived in their welcoming stillness. The house exuded a warm, ataractic feeling that drew him relentlessly to it. And the thought had struck him, an impulsive romantic whimsy:

'This will be our home.'

Arthur curled up under the duvet, closed his eyes and felt himself drift inexorably into the slumber of remembrance, the images of the past sweeping through his mind like black-white negatives on a smoothly moving reel of film, the dialogue a copy-edited manuscript of his life so far.

* * *

Linda had been less than enthusiastic. "That old place? Are you serious? For pity's sake, Arthur, it looks really run down."

He had watched her face as the plucked eyebrows ricocheted with the horror of it all. She sniffed dismissively and pulled up the collar of her mid-length Burberry trench coat. They stood out on the road in sudden silence, looking up at the house as a fine drizzle gently showered them.

Arthur had taken a deep breath and launched a refulgent smile of self-encouragement: "Let's have a look inside first. The place has got character. All it needs is a fresh coat of paint."

But Linda merely snorted and turned away. Arthur followed her back down the road to the station, the April rain sprinkling his face, alternately disconsolate and intent.

Sitting upright in the train on the way back to Belfast she told him what she really wanted, what anyone in their right mind would want if they had the choice: one of those neo-Georgian redbrick residences they were knocking up in Helen's Bay.

'Neo-Georgian egg boxes,' Arthur had muttered. But Linda, Arthur knew, once she had got an idea in her head, was not easily deflected. And she was not averse to employing the aid of special weapons and tactics. In this case, as in so many before, her SWAT force was the redoubtable Moira.

Willowy and dark, Moira differed sharply in appearance and character from the petite persona of Linda, short and fair. But their contrasting aspect belied a uniformity of purpose. Both – it seemed to Arthur – appeared to believe that all men belong to a cloned breed of animal with one throbbing and overriding need that can best be tended – intermittently and circumspectly – by the calculated attentions of an inherently superior species: women. When Linda first broached the subject of a future domicile, as if it were something of no real consequence, a matter of merely passing interest, Moira had erupted into paroxysms of volcanic enthusiasm. As Arthur expressed it later, she had practically wet herself trying to convince him.

"You should see them, Arthur," she breathed, the words bubbling from brightly varnished lips. "They're really classy, with a beautiful façade – and they have these lovely mullioned windows." Her eyes stared at him, bright with conviction, confrontational, challenging him to differ.

"Is that Georgian?" Arthur wondered.

"What?" The look Moira shot him was blatantly hostile. "What?" she repeated. Lamenting his architectural nitpicking, Arthur took a deep breath.

"Well, I thought mullioned windows belonged more to the Gothic style."

Moira twitched her pert little nose as if he had just farted. Then she smiled and shrugged, her small breasts almost popping out of a loosely buttoned, sleeveless blouse that would have fit a five-year-old.

"Gothic, Georgian, what does it matter? They look fantastic."

Her mouth pouted in awe. Arthur noticed with interest how the magenta lipstick crackled on her collagen-bloated lips, like solidified lava from the magma of that rosebud mouth.

"Arthur, we have to go take a look," Linda said, her face crinkling into the kittenish smile that was concomitant with making her husband an offer he could not refuse.

"We? You mean …"

The smile on Linda's face froze, vainly masking the impatience she always felt when he failed to follow the obvious progression of her thoughts.

"Yes, well, Moira's already been there. And she knows the builders."

"They're absolutely gorgeous," Moira purred.

Unsure if she was referring to the builders – she did seem to get around – or the houses, Arthur had agreed to drive them to Helen's Bay and see for himself. Sometimes he felt like a pet rabbit cornered by a pair of playful pussy cats.

The reality of the 'luxuriously appointed neo-Georgian modern residence' was even worse than he could have imagined. A clingy, composite odour of sawdust and fresh paint hung in every room. He had walked around rapping his knuckles on thin chipboard walls you could put your fist through. And the thought had struck him, there and then, that if he was talked into living here with Linda in her neo-Georgian egg-box, he would probably end up doing just that. They went into a kitchen that was so blindingly white he regretted leaving his sunglasses in the car. He almost bumped into the kitchen island, translucently bright in the glare of a battery of ceilinged spotlights.

"You could have your appendix out on that," Arthur said when he'd blinked his eyes into focus.

Moira smiled at him. "Yes," she said, "it's so perfectly clinical, isn't it?"

Perfectly clinical? What did she mean? Clinical? Arthur tried to think of something else to say, something sensible and culinary, but he'd run out of inspiration. Kitchen conversation, he realised, was not his forte. He walked round and made a cursory examination of the kitchen units. His considered opinion was that they had been mounted by a fitter in the latter stages of Parkinson's, but he kept it to himself. And when they beheld the 'Georgian shower cubicle' in the bathroom, he gazed in disbelief at the tiled flooring that sloped *away* from the drain. Despite his better judgement he could not help but point this out, but to Linda and Moira these were simply trivial drawbacks, inadvertent constructional slips to be rectified later.

Sighing at her husband's inability to perceive the domiciliary aesthetic, Linda held out her hands palms up and switched on her feline grin.

"Arthur, you have to see the big picture."

Jesus, she thinks she's in Hollywood, Arthur thought, not for the first time. His wife's view of their life as some sort of celluloid soap opera was a recurring feature of their marriage and he was becoming increasingly unsure as to his role in it.

"Everyone wants to move here," Moira chipped in,

nodding her head energetically. Arthur watched her bouffant hairstyle bobbing up and down, a rudderless yacht adrift in choppy waters. With typical generosity he assumed that her brain was still aboard, though at times he suspected it was somewhere far below deck.

"Everyone," she repeated, fixing him with her challenging, power-drill stare.

The pair of them had ganged up on him, working in tandem like a couple of used-car salesmen, intent on wearing him down, using every trick in the book. Arthur knew that book, knew it so well. 'The book of female wiles,' he called it. What was it his father used to say? 'A woman's guile far surpasses the wisdom of man.' God, there was so much truth in that. He had not really known Linda when he married her. He had not understood who she was – who she really was. You fall in love with a vision, he thought, an apparition, an ethereal being. You are overwhelmed by passion, desire, euphoria – and you succumb, you surrender, you are lost in a self-induced romantic fantasia. Reality comes later. He looked again at the badly aligned floor with its raised drain. Reality is now, he thought.

They wandered back to the kitchen, the women continuing their chorused squeals of adulation. Arthur stared blindly up at the spotlamped ceiling. Like a flashlit photograph in his head he pictured them again as he had seen them for the first time, that mid-winter night years ago at the Orpheus Ballroom in Belfast. He had gone there with his best friend, dancehall dynamo Thomas Cyril Bennett, commonly known – for reasons best known to girls he had gone out with – as Bendy.

Bendy was running a small garage out at Quarry Corner on the edge of the city, selling petrol, doing servicing and carrying out general repairs. In those days, before the onslaught of digitalisation, there was still a need for a petrol station like that. Bendy was widely known in west Belfast for his magic ways with the internal combustion engine and a weakness for souped-up cars. Cars he almost effortlessly souped up himself.

Arthur had known him since primary school, where they shared a common interest in toilet humour and local football. When Arthur had taken his NCTJ diploma in journalism, Bendy had completed his apprenticeship as a motor mechanic at Baird's, one of Belfast's biggest dealerships. Baird's Garage had wanted to keep him on, but Bendy was determined to be his own man. And being his own man had eventually landed him with a two-pump filling station and a sizeable mortgage out at Quarry Corner.

En route to the Orpheus they had first sought the warmth of Lavery's in Bradbury Place, an inviting haven from the permeating damp of the December night. As usual the much favoured drinks emporium with its traditional Victorian-style bar was populated with a bevy of seasoned customers as well as a scattering of glassy-eyed students, all of them smoking, drinking and talking in rapid succession. Arthur and Bendy weaved their way warily through the nicotine mist to the bar.

Boosted by a couple of insulating pints of Treble X and an exchange of snide remarks about the other patrons, they had then driven down Dublin Road, along Bedford Street, round Donegall Square and past St Anne's Cathedral in search of temporary accommodation for Bendy's beloved wheels. Finally they located a parking space in the darkness of a nearby back street. Bendy edged the beat-up Cortina into the gap and switched off. They were parked under a lamp that flickered ominously at two-second intervals. There was no one about. Bleak and grey, the terrace houses lined up in parallel proximity before them, a desolate brick-walled gully in the urban landscape. They sat in silence for a minute listening to the metallic ticking of the engine as it cooled.

"Jesus, Artie," Bendy said at last, looking around him, "this is a dodgy area."

"Yeah," Arthur told him. "You better go back to the cathedral and pray your car will still be here when we get back."

Bendy fired him an aggrieved look. "Thank you, Mr Negative Thinker. Why don't you do something positive for a change – like paying your share of the bloody petrol? And another thing, you'll never get into the Orpheus with that crappy military jacket. Who the hell do you think you are – John Lennon?"

They walked at a steady pace through deserted back streets towards the Orpheus, their breath billowing like smoke signals before them, feathery cirrus wisps vanishing into the night. The December gloom lay like a wet tarpaulin over the city, shrouding the endless rows of terrace houses ingrained with industrial soot. In the sharp breeze flitting spasmodically down the street Arthur caught the grainy smell of urban smut. Hands clutched tight in thin polyester trousers, they hurried on their way, sidestepping the rime frost that edged the pavement.

Passing an entry they glimpsed some figures in the murk swigging from a bottle, ashen shapes moving in some back-street bacchanalian rite. One of them shouted an obscenity, another a coarse guttural threat. They walked faster. Things happened in these quarters. There was mindless brutality. People disappeared. Were never found. Swallowed in the shadows of the night. It could happen to anyone.

Finally they trotted into the muted lighting of York Street. It was another world. York Street formed an extension to Royal Avenue, Belfast's main shopping street, but as Royal Avenue stretched north into the more industrial surroundings of York Street, the avenue's commercial glare dimmed and diffused into a grimier, more besmirched atmosphere in which the stately Orpheus building stood apart. Strolling along York Street Arthur suddenly felt a sense of estrangement, a feeling that he was visiting a place where he could never feel fully at home. But Bendy seemed to adjust readily to the changing surroundings, his humour mounting as they neared their destination. Outside the Orpheus he expressed the opinion that practically all the women there would be student nurses with uncontrollable nymphomaniac tendencies.

"You always say that," Arthur told him. He looked up at the Orpheus, an Art Deco building with a red-brick façade and a grey-stone centrepiece rising to the arched window on the fourth floor where the ballroom lay. Sometimes he thought he should have studied architecture. Buildings, bricks and mortar – they were solid, tangible things you could easily relate to and know exactly where you stood. He had always been interested in construction, in planning the layout of imaginary buildings, creating a network of rooms with functional and aesthetic meaning. How the hell had he ended up in a newspaper office? Words, syntax and semantics – they were so indefinite, ephemeral, insecure. How to express what you mean clearly, succinctly, unforgettably. What do I really mean? Arthur often wondered. Do my words delineate the exact contours of what I want to say, of what I truly mean? What indeed, he sometimes asked despairingly, was the meaning of meaning?

The bouncer eyed Arthur's indigo blue jacket with its imitation brass buttons and his eyebrows shot up.

"Who d'ye think ye are? Ringo Starr?"

Bendy sniggered. Arthur flashed the bouncer a wide-screen version of his conciliatory beige smile.

"My suit's at the cleaner's," he said.

The bouncer deliberated for a moment, then rolled his eyes. "Aw, g'on in."

Climbing to the fourth floor, Arthur took in the more exuberant Art Deco decoration inside the building: the central stairwell with its wainscot wood-panelling and stained glass, and the ballroom with its stucco plasterwork and floral motifs on the curved white ceiling. While all the time Bendy's eyes were admiring other, more mundane attractions.

"It's packed out. Must be a nurses' convention on," Bendy chirped, gleaming his maniacal Jack Nicholson grin from The Shining.

They carved their way through the crowd, cleaving a smoggy discharge of burnt tobacco, cheap perfume and glandular perspiration. The hall was packed with the usual crowd, a cross-section of alcohol-fuelled humanity.

"Time to join the cattle market," Bendy growled.

They had scouted the dance floor for no more than two minutes when Arthur spotted them on the far side of the hall. It seemed that they had spotted him at the same time. He saw them looking over, noticing him and Bendy, pretending not to with exaggerated nonchalance. They were two lookers, he thought, but let's not get carried away here. Plenty of fish in the sea. Arthur was never one to jump in at the deep end. You might end up with a shark. Never one for waiting around, Bendy lit a cigarette with practised indifference and scanned the field.

"I'll take the wee blonde," he said exhaling vigorously.

When the band struck up for the next set of numbers, he marched over, his shoulders swinging slightly to the beat of "His Latest Flame." Arthur stood watching him, wondering if he should follow in his slipstream, wishing he possessed some small measure of Thomas Cyril Bennett's bravado with the female gender.

The six-piece Miami showband was playing mostly up-tempo numbers, but Arthur felt self-conscious – even with drink taken – waving his arms and legs about like an epileptic traffic cop. He waited for a slow number before walking over as casually as he could to the tall dark woman standing on her own, her body-language pose signalling an unattainable female divinity. She blinked when he asked her, eyelashes fluttering like a butterfly about to take flight. Promenading around in what he imagined was a foxtrot, Arthur was pleasurably shocked by the proximity and thrust of Moira's thighs.

"She's givin' you the green lights," Bendy had confirmed when the dance was over.

"Dunno about that," Arthur said, "but she's got these funny eyes. They sortof sparkle when she speaks."

"Your eyes would be sparklin' too," Bendy told him, "if you'd put away as many gin and tonics as she has."

Arthur had been flattered and tempted by the idea, until he realised it was the other one he really fancied, the petite honey blonde overfilling a low-cut maxi dress. So he asked her up next, and it had not taken long to discover she was just as keen as her sparkling-eyed friend. 'Life is a game of chance,' Arthur thought. 'The chances you take and the chances you don't.'

Three months later Linda said she was pregnant and they got married. At the time Arthur was utterly convinced he was doing the right thing. Bendy tried to talk him out of it: "Artie, yer head's so far up yer arse you can't see straight." But regardless of the position of his cranium Arthur had stars in his eyes, which equally distorted his vision, and he went ahead. It was a source of no little amusement to Bendy when the pregnancy turned out to be a false alarm, something he never let Arthur forget.

The onslaught had continued in the car on the way back from Helen's Bay. Didn't Arthur, who was such a music lover, know that Van Morrison was also buying a house there? Van the Man, whom Arthur had known briefly before Van hit the big time.

"I thought he was buying a house in Crawfordsburn," Arthur said. And to distract them, he told the ladies how, in a magnanimous moment many years ago, he had lent his amplifiers to Van the Man.

"Amplifiers?" Linda queried. "What did you have amplifiers for?"

"I was in a group myself for a wee while, played at tennis club dances a few times, that sorta thing."

"You were in a group? Doing what?" Linda's eyes widened with the shock of this revelation.

"I was the singer."

"Singer? You don't even sing in the shower. You never told me about that, about when you were Dickie Rock. Was it classified information or something?"

"It was no big deal. I only did it a couple of times. The group broke up. We were pretty crap."

"I didn't know you knew Van Morrison," Moira said, mouth pouting and eyes dilating. Arthur glanced at her in the driving mirror and shuddered.

"It was really my brother who knew him first. It was before Van got his contract with Decca and moved to London."

"Was that when he was in Them?" Moira wondered.

"Yeah. But before Them he was in another group called The Monarchs and they had just come back from some gig in Germany. He said something about playing in a beer cellar in Heidelberg. It was all very hazy. Well, Van wasn't exactly a mine of information at the best of times."

No, he certainly wasn't, Arthur recalled. Van had needed a couple of amps, Arthur had lent them to him and Van had failed to return them. So Arthur had gone to his house in east Belfast to ask about it. For a while Van had listened to him in grumpy silence, a despondent spaniel with magically upright ears. It was obvious that he had absolutely no idea where the amps were or what had happened to them. Arthur was about to appeal to his sense of decency and fair play, to broach the question of compensation, when Van suddenly pulled a much crinkled £5 note from his trouser pocket and held it out.

"But they cost £10 each," Arthur had protested.

To which Van had responded with a single polysyllabic word that took Arthur completely by surprise and ended all discussion.

"Depreciation," he said.

"Depreciation?" Linda smirked. "Didn't think he'd even know the word,"

"Oh he was sharp enough just then, though God knows he's been ripped off loads of times by the sharks in the music business ever since – which probably goes a long way to explaining his happy disposition," Arthur told them. "Anyway, the amps were gone and that was the last time I spoke to him."

"Well, who knows, Art?" Moira said. "You might become neighbours when you move to Helen's Bay."

'Yeah,' Arthur thought. 'In your dreams.'

There was no way he was going to let them stampede him into buying one of those pretentious chipboard boxes in Helen's Bay. He had set his heart on the house on Carnalea Road and he would not be moved. Not on this. No way. When they got back to the flat, he rang Martin's Property Sales in Main Street, Bangor, and set the ball rolling. Looking back, he realised it was the first and probably the last time he had got his own way in their marriage.

* * *

The estate agent had turned out to be someone Arthur had known at school. In his first year at grammar school Arthur recalled seeing him smoking behind the cycle sheds with the other pimple-faced hoodlums. Undersized Georgie Porgie was the only second-year boy still wearing short trousers and that was how Arthur remembered him: his knees the same chalky white pallor as his face. With feelings of guilt and self-reproach, overgrown Arthur also recalled making fun of the "pasty-faced little pigmy." Now he prayed that George had no memory of his pigmy status.

George Martin had not gone on to university. With mediocre grades in almost all subjects at school, tramping the academic cloisters was clearly not the path he would follow. However, thanks to a highly successful career behind the bicycle sheds, marketing all brands of cigarettes – from Willie Woodbines to Black Russians – he had decided the highways and by-ways of business held greater appeal. George obviously had a knack for selling things. Then it was cigarettes. Now it was property. He glided up the Carnalea Road in a dark green Jaguar coupé. The car stopped beside them and the driver's door swung open.

"What a lovely car," Linda told him.

"Company car," George said, as if that explained its loveliness. He heaved himself out of the driving seat and onto the road. They exchanged introductions. It was decades since Arthur had last seen him. The pale, skinny runt from the bicycle sheds was gone.

Appreciably taller than Linda and slightly shorter than Arthur, George Martin had thickened comfortably into early middle age. He wore a dark pinstripe three-piece suit, the jacket open to reveal a dangling gold chain leading, presumably, to a pocket watch of similar ore. Thus professionally attired, he smiled at them with correspondingly professional ease, his face evenly featured and recently tanned. For a moment Arthur was tempted to inquire if his knees were equally bronzed.

"Just back from Thailand," he had told Arthur on the phone. 'Jesus,' Arthur thought, 'He's certainly landed on his feet. I should have followed his lead, left school after O-levels and gone into real estate.' Writing up the news at the Belfast Telegraph was hardly a lucrative way to earn a living.

"Arthur, there's no money in journalism," Linda always said. "The only payoff is seeing your name in print. And you soon get tired of that." As usual she was right.

"It's a lovely colour," Linda told George Martin.

"British racing green," George said, and his neatly chiselled features angled into another smile. "Toys for boys," he added with a dismissive wave of the hand.

Arthur noticed how his left eye blinked when he smiled as if he was winking at the same time, creating intimacy, letting you in on a secret that only you and he shared. Probably an artifice he had learned on some high-powered sales course, Arthur surmised, a sure-fire way to establish rapport with the customer.

George Martin looked up at the somewhat begrimed, pre-war, red-brick house rising from the shrubbery in front of them and ran a hand up past prematurely greying temples and through his thick raven hair. "Shall we?"

And he flashed his winky smile again as he waved them towards the front door.

"Oh yes, let's," said Linda, smoothing down her tight mid-length skirt as she noted that there was no wedding ring on his hand. The two men followed her, both inevitably noting the pendulous undulation of her buttocks as she cat-walked up the path.

Thirty-five minutes later they had looked through the house from top to bottom. There was much to see, much that hadn't changed in decades. The kitchen was a disaster area, beyond salvage. Even Arthur understood that.

"This would have to go," Linda told him, nodding her head solemnly as if she had just donned a black cap.

"We'll get a new one," Arthur said, overjoyed that she

was even considering it, then apprehensive when he thought of the extra expense. Jesus, you could almost buy a whole house for what a new kitchen cost nowadays. But the rooms were airy, a good size, and he sensed the homely, lived-in character of the place. As they approached the aged walnut staircase, Arthur ogled the elegantly carved balusters and felt his spirits soar. He could almost see Scarlett O'Hara swishing down the red-carpeted stairs to greet them.

Once upstairs, George Martin directed them deftly into the master bedroom. "What a pleasant, peaceful room," Linda remarked after a brief survey.

"Hasn't always been peaceful," George observed. "The old lady told me she's had five children."

They wandered appreciatively round the other bedrooms and the bathroom with its rust-stained washbasin and pink pedestal toilet. Then George urged them out onto the landing and pointed to a trapdoor in the ceiling. As if divulging a state secret, he informed them that there was a view, a minimal glimpse no less, of the sea from the attic window. A wooden pull-down ladder led up to a fair-sized room with a skylight on either side of the pitched roof. Boxes bulging with indiscriminate memorabilia lay scattered around the walls. Floor dust swirled in the air as they ascended into the attic.

Linda, last up the ladder to Arthur's husbandly relief, trawled the attic with minesweeping eyes. She swung round suddenly.

"Arthur, you could convert this and have your music room here."

This possibility had been Arthur's immediate thought as soon as he saw it. His music was the classic crooners: Frank Sinatra, Tony Bennett, Al Martino, Bing Crosby; and he had long hankered after a separate room as a refuge to listen to them in peaceful isolation.

Linda had certainly warmed to the house since meeting George Martin. Arthur noticed with a sigh how she arched her back to accentuate the full curvature of her breasts as she stood peering out of the skylight. It struck him with sudden melancholy that the last time she had done that for his benefit had probably been on a December night in the Orpheus ballroom.

"I can see Belfast Lough from here," Linda crooned on tiptoe from the skylight.

George Martin stood to the side admiring the outline of the powder-blue Gant sweater Arthur had bought her for her birthday.

"Yes," he agreed, "you get a great view up here."

* * *

With George Martin's entry into the property stakes, Linda became considerably more interested in the house on Carnalea Road. A doctor, a paediatric oncologist, lived further down the road; and the next-door neighbour was a Belfast solicitor. These now became significant factors for Linda in choosing a place to live. Arthur had difficulty in suppressing his delight that his wife was as keen on the move as he was.

The next morning he found himself humming and singing some irritatingly catchy hit-parade jingle on his way to work: 'I saw the sign, and it opened up my eyes.' But another family had also seen the sign, the house-for-sale sign, and wanted to buy the house. Wanted it as badly as Arthur, it appeared. Or so George Martin informed him a week later on the telephone. And when Arthur stifled a gulp and said he would pay the asking price, Martin told him the other family had also agreed to pay it.

"So we'll have to increase our offer and bid against them?" Arthur said.

There was a pause at the other end of the line before George Martin spoke again. "Well, yes, in the normal run of things that would be the case."

"And then they will up their offer…"

"Yes, if they still want it."

"Well, of course they want it. If they've agreed to pay the asking price, they obviously want it. They're sure to raise their offer, which means the price will escalate and we'll end up being gazumped and…"

A harsh rattling noise on the line cut Arthur short. He wondered briefly whether George Martin was vomiting or being strangled by a dissatisfied client. Eventually he spluttered to a stop.

"Sorry, Arthur, I can't seem to shake off this bloody cough. It's a high-risk profession this. You meet loads of people all the time and some of them just don't have the sense to stay in bed with their germs."

"Yeah, I know what you mean." Arthur slowed down and lowered his voice to indicate empathy. "It's the same here, George. I take plenty of C-vitamin myself, but now Linda's caught some bug. Don't know where she's picked it up."

"Well, actually it's mostly my own fault this time."

Martin seemed momentarily unsure about how to expand on this before he continued:

"I got a call last week from a widow who wanted to sell her bungalow and that wasn't all she was selling, if you get my drift…"

Arthur rolled his eyes and shifted uncomfortably in his chair. Dear God, the man saw himself as the Lothario of the property market.

"Yes, I follow you, George."

"It's all part of the service, that's what I tell myself. But it can be a slippery slope. You know, there was …"

"But what about the house, George? What do we do

about that? I can't stretch much further than the asking price and that's the truth of it."

Arthur removed the receiver from his ear as it erupted with another sputum-rumbling crescendo.

"Sorry, Arthur," Martin wheezed at last. "I'll have to stop smoking. Don't feel much like them anyway with this cold, but it's a hard habit to break. You know, some surveys say that nicotine is as addictive as heroin."

Arthur bit his lip and breathed deeply through his nose. "I know, George, I know."

"Not to mention the cost of it. Anyway, where were we?"

"The house, and how to stop the price from rocketing if we have to start bidding against another buyer. I mean, I just can't go much higher. And now Linda's set her heart on it as well. She's just about furnished and decorated every bloody room."

"Ah, Linda, she's a lovely girl. You landed on your feet there, Arthur."

He makes it sound as if I took a running jump into the marriage, Arthur thought. A second later he realised that was exactly what he had done.

"Yes, well, I just mean she'll be very disappointed if we don't get this house."

"I know. She told me so."

"She told you? You've spoken to her?"

George delivered a somewhat more subdued cough. "Well, I bumped into her in town the other day."

"She hasn't said anything."

"I think she was out shopping. Anyway I met her just outside my office and she told me how keen she was on the house. Had a few questions and wanted to see the drawings again."

George Martin sounded a little out of breath. He said, "She can be very persuasive, your wife."

"I know, I know," Arthur agreed.

He felt uneasy, unsure of the path the conversation was taking, wondering if George meant something more than he was saying and apprehensive as to what that might be. Linda had a way of getting what she wanted. Arthur felt himself holding his breath. There was a tight pause before George spoke again.

"Listen, Arthur, do you think you could add another thousand pounds to your offer?"

"A thousand? Just a thousand?"

"Yeah, I think so." George cleared his throat with a gurgling growl. "A thousand should do the trick."

"But the other family can easily top that, and then the whole thing will snowball and…"

"Slow down there, Arthur, slow down." George Martin seemed to have got his breath back. "I can fix this so that your bid will be the final one and the one that is accepted. It's the seller who decides who buys the house, and the old lady has the utmost faith in me. So if I advise her to accept your offer of the asking price plus a thousand, I think she'll go along with that. Just leave it to me, Arthur."

"But what about the other family? What if they find out and offer even more?" Arthur heard a wheezy sigh before Martin said, "Don't worry, Arthur, I'll fix it. Can you stretch to another thousand?"

"Well, yes, of course, if that's what it takes."

"No problem. It's a reasonable price for the property, especially when you consider that it's going to need a fair bit of work done on it. And old houses, for all their charm, can sometimes provide a few not-so-pleasant surprises."

"I know, George, I know. But I've got a good feeling about this one."

"Feelings are fine, Arthur, but you need to use your head too."

George's voice was hoarse and dry. It deepened as he launched into professional mode.

"I think it would be a good idea to get a surveyor in. I know a fellow who'll do a good job. He's really thorough, lots of experience and knows exactly what to look for."

Arthur hesitated. What if the surveyor discovered serious structural faults, or rising damp, or dry rot? What if he checked the level of radon and found it was so high you could catch lung cancer within a month? What if…? Arthur realised he was being an ostrich. Why was he such a gloom-ridden pessimist? After all, realistically, what could possibly prevent him from buying the house on Carnalea Road?

As if reading his thoughts, George Martin said: "I'm sure there's nothing seriously wrong with the place, Arthur, but you need to know the facts."

Arthur deliberated for a moment before making up his mind. "The truth will set you free, I suppose."

"Yes, something like that. It's a wise precaution. I know a proper survey isn't cheap – but it's money well spent."

Arthur came to a decision. It did seem like the sensible thing to do. "All right, George. Will you set it up?"

* * *

A week later Arthur was sitting at his desk when the telephone rang. He broke off reading what he had written, testing the syntactic flow, sounding it out in his head, and cleared his throat. Looking round the square, functional contours of the Telegraph's head office he was reminded yet again of how little he liked its boxy, modern character: all movable screens, fluorescent lighting and modular furniture. He sniffed wearily. The resinous smell of computer plastic was battling gamely with his cheese and onion sandwiches in the open landscape of the room. Pushing the floral-lidded Tupperware box to the side he lifted the receiver and said what he always said:

"Belfast Telegraph, Arthur Williams."

The line hummed a short static melody before he heard the voice, muffled yet coldly metallic.

"Arthur Williams?"

"Yes."

"You been writin' about the bombin' in Newry?"

Arthur drew the receiver down over his ear and pressed it closer. "That's right. Who am I speaking to?"

"Never mind about that. You still lookin' into the Newry bombin'?"

"Yes. Yes, of course."

"Well, I have some information that's worth a lot of money."

Arthur expelled a sigh of sad resignation. How many of these calls had he received already? And how many were truly genuine, from people who actually knew something, people who really cared? Zero.

"How can the murder of 23 innocent people be worth a lot of money?"

There was an indistinct scuffling sound before the man answered. "You're offering a reward for information, aren't you?"

Arthur sighed again. "You have information?"

"The information I have makes it clear who was responsible."

The man paused. Arthur could hear his breath rasping in urgent tempo, abrupt and staccato, as if he had been running. "It makes it very clear."

"What sort of information?"

"I've seen things and heard things."

"What sort of things?"

"Things that will tie certain people to what happened."

There was a perceptible hesitancy, a tension in the man's voice that sharpened Arthur's attention.

"What people are we talking about?"

The line droned in nervous silence. Afraid that the caller was about to ring off, Arthur was quick to add: "We're offering a lot of money for just a few names."

The reply came instantaneously.

"I'm not sayin' any names over the phone."

Arthur took a deep breath. "If you've come this far, you can come a bit further." He pushed the phone tight to his head. The man's gravelly breathing seemed to scratch at Arthur's ear. He withdrew the receiver a trifle to ease the pressure.

"Not on the phone."

He said something more about money but the line crackled statically and Arthur could not make it out.

"Sorry couldn't hear you. What was that?"

The crackling receded and there was a moment's pause before he spoke again, strangely hoarse and tense.

"We have to settle the money first."

Arthur fiddled with a ballpoint pen as he pondered how to play it, how to coax the bird out of his cage, how to get him to sing.

"Listen," he said, "I have to know this is on the level before we can discuss money, that you're not just some crank. Suppose I mention some names," he continued, gritting his teeth with concentration, "and suppose they are definitely *not* people that you can tie to the Newry bombing, would you be willing to tell me that now, on the phone?"

For several seconds there was more electrical interference on the line. Arthur scrabbled about in the top drawer of his desk, extracting the list of names he had accumulated from his sources. The man's voice echoed again in his ear, hesitant and tinny.

"You're going to say some names and if they've nothing to do with the bombing, then I say so."

"Exactly," Arthur said reassuringly. "That way, you

won't be fingering anyone, you won't be mentioning anybody's name at all."

There was a short pause and then the man said, "OK."

Arthur breathed out. "All right, what if I say Hugh Maguire?"

At first there was no response. Then, "No, not him."

"How about Peter Cassidy?"

"No."

Arthur worked his way through the list, eliciting solely negative responses until there were only four names left.

"Michael McCann?"

The phone continued to hum. Arthur considered repeating it but held himself in check, counting slowly to five before scrawling a ring round the name. He read out the next name on the list.

"John Cooney?"

The metallic voice was silent. He waited again before ringing it in. He was about to read out the penultimate name when there was a click on the line.

"Are you still there?"

"That's it. I can't speak any more now."

All at once the man sounded extra fidgety and nervous. Arthur jotted down question marks beside the two remaining names.

"We have to meet," he said.

The man coughed briefly and swallowed. "I'll be in touch." There was a sharp intake of breath and the line went dead.

Arthur sat staring first at the telephone, then at the floral decoration on the lid of his lunch box. Except that he saw for the first time that it wasn't flowers at all. It was a collection of bright red tomatoes laid out in front of a large round yellow cheese with a sprig of parsley on top. But food was far from his mind. He jumped up, circled the screens, swerved past some large potted plants and trotted in to see Alf McCurran, as always envious of the fact that he worked in an actual room blessed with a door.

As Arthur told him about the phone call, McCurran lit his pipe and his editorial eyes narrowed into mere slits flanking the bridge of a slightly bulbous nose, which always reminded Arthur of a blue-veined cheese. When Arthur had finished McCurran sat in silence for a moment, looking up at him from behind a burn-scarred desk, his face expectant, as if wishing to hear more.

"Well, what do you think, Alf?"

McCurran pushed his chair back and stumbled to his feet. He walked over to stand face to face with Arthur. He was a tall man in his fifties with a tweedy check waistcoat restraining his stomach like shutters veiling a bay window. His long, greying, curly hair hung like a mop trimmed by a short-sighted barber.

"Well, it could be nothing at all, Artie. And then again it could be something big – could be a breakthrough."

Arthur folded his arms, eyes bright with hope.

"I know, but there's not much I can do now except wait for him to ring again."

McCurran gave him a long look. His clear-blue eyes seemed to cloud over, an intimation of approaching rain on the journalistic horizon.

"You be careful. It could be dangerous."

Arthur raised a shoulder and an arm in a one-sided shrug.

"Well, if McCann and Murphy are involved, I'm bloody sure it will be."

McCurran squeezed his features into an expression of imminent grief. He might have been about to burst into tears. "Then we have to think about the RUC and when to involve them."

"Hold on there, Alf." Arthur could not help raising his voice. "First we get our story."

"Yes, yes of course."

McCurran's face creased briefly into a reassuring smile. He became serious again.

"What sort of accent did he have?"

Arthur pondered for a moment. "Hard to say. Don't think it was Belfast. More country. Armagh maybe. But I'm not sure. He was disguising it. And he'd done something with the mouthpiece."

McCurran looked thoughtful. He rubbed the lobe of an ear as if he himself could somehow imagine the tones of the voice on the phone, as if in some magical way he might be able to identify the countrified accent. Then he sniffed in defeat.

"Well, just watch your step, Artie. And keep me posted, OK?"

"Right."

Arthur was on his way back to his desk, navigating the low-screened, compartmentalised landscape of the office, when he heard the phone ring again. He dashed over and grabbed it. Looking round, he realised everyone in the open-plan prairie of the newsroom was watching him.

"Belfast Telegraph, Arthur Williams."

"Hello Arthur, it's George. George Martin."

"George?"

The smooth, unctuous tones of his voice came as a surprise. Arthur attempted to keep the bewilderment out of his voice. He had been in one world; now he was in another. The feeling of disorientation unnerved him for a moment.

"I didn't know you had this number."

"Got it from Linda." The reply came like glucose syrup. "She's here right now."

Arthur felt a sudden tightness in his chest. His mouth was dry, his tongue a sheet of sandpaper. He coughed and cleared his throat. "She's there? Where?"

"At the office. She called by to see how things were

going. And I have to tell you, Arthur, they're going pretty well."

George Martin's voice oozed even more self-satisfaction than usual. "In fact," he continued, "the old lady has just agreed to sell."

"What? Mrs Walker? She's agreed?"

"Yes, just five minutes ago."

Arthur sat down at his desk and breathed out. All at once his cheese and onion sandwiches looked almost good enough to eat. For something to do, to help him digest the news, he slid the box towards him, staring at the crimson tomatoes on the lid.

"You're sure, absolutely certain. What about the other family?"

George chuckled. "She just wants to sell to you, Arthur. It's all arranged."

"I can hardly believe it."

First the Newry bombing and now this. From horror to happiness in five minutes. Arthur felt the knot of anxiety in his stomach loosen and unwind. The incredible had happened. George Martin, he whispered to himself, the smarmy bugger's pulled it off.

George chuckled again. "Listen, Arthur, I'll draw up the papers and we can all meet here tomorrow morning and settle the whole thing."

"That's terrific. And she's agreed to the price? No problem?"

"No problem, Arthur." George seemed to have shaken off that cold he'd had. His voice had an unmistakably upward lilt, an almost jubilant tone that imparted his commanding role, his total control. He might have been announcing a win on the National Lottery.

"I had a chat with her and she wants you and Linda to have it."

"That's just great, George." Arthur couldn't stop himself

from expelling a heartfelt sigh of relief. He reached over and gripped his lunch box tightly with his free hand in exultation. It had a steadying effect.

"All part of the service. I'll put Linda on now. She wants to have a word."

* * *

Three months later Arthur and Linda Williams moved into the house on the Carnalea Road. George Martin put them in touch with a contact at the Ulster Bank, a short, thickset man with horn-rimmed glasses who closely resembled a barn owl, a man who arranged a favourable loan with a minimum of conversation and a maximum of paperwork. Arthur worried about the renovation work, in particular the installation of a new kitchen, but George knew of a building firm that came highly recommended. Although demanding and troublesome at times, they lived in the house while the work was carried out.

* * *

A weak sliver of light splintered the curtains. Arthur yawned, raised his head and looked round the bedroom. He swivelled his head towards the bedside table. He could just make out the time on the old Sony Digimatic clock radio that Linda had insisted on buying from some strange guy she knew who had owned a shop in the Smithfield Market in Belfast. Twenty past seven.

Linda sighed and rolled onto her back. The radio would come on in ten minutes. Arthur sensed himself becoming rigid, his whole body tautening with apprehension. He felt himself preparing for the charade he had come to play, the game of make-believe that once had been a joyous enactment of reality, a mutual conjoining they shared before the passion he felt increasingly gave way to panic. In his mind the seconds began to tick away like rainwater dripping from a leaky gutter. He heard a honeyed voice singing in the back of his head, Elvis urging him on: 'It's now or never, Come hold me tight.' He began to breathe faster, his heart thumping. It was so loud, she must hear it. 'Tomorrow will be too late.' He turned on his side towards her. He reached out with his right arm under the quilt. His hand brushed across her stomach. He cupped her breast. She didn't move. He tightened his grip ever so slightly and felt the nipple harden in the middle of his palm.

"Oh for God's sake, Arthur, I just want to sleep."

And turned on her side away from him, taking most of the quilt with her. Arthur rolled back over to his side of the bed. Suddenly and inevitably he felt like a stranger in his own bedroom: he wanted to be somewhere else. It was as if he wasn't himself any more, he didn't know who he was, and the man he was pretending to be wasn't a particularly nice person.

Lying on his back as the morning seeped into the room, he thought of something Bendy had once said to him after a singularly unproductive night out: "Rejection, Artie, is the hell we all fear."

"Jeez, that's deep," Arthur had said, gazing into the creamy swirl of his Guinness. Bendy grunted.

"Yeah, I read it in a book."

They had sat in contemplative silence for several minutes before Bendy spoke again. "Artie, it's been so long since I last had it, the next one better have a set of instructions pinned to her knickers."

Arthur smiled to himself. The art of conversation was not dead. Abruptly the droning monotone of the Radio Ulster newsreader interrupted these deliberations.

"... and the condition of the wounded soldier is said to

be satisfactory. Following a telephoned warning, a 635-pound car bomb was defused last night outside the courthouse in Newry. It is believed the Real IRA was responsible …"

Christ, he was fed up listening to this stuff. The Micks and the Prods – the one tribe as bad as the other, ambivalent and treacherous, with only hatred and vengeance in their hearts. And Newry again. Always Newry. Was there no end to it? He heard Linda sigh as he stretched over to stab the off-switch. Briefly he wondered if there was something he should say to ease the tension, a playful platitude to help them both relax, to kick off another day in the perplexing game of marriage with all its complicated rules; but he was offside, he had strayed out of position once again and his mind was a blank. All at once Linda tumbled off the side of the bed and pattered out of the room. Arthur listened to her closing and locking the bathroom door. He lay still for another minute before getting up.

* * *

The bacon was sizzling in the pan as he sat down to the dish of cereal and skimmed milk before him. He drew the skin off a bruised banana and sliced it surgically into the dish with his table knife. The salty pork smell of the rashers frizzling in their fat always made him feel good. There was something indefinably reassuring about it, sparking memories of family breakfasts in his childhood, telling him he was safe in the warmth of his home and that all was well with the world. He smiled to himself as he poured a little more milk in the dish. The much-discussed Swedish-style kitchen they had installed was reassuringly bright and cheerful, a major investment but not one he had regretted.

Until Linda turned from the induction cooker and stared at him. He watched her face tighten with that Armageddon look he knew so well.

"What?" he said. "What is it?"

Linda's eyes darted piranha-like round the room. Arthur saw that she had already eaten. Her grease-mopped plate lay across from him on the table, the egg-yolk already congealed in a vaguely circular pattern. She nodded her head slightly and sighed.

"We'll have to do something about this kitchen," she said, as if uttering the final rites, a sacramental expression of extreme unction.

Arthur simply could not believe it. He dug his spoon fiercely into the sodden bales of Shredded Wheat. The kitchen fittings were no more than four years old: the table, cupboard doors and shelves in blond Swedish pine, the flaxen wickerwork chairs only so slightly sunken from everyday use, the induction cooker, fridge, freezer and Miele dishwasher all still gleaming pristine white.

Swinging the breadknife like a Samurai sword, Linda cracked open an egg and upended it to sizzle in the pan. Arthur took a deep breath, sucking the premonition of doom down deep into his stomach.

"The kitchen?" he said at last, his chair creaking uneasily as he sank deeper into it. "What's wrong with it?"

A south-facing room at the back of the house, the kitchen was normally a bright, well-lit place; but on this drab December morning the light sifting in from an overcast sky hung grey-grained and wan in the room. A single bulb flared within a glazed pillbox of cut glass, the central light fixture in the ceiling. Arthur looked up at it in what he already knew was a hopeless quest for enlightenment.

"What's wrong with it?" Linda echoed.

The fretting features of her face combined in a look of sheer incredulity. "Arthur, you simply don't have a kitchen like this nowadays."

She made it sound like the eleventh commandment: Thou shalt not covet this kitchen.

"Nobody has a kitchen like this anymore," she elaborated, placing special emphasis on the first word, dark shadows clouding her eyes.

But I want to be nobody, Arthur thought, anticipating the coming storm. Why can't I be nobody?

"Linda, I thought this Scandinavian style was all you ever wanted."

He held his hands out imploringly, fingers stretching in desperate appeal.

"This was the Dream Kitchen," he reminded her, "the one you'd always wanted."

"Arthur," Linda summoned all her reserves of patience, "this was a popular kitchen ten years ago. But look at it now. It's hopelessly outdated."

With furrowed brow she glared at him, her face a wrinkled road map pointing unswervingly in one direction. Then, perceiving the lack of compliance in his face, she added: "Everyone says so."

"Everyone?" Arthur queried tight-lipped. "Everyone being Moira, I suppose."

Linda's manicured eyebrows rose in long-suffering forbearance. "Moira's just being honest. That's what best friends are for." She paused to take a breath. "You have to admit the layout is ancient. The dishwasher's in the wrong place for a start. You have to carry the dishes miles to put them in the cupboard. And nowadays you have to have an island."

When he stared at her in total incomprehension she hurried to explain, to strengthen his grasp of culinary terminology: "A kitchen island."

The added attributive seemed to shed no light. Arthur looked at her blankly.

"A kitchen what?"

Linda grabbed the frying pan and a spatula, swept the eggs, tomato and bacon onto his plate and took a deep breath.

"A kitchen island. It's a unit you have in the middle of the kitchen to give you more workspace. They have them in all sizes and designs. You prepare the food on them."

Arthur looked down at his plate. The egg was broken, the bacon was burnt and the tomato had burst. He looked up again, his caterpillar eyebrows wriggling in a vertical shift.

"But if we had an extra unit in the centre of this kitchen, we'd have nowhere to sit."

Linda closed her eyes briefly before clarifying the obvious.

"Arthur, the right sort of kitchen island can also function as a dining table for the whole family. It makes the kitchen a more social place where the whole family can gather."

Ah, that's something she's read in a glossy brochure, Arthur thought. Word for word.

"And you should see some of the cupboard designs they have today," Linda continued. "They have whole shelves that just fold in and out when you open and close the door. It's so practical and you save masses of space."

"You save space," Arthur suggested, "I spend money."

"We save space – and money too. It's very reasonable, Arthur. They've got tremendous offers. The market's very competitive and they're all cutting prices."

Arthur attacked the food on his plate. He searched his mind frantically for the right argument, a parrying word or phrase to deflect her, anything to knock her off course. But in his heart he knew he would not succeed. She had it all mapped out already; the route was predetermined and he did not even have a compass. As usual, when Linda's mind was resolutely set to move in one direction and he attempted to move in another, he ended up in a cul de sac.

She was standing over him now, her pop-up bra straining the buttons of her blouse, the spatula still raised in her hand. For a moment Arthur thought she was actually going to beat him into submission.

"Art, we do need a new kitchen."

Art. He shuddered at the word. She always used it when she was about to deliver the coup de grâce. Somehow he sensed she would deal him one final blow, an act of marital euthanasia to put him out of his misery: the misery of not understanding what she wanted, what she needed, what she had to have. He felt his head sag forward towards the greasy plate. With any luck she might go for his neck and behead him with the spatula. Put an end to it all. Dear God, it would almost feel like a release.

But wait a minute, hold on, all was not lost. There was still one line of defence left, well-tried in the past, and he used it.

"Linda," he asserted bravely, "we simply can't afford it."

He assembled the features of his poor-as-a-church-mouse face as he said it, leaning back, screwing up his eyes and tilting his head weakly to the side. But Linda ignored this posture of abject destitution. She turned to jab the spatula into the dishwasher and when she whirled round again, she had a smile on her face that made Arthur wary with fear.

"Don't give me that, Arthur. I know your mother left you everything."

"Then you also know we have to wait for probate now that the original will has finally been found. And if Doug fights the will, which I'm bloody sure he will, then we could be waiting for years."

But, as Arthur knew in his heart, that wasn't the real problem. In this case it wasn't brother Doug at all. The real problem was that Linda couldn't wait. Couldn't wait for anything. Had to have it now. Even now was too late. She wanted everything five minutes ago. And sure enough, Linda had another proposal to hurry things along.

"Okay Arthur, but we don't really need to wait. We could easily sell this kitchen and put the money towards a new one," she told him.

"What? Sell this kitchen?"

"Yes. What's so strange about that?"

Arthur saw his chance, and he took it. "But if this kitchen is so unfashionable, decrepit and outdated, how are we going to sell it? Who on earth would want to buy it?"

Yet even as he posed the question he saw from the ill-controlled smirk on her face that Linda already had the answer.

"I'll sell it." she declared. "No problem. There are hundreds of families looking for a kitchen like this."

'Yes,' he thought, 'you'll sell it all right, you're good at that. But you'll sell it at a giveaway price, the way you sold the lounge sofa and the sideboard, just to get rid of them.'

"Hundreds of families looking for a grotty, old, has-been kitchen like this?" he rallied.

Linda took a step towards him, swept her plate off the table and turned to jam it in the dishwasher. She swung round to face him again, her forehead a decorative frieze of utter conviction.

"Arthur, believe me, it won't be a problem. Glenda Stevens down the road just loves our kitchen and they're talking about getting a new one. And Ian's a plumber so he's got all the contacts and can easily install it."

Despite himself, Arthur felt his jaw drop. "You mean they might buy this one?"

"There's a strong possibility, yes."

The truth finally hit him and he groaned.

"You've already talked to them about it."

His wife's eyes widened and her eyebrows shot up as if he had just jogged her memory.

"Well, yes, I did air the idea with Glenda a couple of days ago."

"Yeah, and she won't have any trouble convincing Ian."

Linda's features morphed into a portrait of cherubic innocence. "I'm not sure she's even mentioned it."

Arthur mopped up the last of the egg yolk with a piece of wheaten bread. So now it was the kitchen. With Linda it was always something. Six months ago it had been the bathroom. A new bathroom had been the sole item of conversation for a month. Every morning, every evening, every weekend. He had suffered a narrow escape there, finally fobbing her off with a new "ocean blue" moulded-wood toilet seat and cabinet unit instead of the complete bathroom suite she had originally craved. It was a triumph he was not likely to repeat. All at once the realisation dawned on him.

Holy Jesus, had he totally forgotten how her mind worked, her genial ability to pursue her goal with relentless energy, her inherent talent for condensing a five-year plan into a five-day accomplishment?

"Linda, you've already chosen this new kitchen, haven't you?"

She stopped wiping off the draining board and smiled at him conspiratorially. Sometimes he understood her so well.

"Well, as a matter of fact, there is one I rather fancy." She reached over to the bookrack on the wall beside the table and, like a magician pulling a rabbit out of a hat, whipped a magazine off the shelf. It was already open at the relevant page. She placed it carefully on the table before him.

"Look here, Art. They've got this fantastic offer. You get all the wall units free plus a dishwasher at half-price."

Arthur cast his eyes over the glossy kitchen interiors spread across the double page. There was something unreal about the pictures, the units and appliances sparkling with consumer avidity. The women in them had never worked in a kitchen in their lives. Some of them were so thin they might have come out of the food processor. He suppressed a sigh and decided to go with the flow.

"Which is the one you fancy?"

Linda beamed him a measured smile. "This one here – Taunton cognac oak. Look, read here: 'Even the leaded glass units are free.'"

Arthur released an uncomfortable cough. "Linda, nothing here is free. They just dangle that at you like a carrot. Then they increase the price of the base units to cover themselves, that's all."

"But it says here you save over £1,000. Now that can't be a lie, can it? I mean, there's a law against making dishonest claims, isn't there?"

Arthur's brow assumed the contours of a well-ploughed field. The light in his eyes revealed intimate knowledge of the wily ways of a wicked world. His lips crouched briefly in bitter preparation before taking a run at the truth.

"Yes, but it doesn't say how much everything costs to begin with. They can just add a thousand to the original price and then tell you that's the normal selling price. It's incredible how people will grab at things when they think they're getting something for nothing."

"Oh come on, Arthur, you're so cynical."

"No, not cynical, Linda," he retorted. "Realistic."

Linda glared at him and placed her hands on her hips. "Well, I rang them up yesterday and they were very nice. And they're sending a proper catalogue and a price list, so you can see for yourself. And then they'll come out and have a look at our kitchen, you know, take measurements and so on."

"Dear God in heaven, I might have known."

"Arthur, nothing is decided yet."

"Really? Well, you could have fooled me."

"Oh I knew you'd be like this."

All of a sudden Linda's eyes blazed black and blue anger. With grim foreboding Arthur watched her clench her fists.

"You're against anything I ever want to do."

She emitted a high-pitched squeal of anger and frustration and stomped out of the kitchen. Arthur heard her in the hall, calling up the stairs to Max, telling him to get up. There was a grunted reply and then silence.

Arthur stared out of the kitchen window. Tears of condensation trickled, raced, burst down the refracting lens of the glass. He sat absolutely still, as if searching for some far distant place, gazing out past the crumpled privet hedge over the bare, disjointed limbs of the neighbour's apple trees to a point of focus, perhaps a haven, not just on the horizon, but somewhere further away, a possible refuge just beyond his field of vision.

Linda walked back into the kitchen and shot him a look of open irritation. Abruptly he drained his teacup with a short, indrawn slurp.

"Christ, look at the time. I've got to run."

Scraping the chair backwards with the underside of his thighs, he rose to his feet. For a lanky man three inches over six feet, the procedure resembled an aerial ladder gradually unfolding itself. Linda snatched up his teacup and dumped it in the dishwasher.

"Will you just be at your desk today – no outside jobs?" she snapped.

"Yeah, I'll be in the office. Few loose ends to tie up. And Alf's lumbered me with tomorrow's editorial."

"He's always doing that. Every Friday, regular as clockwork."

"I know, I know. So I may be a bit late. I sure as hell don't want to have to go in again tomorrow."

"Arthur, sometimes I think you live in there."

"Linda, sometimes *I* think I live in there."

Out in the hall Arthur eased his trench coat off the hanger. He had bought it on impulse during an extended lunch break in the city centre. He thought it gave him the cool but clever look of one of those TV detectives. Was it Lieutenant Colombo? Somewhat slow and rumpled in appearance, but intellectually miles ahead of the opposition. Linda watched as he put it on. The sleeves were a trifle short and one of the shoulder straps was hanging loose. Linda sighed as she buttoned it up.

"Have you still got that old scarf?" she said as he tucked it inside the collar. She had tried on a number of occasions – periodic attempts to rationalise his wardrobe – to persuade him to give the bedraggled woollen scarf to Oxfam, the Red Cross, to anyone who would have it, but he refused to part with it. He did not give things up easily, she thought. With things and people, he was a man who liked to hold on. It was a quality she did not always appreciate.

"Where's Max?" he asked, glancing up the stairs. "Is he not up yet?"

"He's got a late start on Fridays, Arthur, remember?"

"Late start?"

"Yes, he has a free period every Friday morning."

"Free period? Sounds more like a holiday camp than a school."

"It's good for him to be able to sleep in," Linda said in her modulated voice of reason. "He's only fifteen. Some experts think that teenagers need more sleep than adults and that it helps them to excel in school."

"Don't wake him till lunchtime then."

The potential humour of this remark seemed to escape

her. "Oh come on, Arthur. His last report was pretty good."

"Pretty average, you mean. He's capable of much more. If he didn't spend half the night surfing the Net…"

"You're exaggerating. He's a teenager. They all do it."

"Well, that's a perfect justification. Anyway, tell him I'll see him tonight."

"It's Friday. He'll be going out."

"Well, I'll try to get back before he leaves. Now I've really got to go."

As he turned towards the front door, Arthur caught sight of his reflection in the hall-stand mirror, his image momentarily frozen in the dust-hazed glass, a constant source of vanity and doubt. It was him, yes it was certainly him, and yet he was also gazing at a total stranger, a man in a beige gabardine trench coat and fluffy woollen scarf, his forehead furrowed with the same question he asked himself every morning at this juncture: Is this my life, this 9-to-5 existence, this mechanical write-the-Saturday-editorial chore, this buy-a-new-kitchen suburban charade?

Linda dutifully proffered her cheek as he bent forward, but he tilted his head and kissed her full on the mouth.

"Ugh, you haven't brushed your teeth," she said.

"Haven't got time."

"That's disgusting."

"Oh for God's sake."

He grabbed the umbrella, opened the front door and stepped out. A sudden light breeze gusted the waxy green smell of wet privet leaves into his face. Linda followed him onto the porch. The early morning mist was lifting. Beyond the tattered branches of the elm trees murky cloud swells drifted across the sky. A dank stillness hung in the air. Linda shivered.

"Ring me if you're going to be late."

"Yeah, right. See you this evening."

"Bye."

He tramped down the gravel path to the gate, turned and half-lifted a gloveless hand to wave, but she had already gone. He slammed the garden gate and set off for the station.

* * *

Linda stood at the living-room window, watching her husband as his head and shoulders undulated along the glossy green oblong of the privet hedge and disappeared from view. She turned, tripped quickly back into the hall and lifted the phone. For a second she hesitated. Then she dialled the number.

He answered almost immediately.

"It's all right," she said, her voice low and husky. "He's gone now."

TWO

Arthur stood poised on the damp kerbstones, waiting for a break in the traffic before crossing the Crawfordsburn Road. The mist had lifted, but the sky was still overcast, ridged with long ranges of blue-grey cloud. The stream of vehicles towards Belfast flowed in a never-ending torrent, exhaust fumes purling in their pungent wake. Arthur sniffed fearfully and took a series of short, swift breaths in the mistaken belief that it would reduce the amount of carbon monoxide he inhaled. Unwitting passers-by might view him with alarm, afraid that he was suffering cardiac arrest.

Arthur had decided to take the train from Carnalea Station. He could just as easily have gone to Bangor West – the two stations were equidistant from his home – but he preferred the downhill walk to the coast and Carnalea, and it would give him a few extra minutes as the train from Bangor stopped first at Bangor West. It also took him off the busy main road, away from the exhaust fumes and past the little newsagent's shop where he sometimes bought the Guardian for more detailed coverage of the national news.

Teetering there on the kerb, he came to think of himself as a boy in short trousers lying in a crumpled heap on another roadside, his bicycle spread out beneath him, the handlebars askew, the front wheel bent, spinning disjointedly. At the back of his head he could still hear the Gorman brothers laughing at him as they cycled off, leaving him to pick the grit out of his bloodied knee and peer through his tears at the skin-torn heel of the hand he had instinctively jabbed down to break his fall.

Arthur sighed as he recalled what had happened next: his brother meeting him the next day outside school, with that hard, stony look in his eyes, walking home with him and rounding the corner near the Methodist church, to meet the Gormans cycling towards them as if they were simply out for a Sunday spin, as if yesterday's attack had never taken place, as if it was an ordinary day just like any other. And as they drew level, he saw again how Doug had sidestepped to the kerb and punch-kicked the bike nearest him causing Brian Gorman to swerve out of control into his brother's bike outside him so that the two of them crashed steel and flesh into the asphalt grindstone of the road.

Doug had that streak of violence in him, that conviction that his pain derived from other people and that they deserved to be punished, to be made to suffer: they had it coming to them. Arthur had stood there, looking askance, waiting for him to go in for the kill. But this time he had not moved, had held back, watching them pick themselves up, leering at them, wishing they would make something more of it. Humiliated, backing off down the street, they had screamed obscene threats of foul brutality and bloody revenge; but the truth was nothing ever came of it, nothing happened and they had never bothered Arthur again. Ever.

And as he thought of his brother he felt the same sick, gnawing ache in his stomach over what had happened between them. The whole thing made him think of one of those bloody soap operas Linda watched on television – so mundane, so predictable, so utterly pathetic. He had seen it coming, like a train thundering towards him in a tunnel, and still he had done nothing to avoid it. He had just stood there in its track, irresolute and helpless. God, he had wanted to honour his promise, his gut feeling told him he should, but Linda had kept on at him, never letting up: "You don't owe him anything. He's got plenty already. He doesn't deserve it and you do. He'd never do the same for you."

Further down the road he saw the gap in the traffic he

had been waiting for. Glancing both ways and then, just to be certain, once more, he launched himself off the kerb and out into the road. He half-glimpsed a woman just behind him, scurrying across after him, raincoat flapping like a chicken's wings.

Having gained the refuge of the far pavement he proceeded more leisurely for some hundred yards before turning right onto Station Road. Now he could almost see the lough down below and the coastal path where he had taken his mother on her last outing just two months before. Loping down Station Road, that final day came back to him, the sea lapping with short, ruffled waves in the morning sun as they looked across the lough to the blackened chimney of Kilroot power station, rising like some dark sentinel on the far shore. And he remembered how the autumn breeze had lifted her wispy grey hair as she drew the blanket tight around her in the wheelchair, how she had reached over and taken his hand, her fingers dry and twisted with the years.

Above their heads the gulls soared in the endless sky, gliding, diving, crying warning. And the passenger ferry drifting out to sea, full of people, bearing lives moving forward, into the future; while she sat still, alone with him, eyes yellowed with age, seeing only yesterday. He could almost hear again how she had laughed in fond remembrance at some distant memory, and he recalled thinking, knowing there wasn't long to go: 'We still have this day, these seconds of tactile contact, these hours of final closeness.' Arthur had looked at her then, suddenly glimpsing the young woman again, the mother of his childhood, and she had smiled at him, smiled at life, smiled at their last moments together in time.

Her death, her non-existence was the absolute hardest thing to comprehend. The incontrovertible fact that he would never see her again, never watch that crinkly smile ripple across her face, never have her reach out to hold his hand in comfort. To his amazement he felt quite shocked by the knowledge that the physical reality of her being was gone for ever, that they would never meet again.

Yes, he missed her. Missed her most as she once had been. But God knows she had not always been easy, not in the last years, not with her mindless drinking and her uncontrolled animosity towards Linda. Doug had no idea of the hell she had put him through, her drunken outbursts in company, her virulent dislike of anything Linda said or did, her destructive rage when he dared challenge her about her drinking.

Linda was right. He deserved the money. All of it. Sure, he had always been his mother's favourite. Behind his back she spat venom at their father, derided his meanness, mocked his rigid principles, despised his inability to show affection, not to speak of love. And in the next breath she would say that Doug was just like him.

Arthur had felt sorry for Doug: it wasn't Doug's fault the way he was. But then it wasn't Arthur's fault either. It would never have turned out this way if his father were still alive, if he hadn't suffered that massive brain haemorrhage. Christ, who could have foreseen that, the way he looked after himself? Moderation in all things, he would say, and you'll live to a ripe old age. Well, he got that wrong. And everything going to the tearless widow. And now to him.

He had earned that money, done more for her than Doug had ever done, mopped up her fetid vomit and cleaned up the mess of shattered crockery when Doug was away on his endless business trips to the back end of beyond. It was weird, the sense of timing his brother had: he was simply never around when things happened, the countless times she had stumbled insensible to the brink and toppled over the edge. Like the time she smashed the frosted glass door in the hall in a frenzy and he had to rush her to hospital with the bloodied shards sticking out of her arm and her hysterics and the endless, despairing, repentant tears. Where were you then, Doug?

Why in God's name had he ever promised him that share of the money when she wanted to give it all to him? He's got plenty already, Linda always said, more than enough: 'Christ, Arthur, he's loaded.' To be sure it's not what their father would have wanted. 'Give Doug his rightful share, Arthur,' that's what he would have said in his fire-and-brimstone tones. But who was to say what was right and what was wrong? Doug had no money worries. Doug with his commercial drive and his sharp business brain. "He could buy you and sell you, Arthur," Linda said. "And never bat an eyelid." She had never liked him. "He's a cold fish, Arthur. Chip off the old block. Another fucking go-getter." God, it had turned into one bloody mess. Worst of all, he knew Doug would never forgive him.

Station Road sloped all the way downhill to the railway line and, beyond it, to the coastal path and Belfast Lough. As he marched along Arthur glanced idly at the detached chalet bungalows with their smug residential presentation – regimented lawns, manicured borders, pleated curtains and drapes – and he thanked God that he had not chosen one of them five years ago. Prim and proper they certainly were, but they lacked character, distinction, a soul. There was a bland antiseptic aura about them that made Arthur think of living in a health centre or a dental surgery. Live your commuter life here and have your domestic well-being gradually expunged, piece by piece, day by day until you became just another suburban robot.

Every time he passed by he was reminded of his good fortune in acquiring the house on the Carnalea Road. What a piece of good luck it was that he had known George Martin from school, that he had hit it off with him. Though when he thought about it, it was really Linda who had done that, wasn't it?

She'd certainly changed her mind about the house when George Martin had turned up as the estate agent. George had said she could be very persuasive but Arthur had an uneasy feeling that it was George who could be the more convincing in certain situations. But he dismissed these thoughts from his mind half-way down the road as he turned into the Mini-Market to buy the Guardian. "Arthur, you're just a closet socialist," Linda had sniped the last time he brought the paper home.

"That's a foul mornin'."

True to form, Billy Simpson, the newsagent, greeted him with a succinct meteorological observation. A short, dumpy man in his late forties with grey-streaked black hair, he had a powdery, soft-pastry face baked round a punch-flattened nose. Having exhausted the weather as a topic, he would often extol his former career as an up-and-coming welterweight. Yes, he had been good, no one denied that, just not good enough to reach the top. When he saw him, Arthur invariably thought of Oliver Hardy, minus the bowler hat.

"Deadly," Arthur responded mechanically and reached for the newspaper on the counter before him. It was the last one; he only stocked half a dozen. Magazines, bags of nuts, potato crisps, boxes of chocolates, cigarettes, snacks, stationery and greeting cards were all arrayed in an amorphous collection of shelves, racks and stalls around the shop. The sugared scent of long-stored milk chocolate fought a losing battle with the disinfectant Billy used to mop the concrete floor.

"Supposed to brighten up this afternoon," Billy continued.

Sweet Jesus, Arthur thought, next thing you know he'll roll down a weather map from the wall, grab a pointer and give you the regional forecast. Arthur paid for the paper, turned, ambled towards the doorway, looking down at the headlines, and collided with a woman on her way into the shop.

"Oh sorry."

"That's all right."

The woman responded without smiling. Not yet middle-aged, she was wrapped in a crumpled beige raincoat – not unlike Arthur's – with rust stains around the collar and a blue headscarf over wiry dark hair that seemed to be cropped short. Arthur had started to walk on when she said:

"'Scuse me, maybe you could help me."

"Help you?"

"Yes. I have to meet a fellah at the station and I'm new in the area. Could you tell me how to git there?"

She spoke in the broad meandering tones of the Belfast dialect, stretching the vowel sounds to breaking point so that they ended up almost as diphthongs.

"It couldn't be easier," Arthur said. "It's just straight down to the bottom of the road. There's a bend at the bottom and you... But I'm going there myself so I can show you, if you like."

The young woman looked at him keenly, as if making her mind up about something. Under a corrugated brow her eyes became watery and flustered, as if struggling to pinpoint a new target in her field of vision. She glanced down at Arthur's umbrella.

"I'm drivin'," she explained. "Maybe I can give you a lift. It looks like rain."

Jesus, Arthur thought, it's dead easy to find the station.

"Well, yes, okay," he said finally. "I'm a bit late myself."

The woman cracked her features into the semblance of a smile, skeletal ice breaking across the frozen pond of her face. "Good," she sighed. "I'm hopeless at followin' directions."

Arthur followed her out of the shop, Billy Simpson calling after them, wishing them a nice day. A white, four-door Sierra, rust-splotched round the wheel arches, stood parked at the kerb. There was a man sitting in the driver's seat. When he saw them coming, he climbed over into the passenger seat.

"Would you mind sittin' in the back?" the woman asked. "I've got my brother wi'me."

"No problem," Arthur said and opened the nearside door at the rear.

The man in the front seat did not turn round. Arthur noted how his grey, shaggy-rug hair sprouted over the fake fur collar of a black bomber jacket, so that the whole garment looked like an extended hair piece hanging over his shoulders. The man made no attempt to speak. Stale cigarette smoke hung in the air. Arthur coughed and tried to roll down the window, but it would not budge. The woman climbed in and caught his eye in the driving mirror.

"You just continue straight down the road," he told her. "It bends a bit to the left further down, but just follow it round."

The woman turned the ignition key, found first gear and let the clutch out too fast. The car jerked forward and stalled. The man in the passenger seat muttered, "For fuck's sake," and glared at her. Arthur watched him in profile, his nose jutting out like the prow of a battleship. Sitting right behind him, he caught the fusty whiff of unwashed bodies. There were a few moments of strained silence before they started off again and the man in front of Arthur spoke again.

"On your way into Belfast, are you?"

This time he swivelled his head slightly to the side as he spoke. His voice had the flat singsong whine of the native. Arthur gazed at the bedraggled tufts of hair sticking out in random array on the back of his head.

"That's right," he said.

The Ford had almost reached the bend in the road. The woman, still silent, changed down into third gear. Arthur noticed she was wearing pigskin gloves, a light rodent-grey colour with dark oily stains. A thumb protruded from a burst in the right-hand glove on the steering wheel. The nail was bitten, painted with crackled lacquer that had once been pink.

"You're not a teacher, are you?" she said suddenly, glancing at him in the mirror. "On your way to school?"

Arthur smiled to himself. "What makes you think that?" Her eyes met his in the rear-view mirror.

"Like yer clothes. An' the umbrella. You look just like a teacher I once had."

Arthur chuckled feebly. "Well, you're a bit off the mark. I work for a newspaper. I'm a journalist."

"Really?" the brother whined. "The Belfast Telegraph?"

"Yeah."

The brother turned his head sideways to squint round at him. Above the blunt-axe nose, steel-wool curls hung like a valance over the man's forehead. Pitted acne sores fired his chin and cheeks that hadn't seen a razor for the better part of a week. As Arthur watched him, he thought of a scalded warthog minus the horns.

"Is that so?" the man said and turned again to face the front.

Arthur felt himself becoming irritated by their questions. "What about yourself?" he said, eager to switch the direction of the conversation.

There was a slight pause before the brother sniffed and mewled, "Self-employed."

They were almost at the station now. Drops of rain began to shatter on the windscreen. Arthur took a deep breath and fumbled for the handle of his umbrella, gripping it tightly.

"It's just a bit further down," he told them. "You'll see

the underpass in front and you turn in to the left just before it."

The red-brick station building with its white-framed windows loomed up as the Ford swung in and lurched to a stop.

"There's Des," the woman breathed, rolling down her window. Arthur saw a heavily built man in a motorcycle cap, black jerkin and jeans striding across the parking lot towards the car. The man increased his pace as he approached.

"Well, thanks for the lift," Arthur said, opening the door behind the brother and starting to get out.

"It's him," the woman hissed as the man reached the car.

Arthur glimpsed him coming swiftly round the car. He had one foot on the ground when he realised there was something wrong. In the same instant as the man's fist swung towards his face, Arthur snatched up his hand with the umbrella to ward off the blow. He felt the shaft shudder as its rapier point tore between the man's knuckles and buried itself in the palm of his hand. The man gave a sharp involuntary gasp, jerked backwards and wrenched the umbrella from Arthur's fingers with his other hand. At the same time Arthur somehow managed to fall forwards out of the car and into the roadway. In a frenzy of fear he grabbed his assailant tightly round the legs and succeeded in toppling him over and onto the ground. As he fell, Arthur heard the train coming to a halt beyond the parking lot. 'Got to get on the train,' a voice screamed in his head. 'Got to get on the train.'

Frantically he began to rise to his feet, a sluggish sprinter in his starting blocks, when he sensed a movement to his left and his legs were kicked from under him as the other man, the brother, rushed at him swinging a steel-tipped boot ferociously into his ankle. The abrupt pain seared from his shins to his head like a needle being thrust into his temple, blinding him. Involuntarily he blinked his eyes once, twice, opening them only to see a monkey wrench descending upon him. He jerked his head to the side and felt an agonising pain as the wrench smashed into his shoulder, splintering the bone. Almost as a reflex he kicked out blindly and caught the brother a lucky blow on the kneecap with his heel. Cursing, the man staggered backwards, almost dropping the wrench, and Arthur made a final effort to get to his feet.

As he struggled to his knees, hands on the asphalt for support, he looked through a mist of pain to see the woman come at him with the umbrella, jabbing savagely at his face until the steel tip burst into the socket of his left eye, gouged up behind the forehead bone towards the temple and ripped out again with blind ferocity.

His scream of agony was terminated only when the man in the bomber jacket struck him over the head with the wrench, a pitiless cracking blow that seemed to echo against the station building. As he swung his arm back to strike again, the woman rasped, "Get him in," and the brother seized hold of Arthur under the arms.

With frenzied haste the two men bundled the limp body into the back seat of the car as commuters ran past, barely daring to look, dashing towards the waiting train, rushing to reach the security of their carriage. Seconds later the Sierra slewed round in a tight U-turn, scorching the asphalt as it accelerated up the hill, round the bend and out of sight. The doors of the train emitted a pneumatic sigh and closed. Wide-eyed faces stared through the windows, rigid with fear, frozen in disbelief. Slowly the train moved off, leaving the station, gathering speed down the line towards the city.

Two teenage girls in school uniform waited until it had gone. Then they went over hesitantly to the blue and yellow umbrella lying in the road. Blood and an opaque jellied substance smeared the tip. The safety catch had come off and the thin polyester canopy flapped spasmodically in the morning breeze.

THREE

Quinn stared at his image in the mirror. The scars were almost healed. Superficial wounds, you were lucky, they'd said. Surgical tape should be enough, if you're careful and don't laugh too much. Jeez, everybody wants to be a comedian.

Well, no fear of that now. He looked all over his face, intently, from the top of his forehead to the tip of his chin. It was a sombre face, with a square jaw and searching eyes under dark, incipiently greying hair. "You'd almost be good looking," his ex-wife had remarked at one point, "if you didn't look so bloody cynical."

But this morning there was something about himself that he didn't quite recognise, something different that hadn't been there before, an alien quality that simply didn't belong. 'Am I me?' he wondered. His right eye seemed smaller than the left, but hadn't it always been like that? He wasn't sure. Didn't he always look like that when he was tired? Or hungover? Or both? Like now. The sagging skin under the eyes didn't help either, hanging there like small, limp, deflated bladders. And those little brown spots of hyperpigmentation just below the hairline, they hadn't been there before. Christ, he wasn't a young man any more.

Maybe he was coming down with something? Jesus, he should be so lucky. His whole world was coming down. Right now it actually felt as if everything was breaking apart. He had been a fool to get involved, he knew that. He had seen the warning signs, heard the danger signals. And still he had gone ahead.

The cabinet mirror was cracked at the bottom, cleaving his stubbled chin like a sabre slash. He reached up and swung the door open, scanning the glass shelves with bleary eyes. All her things were gone: the creams, the lotions, all the flotsam and jetsam of cosmetic application that had cluttered the shelves had now vanished save for one small, grey plastic bottle of acetone standing solitary before him. He lifted it and stared at the label. It said Remover. 'You forgot to remove the Remover,' he muttered stupidly. He shook it. The bottle was almost empty. He stamped on the bin pedal under the wash basin and flipped it in.

He walked into the bedroom alcove and opened the top drawer of a small walnut-veneer dresser that doubled as a bedside table. A torn cellophane wrapper gaped back at him. It was the only thing there. He remembered the running tights she had bought to go training with him. He wrenched open the other drawers, closing them again as he worked his way down. The bottom drawer jammed first. Mechanically he cursed it and pulled again. A gilt-framed photograph lay face-down on the pink drawer liner with the floral pattern. He turned it over and gazed at the happy expression on his wife's face. Ex-wife, he reminded himself. You screwed that up too. Big time.

When he looked up, his sudden reflection in the mirror startled him. 'I look unreal,' he murmured to himself. He sat down on the edge of the bed, sinking deep into the lumpy mattress, looking round the blank expanse of honey-milk white walls he had painted himself when he moved in.

The flat was at the top of a refurbished Victorian house on Eglantine Avenue, a long, undeviating, tree-lined street that ran up and over a gentle hill close to the university. It had been advertised as a 'studio apartment'. "That means it's small," his solicitor had told him, and that had been his first thought on entering it. He liked the blond parquet flooring in the living room, extending into a kitchenette and an oblong alcove into which he had just managed to squeeze a bed and the slender dresser. The cobalt-blue tiled bathroom contained a toilet, a washbasin and a shower cubicle he could barely turn round in.

"Compact living," Joe had remarked.

"You could hardly swing a mouse in here, never mind a cat," Quinn said.

Joe Stewart had provided Quinn with judicial support in his divorce and, following on from that, with finding a new place to live. Often termed Wee Joe because of his diminutive stature, Stewart ran a successful legal practice that the Troubles had blessed with an abundance of lucrative work. They had resolved an importunate police matter together while Quinn was still married and Quinn had looked Joe up again when, as he put it, "the shit hit the marital fan." The studio apartment had been the next item on their common agenda.

What actually caused the decade-long marriage to disintegrate was something Joe had never really discovered, though it wasn't for want of trying. The closest he came to an explanation was one night in a cubby in The Crown, halfway through a bottle of whiskey and a probing discussion, when Quinn had muttered, 'It had just gone dead between us.'

"Aha," Joe had said knowledgeably. "The spark had gone."

"Spark?" Quinn had slurred. "Whaddy ya mean, spark?"

"The sexual spark. That's what keeps marriage alive."

Quinn had just stared at him and nodded slightly, and they had left it at that.

Viewing the flat had taken no more than five minutes.

"I suppose it has a certain *je ne sais quoi*," Joe had said, looking round the living room.

"I don't know what either," Quinn stated, "but I need a place to live and it's available."

"Yeah, it's got that," Joe agreed.

* * *

Quinn had been living in the apartment for almost four years when Joe Stewart had introduced him to Renée: "I'd like you to meet someone. Could be good for you. She's an English journalist, Renée Vega."

"English? With a name like Renée? A born-again journalist? And Vega? Where does that come from?"

"Look, she just wants to interview a typical Belfast policeman about the job."

"Typical?" Quinn had queried. "Am I typical?"

"Yeah, you're a typical pain in the ass."

"So give it to someone else."

"You'll regret it, believe me. Wait till you see her. Hourglass figure, knockout knockers. She's a real honey."

"Forget it, Joe. I've seen that movie."

Joe took in the expression on Quinn's face and decided to change tack.

"Look, she doesn't know anyone here. I imagine Belfast has been a bit of a shock to her. You'd be doing her a big favour. Me too. I may be doing some business with her father. Come on, Quinn, I can't believe you're not going to help a damsel in distress. First time in Belfast can be a bit unnerving. You don't know what you're passing up."

"You told me already," Quinn said. "Hourglass figure, knockout knockers."

"Okay," Joe admitted. "That was just the soft, sexist sell."

"Like I said, Joe, forget it," Quinn said, waving a hand as if at a non-existent fly. But this was friend-in-need Joe Stewart, not just any old Joe, and Quinn felt a need to explain.

"Fact is, I've just started on a Special Forces training course and it's killing me. This is just between you and me. They've got me training the other guys, y'know, I've got to put them through their paces. And it's all about leading by example."

He looked at Joe's face, seeking a sign of mutual understanding. They were about the same age, he judged; surely that should count for something.

"Joe, I'm getting too old for this sort of thing and I just don't have the time to mollycoddle some culture-shocked Martha Gellhorn."

"Martha who?" Joe glared at him.

Quinn constructed a concessionary smile and added, "But what I could do is put her in touch with a local journalist – Arthur Williams."

One of Joe's eyebrows rose in an archway of semi-interest.

"The guy at the Belfast Telegraph? The one who exposed the Newry bombers? I remember you were in on that. You know him?"

"Yeah, sort of. Haven't seen him for a couple of years, but I could give him a call. I think he'd help. He's a really good guy."

"The real deal, eh? Well, that would be a start, though they might be competing with each other – she's a freelancer."

Quinn shrugged his shoulders. "That's the best I can do, Joe. I simply haven't got the time."

"Or the inclination," Joe snorted. "Well, it's a start anyway."

* * *

Joe Stewart, however, never one to hang around, arranged for Renée to come to his office one evening later the same week when he knew Quinn would be there. He was sneaky like that. It was the way he got things done.

The office was central, one flight up in a side-street off Royal Avenue. Joe said he had got most of the furniture from the Europa Hotel after the Provisional IRA refurbished it with a 1,000-pound bomb in 1993. "They practically paid me to take it away." He was known to point out the scorch marks on his desk to interested clients.

A low-backed tan leather chair crouched opposite the desk. Two identical cloth-seated chairs sat on either side of a fireplace with a blackened, empty grate. The walls were enlivened with a milky emulsion patterned in a random array of bubbles and blisters. These were partly concealed by a ceiling-high glass-fronted bookcase against one wall and a row of gilt-framed paintings, colour copies of pastoral Irish scenes that continued round the other walls of the room. The irregular one-up one-down alignment of the pictures suggested that Joe had enlisted the help of John Jameson in hanging them up on the walls.

As if on cue, Joe stood up when Renée came in through the open door.

"Well, hello there," he cooed. His patently surprised look came from an extensive repertoire of facial expressions he had honed to a fine art in the line of duty. Unsuspecting, Quinn swung round. Joe was right, he thought, she is a looker: tall, slender, olive skin, attractive features, intriguing in a dark Latin way.

"This is Quinn," Joe told her and nodded at the man in the opposite chair. She grinned, as if merely to show him her perfect teeth.

"So you're the elusive Inspector Quinn," she said.

Quinn smiled. "You must have confused me with someone else.

"No uniform," Renée observed.

"That's right," Quinn said. "No uniform."

"He's a senior policeman," Joe added, "one of the Specials."

"No first name?" Renée observed further. "That's it? Just Quinn?"

"That's me," the policeman said, deciding at last to rise to his feet. "Just Quinn." Her olive cheeks dipped in a sardonic smile as she took his hand.

"You think you're Inspector Morse or something?"

"Yeah. Something like that."

There had been ups and downs in the relationship right from the very start. If he was honest with himself, that had been part of the attraction. A large part. The making-up sex had been explosively memorable. But he was assigned to the Specials, got called away for days on end leaving Renée on her own; and Renée was not a woman who enjoyed being on her own, not a woman who could forgo the company of others. The Specials demanded more and more of Quinn's time and things did not improve.

That was all he had told her: the Specials. Renée had assumed he meant the B-Specials, which she had heard about. He did not correct her, did not tell her the B-Men had been merely a semi-military reserve force, disbanded years ago. The new unit was totally different; its existence was not officially acknowledged. Known among the men as the D-Specials it was a full-time covert force. No uniform, just civvies. The three-month training programme had been murderous, murder being the operative word. The men had their own ideas on what the D stood for.

He thought of her words to him, almost the last thing she had said, just before she left: "Listen Quinn, not so long ago I thought you were someone special, really special. There was something about you that made me think I might want to spend the rest of my life with you. But that simply isn't true anymore. Sadly, the facts speak for themselves. Of course I realise you aren't a perfect person, but there are limits. The way you look at me sometimes, at night-time, when we argue, it frightens me.

"You're a powder keg, Quinn. You can just explode, without warning. You scare me. You're like a road accident that can't stop repeating itself. Believe me, it hasn't been easy finding out the kind of person you really are."

Yet he had tried. He had gone to that shrink, that doctor in the top-floor office with the slippery Chesterfield sofa on the Malone Road. Was Dr Benjamin Musgrave a psychologist or a psychiatrist? Quinn was never quite sure of the distinction. Strangely, it was his mother who had recommended him. She had always been obsessed with the medical profession in one way or another. Hence his Christian name from a certain street in London, which he had always detested. And Benjamin Musgrave was a doctor who hardly made him feel better about his baptismal sobriquet. Buttoned up in a mossy three-piece tweed suit criss-crossed with a thin red-lined check, Dr Musgrave could easily be mistaken for a country squire. Quinn found himself looking under the leather-topped writing desk for a gun-dog, but the only object on the Gabbeh rug was a pair of Musgrave's burly brogues.

The doctor was a man of full-bearded, iron-grey authority, a professional physician who commanded distance rather than inviting intimacy. He seemed particularly interested in Quinn's memories of his teens, which he called his 'determinative, late-formative years,' leading up to his curtailed university studies. As he saw more of him and accustomed himself to his elevated, doctrinaire way of talking and behaving, Quinn could not conceive that his wife would ever address him as anything other than Benjamin, or possibly Doctor – but definitely never as Ben or, even more unthinkable, Benny.

With growing unease Quinn recalled the series of consultations, the attempts to assess what actually ignited his temper, the concomitant factors that unleashed his rage, his relentless fury, and the disturbing queries about his relationship with his mother and the loss of his father, killed in the McGurk's Bar bombing when Quinn was 18, in his first year at university. The doctor had talked around his father's death, inquiring about his background, his habits and beliefs, plumbing Quinn's relation to him, finally wondering what he thought his father was doing in McGurk's Bar on that particular evening. It was a mystery that had plagued Quinn to the present day. Had he been involved in the bombing? A volunteer? An infiltrator? A spy? A double agent?

And when Quinn professed his ignorance and frustration at not knowing, Benjamin Musgrave had delved deeper into the enigma, relentlessly probing the mystery of the bomb explosion that had killed him, as if he suspected the son might unwittingly possess information that could resolve the puzzle. Who did his father work for? What sort of company was Kennedy Construction Ltd? How long had he worked as a materials buyer? Quinn had the distinct feeling Dr Musgrave was endeavouring to lead him to some conclusion that he himself had come to, but he had no wish to go there.

It brought it all back and he began to understand why he had opted out in the first place, all those years ago, how the death of his father lay behind most of his actions, fuelling his anger and playing a significant part in his decision to move away from home. The doctor was an attentive listener, periodically scribbling in the ledger on his imposing desk. No one in the Quinn family had even taken A-levels before, never mind gone to university. It was expected of him – yes, he had felt that pressure, that somehow he also owed it to his father – and English was his best subject. Well, Beowulf and the historical development from Old English to Middle English didn't exactly grab him, but there were other courses – like the creative writing option – that he found challenging, stimulating, sometimes really interesting, that kept him going to the lectures and seminars, doing barely ample work for the exams and usually getting through on that.

He didn't have the staying power though, and he realised that this lack of academic tenacity had been his problem all along. There were too many distractions of one kind or another, and he let himself be distracted. He understood now, with Dr Musgrave's help, that the death of his father had been by far the biggest distraction, underlying everything else that happened to him even though he wasn't always fully aware of it. And the mystery of his father's presence in McGurk's Bar that evening was something that had pursued him to the present day.

The product of a mixed marriage, Quinn was never entirely sure where his father's political convictions lay. And when the mixed part of his parents' marriage cropped up in conversation, Quinn would usually try to wisecrack his way out of difficulty by saying: 'Yeah, my dad's a man and mum's a woman – you can't get more mixed than that.'

From his childhood he remembered his father as the man with warm, grey eyes who often made him laugh at bedtime when he told him outlandish stories with much histrionic finesse; then, during his teens, his father became a rather stern and dominating figure, a strict but respected taskmaster when it came to his schoolwork and his general behaviour. In retrospect it made little difference whether the bomb had been planted by the UVF or exploded inadvertently by the IRA. It had all seemed so meaningless then, and it was just as meaningless now. His father was gone – gone before he had even got a chance to know him properly, as a man. And he would always wonder how his father, never a pub man, came to be in McGurk's Bar that evening in December 1971; it would always torment him.

As far as university was concerned, he concluded in the end that he didn't have the collegiate discipline required, simply couldn't knuckle down to the academic grind. His marks weren't great – they were okay, yes, but the fact was, he wanted out. He wanted to travel, to see something other than the university library and the Union – above all, he sought adventure, excitement, an active direction in life.

Things came to a head after a brawl in the Botanic Inn at the end of the summer term. He had difficulty explaining to Dr Benjamin Musgrave explicitly how he had felt when he snapped, as the red mist enveloped and blinded him, as his rage took complete control. Significantly, it was when his father's name was maligned that he utterly lost it. Two men ended up in hospital – one with half a shattered beer glass in the face, the other with a multiple brachial fracture – and for a time there was an intensive RUC hunt for the perpetrator.

Almost by chance he had managed to slip away, avoid identification and disappear to England. His departure coincided neatly with the start of the summer vacation. He worked on a building site in Birmingham, intending to stay just over the summer before returning; but one thing led to another and when the autumn term approached, he decided he wasn't going back. But the good doctor wanted to delve deeper; he wanted to know exactly how one thing could lead to another, what sort of thing and the effect it could have on a man with Quinn's background and disposition, a man with such an apparently volatile personality.

Quinn was careful to ascertain Dr Musgrave's professional confidentiality before divulging his former membership in the Special Air Service and the disturbing series of pain barriers he had to break through in order to join. He discovered, almost to his surprise, that he possessed the determination and mental stamina needed to survive the relentless torture of the physical fitness trials, the endurance tests and the jungle training in Belize.

Afterwards Quinn experienced a surprising sense of release, of liberation, as a result of having discussed his time in the SAS in some depth, culminating in the Iranian Embassy siege in 1980. The subsequent step – authorised at the highest level – from liaising with the security forces in Northern Ireland to becoming an RUC inspector instrumental in setting up the covert D-Special unit had been both short and, given his track record, natural.

Out of all of this had crystallised one concrete piece of advice: the good Dr Musgrave suggested that he should write down in a notebook an account of the occasions when he suffered these 'rabid attacks', as he put it. Treat it as an exercise in that creative writing course you told me about, Musgrave had said, his words emerging miraculously through a thicket of overgrown follicles that sprouted round his mouth. But be truthful, he had added, peering admonishingly over his half-moon eyeglasses. Be truthful.

Quinn suspected that writing and reading these accounts, whether alone or together with Dr Musgrave, was designed to provide a therapeutic effect; but the very day after the advice was given, Benjamin Musgrave had suffered a fatal cerebral aneurism coming out of his surgery at the top of the stairs in his Malone Road residence. The subsequent fall and broken neck constituted a clear case of overkill. The news of his death and the realisation that they would not meet again, that he would not have to endure another of those probing, unsettling consultations, engendered an unmistakeable sense of relief in Quinn that both surprised and in some way emancipated him. Nevertheless, he had felt inexplicably obliged to follow the final admonition from the good doctor and had bought a lined notebook in the nearby university bookshop for this very purpose.

Quinn wasn't really sure why he did it. But he supposed, in a way, it was Benjamin Musgrave's death that sparked him into action. The whole business quite shocked him and he came to see the notebook as a kind of legacy. The doctor had seemed so permanent, immutable, manifest, like the nose on your face. And, all of a sudden, he was gone.

The kind of person you really are. He looked again at his image in the mirror. It was like a sepia photo of himself as a boy, staring at him from another lifetime. The boy stared back at him, a lost child searching for a friend.

He felt his breath coming heavy and deep. The words reverberated in his head like bullets smacking into the target on a shooting range. The kind of person you really are. And in his mind he was back that night three weeks earlier in the Café Vaudeville on Arthur Street, a dog leg's walk from Belfast's City Hall.

FOUR

Three weeks earlier

It had been some time since Quinn had taken Renée Vega out to dinner. He had been involved in an intensive RUC training course and she had been in London for a week working on a freelance project for the Illustrated London News. On the same day that Renée flew back to Aldergrove, Quinn took her out for what he had hoped would be a celebratory dinner.

The Café Vaudeville in the middle of Belfast is supposed to be a homage to the Art Nouveau movement, and Quinn takes Renée there to impress her, for her to breathe in its 'authentic Parisian atmosphere,' the glass-domed sky-high ceiling, the chandeliers with their tassel-draped lampshades, the marmoreal pillars and the sinuous lines of the tapestries. It's just a lot of bloody kitsch, he thinks, but he doesn't say this to Renée.

He's sitting watching her across the table, thinking how beautiful she is with her ebony hair pinned up like that and her neat little nose sniffing in the authentic Parisian atmosphere under a pair of deep tarn-brown eyes you could drown in. Despite himself he feels drawn into another world in those eyes, a mysterious place that he doesn't fully comprehend and cannot forgo. He knows she's English, with a French name, but with that Latin look she could be Catherine of Aragon. First time he took her out, he said, before he could stop himself, *'Buenas días. Como está?'* And she turned those eyes on him and let fly with a string of Spanish expletives that left him standing there with his mouth open like a letterbox someone's dropped a turd in.

So eventually he finds out she comes from Sevenoaks in Kent but has a grandmother from somewhere in South

America and doesn't want to be taken for anything other than English. 'I'm English, you dumb Mick. Got it?' Not with that temperament, you're not, Quinn thinks, not with that temperament. But he just smiles at her the way he does when he's not really sure what's going on. It's a habit he has acquired over the years, a defensive ploy he uses to give him time to think.

They're dining sumptuously, to Quinn's way of thinking, on farm duck liver parfait for starters, and he seems to press a button when he asks Renée how she came to be a journalist. "Jesus, haven't I told you already?"

Her face lights up with anticipation at telling her story, and she reveals right off that her choice of profession wasn't exactly popular with her father. Quinn is somewhat taken aback when she refers to him as a sonofabitch, but lets it pass for the moment. Instead he asks her what line of work her father would have preferred for his darling daughter. Somehow he's not surprised to hear that Vega père was determined that she, as his only child, should be a banker, a corporate lawyer, or a doctor at least.

"But you became a journo."

"No, not even that, not at the start. The fact is, when I left uni, with English and Spanish, the only thing I could actually do – get a job doing – was teach."

Quinn is taken aback. Renée as a teacher is a trifle hard to imagine. "You were a teacher? Really?"

"Yes, I was a teacher. What's wrong with that? Why are you so surprised?"

"Well, of course there's nothing wrong with it. I just don't really see you in the classroom."

"I was bloody good in the classroom."

Quinn runs a nervous finger over the bridge of his nose "I don't doubt it, but …"

"But what?"

Quinn has noticed this tendency with her before, this

inclination to interpret the most benignly expressed opinion as some form of vindictive, personal criticism. He had hoped it would slacken off as they became better acquainted, but the penchant was still there and it invariably led to a tension between them.

"Well, I suppose I just have difficulty seeing you looking after a bunch of stroppy kids."

Renée recoils in mock surprise.

"What? Think I couldn't keep control?"

"I don't know. What level did you have?"

"It was an inner-city comprehensive."

"So you had mixed-ability classes with gangs of insecure, spotty-faced adolescents from all sorts of multicultural backgrounds."

"I did. And there was no problem with discipline."

Her eyes glare at him, brown gauntlets tossed down in a death-defying challenge. Quinn wonders briefly if he should pursue this. He puffs out his cheeks slightly, exhales and goes ahead anyway.

"But it was still 'Goodbye, Mrs Chips.' Why?"

She shrugs her shoulders with Latin levity.

"Simple. I wasn't teaching them anything."

"What do you mean? You speak perfect Spanish, as far as I can judge. And your English is pretty good too."

"Funny."

She stresses the second syllable and gives him her adoring-fan smile. Then she's serious again.

"No, no matter how hard I tried, they just weren't interested. It was a dead end. I didn't get anything back."

Quinn tugged gently at the lobe of an ear. "One-way communication?" he ventured.

"That's it, exactly. They weren't interested and I couldn't get them interested. I was banging my head against a brick wall. It took just over a year, and then I realised it simply wasn't what I wanted to do. It wasn't me."

This makes sense to Quinn. In school she was trying to give the kids something they didn't want, something they felt they had no use for. He knows she thrives on human contact, is dependent on it. He understands her need of intercourse, the social kind often being the most important variety even with him.

They pause briefly to eat and drink some wine. The wine is good: Amarone, Italian. He's read up on it beforehand. Joe Stewart had given him one of his wine catalogues, recommending it. Fancies himself as a bit of a connoisseur, Quinn thinks. Come to think of it, Joe fancies himself as a bit of everything. But the wine is good, full bodied, strong. Quinn swallows it and smiles tentatively.

"I get the impression you're not on the best of terms with Daddy."

"Jesus Quinn, you really are quite the detective."

"I've been called worse."

"I'll bet you have."

"Mostly by you."

"That's true, and not without due cause."

"Debatable. Now, are you going to tell me about your old man?"

Renée pushes a strand of hair back from her forehead and expels a short sigh.

"Well, in a previous life I did a semester at Princeton. It wasn't long after I finished school and I was looking for a year away from it all. My father was on at me to do an MBA, to follow him into the business. There was a lot of pressure. So I let myself be bribed into crossing the pond and doing business admin and economics, y'know, all that Ivy League bullshit, something that I immediately regretted."

"You abandoned the good ship Mazuma?"

"Yeah, and never heard the end of it. Fact is, any time I have dealings with my father it always seems to end in a shitstorm. My mother used to say that we were too much alike to be able to get on."

"But you get on with your mother?"

Renée is lifting the Amarone to her lips but stops and returns the bulbous glass to the table. She regards the dark wine swilling gently to and fro before she tells him.

"My mother's dead."

She suddenly looks Quinn straight in the eye, daring him to speak, forbidding him to say anything before she continues.

"She opted out when I was 14. Cut her wrists. Well, it wasn't exactly an idyllic marriage to begin with. My father didn't really have time for her. Let's face it – he was married to his business. Still is. And I suppose she was very highly strung, very high-maintenance. They had this weird relationship. There were issues, lots of hang-ups. Looking back, I think a lot of the time my mother was more or less teetering on the brink. Anyway, I'd just gone to school as usual that morning when it happened. My father was in Switzerland on business. Of course. And I found her in the bath when I got home from school."

She utters this last sentence as if telling him she had found a letter lying in the hall. He can't believe it, can't believe the equanimity with which she tells him. She looks down at her hands clasped together on the table. Quinn watches her knuckles whiten. Her face is expressionless, betraying nothing.

"Jesus Christ, I had no idea," Quinn says eventually. "You've never said anything."

She looks up to stare at him, her eyes cold and dismissive.

"You've never asked. Anyway, it's not something I want to dwell on. It was a long time ago and it's over. Quinn, we've only been together a couple of months. We hardly know each other. And you've been away a lot, you know, that training course with the Specials, or whatever. I don't know what else you get up to. Anyway, we had other subjects to discuss when we met."

"Yeah, when we discussed anything at all," Quinn says, diving into the tarn-brown pools of those eyes.

She gives him a half-roguish smile and he feels childishly pleased. But this news about Renée's home background comes as a bombshell. What a childhood she must have had with those parents, all the emotional baggage she must be carrying around with her. And he sits thinking about it, wondering what to say, pondering when to say it.

He waits until she lifts her wine glass and drains it.

"I know your father's in some sort of investment business, but what exactly does he do?"

Renée Vega peers at him as if she's having trouble focussing, takes a demonstratively deep breath and places her wine glass carefully on the table.

"He thinks he's Britain's answer to Donald Trump in America."

"Bigshot billionaire businessman?"

"Exactly. Calls himself an investment banker, has his own company, buying and selling, makes oodles of filthy lucre and — yes — he's an extremely successful businessman. His favourite smartass saying is: 'Money isn't everything. It just buys everything.' And that just about sums him up."

* * *

The waitress arrives to clear the table and soon they are dissecting a rump of Lough Erne lamb with quinoa, aubergine, feta croquettes and tarragon aioli, washed down with another bottle of Amarone della Valpolicella. Quinn looks over at Renée but she's engrossed in the food, avoiding eye contact, and they eat in silence.

To his considerable dismay, it seems as if the evening may be ending with a whimper, when in fact a bang is just around the corner. It begins with the clatter of fallen cutlery on the square-tiled floor. They turn their heads and look at the waiter who has been gingerly navigating his way from the kitchen to a table in a far corner of the room. He stoops to retrieve the tableware. As he straightens up again they note that he is unusually tall and, to be someone employed in the kitchen of the Café Vaudeville, looks inappropriately undernourished. His features are gaunt, almost emaciated, as pale as curdled cream and, in his tight-fitting waiter's waistcoat and trousers, he rather resembles a life-size matchstick puppet. A voice behind them murmurs, "He's like a herring wi' the back ate out of him."

"What's that?" Renée whispers. "A herring…?"

Quinn translates from the local patois: "He's a rather thin gentleman."

The waiter really is exceptionally tall and thin. His disjointed gait makes Quinn imagine a puppeteer pulling on a set of strings from the ceiling, but there is no one behind the burgundy lampshades on the chandelier above. This flight of fancy has a simple and obvious explanation: Quinn has fortified his appetite with several double whiskies before leaving home, which also tends to amplify his imagination.

As the waiter passes by on his way back to the kitchen, Renée turns to her dinner partner and says, "Listen, Quinn, I have something to tell you."

She gives him a worried little smile and leans into the curved back of her Art Nouveau chair.

"Sounds serious," he says, trying to assess her body language and becoming a little anxious when he notes her nervousness.

"Well, it's important," she says. "For me, anyway, it's

an important …" She draws in a breath, searching for the right word, *le mot juste*, as she would say.

"… development," she breathes out at last. But her olive cheeks clench with discontent and Quinn can see she is somewhat dissatisfied with her lexical choice. Or something else.

"Okay," he says, a vague unease now constricting his somewhat bloated midriff. "What's your… development?"

She looks down at the dessert spoon in front of her. For a moment he almost believes she's going to say, "I've decided to have the warm, soft-centre chocolate cake with peanut ice cream," but that's just the whiskey and wine playing ball with his imagination again. Much later he thinks, if only she had said that, and nothing more. Just that, and nothing more. But there was more.

"I've been offered a job in Madrid," she tells him at last and pauses briefly to let this sink in. "I'm pretty well bilingual in Spanish, as you know, and they want a correspondent there to cover Spanish affairs, economics, politics, the works. I'd also have to travel to the EU in Brussels every so often when there were issues of particular interest to Spain."

Quinn licks his lips and swallows hard. "Who's 'they'?" he asks. She mentions one of the big national dailies, one that he knows she's done some freelance work for, and he remembers.

"You used to work with some guy there, didn't you, when you lived in London?"

She hesitates, plays a little with her fork on the side of the plate before she says: "Robert Sinclair. He's a senior editor there now. I met him when I was over this week and he said there might be something coming up."

Quinn takes a deep breath before he asks her. "Are you going? Have you decided to take it?"

Renée sits back in her chair and dips her head forward

slightly to apprise him of the seriousness of what she is about to say.

"It's a proper job, Quinn, full time, with a good salary and expenses. Christ, it's better than being a freelance, hawking stuff around like I've been doing, trying to sell an article you've sweated your guts out over and getting paid peanuts for your trouble. I've done all I can do here. I've seen Northern Ireland, seen your Troubles, met the people. My God, half the time I don't even understand the bloody language. This is the chance I've been waiting for. I can't pass it up. Bobby says it's an opportunity that won't come again."

There's something in the way she says his name, its diminutive form, something in the set of her face and the way she averts her eyes that causes Quinn to stumble, makes him crumble.

"Bobby?" He searches her face for a clarifying clue. "Bobby?" He looks her square in those deep brown eyes of hers, those mountain pools, and he sees at once that he's fallen in, he's sinking, and he lies there drowning. "You've fucked him?"

He chokes it out through the surging fury, louder than intended and, as he says it, the soft bistro tones of piano-accordion Muzak seem to fade away. People stop talking. Even the couple behind them who've been chattering non-stop since they arrived.

"Don't do this, Quinn. Please don't do this."

He watches a saddening, pained expression circumnavigate her face.

"It's a simple enough question. Did you fuck him?"

She shoots him a look of undisguised animosity.

"Why do you always have to destroy everything?"

"Just tell me the truth. Did you fuck him? Yes or no?"

"No," Renée tells him. "He fucked me. It was more fun that way."

She glares at him now, challenging, defiant, her eyes somehow becoming larger, wider, stronger.

"You know," she says, "I hadn't absolutely decided before tonight, before now, about the job. But I'm going to take it. You just talked me into it, and there's not a damn thing you can do about it."

"No, probably not. Not now that you've already made up your mind. Not now that you've decided to fuck up everything between us."

Quinn is uncertain now, dangling between her possible irony and her probable honesty. She sighs suddenly. It sounds like a sigh of defeat, even though she's won.

"You don't know me, Quinn, and you sure as hell don't own me. Somehow I knew you'd react like this."

"What did you expect?" he says. "The Hallelujah Chorus?"

The lanky, cadaverous waiter is treading delicately past their table, like some mutant daddy-long-legs in a waiter's suit. He bears an array of hot dishes arranged along his right underarm, a bowl of steaming County Down potatoes held in his left hand. And he cannot help but hear the angry voices, he cannot help but glance at Renée, then at Quinn, and all at once in his distraction he falters, jerks back his right arm, attempts to regain his balance, but fails and a hot assortment of peas, carrots, roast turkey, gravy, cranberry relish and boiled potatoes comes cascading over them.

"Oh for fuck's sake!"

"Jesus Christ!"

All but one of the dishes shatters across the mosaic tiled floor. The unbroken dish clatters to a stop beside Quinn's chair. Painstakingly he picks a slice of turkey breast out of his top pocket and, rising to his feet, brushes sticks of carrot and mushy peas off his trousers. Most of the gravy and cranberry relish has splashed on to Renée's dark-blue velvet jacket and black skirt. She looks down at the mess, at the hapless waiter stammering his apologies, at Quinn wiping himself off.

"Let's get the hell out of here."

Quinn pays the bill while Renée goes to the Mesdames to clean up. There is no talk of compensation. They just want to leave the premises. Management just wants to get them off the premises. Quinn brushes himself off with toilet paper in the Messieurs. Miniscule fragments of the soft tissue remain attached to his clothes even though he endeavours frantically to brush them off with his fingers. This infuriates him even further. As they get their coats and leave, the volume of the piano-accordion Muzak is switched up as if to melodiously eradicate their presence and regenerate the authentic Parisian atmosphere.

* * *

They walk up Arthur Street in silence, turn right into Chichester Street and hurry along into Donegall Square and the City Hall. Cars and buses trundle past, their headlamps projecting spectral beams in the late November gloom, their fumes reeking foul and smoky in the wintry air. Hundreds of Christmas lights are blinking around the City Hall, linked and twinkling from lamppost to lamppost. The street lamps are adorned with green wreaths entwined with red ribbon, glowing beacons of seasonal cheer. From loudspeakers on every lamppost children's voices sing out Jingle Bells and Rudolph the red-nosed Reindeer. Quinn feels ill at ease, out of place. The Yuletide merriment is almost too much to bear. He scours the street for a taxi.

"You won't get a taxi now," a newsvendor tells him. "Van Morrison's just had a concert here."

"Is he still on the go?" Quinn wonders. "Why doesn't he

just stay at home and mope?"

"He's making a pile of money," says the news vendor.

"We'll take the bus," Renée says. "I'm not walking home like this."

They jump on a double decker and climb up the metalled stairway. The top deck is deserted except for an elderly woman sitting halfway up the bus on the left-hand side. She turns round briefly to see who's got on and adjusts a scarf over her ruffled grey hair. Quinn notices a half-smile on her face, as if she knows them from somewhere or she's just relieved to have company. He suddenly thinks of his mother and the way her face would light up any time he arrived home unexpectedly. She would stand there in the doorway holding her arms straight down by her sides with her hands open and slightly raised, waiting for him to come forward and embrace her. He hated himself for the guilt he felt every time he realised it had been months since he visited her grave out at Drumbeg.

Without warning the bus jolts forward and they topple onto the back seat, and then it shudders to a stop again and they hear voices down in the street shouting profanities followed by the grating sounds of metal-tipped footwear on the platform and the bus lurches forward again. Seconds later two men in their twenties clamber up the stairwell, jabbering as they climb.

"Holy fuck, I'm full."

"No fuckin' wonder, the way you were knockin' them back."

"For chrissakes, a party's a fuckin' party, innit?"

"Just don't you puke all over me the way you did last time…"

"Or you'll do what, you dumb fuck?"

As they swagger past and move up the bus to slouch down on the front seats, one on each side, Quinn notes the black bomber jackets, the BDU camouflage pants and the

Doc Martens boots with steel toes. Both have shaven heads, one with a dragon tattoo in a ring of fire at the back, the other entirely covered with a lifelike skull and the text *No Surrender* in Gothic script across the neck. And Quinn thinks: Christ, these guys are locked in a time warp from the seventies.

They have no sooner sat down than they pull out cigarettes and light up. Quinn ponders the smoking ban. Does it just apply downstairs? They keep up their Neanderthal banter until a shrill voice cuts through the cacophony of obscenities.

"Excuse me, excuse me."

The woman sitting further up the bus has half risen from her seat.

"Please, would you mind not smoking up here? There's a smoking ban and I suffer from asthma."

They turn round and stare at her until the Neanderthal with the skull tattoo decides to answer her question.

"Listen, missus. We can smoke here if we fuckin' want to. We can burst into flames if we want to." He laughs with the vacant face of a corpse. "There's no fuckin' smoking ban up here."

"Please, I'm sorry to have to ask you. I usually have my nasal spray with me, my inhaler, but I forgot it. I've left it at home."

Her voice is thin and without inflection. She slumps back in the seat. The skinhead with the dragon tattoo looks at the other one and shakes his head resignedly.

"The aul' bitch wants us to put our fags out. Can you fuckin' believe that?" The skinhead with the skull tattoo can't believe it and says so.

"What's the world comin' to when a fella can't have a quiet smoke in a public place anymore?"

The woman pulls herself up using the back of the seat in front. "Please, I think I have an attack coming on."

Quinn can detect a slight wheezing in her speech. The skinheads turn away, facing front again, and continue to babble abuse.

"Hey, fellas," Quinn calls out. "Why don't you give the lady a break?"

There is a moment's silence before they both whirl round, eyes agog with instant aggression.

"Mind your own business, cuntface,"

"Yeah, why don't you give your own lady a break, Grandad? Give that piece of hot chocolate a bit of a stir, know what I mean? You're not too old for that, are you?"

They chortle uproariously at this suggestion and, when Quinn doesn't respond, turn back to look out the front window at something happening down in the street. A car horn blasts a jagged peal of protest and the bus slews to a halt once again.

As the woman starts coughing Quinn swings round, grabs the red cylinder and wrenches it from its metal clasp. Renée touches his arm. "What are you doing?"

But he's off the seat and up the aisle and on top of the shaven heads before they even know he's there. As they begin to turn their heads, Quinn rips the safety pin from the handle, aims the short hose and squeezes the trigger. He aims at the cigarettes, sweeping from one to the other, back and forth. Skull-head has a cigarette in his hand, but his companion has his in his mouth, which is where Quinn directs the spray. The chemical powder spews out of the nozzle engulfing them both and they slide off the seats and onto the floor in a bid to escape. Quinn presses harder and harder until the powder spray is exhausted.

"Holy fuck," Skull-head gasps. The other skinhead is busy frantically wiping the powder out of his eyes, off his face, up over the dragon etched in the crown of his head. The cigarettes lie extinguished in a puddle of foam on the floor.

"Oh thank you," the asthmatic woman croaks from her seat. The bus is moving forward again. Quinn half turns his head towards her. When he looks back, Skull-head is rising to his feet with a knife in his hand. Quinn recognises it as the same knife he has used in training: a standard British Army combat knife with a seven-inch blade. Skull-head makes a forward slashing movement and Quinn lifts the fire extinguisher to ward it off, but it's heavy and he's too slow and he feels the knife slice his cheek and chin as he backs off in desperation.

"You're dead," Skull-head hisses, and he draws his arm back to make a darting thrust at the policeman's chest but Quinn has control of the cylinder now and the fury fires him as he launches it at his attacker and feels the crunch against nose and cheekbone as it smashes into his face with everything Quinn can put into it. But as Skull-head goes down the other skinhead comes at him from the side with a hawksbill spring blade, slashing him on the other cheek though he manages to avoid the worst of it by spinning round using his lunge with the fire extinguisher to gain momentum. And as he rotates to face him, Dragon-head makes an upward backhand swipe with the hawksbill, which is blocked as Quinn follows through with his impetus, swinging the cylinder into his elbow and there is a crack and a scream of agony and the knife falls to the floor.

The fire extinguisher clangs to the metalled floor as Quinn drops it to grab his assailant's right ear with the fingers and palm of his left hand, pressing his thumb across and into his eye. Dragon-head tries to twist his head away but only makes it easier for Quinn to thrust his thumb deeper into the eye. Suddenly the bus brakes and as he loses his left-hand grip Quinn slams him against the front window and jabs the index finger of his right hand like a screwdriver into his windpipe just below the Adam's apple.

He stops whimpering then because he can't breathe and Quinn watches his one good eye lose focus and his body sag until he hears Renée behind him yelling, "Quinn, for Christ's sake, you'll kill him!" and he shoves him to the studded metal floor, whips round and jogs down the aisle and down the stairwell with Renée in front of him just as the bus pulls up at Shaftesbury Square and they jump off and disappear into the night.

FIVE

Quinn stood at the dormer window and peered out at the morning. A pregnant cloudbank purpled half the sky, a murky backdrop to the row of houses and ash trees on the other side of the street. Behind him, from an unseen horizon, the sun shone on the tops of the avenue trees, casting long, translucent shadows through the morning rain. The slate-cloaked rooftops glistened blue-black in the downy drizzle.

He walked back into the room, into the compact bathroom and into the broom-cupboard shower cubicle. He recalled Renée being in there with him, tight together. He hadn't noticed the slightly stagnant, drainage-pipe odour then, but he noticed it now.

There had always been ups and downs in the relationship, and he realised with a start that it had been the downs that had made the ups so good. So let's face it, he thought, recently there had been more downs than ups. The water helped to wash away the sleep and most of the hangover, but he felt empty, utterly drained. All the strength had seeped out of him, leaving him immobile, quite still, unable to move. He stood there lifeless in the misty glass coffin of the cubicle, listening to the water gurgling down the drain. After a while it began to turn cold and he switched it off. He was still standing there like an upright corpse when he heard a key turn in the front door. He slid the glass door to the side and called out, "Hello?"

There was a momentary silence before she spoke. "It's me," Renée said. "I forgot a couple of things."

Quinn dabbed himself swiftly with a towel and wrapped it round his middle. Renée was crouched over the CD player when he padded into the room. He went over to the small wardrobe closet beside the alcove, took out a clean shirt and put it on. Then he hesitated with his boxer shorts and chinos. "What'd you forget?" he asked, walking over to the window and fumbling with the buttons on his shirt.

"Well, I forgot to leave the door key for starters. And my CDs are still here," she said fishing them out of the stand. He thought of the times they had lounged intertwined on the two-seat sofa, listening to them, happy that they at least had the same taste in music.

"Dire Straits and Gerry Rafferty."

"Golden oldies," she said with a penumbral smile that he couldn't quite read. She turned back to the CD rack. "I think I had another here somewhere."

Quinn watched her skim through the titles. She plucked out a couple of the plastic boxes, then checked through everything once again, more carefully, taking her time. He might not have been there, in the same room, listening to his heart.

Renée was dressed in bleached blue jeans and a turquoise polo shirt under an unzipped brown suede jacket. Her black hair hung loosely and evenly over the collar. He tore his eyes away and glanced out the window.

The rain had passed, and a light breeze was shaking the ash trees free of raindrops. The cloudbank had sunk below the houses opposite and the sun shone out of sight behind him in a desolate blue sky. Fragmenting raindrops trickled erratically down the mottled pane. He shivered in the coldness of the room.

"That's the lot I think," she said.

Quinn looked at the half dozen CDs she had clasped in her hand. She held the door key between thumb and forefinger in the other hand. She placed it carefully on top of the player. "There's your key," she told him.

She stood up straight and made ready to leave. For a moment she seemed to look at him questioningly, her deep almond eyes seeking a response. He sensed a band of panic tighten between his temples. His throat felt lined with gravel, his lips cracked with dry cement.

"I don't want you to leave," he said suddenly.

She stopped then, stood still and let him speak. The words poured out like a cloudburst of rain.

"I know I can't stop you. I shouldn't have tried. Of course I don't own you, but the fear made me act as if I did. It was stupid. If you really want this job, then take it. Go ahead. Take it and give it all you've got. But, at the end of the day, it's still just a job. So don't forget what we've had together. I realise you probably see me as being a lot like your father, trying to stop you from doing what you want to do, force you into something you don't want. But the fact is I've always looked up to you for your independence, at the same time as I suppose I've felt threatened by it."

He tried to smile at her then, to camouflage the embarrassment he felt, but it was a tight grimace that dented the corners of his mouth and froze in the abrupt silence of the room. He still had the towel round his waist and the clean shirt on his back, but standing before her with his discomfiture and his crooked smile, he was naked.

"Jesus, Quinn, I didn't know you could make such a long speech."

He felt a surge of wonder and excitement as she came towards him. She caught him by the collar of his shirt and his hands were in her hair and he felt the tears in his eyes and his heart ached with the love of her until the towel and the CDs lay scattered across the floor and they were together again in one electric moment as they had been in the beginning when they were close and he was sure that she was all that he had ever wanted.

The telephone woke them, a shrill double echo piercing the cocoon of midday slumber. Quinn creaked his eyes open to see the low December sun creeping in through the window, casting a shaft of hazy light across the room.

"Let it ring," he mumbled, wriggling closer, his arm tightening its hold on her shoulder.

"God, is that the time?"

Renée pulled away from him and peered at her wrist watch on the dresser, then reached for her clothes. "I have to go."

"Can't you answer it? It's right beside you."

"It's your phone, in your flat. You take it."

She slid out of bed, scooped up her clothes from the floor and disappeared into the bathroom. Quinn sat up staring at the bathroom door as it closed behind her brown buttocks and he heard the bolt sliding home. Then he groaned and rolled over to the dresser. He was just about to pick up the phone when it stopped ringing.

Relieved, he lay back in bed and thought about what had happened and what it could mean. He was never sure where he stood with her, was always uncertain as to what she really wanted. Often he wondered if she really knew herself. He was both drawn to her and rebuffed by what he saw as her erratic mood swings. He had sought an easy familiarity which she was apparently unable to give. It was as if she was always on her guard. There were just so many ups and downs.

The sleep meant his hangover was no more than a fuzzy memory. He listened to the shower running and thought about what to say when she came out. A faint ray of sunlight had fallen obliquely across the room, slanting weakly into the kitchenette. He saw the dust everywhere and tried to remember when he had last cleaned. When the shower stopped he got out of bed and started to dress. He put on his dark blue chinos and a soft check flannel shirt Renée had given him shortly after they met.

He had just buttoned up when the bathroom door burst

open and Renée strode fully dressed into the room. She glanced at him, then at the dresser where her silver-banded wrist watch still lay.

"I'm in a hurry," she told him, making for the dresser and snapping the bracelet round her wrist. She sat down on the bed to put on her shoes. He started to ask her where she was in a hurry to, when the phone began to ring again. She snatched up the cordless receiver from the dresser beside her.

"Yes?"

Quinn could hear the plastic echo of a voice, a woman's voice, speaking fast, loud and shrill. Renée swung round to him, extending the receiver.

"It's someone called Linda," she said, giving him a quizzical look. "Seems to be in quite a state."

He took the phone wondering what the hell was going on. Linda? He only knew one Linda. He couldn't remember the last time she had rung him. An uneasy feeling took hold of him. He went over to the window and looked down at the street.

"Hello. Linda?"

"Thank God you're there. I don't know what to do. Arthur's disappeared. They think it's the IRA. Or the RIRA. They've lifted him. You remember, five years ago, he did that piece about the Newry bombing, the big exposé that put some of them away. Well, they're out now, all part of the bloody Peace Process. Jesus, all those murderers are being let out on the street. Anything can happen. They can —."

"Hold on, Linda, hold on. Have you contacted the police?"

"They contacted me." She spoke quickly, forgetting to breathe, her speech broken, punctuated with short gasps. "They're here now. It happened at the railway station – he was on his way to work – they attacked him – he was abducted. I didn't know. I heard about it on the news. Then Alf rang – Alf McCurran, his boss – said he hadn't come in – asked me if he'd been taken ill. And I tried to ring you – but then the police came. They're here now. Alf had rung them and –."

"OK, OK, I'll be right over."

There was a sharp intake of breath on the end of the line and what sounded like a sob. Then she seemed to gather herself.

"Please come as quick as you can."

"I'm on my way."

He disconnected the call. Down in the street he saw students on their way to the university, hurrying along in the thin December sunshine. It must be near the end of term, he thought distractedly. They'll be breaking for Christmas. His mind was racing.

He had to get to Bangor. He turned to replace the phone in its cradle on the dresser when he realised that the front door was wide open and the room was empty.

SIX

Ards Peninsula

The rain falls from a dark, restless sky, soft and grey like a threadbare veil shrouding the land. Mid-winter clouds scurry past, high in the heavens, pushing on and out across the Irish Sea. The road ahead runs forward wet and black into the sleeping landscape.

Michael McCann gazed out the window as the car undulated over the green hills of County Down, rising and falling it seemed almost in time with the slow, sweeping scrape of the windscreen wipers. Ireland is a world of rain, he thought, looking up at the flurries of cloud gusting past in the fresh west wind. Beyond the naked hedgerows he watched the farmlands parcelled out in tattered allotments, skimming by in the early-morning gloom.

Lights still shone in the whitewashed houses, and once he glimpsed dark figures hurry across the yard to a nearby barn. Later he saw headlamps in the wing mirror as a van sped up behind them, followed almost bumper to bumper, then overtook them on a short straight stretch in a deluge of churned-up drizzle, leaving them temporarily blinded

"Holy fuck," Michael breathed.

"Keep yer hair on," Brady said, clenching the wheel. "You're safe now."

Michael stared at the side of Francis Brady's ruddy face. In profile, from his wispy beard, snub nose and craggy forehead up over the flat, thinning, sandy hair down to his long, flossy ponytail, he closely resembled a Woodstock hippie roused from a 30-year slumber. What the fuck did he know about being safe? Try sitting a couple of years in the Maze with all those vicious bastards you couldn't trust for two seconds. Christ, they'd slit your gullet as soon as look at you, stab you in the eye with a ballpoint pen, mash your fingers in the iron slit of the cell door. He'd seen it done. More than once.

And the warders were out of control. You weren't safe anywhere. Those UFF fuckers were always looking for a chance. In the Maze everyone knew Tommy Sutton was after him. "McCann is number one on my list," he'd told them. It was like an execution about to happen. Jesus, they reckoned Sutton had murdered at least 40 people. There'd been more than half a dozen attempts to kill him, but they'd all failed. The guy led a charmed life. Sutton was a bloody demon, they said. A demon of death.

Michael used to think about that sitting alone in his H-block cell. Anything could happen. And more often than not, it did. There was the daily outing for exercise, and all sorts of people coming on visits when you felt extra vulnerable, more exposed, often utterly defenceless. You didn't know who was coming, who would be there. And in the beginning there'd been the court appearances.

It was open season on him then. Prisoners would come and go in a constant stream of releases and arrests. Sometimes, for a while, the Irish classes and the reading and the sexual frustration took his mind off it. But then he'd be back in his cell, sitting there, looking up at the five vertical slits of light that formed the window, and he'd be thinking about it again, listening to sounds outside, fantasizing about how they would do it, wondering when it would come. Sutton had sworn to get him.

He remembered waking in the middle of the night, sitting suddenly upright in the deafening silence with a voice in his head that screamed of guilt and blame and unyielding remorse.

He simply could not believe he was now out on the street because it was still with him. It was like a death sentence that hadn't been carried out yet. And Brady sitting there with his "You're safe now" and his hair hanging limply down to his arse like a donkey's tail. Brady didn't know shit.

Michael McCann gazed in wonder at the passing countryside. It was years since he had last travelled this same road down the Ards Peninsula, the endless hedges ventilated with occasional iron gates, lanes and potholed side roads. Down through the little cottaged village and townland of Kircubbin on the lough shore and on to Portaferry and the ferry boat across the Narrows to Strangford.

Brady had picked him up when he got out of the Maze. The warders had broken them into two groups and staggered the release times so the Micks and the Prods wouldn't meet at the exit. Michael hadn't felt as nervous since that day in Newry all of five years ago. Brady had been their armorer then. It was all so unreal, so hard to fathom. Then and now. Fifteen years commuted to five, thanks to the Good Friday Agreement. Somehow the sudden, boundless sense of freedom made him feel unsteady, fragile, increasingly uncertain.

Yesterday they'd driven to Newtownards at the northern end of Strangford Lough, then down the coast road to Greyabbey where they'd stopped at the Wildfowler Inn for beef and mushroom pies and a pint. Michael had felt like a kid at his own birthday party. Brady looked at him and smiled. Michael gazed around at the other people living their normal everyday lives. He watched them talking between eating their lunchtime food and drinking their lunchtime pints. Brady had to tell him his pie would be cold if he didn't eat it soon.

From Greyabbey Brady had followed a back road across the peninsula to a solitary farmhouse at the end of a lane where he lived alone. Michael wondered how anyone could live on their own in such an isolated place, but then Brady had always been the ultimate loner. They swung round the house and parked in a concreted yard at the back.

The building was funereal, ice-cold and bare: a mausoleum. They had sat before the massive stone fireplace, the flames crackling and spitting round half-dry logs in the grate, wood-smoke drifting round the room, and they had talked about the old days, about the fluctuations of fortune in the campaign against the Brits, the Good Friday Agreement, and about Cassidy, Cooney and Collins, already released, what had happened to them and – ever in their minds – who had betrayed them. The word had long been out that an informer had rung a journalist at the Belfast Telegraph, had mentioned names, dates, places, revealing incontrovertible evidence leading to mobile phone traces and contacts linking them to the blast, implicating them beyond the shadow of a doubt. A Judas had nailed them to the cross.

Michael pushed his feet into the passenger well of the car and felt his shoulders rubbing against the softly yielding seat back and his head hit the supple leather support. What was Brady doing driving a big BMW with nappa leather upholstery and several hundred horses galloping under the bonnet? It was a far cry from the old Vauxhall Cavalier he used to have. It's an M6 Gran Coupé, he'd said on the way from the Maze, as if that meant something. Well, he always was crazy about cars – guns and fast cars. All the same, it was funny he'd never been fingered like the rest of them. His name had never been mentioned. And whoever had grassed on them had undeniably been rewarded for the information, that's what they said. Handsomely rewarded.

Daylight brought a light breeze that ruffled the water as they crossed on the ferry to Strangford, the hidden sun edging its way over the horizon behind clouds swollen with rain, the tide on its way out. They sat in the Gran Coupé without speaking. The ferry ploughed its way through the bottle-green water, steady and firm in the lough-mouth swell. Michael stared straight ahead at the van that had passed them earlier: a dark blue Ford Transit with a Belfast registration. For a moment he thought he saw a face at one of the rear windows, but when he looked again it had gone.

As they approached the small harbour below the rows of Victorian cottages, Michael felt himself grow tense with the questions buzzing in his head. He was about to ask Brady about his car, how he had acquired it, when Brady reached across in front of him, snapped open the walnut-burr lid of the glove compartment and pulled out a package wrapped in an oily flannel cloth.

"You may be needing this, Mickey," he said, handing it over. "But I hope you won't."

He switched on a thin smile before adding, "Best to be on the safe side."

Michael lifted the cloth carefully and uncovered a Ruger SP-101 revolver with a short barrel and an ebony handle.

"That's the .357 Magnum," Brady told him. "The big one. It'll stop anything short of an armoured car."

Michael held it in his lap. He saw it was loaded. Five bullets. It was heavy. "There's an ammo carton in there," Brady said, nodding at the open glove compartment. "It's full."

Michael slipped the Ruger into the right-hand pocket of his quilted jacket, pulled the ammo carton from the glove compartment and stuffed it into the other deep pocket. He couldn't deny the increased sense of security they bestowed.

"I'm just looking out for you, Mickey," Brady said as the ferry docked.

"Yeah, Francie, thanks," Michael said with an awkward nod, his misgivings receding with the outgoing tide. "Quick crossing," he added, as Brady started the engine and he searched for something to say to allay his confusion. "What was it, ten minutes?"

"Yeah, that's all. It's a wonder they haven't built a bloody bridge and ruined it." When Michael looked at him askance he continued: "This is an historical site, Mickey. Did you know there's been a ferry operating here since the 12th century?" Brady glanced at him as he drove off the ferry and up the slipway into Strangford.

"You're a fuckin' mine of information," Michael told him, now reassured by the contents of his pockets.

Brady shook his head in rebuke, his ponytail wagging like a dog's tail. "History is important, Mickey. Our history."

"Well, it looks like our history is changing now."

"Yeah, but is it for the better?" Brady's ponytail swung again in bristly dissension.

"Five years instead of fifteen in the Maze. That's a fuckin' sight better, I'd say. I've nothing against the Good Friday Agreement."

Brady gave him a derisive look. "That's just you – your life. What about Ireland, the people of Ireland? We're no closer now to what we wanted five years ago."

"Yeah, makes you think, doesn't it?" Michael said. "There's what we want, and there's what people want – ordinary, everyday people, not your Marxist-Leninist counter-revolutionaries fighting for an all-Ireland workers' republic."

He stopped abruptly, taken aback by his own verbosity.

"Jesus, you've changed, Mickey. You were singing a different tune five years ago."

Michael felt his stomach coil up in a rigid knot, his chest clamp tight with anguish. With clenched fists he expelled his breath in a short hiss, his lips a taut slit slashed across his face.

"What happened five years ago was a monumental fuck-up. Have you forgotten that? Have you any idea what it feels like to have been a part of that? Twenty-three ordinary people – not soldiers, not police, not the fuckin' UVF, but ordinary men, women and children blown to kingdom come. One was a woman pregnant with twins. Have you any idea? Some of the bodies were never even found because the force of the blast was so fuckin' ferocious. But you wouldn't know about that, would you? Because you weren't even there."

"You know I wasn't there. I'd done my bit," Brady retorted, a defensive frown rippling his forehead.

"Too right you had," Michael shouted. "You'd fuckin' *over*done it!"

"Well, for Christ's sake, you weren't there either. You were just in the scout car, checking the route. It was Cooney and Campbell in the bomb car."

"Yeah, and they fuckin' parked it in the wrong place," Michael said. The memory of it made him squirm. "Three hundred yards from the courthouse, at that shopping centre."

"They couldn't park at the courthouse, like they thought. It was cordoned off. Liam had phoned the warning in too early," Brady said, angry at telling him what he already knew. "For fuck's sake, this is history. You know all this. The Brits were everywhere, soldiers and police. The lads panicked. They drove on and just parked at the first place they could find."

"And people were moved there, away from the courthouse. The warning was for the courthouse. Jesus, talk about lambs to the slaughter."

Brady sat back in his chair, shook his head and sighed.

"OK, you're right, Mickey, you're right. It was a monumental fuck-up like you say. But there's always casualties in a war. What's the use of going over all that again? There's no point in looking back, nothing to be gained by that. It's over, Mickey, it's done. It's the past."

Michael swung round to face him. "The past is the one thing you can be sure of, Francie. The only thing."

A pained expression crossed Brady's face.

"Christ, you going to get all philosophical on me now?"

"At some point you have to face up to things. That's one thing I've learned in the last five years. Don't you ever regret things you've done? For fuck's sake, Francie, you can't pretend it never happened."

By way of answer, Brady pulled up outside the Cuan, a grey-walled, two-storeyed inn on the square. He looked Michael square in the face.

"We need some breakfast," he said. "I'm not going to try and talk some sense into you on an empty stomach."

They entered the Cuan under a stained-glass transom window above the entrance. Inside, in the tea room that felt like a homely living room, a coal fire was burning under a smoke-blackened iron mantelpiece. They sat in a corner near the fireplace, watching the low-burning flames, smelling the fire and the polished wood of their surroundings. Varnished wall-panelling enclosed the room together with a broad band of patterned, russet-red wallpaper. A pot of tea and toast with a dish of butter curls and thick-cut marmalade were brought by a tall, handsome woman in middle age who might have been the manager or the owner or both. When she left they sat in silence looking round the room. They were alone. Gilt-framed pictures of local sights hung high on the walls: Strangford Castle, the lofty Temple of the Winds overlooking the lough, and an old sepia photo of Castle Ward.

"Ever been there?" Michael said, nodding at the photo above them. Brady followed the direction of his gaze and sniffed.

"No," he said. "Gentrified houses aren't really my thing. What is it?"

"Castle Ward. It's only a couple of miles from here."

"You've been there?"

"I was there once," Michael told him. He hesitated before adding, "With Mary Devlin."

"Mary Devlin?"

Francis Brady's sandy eyebrows shot up like fertilised weeds. He smiled knowingly. "Yeah, I remember you had the hots for her, long time ago. Well, whaddya know? Is that why you're going back to Ballyfoil? To see her?"

Is that really why I'm going back? Michael thought, I'm not sure. I'm not sure of anything anymore.

"I don't know. My mother's there," he said, shaking his head. "And it's where I come from. Ballyfoil's my home ground. Anyway, I haven't seen Mary Devlin in over five years. She wrote a couple of letters at the start, but then they stopped coming. I mean, fifteen years in the Maze – what was the point?"

"Yeah, you can appreciate that." Brady nodded understandingly. "Not even Mother Teresa would wait that long."

"Mother Teresa?" Michael's features contracted until his face resembled a dried prune. "Mother Teresa? How does a nun come into it? A nun's not going to be there in the first place. For God's sake, Brady, how does your mind work? That's sick, man, sick."

"I just mean nobody would wait that long, Mickey, no normal person," Brady said, backpedalling desperately. "You can't blame her." He stabbed at a butter curl, as if to emphasize his point, and transferred it to a slice of toast.

Michael said, "I'm not blaming anybody. There's nothing to be blamed for."

"No. And now it's been five years, she may not even be there anymore."

"No, probably not. I mean, what would keep her in Ballyfoil?"

"What would keep anybody in Ballyfoil?" Brady snorted. "The armpit of Ireland."

"Aw come on, Francie. You've only been there once. Maybe twice. How would you understand living in a village? You belong in a jungle. I grew up there, remember?"

"You had to grow up somewhere, Mickey. Not your fault. But let's face it – it's a one-horse town. I'm surprised there's anyone still living there. What do people do? I mean, the industry's gone. There's nobody cutting Mourne granite anymore."

Michael raised his hand and inclined his head remonstratively.

"Hold on there, hold on. I know there's at least one firm still making work tops, floor tiles, memorial stones, that sort of thing. And I know people who work there. At least I used to."

Brady spooned a substantial dollop of marmalade onto his toast and distributed it as evenly as his shovel-like hand would allow.

"Yeah, well," he began, "I can see the need for memorial stones with the way the business is dying off, but there isn't much else to keep people living in the Mournes."

"You obviously haven't heard about the Whitewater Brewery," Michael said, "which surprises me, knowing your fondness for the brown stuff."

Brady half-raised his left hand, palm up, in surprise; the right hand was busy holding his slice of toast, plastered with butter and marmalade.

"The Whitewater Brewery's in the Mournes?"

"It's in Kilkeel, and it's taking off in a big way."

"OK, OK, I stand corrected. I had a couple of pints in Belfast last week. It's a drop of good stuff, I'll grant you that."

"Well, Francie, you may think it's daft but most people

today don't give a tinker's about the high and mighty ideal of a United Ireland. Not anymore. Maybe twenty or thirty years ago they did, but not now. What they care about now is jobs. And that means industry – light industry, heavy industry, any kind of fuckin' industry."

"So there's an industrial revolution going on in the Mournes," Brady sneered.

"I'd say it's a fuckin' sight better than your kind of revolution," Michael retorted. Brady glared at him and seemed about to say something. In the end he took a savage bite of his toast and started chewing like a horse eating a wild crab apple.

Michael refilled their teacups and they each topped up with milk. Brady pointed a scuffed, nail-bitten finger at the picture of Castle Ward.

"So what were you doing there with the lovely Mary Devlin?"

Michael sat gazing at the photo for a couple of moments before he answered.

"Aw, it was just an outing. It was a good day to begin with, but we ended up having a row." He seemed to think about this, before adding, "A bit like the people who built that house."

"What do you mean?"

"Well, they were an odd couple."

Michael cast his mind back, trying to recall the details of the story.

"They wanted to build a fine, impressive house but they didn't have the same taste. He wanted one style of architecture and she wanted another. Anyway, it ended with the front of the house being built the way he wanted it. But, if you go round to the back, you'll see that she had the last word there because it's a completely different style – the way she wanted it."

Francis Brady discharged a humourless chuckle.

"So they both got what they wanted and everybody was happy."

"No, not really. They ended up getting divorced."

"Yeah, tell me about it," Brady said with a leer. "And what did you and Mary quarrel about? I can't believe it was the architecture."

Michael drained his teacup, placed it on the saucer and sat looking at its antique rose pattern as if he was seeing it for the first time.

"It was Newry," he said at last in a whisper.

Brady jerked back in his chair. "What? Newry? You told her about Newry? Were you out of your fuckin' mind?"

Michael raised both hands in a gesture of pacification.

"Keep yer hair on. And keep yer voice down." He glanced at the door, as if expecting it to open at any second.

But Brady was not to be pacified. "She's the fuckin' squealer, don't you see that? Are you fuckin' stupid? It's her. And you told her, you dumb bastard. You told her."

"I didn't tell her. Will you just listen? I didn't tell her. This happened way before Newry. We went to Castle Ward a month or more before Newry."

"You didn't tell her?" Brady looked at Michael almost beseechingly.

"No, I didn't tell her. We were talking about the different ways of doing things, y'know, like the way Castle Ward turned out, with two different facades because they couldn't agree on just one style. And then we started talking about the cause, about getting the Brits out and how to go about it."

"What exactly did you say?"

There was an undertone of menace in the way Brady asked the question. Michael stared back at him before answering.

"It was maybe more what I didn't say that caused the trouble."

"How do you mean?"

"Well, she knew of course where my sympathies lay. I mean, she knew I was a member. You can't keep that a secret in Ballyfoil, and I wasn't the only one by any means – Jesus, you know that. Anyway, after a bit of shilly-shallying, she asked me point blank if I thought that the end always justifies the means."

"What did you say?"

Michael lifted his teacup, drained it and placed it very carefully back on the saucer.

"I told her what I believed then, what I was absolutely convinced of at the time. I told her that bombing the bastards was the only way to get the Brits out, that this was a war and in a war there will always be casualties and innocent people will get hurt."

Francis Brady shot out a freckled hand and took the last piece of toast without taking his eyes from Michael's face. "How did she take that?"

Michael hesitated before he answered. "It's strange, I remember exactly what she said, even though it was all those years ago. 'Michael,' she said, 'you won't be making me into the Blue Lady, will you?'"

"Blue Lady?" Brady looked down at the little dish on the table. He speared a butter curl and spread it on the toast. "What the fuck's that?"

Michael was irritated. He was about to skip an explanation but decided to tell him anyway.

"It's one of those myths in the Mournes – folklore I suppose you could call it. The Blue Lady is a woman who was abandoned by her husband – I don't remember why exactly – but she never gets over it and they say her ghost still haunts the mountains, searching for him."

They sat in silence for a few moments while Brady excavated the marmalade dish.

"And then, a few weeks later, 23 innocent people were

blown up in Newry," he said, his voice quiet and steady. "What did she say?"

"Well, I was lying low in Monaghan, remember, afterwards?" Michael reminded him. "So I didn't see her for some time. But when I got back to Ballyfoil I met her at Shannon's Grocery one morning and she followed me out into the street, and I could see it was on her mind. She looked around to make sure there was nobody else listening, and then she asked me straight out if I'd had anything to do with it. I denied it of course, told her I'd been down at my cousin's in Virginia, helping him with the hay. It was that time of year and I used to go down every summer and help out. It was common knowledge in the village."

"Did she believe you?"

"She didn't say. She just stared at me for a few moments, like I was a stranger or something. Then she turned on her heel and walked away."

Brady drank the rest of his tea without taking his eyes off Michael. To avoid his stare Michael looked up at the dusty, gilt-framed pictures hanging slightly lopsided on the wall.

"Was that the last time you saw her?" Brady asked.

"Yeah, it was." Michael turned his gaze back to Brady. "She wrote me a letter when I was standing trial. Of course I had sworn blind I was innocent and she said she deeply hoped that was true. Then, when all the evidence had been presented and I was found guilty, I got another letter from her."

"What'd she say?"

"It was a short letter. She was sorry she had believed me and she would pray for me. It was a letter of farewell."

Michael sat gazing at the flames flickering spasmodically in the fireplace. "She signed it 'The Blue Lady'," he said.

That had been the best time, he realised, the best time of his life: those warm summer months together with Mary, just the two of them in the high mountain lands of Mourne. And he recalled how he had held her head in his big bony hands and run his fingers through her hair, saw again the open expression of her face, the features clear and regular yet extraordinary, the trust mirrored in her eyes, the palest blue imaginable, and how she had given herself so unreservedly to him; and he was filled with a sudden, resurrected feeling of guilt and black despondency.

It was as if the years in the Maze had coarsened him, had deprived him of human qualities, inoculated him from the sentiments that were in his heart. And he was overcome by a sense of the irrevocable past, the thought of how unfair life can be, the realisation of what a good person Mary had been to him, the loss of what they once had together, how everything changes, how we change, and it's not always for the better. It all came back to him and he was overwhelmed by his freedom, assailed by his vulnerability. He turned away from Brady, half-rose from the table, hiding the tears in his eyes.

"Back in a sec," he mumbled and made for the door.

When he came back Brady had paid and the woman was clearing the table. Outside a shower had passed and the sun peered out warily from fluffy billows of cloud. Michael smelt the wetness of the grass and the low evergreen bushes dripping raindrops in the triangular green. He gazed round the square and up at the sky. Everything could change in an instant, he thought. He looked at the Georgian terrace across the square, noticing how finely sculpted it was, its symmetry and harmonious lines, the small-paned windows reflecting the weak rays of the sun. There could be a beauty in the order of everyday things. Abruptly he was struck with the understanding that he longed to see Mary again, and he felt a remarkable sense of hope and liberation surge through him. He couldn't explain it, but he was convinced that he would meet her again, that somehow she would be there in Ballyfoil, waiting for him to come back. He felt bewildered and confused by these sudden mood swings. As he walked to the car he kept asking himself: 'What the hell's happening to me?'

Brady was standing by the driver's door about to get in. He paused to scan the square with narrowed eyes.

"No sign of that bloody van," he said.

They got in the car and drove slowly out of Strangford.

SEVEN

Linda replaced the receiver in the cradle and looked thoughtfully at her reflection in the hall mirror. A hesitant smile flitted across her face. A police inspector in the Royal Ulster Constabulary was a useful person to know, particularly if you'd had him in your bed. Just the once, admittedly, and it was years ago, but even in Linda's unfettered experience it had been memorable. That Saturday morning as she stood there in her aerobics outfit with the short shorts and the tight, white, Girl-Power T-shirt, she had felt an instant attraction as soon as she had opened the front door and looked into his slightly puzzled face, the darkly steadfast eyes staring at her as if he could see right through her, as if he knew exactly who she was.

She took in every inch of him: a sturdy, tallish man conventionally dressed in a dark blue suit, white shirt with cutaway collar and a woven green tie. He had just stood there for a moment gazing at her before he said, "Mrs Williams? It's about the Newry bombing. I was told your husband would be at home."

"I've been cleaning," Linda had said, her eyelashes fluttering like hummingbird feathers. "You'd better come in."

Arthur was not at home. He was at his brother's discussing the property transfer that had caused so much enmity between them. Linda had foreseen the inevitability of a conflict when her mother-in-law had decided to transfer ownership of the parental home to Arthur without any exchange of money. And she was not dilatory in pointing out that Arthur's brother was already an affluent and highly successful businessman, while Arthur himself had always been the one on the commercial sidelines taking care of their mother. If the truth be known – and

Linda knew it intimately – he had always been the favourite.

The gift deed had just been registered and the two brothers had been having sporadic, often infected dialogues over a period of several months. Arthur was likely to be gone for some time, while Max was away playing a football match for his school. Later she would readily admit to Moira that glimpsing the semi-automatic pistol inside Quinn's open jacket had injected a certain frisson of excitement into the encounter, a feeling that had been instantly revived any time she had rung him up after that first meeting. And she had rung him up on a number of occasions. But Quinn had resolutely refused to see her again, realising the impossibility of secrecy, and knowing full well the inescapable consequences for his marriage and his career. Over and above these significant factors he was also troubled by his quaking conscience, a feeling of self-reproach which only worsened as he came to know Arthur Williams and ultimately hold him in high regard.

Following the breakthrough in the Newry bombing investigation, he had conducted a series of interviews with the journalist, both formal at RUC headquarters and informal at the Belfast Telegraph head office in Royal Avenue. During these discussions it had emerged that the bulk of the reward money being offered had been put up by a prominent local businessman whose daughter had died in the bombing. In view of the cardinal importance of the case, Quinn had made an extra effort on these occasions to assess Williams' competence and his character, both as a journalist and in a more personal capacity. He recalled a talk he had had alone with the chief editor at the Belfast Telegraph, Alf McCurran. Since there was no way that Arthur Williams as a journalist would reveal the identity of his source, if in fact he knew it himself, it was vitally important for the progress of the investigation that the information being passed could be classified as both authentic and reliable.

"There's a hell of a lot at stake here," Quinn had said. "I need to know that I can count on Williams and the intelligence he's receiving. The whole country's in uproar. We have to nail the bastards who did this."

McCurran sniffed aggressively, his spider-veined nose veering abruptly sideways as if in disgust at the topic of conversation.

"Obviously Arthur can't vouch for the veracity of what he's been told," he stated. "You must realise that yourself. But he seems to rely on his source and, all things considered, I'd go along with his instinct. Listen, Inspector, I've known Arthur Williams for the guts of twenty years. I can't say he's never put a foot wrong – he's only human. Sure he's made mistakes, but they've been wee footery things, not worth a fiddler's fart. Can you count on him? OK, let me make it simple for you – in my book Arthur's definitely one of the good guys. So, yes, I'd say you can trust him in this."

In the end, Quinn did. Despite his customary determination to maintain an objective distance, he couldn't help liking and admiring Arthur Williams for what he was doing and the professional way he went about it. Accordingly, he acted on the information supplied to him. He never regretted it. But that episode with Linda …

Linda tripped upstairs to the bathroom. He'd be here soon. If anyone could find Arthur, it was Quinn. There was something intense about him, something fierce and relentless that both attracted and in some way repelled her. But who had taken Arthur? And why?

As she fiddled with her foundation stick, Linda's mind wandered back to the early morning in the bedroom. She sighed. The same scene had enacted itself just last weekend, on Sunday morning, after a prolonged restaurant dinner on Saturday night with Glenda and Ian Stevens. She remembered lying there in the dark, flicking frantically through her catalogue of favourite fantasies, searching desperately for one to do the trick. In vain. What was it she had said then, in an attempt to sidetrack him, to take the sting out of it? It had come to her quite suddenly, a lightning bolt of wifely inspiration.

"Are you working for British Telecom?"

"Telecom? British Telecom? Whaddya mean?" His voice was a gruff whisper. She could feel his heart pounding like a steam hammer.

"I mean with that telephone pole you've got down there."

That paused him, diverted him briefly before he replied. "Uh, just a slight swelling. Nothing to worry about."

Poor Arthur,' Linda thought, reaching for the liner. 'What the hell has happened to him?'

Swiftly, expertly, she applied the liner just outside her natural lip line, then dabbed a smudge of gloss on the middle of her bottom lip and smacked her lips together. It was a trick she had learned from Moira to give the impression of plumper lips. "It'll give you that 'bee-stung' look," Moira had promised. And she was right.

'Poor Arthur,' Linda thought again. He was convinced that she was secretly injecting Botox or some other filler into her lips and, despite her protestations, assured her repeatedly that he liked her lips just the way they were, in their natural state. "Why would you want to look as if you've been stung by a bloody bee?" he'd asked.

Poor Arthur, she thought yet again, he simply didn't understand these things. It was so much easier to discuss such matters with Moira – well, with any of the girls: Glenda, Carol, Maria, Anne, whoever. The G-string Girls, as they liked to call themselves in a bold attempt to glamorise their 40-year-old-plus lives. And they all seemed to be having a similar problem with their men. Just a week ago Linda had invited them round for a 'perfume party,' her latest project in a long line of schemes to bring in some extra cash. This time she would be selling a new brand of fragrant scents that women were "simply going to fall over backwards for."

"That's the old Tupperware strategy," Arthur had remarked somewhat disparagingly when she broached the idea, "using social blackmail to sell the product."

"Nonsense," she had fired back. "Their perfumes are first class, so what's wrong with telling your friends about them?"

She had tried to laugh it off, but she realised that had been her own reaction when the company had launched the idea. Now, despite her misgivings, she had gone ahead anyway. When she thought back, she remembered the whole thing rather like a dream sequence, an incoherent series of pictures in her mind, a rather repugnant charade in which she had willingly taken part.

They had all somehow contrived to arrive at the same time. Linda had been hoping they would come in dribs and drabs so that she could attend personally to each one, re-establish the rapport they had, explain this embarrassing business of the perfume – that it was just an excuse to get them all together again, nothing else – and reassure herself that everything was going to be all right. But when they all simultaneously converged on the front door as if by some unseen signal, she had let it all just wash over her and, in retrospect, it was probably the best thing that could have happened.

Glenda Stevens was first to the door, deftly emerging through a flurry of poplins and Burberrys, her gold-hoop earrings dangling indecisively, thin lips crinkling in a tenuous smile.

"Hello Linda. Am I the first?" She didn't wait for a reply.

"Lovely idea, all of us meeting again."

At this point Linda was not so sure, but this was no time for second thoughts. She grabbed their coats and scarfs and ushered them into the dining room. There was a moment's hush as they surveyed the oblong pine table garnished with sets of silver-plated Swedish cutlery, Orrefors wine glasses and a collection of Bordeaux and Gewurztraminer wines forming a bottleshop high-rise up the middle.

"I thought we could eat straight away," Linda said, taking advantage of the momentary silence. "The food and plates are in the kitchen. Please, go right in and help yourselves."

Then she was swept up in the ceaseless swirl of identifying the various foods for them and seeing that everyone got enough to eat and drink, serving themselves from an assortment of dishes on the kitchen table and picking their way with plates heaped high back to the dining room. Eventually they were all seated and Linda nipped back into the kitchen to get herself something to eat. As she spooned a piece of foil-poached salmon, some beetroot and bean salad, and a slice of courgette and goat's cheese tart, she grew uneasy at the sudden silence that had fallen in the next room. Then Carol stuck her head round the door: "Come on, Linda, we're all waiting for you."

As soon as she sat down, Moira rose ceremoniously and called a toast in her name for having successfully gathered them all together again. There were many toasts after that, the others taking their cue from Moira. Before long it was difficult to get a word in edgeways: so many memories to recall, so many personal experiences to describe, so many incidents worthy of retelling. The fiery glow of the past was upon them and they warmed themselves gladly in its embers. In due course, from the sentimental evocations of lost youth, they worked their way up to the present day.

Afterwards Linda was never quite sure how they got on

to the subject, but when they opened the fourth bottle of wine, the cork popped out of the bottle in more ways than one. Linda had been in the kitchen mixing a bowl of fresh salad, splashing it liberally with classic vinaigrette. She was pondering the business of the perfume. She had not even shown them the products yet, much less tried to sell anything. Perhaps she would spoil everything if she did, cast a wet blanket over their buoyant mood. They certainly seemed to be enjoying themselves as things were.

She stepped into the dining room with the salad bowl, thinking about the perfume, wondering how to introduce it.

"Yes, isn't it awful?" Glenda was saying. "You know, I was over at my mother's the other day and she asked me how things were between Ian and me, so I told her."

"You didn't?" Anne said, grasping her wine glass for support.

"I did. It was a bit difficult at first, but she knew exactly what I meant."

Linda stood by the table, the salad bowl in her hands, looking over at the small mock-leather attaché case of perfumes on the sideboard, half-listening to what was being said.

"Well, what did she say?" Carol wanted to know.

Glenda took a deep breath. "She said, 'You have to go through with it – for their sakes'."

"You mean, like, fake it?"

Glenda shrugged. "Well, yes."

They all looked at one another, then at Linda.

"More salad anyone?" Linda ventured.

Anne snorted and tossed her urchin-cut, blond-streaked head.

"Tom would spot it a mile off. He can read me like a book. Definitely out of the question."

But Glenda would not be put off. "Then just go along

with it. Don't bother trying for an Academy Award. Just do your marital duty."

"You mean, lie back, grit your teeth and think of England." Anne protruded a stiff upper lip. "Oh jolly hockey sticks."

The other G-string Girls chuckled. Linda placed the salad bowl carefully in a vacant space on the pinewood table.

"Would someone mind telling me what you're all talking about?" she asked. For a few suspended seconds no one said anything; then they took it in turns to respond: "Desire." "Passion." "The urge." "Lust." "Sex."

They looked expectantly at Linda. "Oh," she said. "That."

"Yes," Moira said. "That."

Linda grabbed the nearest bottle of Bordeaux and set about filling up the promptly extended glasses of the G-string Girls.

"Well," she began, thinking quickly, "I met an old friend the other day and she reckoned it was the children who put the brakes on that."

"How many has she got?" Glenda asked.

"Three," Linda suggested, after a perceptible hesitation. "She had the last one a year ago," she added cleverly, "and she still hasn't got a glimmer of it back."

There was a brief pause while they drank their wine and thought about this. Then Maria said, "I'm not so sure you're right about that. I mean, that it's having children that puts a damper on things."

There was a longer silence. Maria was the only one who did not have children – whether by choice or by accident no one quite knew, though there was abundant speculation when she wasn't there to hear it. Her husband, Brian, was a sales representative and travelled a lot. Maria worked as a nurse in the A&E department at the City Hospital. She was good at emergencies.

"What do you mean exactly?" Anne said finally. "Are you saying we're all in the same boat?"

Maria smiled and took a deep breath.

"I mean, I think it might be as simple as recognising that men and women are biologically different."

"Well, I'll be a monkey's uncle," Anne said. "Why didn't I think of that?"

Maria's smile congealed for a second, then dissolved into an aggrieved frown. "My sister is just five or so years older than us, and she's already hitting the menopause. She tells me she suffers from 'emotional incontinence' – that's what she calls it – and says she often feels she's drowning in a tsunami of hormones. A tsunami of hormones? Some of us have that already every month. Do you think men go through that? Or anything like it?"

'Christ', Linda thought, are we really having this conversation? In vino veritas. "Okay," she said. "So we're different."

"Yes, we're different." Maria's frown was slackening. "Look, all I'm saying is that men and women have different sexual appetites. And, as we all know, the men are hungry most of the time while we, if we're honest – after ten or fifteen years of married life – can generally make do with the occasional snack."

"You realise, of course," Moira said, "that's an extremely sexist point of view."

Maria reassembled her features into an expression of light amusement. "Of course. But there's no such thing as sexual equality. Haven't you noticed?"

This was a question that did not seem to require an answer. They sat glancing at one another and reaching for their glasses. Glenda was the first to speak.

"It's ridiculous," she said. "Here we are, gathered together in order to sample all these musky perfumes, these sensual scents, every one of which is designed to make us incredibly alluring and seductive. And yet none of us can be really interested in turning on the man in our lives when we can't even manage to get turned on ourselves."

"Yeah, it's crazy, isn't it?" Carol declared. "I mean, half the time I feel like the victim of a traffic accident or something. You know, paralysed from the waist down."

"You make it sound as if it's our own fault," Moira protested. "What about the men? Haven't they any part in all this?

"Maybe they're the ones who should be wearing the perfume?" Glenda suggested. They snickered a bit at that, then got serious again.

"No, of course I don't mean it's all our fault," said Carol. "I mean, how much have we left to give at the end of the day? How many of us have the energy left to take any sort of initiative, sexual or otherwise?"

Glenda sighed audibly for all to hear. "Speaking for myself, I can tell you I'm absolutely knackered come six o'clock in the evening. Every evening."

Linda was surprised to hear her say this: Glenda who was interested in buying their kitchen, Glenda who was usually so much in control of every domestic situation, Glenda who continued, saying, "What with the kids and the washing and the ironing and the cleaning and the shopping – God Almighty, you have to be bloody Superwoman to cope with a randy man at the end of the day."

"You know what they say about Superwoman," Moira said. "Love is like kryptonite. When it shows up, all your super powers disappear."

"That's smart, Moira," said Carol. "But what the hell does it mean?"

Linda smiled mysteriously. "I'm not so sure that the real question is: How much have we left to give? Perhaps we should be asking ourselves instead: How much do we need to take?"

They talked about that, about their feelings of inadequacy and guilt, about all the labyrinth twists of married life. And they discussed their men – modern men with boxer shorts and snappy nappy changes – men who occasionally confessed that something had gone out of their marriage and they were living on the memory of the hot raunchy woman they used to know. Which brought them back to the old days again – B.C. as Glenda called it: Before Children. There was so much to say, so much to catch up on. After a while Linda had slipped out to the kitchen to make the coffee and collect her thoughts.

Well, she surmised, all things considered, the perfume party had been a reasonable success. When she had finally managed to open her attaché case and demonstrate the products, the girls had lapsed back into personal-appearance mode. One of the scents, Peony Passion, had won particular praise with several purchases being made on the spot. Yes, Linda had felt somewhat uncomfortable as money changed hands, but reminding herself of the expenditure for food and drink swiftly alleviated that feeling.

She drew the metal comb through her long blond hair, wishing it weren't quite so curly, and glanced at her watch. God, he would be here soon. Despite herself, she experienced a buzz of anticipation – and was immediately reproachful. Jesus, what was she thinking? Arthur had been abducted. She had no idea where he was, what had happened to him. The idea unsettled her as she opened the little phial. Shit, that Peony Passion was powerful stuff. She dabbed a little more behind her ears.

The sun had somehow shuffled up past the clouds and into the sky when Quinn got off the train from Belfast. The area outside the station had been cordoned off with crime-scene tape. A technician was sniffing around for clues and criminal traces on the site apart from the bloody stencil left in the tarmac. The umbrella was bagged and gone. Quinn had rung the chief superintendent to clear his involvement in the case. Given his background history with the family and the whole Newry bombing investigation, the chief had virtually given him carte blanche. He had skipped his car and taken the train to Bangor with the idea of following Arthur Williams' path from his home down to the station.

Quinn exchanged a few words with the sergeant overseeing the crime scene outside Carnalea Station. A couple of schoolgirls had witnessed the abduction but they were long gone. The sergeant had taken their statements and sent them on to school. Quinn took some notes. No one had got the number of the car, a white Ford Sierra. The colour and the make, but no number. Quinn left him, saying he'd be back within the hour to get more details. He took a narrow side-road running parallel with the railway and lough, then cut up onto a path through the hillside wood, a shortcut to the house on Carnalea Road that he still remembered from his previous visit. As he entered the woodland, he began to wonder if this was the path Arthur Williams had followed. There were several routes he might have taken.

Quinn walked swiftly uphill through the trees. The mildewy smell of vegetation hung in the gloom above the forest floor. Overhead the wood rose high, a towering edifice with unfurling cracks in its splintered roof, a timbered building forever shifting in the wind. At times the winter sun slanted down through the cracks, its distant light slicing myriad shafts through the trees. He walked beside a winding stream for part of the way. The path was verged sporadically with ferns that had browned and withered, their fronds dead, misshapen and broken. It took him almost ten minutes to reach the Crawfordsburn Road at the top of the hill. He followed the pavement for a hundred yards before crossing over to branch off onto the Carnalea Road.

The sun had slipped behind a murky cloud mass on the edge of the sky. Quinn buttoned his serge overcoat and increased his pace. He felt uneasy about the impending meeting. He should have brought one of the policemen from the station with him to keep things official, to help him relax and do his job.

The Williams home came into view gradually as he came round a bend, a pre-war red-brick house rising among the trees at the end of the road. As he approached, Quinn saw that the Williams seemed to be fighting a losing battle with the front garden: beyond the privet hedge the area nearest their neighbour was being gradually strangled by a metastasizing tangle of shrubbery, sprawling and unrelenting. Contrasting sharply with the red brick, the window frames had been newly painted white, as had the wooden gate he opened midway along the hedge.

With some foreboding he walked up the gravel path and onto the tiled floor of the porch. There was an electric push-button bell beside the front door and a tarnished brass knocker below the windowed top panel. On past experience Quinn distrusted the functionality of electric door bells. He lifted the brass hoop under the lion's head and let it fall. It resounded with a gibbeting clunk in the stillness of the porch. Quinn took a deep breath and waited.

EIGHT

The blue Ulsterbus with its white roof squealed to a halt at the crossroads. Michael McCann held his travelling bag in front of him as he made for the exit. He clambered down onto the grassy verge and stood in the pale light of the afternoon. No one else dismounted. The bus shuddered off again, strained up the hill and gradually sank beyond the summit.

Michael stood at the crossroads and listened until the engine drone dwindled and died in the dip of the next valley. Turning away from the mountain, he looked out over the lowland area of the Mournes with its patchwork quilt of green fields crisscrossed with drystone walls. It was just as he remembered it. Cushioned in a pillow of blue-grey cloud, the sun lurked low in the sky as it slipped to the horizon.

Michael swung round to face the mountain road behind him, a pockmarked tarmac track up to Ballyfoil, and started walking. It would take him around twenty-five minutes, he reckoned, to make it to the village. Francis Brady had dropped him off at the Ulsterbus station in Newcastle, saying he had to "make a delivery." What the "delivery" consisted of, he wouldn't reveal.

"What you don't know, can't hurt you," he'd clichéd. Michael wanted to smack him on the head with a lump of Mourne granite, but he made do with a suggestion that he perform a physically impossible sexual act. The mean bugger could easily have driven him out to Ballyfoil and then made his delivery. A half hour there and a half hour back. At the most. When he had pointed this out, Brady said he had "a time to keep."

As he went to take his bag from the back seat of the car, Michael recalled that Brady had insisted he put it there instead of in the boot. Looking at the BMW M6 Gran Coupé as they shook hands, he noticed that the rear end sank appreciably closer to the road surface than the front. Brady saw him looking, adding two and two together, wishing he didn't already know the answer.

"Take care, Mickey," he said and slid across the burgundy leather seat and into another world. Michael had watched him drive off and wondered if he would ever see him again.

The narrow road twisted its way up the highland slope. As he trudged uphill Michael felt a light mountain mist in his face and the soft, smoky smell of the damp turf brushed his nostrils. On both sides of the road evergreen gorse and wintered bracken skirted the drystone walls. He was looking around, getting his bearings, when he stumbled into a pothole and almost fell. Mouthing an obscenity he switched hands to hold his bag and tramped on. At the bus station he had transferred the Ruger and the ammo carton from his deep jacket pockets to the travelling bag. The extra weight seemed somehow to more than double the heaviness of the bag.

Picking his way between the potholes, he relived in his mind the summer evening over five years ago when he had walked up this road with Mary Devlin after their excursion to Castle Ward. He could almost feel the lasting warmth of the evening, see the sunlight golden on the gauze of Mary's hair, picture the strong curve of her back when he put his arm around her and how she twisted away from him. Most of all he remembered the crushed look in her eyes when he told her about his commitment to the cause and the heated discussion that followed.

"None of that will change anything," she had said finally. "How will you get a million people to become part of a united Ireland? Will you kill them all?"

"Mary, we're just looking for a strategy, an effective way

to get the Brits out."

"Looking for strategies, are you?" She glared at him defiantly. "That wouldn't include murder, would it? The indiscriminate murder of innocent people?"

Michael had tried to explain, but Mary was already moving away from him, marking the distance between them, hurrying on up the road to Ballyfoil. You've sacrificed yourself, she had said, sacrificed yourself on a shrine to misbegotten idealism. Now, when he thought about all that had happened, when the raw memories came to haunt him, Michael sometimes felt he was being stretched on a rack: the rack of regret. Stop it, he told himself, stop it. Don't waste your energy.

The sudden guttural rumble of a diesel engine and the harsh grinding of cantankerous gears told Michael he was not alone on the road to Ballyfoil. Turning to look back down the mountainside he watched a battered white van navigate the bends and potholes of the tarmac track below him. He stopped and stood still, watching the van approach. With a flick of his wrist he unzipped the side pocket of his travelling bag. The rust-blistered vehicle finally rattled to a stop beside him and the driver's window was rolled down.

"Is that you, Mickey?"

When he didn't reply the driver leaned his head out the window.

"It's Michael McCann, isn't it?"

Liam Hogan's bushy hair had gone snowflake-white since Michael had last seen him. He must be close to retirement age now. He peered out at Michael from behind metal-rimmed glasses. His eyebrows flared like a pair of ragged toothbrushes, much used and bristling with curiosity.

"And sure who else would it be?" Michael responded at last, zipping up the side pocket.

"I heard they were letting you out," Liam said. "The Good Friday Agreement. Jesus, how long were you in for?"

Michael realised it was a question many of the inhabitants of Ballyfoil would be asking him.

"Five years."

"God Almighty, Mickey, that's a long time, especially when you're young." The look of concern on Liam's face was reassuring.

"Liam, are you going to sit there blethering all day long, or are you going to give me a lift?"

"Well, stop standing there like an aul' bag of spuds and get in."

Michael walked round the van, cranked the chrome-flaked door handle and climbed up into the passenger seat. The van smelt of diesel and fish and chips. There was a scrunched-up newspaper on the floor at Michael's feet. Liam found first gear and they jerked forward. Soon they were up over the ridge and coasting down through the valley to the village. As the stone-walled fields rolled past, Michael took an edgy breath and asked the question in his head.

"Is Mary Devlin still in the village?"

"Mary Devlin? Yeah, she's here. Why?"

Michael was surprised at the question. "I used to know her," he said after a pause. Liam was silent. He seemed to ponder whether to pursue the subject, and thought better of it. Then he glanced over hesitantly. "What was it like in there, Mickey, in the Maze? I know it was pretty fuckin' awful during the hunger strikes in the eighties."

Michael thought about it for a moment. It was hard to believe he was no longer there. Bumping along the country road to Ballyfoil in a van after five years in the Maze was somehow unreal, something he could never have imagined a week ago.

"Well, it wasn't exactly the Europa Hotel."

Liam chortled. "They've blown that up more times than you've got fingers on yer hand."

He sneaked a look at Michael's hands, as if to check they were all still there. There were stories about atrocities, savage beatings, brutal interrogation methods at the Maze. You didn't know what to believe.

"Liam, things changed in the Maze in the nineties."

"You're telling me." Liam Hogan's rubicund face broke into a sudden flurry of agitation. "Jesus, it was like a bloody holiday camp when you were there."

"Whaddya mean?"

"Well, you weren't even locked in your cell, were you?"

"No, nobody was. Unless there was a security alert or they did a head count."

"That's what I mean."

"Holiday camp?" Michael felt a surge of anger. "You must be fuckin' jokin'. You could get murdered in there, dead easy. The doors not being locked just made it even more dangerous. Anyone could get in. Tommy Sutton was there and guess who was number one on his hit list."

Liam glanced at him and shook his shaggy head.

"Jesus, you're lucky you're still here then. But that worked both ways. The boys got Gordie Bell."

"Gordie Bell? Yeah." The name brought back memories, dark visions from the past. "It was ironic really. Both the IRA and the INLA had tried to kill him half a dozen times, and failed. Badger Bell always escaped. Then, when he was put in the Maze, he couldn't get away anymore. There was nowhere to hide. The Badger was caught in a trap."

"It was the INLA that got him, right?"

McCann nodded. "Three of them were in on it. It was well planned. One of them shot him when he was being taken for a visit with his girlfriend."

"They executed the fucker in the prison van."

"Yeah, that's how much of a holiday camp it was."

Liam Hogan's toothbrush eyebrows rose in dissension. "It was a completely different setup in the eighties when the hunger strikes began."

"Well, you were locked up in your cell for a start. The warders were hard as fuckin' nails."

"I know, Mickey, I know. I was there."

Michael McCann's head executed a sharp right-hand turn. "You were there? Whaddya mean, you were there?"

"My nephew was in there then," Liam said. He looked affronted, as if this was common knowledge, something Michael should have known, and didn't. "He was one of the hunger strikers. I went there to visit him."

"You're joking."

"No joke. It was just after the Dirty Protest, you remember, when they were smearing their own shite on the walls of their cells to try and get political status again."

Michael remembered it well. He had been in his last year at school. "So you went up to Belfast to visit your nephew at the Maze?"

"Aye, I did."

Liam was quiet for a while, concentrating on the road ahead as if it required his full attention before he spoke.

"You know, it's a funny thing," he said, "but I still remember the way the turnstile at the entrance creaked when you went through it. It was eerie. Made me think of torture, that squealing noise, like someone being hanged, drawn and quartered. Gave me an uneasy feeling, as if something bad was going to happen."

He turned to look Michael straight in the eye. "And it did," he added. Staring ahead again, he made a clumsy gear change from fourth down to third as they approached a sharp bend on the outskirts of the village.

"Gave me the willies, goin' there. We were crowded into a van, all of us including women and children, and it took us from the reception area to the H-blocks. The van had no windows, you were in the dark, couldn't see out, so you felt like you were on a fuckin' ghost train or something. It was scary."

They approached the cottages on the edge of the village where Michael's mother lived.

"Do you want off here?" Liam asked. His eyebrows lifted in hopeful appeal. "Or at the pub?"

"O'Leary's will do fine. I've a bit of a thirst on me."

Michael glanced out as they passed the cottage where Mary Devlin had lived. There was no sign of life. 'What did you expect?' he thought to himself. 'Yellow ribbons round the old oak tree?'

"We were counted in and counted out," Liam continued, slowing down. "And sometimes the van would stop on the way and a warder would come in to double-check the numbers inside."

Michael thought about all the people in Ireland who came to be counted then. "I heard there were 100,000 mourners at Bobby Sands' funeral," he said.

Liam removed his left hand from the wheel to give a disgruntled wave.

"Mickey, to hear people talk, you'd think Bobby Sands was the be-all and end-all of the Maze prison."

"Well, wasn't he? At least at that time."

Liam nodded. "He might have been the figurehead – he was the first to die – but there were ten republican prisoners who starved themselves to death in the name of political status, and my nephew was one of them."

The thought entered Michael's mind that Liam Hogan hadn't mentioned his nephew by name, but at that moment Liam braked and swung in to park behind a black BMW saloon outside O'Leary's pub.

"This is it, Mickey," Liam said. "Downtown Ballyfoil."

"You'll be singing the song next," Michael told him.

"Think I'm past it, do you?" Liam said, remembering the lyrics. "Just listen to the music of the traffic in the city," he burbled, "linger on the sidewalk where the neon signs are pretty."

Michael smiled at him. It was lucky meeting him on the road like that, good to see him again; suddenly it also felt good to be back in Ballyfoil.

"Could you take a jar, Liam?" he asked, nodding towards O'Leary's pub, its peeling façade encrusted with the grime of protracted neglect. Hogan's craggy features creased into a vermilion smile.

"Can a bird fly? Can a fish swim?"

"Be easier to talk if we had something to wash the words down with."

"Aye, and to flush them out with too."

Michael gazed across at the front of the pub. "The place could do with a bit of a clean-up. Maybe not a neon sign, but a coat of paint wouldn't do any harm. O'Leary always was a bit tight."

"Ted O'Leary doesn't have it any more, Mickey. He sold out."

"You're kiddin'. When was that?"

Liam Hogan stared at the fingers of his left hand, still holding the steering wheel. Michael got the impression he might be counting them.

"About four years ago. Well, he was getting on a bit – like me, you could say, 'bout my age. Wanted to see more of the grandchildren. So he sold out. Him and Teresa moved up to Belfast. They haven't been back since."

"Sold out? Really? Who to?"

"Gerry Savage. You know him, don't you?"

"Savage? Yeah."

Michael recalled a tall, athletically built youngster from school with an unruly mop of blond hair, a sullen attitude and a disposition towards bullying. "We were at school together. He was a couple of years ahead of me. Fancied himself as a hard man. Was a pretty good Gaelic player, though."

"Yeah, he's played centreback for Down – one of their best players."

Gerry Savage has come up in the world, Michael thought. "How'd he get the necessary to buy O'Leary's? There's not much money in playing Gaelic. I mean, it's not like playing for Man United, is it?"

"Dunno. There was talk of a legacy from some uncle in America, but nobody knows for sure."

"Can't have been cheap."

"No, it's the only pub around here, and popular. At least it was."

"Not now?"

"Well, like I say, it's the only pub to go to, so people still come. But Gerry Savage isn't exactly known for his irrepressible charm and winning ways."

"Still playing the hard man, is he?"

"Pretty much."

They looked out at the approaching evening. The long, evanescent shadows of the stone houses fell far across the street. Above the grey slate roofs the darkening slope of the mountain reached all the way up to the sky. The village was as it always had been, thought Michael, an elongated cluster of small country houses and cottages nestling under the brow of a hill.

"We better go in while you've still got the thirst on you."

"Aw Mickey, there's no danger of that goin' away."

Michael McCann followed Liam Hogan into the dim, low-ceilinged room that was O'Leary's pub. The roasted treacly smell of porter seemed to rise from the floor, reminding him of past times. There were only two other customers. Crouched together in a window seat, they looked up briefly before returning to their conversation. In a large Mourne-stone fireplace flames fluttered sluggishly round several sods of turf. The dimness at the far end of the wood-panelled counter dissolved suddenly when someone switched on a globe-shaped brass lamp. The same dusky brown panelling extended half-way up the walls with wall-bench seating all around. No carpet, no TV, no fruit machines. It looks a damn sight better than it did when I was last here, Michael thought, as he crossed the quarry-tiled floor to the bar.

Behind the bar he could see no one. Then, into the light of the brass lamp at the end of the counter appeared the considerable frame of Gerry Savage as he straightened up with an empty glass in one hand and a drying towel in the other. Crowned with a shock of blond hair like a half-shorn sheep, the former Gaelic football centre back gave instant credence to the oft-whispered notion that he had "Viking blood."

Catching sight of Michael and Liam Hogan at the bar, Gerry Savage stood for a moment as if transfixed. Then he moved slowly towards them along the counter. Michael noted that he hadn't put on any flabby weight since his schooldays. Gerry Savage was still a fast-running muscled powerhouse with shoulders like a brick shithouse, and the opposition on the football field would clearly have their hands full trying to stop him.

"Didn't expect to see you back here, Mickey," he said, contorting his mouth into what he imagined was a smile. The icy pale blue eyes stared unremittingly, devoid of merriment.

"Nice to see you again too, Gerry," Michael said, pointing at the tap tower in front of him with its Whitewater Brewery medallion. "We'll have a couple of pints of Hoppelhammer."

"Hoppelhammer?" Savage inclined his head to one side in admonitory posture. "You want to watch your step there,

Mickey. That's powerful stuff."

"I believe in supporting local industry. It's strong beer, is it?"

"It is that. Careful though, you don't want to be losing control."

"I've been keeping control for the past five years, Gerry. I don't think a pint of beer is going to change that now."

"Well now, you never know."

Gerry Savage pulled the beer with exaggerated care and concentration. Michael watched him as it gurgled into the glass. The knuckles of his hands were skinned and blemished with faint traces of dried blood.

"Still playing the Gaelic, are you?" Michael said, nodding down at the hands holding the glass and the tap. Savage caught his glance, topped off the beer and sat the glass down on the counter.

"Bit of trouble here last night."

He lifted the other glass and began to pour.

"I understand you're the publican here now," Michael said.

"That's right. The O'Learys moved up to Belfast."

"Grandchildren up there?"

"So I believe."

Michael half-turned to survey his surroundings. "You've done the place up, I see."

"Wasn't before time. We'll be doing the front in the spring."

His voice was gruff, not unfriendly, but not friendly either. He placed the second pint on the bar counter, looked up and stared fixedly at Michael. There was fire in the ice of those eyes.

"Will you be stayin' long?"

"I'm not sure," Michael replied. "It all depends."

Savage stood with both hands flat on the counter. His eyes never left Michael for a second.

"Anything else?"

"Got anything to eat?"

Michael could feel his stomach groaning for sustenance. He hadn't eaten since Brady had left him at the bus station in Newcastle. Waiting for the bus, he had ordered sausages and beans on toast at a nearby transport café. It had been a gastronomic experience of debatable merit. He'd sat there for over an hour reading an old newspaper and digesting the food.

"Cheese and pickle sandwich?"

"Fine. How about you, Liam?"

"Thanks Mickey, I'm all right with just the beer."

Gerry Savage swung round, opened the service hatch in the wall behind him and called: "Bring us a round of cheese and pickle, will you?"

He turned his flaxen head back to his customers. "Won't be a moment."

Liam Hogan raised his glass carefully off the counter, intent on not spilling precious drops. He glanced up at Michael.

"Here's lookin' at you, Mickey. Welcome back."

He tipped up the glass and drank, leaving a thin, foamy moustache on his upper lip. Michael had just lifted his glass, the condensation wet on his fingers, when the door at the end of the bar opened and Mary Devlin walked into the room carrying a tray. As she placed the tray on the counter, Michael saw the steady swell of her stomach under a loose-fitting, navy blue blouse with white dots.

"Hello, Michael," she said. "Did you find what you were looking for?"

NINE

Quinn felt somewhat relieved when the door opened and he saw Linda Williams standing there in her snug blue Armani jeans and mauve V-neck sweater. Of course he glimpsed the sweater's dangerous dip between her rather swooping breasts, but he deliberately and steadfastly ignored this distraction from then on and for the duration of his visit. His feeling of relief emanated from the memory of their former meeting when she was merely clad in a scanty aerobics outfit that played erotic havoc with his imagination. He was there to do a job – as indeed, to his shame, he had been on the previous occasion – and the last thing he needed was such a blatant attempt at sartorial seduction. She still looked good though, he thought, and she must be pushing fifty. Well, maybe just forty-five. And, apart from anything else, she took his mind off Renée. For a while.

She wavered in the hall, her arms hanging loosely, waiting for Quinn to step forward, to approach her. In the hall mirror behind her he glimpsed his partial reflection, the fragmentary image of a man on the threshold. Of what, he asked himself momentarily. Of what?

Linda stared at him as if she was looking into and beyond him, looking for something she saw in the darkness of his eyes. A clock chimed somewhere in the house, a distant, beckoning sound. But he stood his ground in the porch, waiting to see how this would play. He sensed the tension, recognised the indecision in her face, wondered what she was feeling.

"Thank God you've come," she said at last, moving slightly to the side, opening the door a little wider for him to enter. Her voice was husky, just as he recalled it, as if she were suffering from a touch of laryngitis.

He stepped into the hall. She closed the door behind them, the flowery scent of her perfume wafting over him with the forward movement of the door. Good God, what was that balmy aroma? He felt immersed in a cloudburst of pollinating raindrops, drenched in a shower of almost liquid fragrance. It was quite overpowering. She dabbed an index finger behind her right ear, as if to indicate its proximity.

"I was going to make some coffee," she said. "Would you…?"

"Yes, that would be good," he told her.

"We can have it in the lounge."

She meant the living room, of course, where they had been before, where it had begun that last time, and the memory of the spongy sofa with its ill-tuned springs helped restore his equilibrium.

"Perhaps we could just have it in the kitchen?"

Her carefully polished features crinkled into a kittenish smile.

"Yes, all right," she acquiesced. Her expression changed. Did he imagine it or did her eyebrows shift with a slightly querulous twinge?

The kitchen was all pine cupboards and light grey laminate worktops. He looked around and a covetous voice whispered in his ear: 'This is a big step up from your pint-sized kitchenette.'

"Nice kitchen," he said.

She looked a trifle shame-faced. "It's Scandinavian," she told him. "Years old. I'm thinking of changing."

"Changing? Really? Looks bang up to date to me."

He surveyed the cooker, fridge, freezer and dishwasher all gleaming creamy white. "You've everything you need here," he said.

"I used to think that," Linda said, and somehow he got the notion she was referring to more than just the kitchen.

He sat down in one of the wickerwork chairs around the pine table and took out his notebook. He was entering the time of day and the location when Linda asked him if instant coffee would be all right.

"Actually," she continued, "I'd like one of those automatic espresso machines to make real coffee. Bit fancy maybe, and they cost the earth, but the coffee is a dream."

"Instant is fine with me."

"I usually make it with milk. Is that okay?"

"Perfect. Milk or water, it doesn't matter. No sugar."

She swung open a glass cabinet door and stretched for a jar of Nescafé Gold Blend. Quinn felt an unsettling déjà-vu tremor as he watched the outline of her body in the clinging jeans and sweater.

"Anything else you want?" she asked, catching his reflection in the glass pane of the cupboard door.

"I was just admiring the porcelain handles on the cupboards," he extemporised with sudden inspiration.

"They're just plastic," she snapped.

She unscrewed the round lid of the coffee jar and pulled out a pair of English ironstone coffee cups from another cupboard. As she rolled open a cutlery drawer and whipped out a spoon, he savoured the dusty scent of the coffee granules and realised he was looking forward to his caffeine rush. Then she whirled round to the fridge to extract the milk. She moved with snappy, almost jerky actions, a twitchy St Vitus dance of her own making. Watching her, Quinn suspected that her plan of action for most things in life was: 'Immediately, if not sooner.' And, in recollection, he understood that had been her agenda the last time he was there. He sighed inwardly and decided it would be best to keep the tone as official as possible. He pondered how to address her: 'Linda' would feel too intimate, despite what they'd done in there on the sofa and upstairs in the bedroom; Mrs Williams too formal, as if they hadn't done it at all. He opted to postpone the dilemma.

"So you last saw your husband when he left for work this morning?"

She paused for a moment before replying, as though it required an effort to call the recollection to mind.

"Yes. He was in a bit of a hurry. He was late."

"Any special reason why he was late?" Quinn had no sooner asked than he conjectured some early morning heavy breathing and swiftly added: "Did he get a phone call, anything like that?"

"No, no phone call. We'd been talking and he just forgot the time."

"Did he seem worried about anything? Was something troubling him?"

Again she paused. Her forehead twitched with apparent concentration.

"Well, if you must know, he was pissed off because I told him I'm fed up with this kitchen and want a new one. That's all. Is it important?"

Too much information, Quinn thought, somewhat surprised by the colloquialism and the needless domestic data.

"Well," he mitigated, "it's important to establish his frame of mind before he was lifted. There might be a connection."

Linda froze in her coffee-making preparations, her eyes flared up and she bowed her head forward slightly in a look of open incredulity.

"Wait a minute, wait a minute," she said, looking up with dark, dilated pupils.

"Surely the obvious connection is all those bloody murderers they've let out of the Maze?"

"You mean, you think this is linked to the Newry bombing?"

"Jesus Christ, what else can it be? They've all been released. McCann was the last one and they let him out yesterday."

"Michael McCann?"

"Yes, Michael bloody McCann. They're looking for whoever informed on them and they think Arthur knows. They obviously think he had direct contact with the informer."

Quinn took his chance. "Didn't he?"

"No, he didn't. At least, not that he ever told me. You know as much about that as I do, for God's sake, you were working on the case."

As her irritation grew, her allure diminished and he began to feel more at ease. "I just thought he might have told you, as his wife, more than he told me."

"Well, he didn't. But you must have asked him. All those interviews you had with him, the talks, interrogations."

Quinn recalled with vexation the pressure he'd been under then to secure the identity of the informer, how he had been urged to "go to any lengths" to at least get a sketch, a location, a name – any name.

"Yes, I pushed him really hard about it but I knew that, as a serious journalist, he wouldn't give me any names. Truth is, he probably didn't even know the guy's name. What I really wanted to know was if he'd actually met him face to face."

"What'd he say?"

"He swore to me that he hadn't."

"Did you believe him?"

"No, not really, not at first. But in the end, when I'd got to know him a bit, I think I did."

"You're probably right there." She seemed to think about this as she poured milk into a saucepan. "When all's said and done, I think Arthur's an honest person."

And Quinn thought: yeah, well, that's more than you are.

Or me, for that matter. He's an honest, serious guy that you can count on, someone with courage and a conscience. Maybe that makes him dull and boring in your eyes, but not in mine.

"So you believe the Newry bombers are behind this?

Linda Williams looked at Quinn as if he had just crawled out of a toilet bowl.

"Come on, get real. Is it just a coincidence then? McCann gets out of the Maze yesterday and Arthur gets lifted today? Is that just a fluke?"

"What about the rest of them? John Cooney and the others? They've been out for over a week."

Linda took a deliberately audible, deep breath before she continued. Quinn had already deduced that patience was not one of her more salient virtues. Then again, her husband had just disappeared and she was probably not her true self. Whatever that might be.

"Didn't they say that McCann was the leader, the mastermind behind getting twenty-three people blown to smithereens?" she said, her voice rising with each word as if she were practising some musical scale of her own designation. "I'd say they've been waiting for him to be released. I'd say it's all been planned in advance from within the Maze."

"You think they've just been waiting for McCann?"

"I'd put money on it. And another thing... Oh shit!"

The milk had frothed over the rim of the stainless steel saucepan and was sizzling on the ceramic glass cooktop. Linda grabbed the handle and jerked the saucepan off the cooker, causing more spillage across the top.

"Shit!" she said even more vehemently. "I deliberately put it on low heat so that wouldn't happen.

"Shit happens," Quinn pointed out, somewhat unnecessarily.

Linda snatched a cloth from the sink, squirted a creamy

liquid from a plastic bottle and began rubbing frantically on the cooktop. Unable to rub the hot plate, she gave up, tossed the cloth in the sink and popped the plastic bottle back on the narrow shelf above the extractor fan. As an afterthought she switched the fan on full blast. The acrid aroma of cindered milk lingered nonetheless in the room.

"I think there'll be enough," she said, digging the teaspoon into the coffee jar. "Two spoonfuls?"

"One's enough," he said, observing the brown anthill heaped on the teaspoon. "You can always top up with cold milk to make up for the spillage."

"Yeah," she said. "The milk's boiling hot as it is."

Finally, with coffee cups on the table topped up with cold milk, she sat down and forced a rueful smile.

"This is fine," he told her, sipping the simmering brew.

Linda looked only slightly reassured. She tasted the coffee, poured more milk in her cup and stirred with the teaspoon. As she spoke, Quinn realised he was seeing a new side to her, a side she hadn't shown before.

"Listen, Quinn," she said, "it's pretty obvious what's happened. The Newry bombers want revenge on the guy who informed on them. And they believe that Arthur has met him personally and knows who he is. Maybe not by name, but he'll be able to identify him. And they, no doubt, have several suspects in mind, so they'll be using Arthur, moving him around maybe, so that he will eventually meet whoever it was who sold them out."

"You think that's it? Arthur has been abducted so that he can finger the informer?"

"Absolutely. What else could it be? Why else would anyone lift him?"

Quinn thinks about this. Because, if Arthur Williams really hasn't met the guy, has never seen his face, then he's in a bad place. A really bad place. Why? Because we know for a fact that he's seen the faces of the people who lifted him. He can identify them, no problem. And that's not a good omen.

If he really can't identify the informer, then he can't give his abductors what they want and, consequently, he's of no further use to them. That, combined with the fact that he can identify them, means that they have no reason to keep him alive. But if he's smart, if he realises that his life hangs on the slender thread of him leading them to the snitch, then he will play that card for as long as he possibly can, because that's all that's keeping him in the game. Without it, he's lost. He's gone.

An almost indiscernible metallic noise from the direction of the hall was followed by the wrenching sound of the front door opening. Linda rose from her chair like a helium balloon and flew out of the kitchen yelling, "Arthur, Arthur, is that you?"

Quinn was about to follow her when she returned pulling a lanky teenage boy by the sleeve. He pulled free and straightened his crumpled nylon jacket. He had the fair hair and slightly upturned nose of his mother, together with the prepossessing height and mien of his father.

"My God," Linda wailed, "I'd forgotten about Max."

Max looked apprehensively at the man sitting at the kitchen table. "What's going on?" he said in a tight voice. "Who are you? What's happened to Dad?"

"He's a policeman," Linda told him, her voice almost breaking. "Your father's been lifted by the IRA."

Quinn rose and stepped over to the lad, holding out his hand.

"My name's Quinn," he said. "I'm afraid your father's been abducted."

The boy reached out to take Quinn's hand. His fingers were long and slender. Quinn thought of a pianist. The grip was surprisingly firm.

"I got a message at school," he said, "to come home.

They just said something had happened to Dad."

"It's the bloody Newry bombers," Linda blurted out, tiny bubbles of spittle forming on her lower lip. "They've been let out of the Maze and…."

"That's a possibility," Quinn intervened.

"The Newry bombers? But what has Dad got to do with them?" Max asked.

Quinn realised that the boy must have been in short trousers when the bombing and its aftermath took place.

"They were exposed by an informer who contacted your father in return for a reward," Quinn told him. "They don't know who the informer was, but they probably believe your father can lead them to him."

Max pondered this for a moment before he spoke. "And they want revenge. They're going to kill him."

"The informer? Probably, but we don't know that for certain. In fact, we don't know anything for certain at this stage."

The boy gazed at Quinn wide-eyed, as if he'd just been told the truth about Santa Claus. Then he blinked several times and said, "Where did they lift him?"

"Outside the station," Quinn said. "Carnalea Station."

"He was on his way in to work." Linda snapped the words out. "He was late."

"Outside the station?" Max said. "Then someone must have seen it happen. There must be witnesses. Somebody must have seen who took him."

Quinn glanced down at his PNB and read: "Two men and a woman, late thirties or early forties, in a white Ford Sierra."

"Anyone get the number?" The boy's eyes were sharply focussed on Quinn.

"No. As usual, it all happened too fast. People are paralysed when something like that happens. They stop thinking."

"What about CCTV?"

"Out of action. It'd been smashed."

The word 'smashed' seemed to strike a chord. His eyes narrowed. "Did they hurt him? Was he injured?"

"I don't think so," Quinn lied, and compounded the lie further. "Nothing serious." Quinn swallowed the last of the coffee. It was less than lukewarm now. He didn't feel a caffeine rush. He didn't feel anything much at all.

"How can you find him?" Linda asked. "What will you do?"

"I'll need to speak first to Arthur's boss. What was his name again? Alf Mc-something?"

"McCurran," the boy said. "Alf McCurran."

He wrote the name down. "I'll find him," he said, trying to configure a reassuring expression on his face. "Your father, I mean."

Both mother and son had sat down at the kitchen table. They stared at him, the light of hope tindering in their eyes, a hope that he could see was born of desperation. It did not take a vivid imagination to conceive what the Newry bombers were capable of, what they might do to extract the information they wanted from a defenceless man.

"Mrs Williams," he noticed how she started when he addressed her as such, "can you think of anyone else who might hold a grudge against your husband, anyone at all who might have a grievance against him – for whatever reason?"

She didn't give the question a moment's thought. "No, I can't. There's no one who would want to do Arthur any harm, no one at all. In fact, …"

The double jangle of the telephone cut her short. The boy leaned over to the worktop and plucked the cordless receiver from the cradle.

"Hello?"

He listened while a muzzled voice spoke to him briefly.

He turned to his mother, reaching her the phone.

"It's that man again. Says he has to talk to you."

"What man?"

"He didn't give his name," the boy said, scowling. "He never does."

Linda Williams looked distinctly uneasy as she took the phone. Her eyebrows twitched and her face assumed the querulous expression Quinn had glimpsed earlier.

"I'll take it in the lounge."

She hurried out of the kitchen and a door closed deeper in the house. Quinn seized his chance. "Phones up a lot, does he?"

Now the boy looked uneasy. "Dunno. I just seem to be in the house when he rings. Mum's out a lot."

"She's got a job?"

"Yes, she's working for some company selling perfume."

"Really? On a freelance basis, is it?"

"Freelance? Yeah, I think so."

The boy gave Quinn a lingering look without saying anything more. He seemed to be making his mind up about something. Quinn nodded encouragement.

"Mr Quinn," he said, finally, "you asked if there was anyone else who might hold a grudge against Dad."

"Yes. Does anyone come to mind?"

"Well, actually there is someone who fits the bill." He paused suddenly, seeming uncertain of how to continue. A long forefinger rubbed thoughtfully at a coffee stain on the pine surface of the table.

"And who would that be?"

He didn't hesitate now. "My uncle."

"Your uncle?"

"Yes, Dad's brother, Doug."

"Has there been some trouble between them?"

"You could say that. A helluva lot of trouble, in fact."

He looked a trifle doubtful at using the mild expletive,

but when Quinn didn't react he continued: "It's about the house. It started about five years ago. Gran had been living in the big house since Grandad died and she decided to give it to my dad."

"The big house?"

"Yeah. It's a sort of ranch-style place, y'know, like Southfork in Dallas, with pillars and arches and stuff. It's just outside Bangor, in Crawfordsburn. Grandad had it done up, spent a fortune on it. Everyone said it was like a mansion."

"And then he died?" Quinn prompted.

"He had a massive brain haemorrhage." The boy shrugged his shoulders with the mystery of illness, the helplessness of death. "It was totally unexpected. Everyone thought he was indestructible. He was like an institution. One day he was running things, king of the castle. Next day he was gone."

"I'm sorry."

Quinn looked at him closely, trying to gauge the extent of his feelings.

"That's all right," the boy said and shrugged again. "I didn't really know him that well."

His forefinger now appeared to have erased the coffee stain on the table in front of him. He sat staring at where it had been.

"So your gran was left in the big house."

"Yeah. But it was far too big for her and she wasn't ... well."

"In what way? Was she ill? Seriously ill?"

The boy's face was momentarily clouded with doubt, with uncertainty. He hesitated, looked over at the kitchen door, then once again made up his mind. He shuffled forward on his chair, closer to the table, and lowered his voice.

"She had a drinking problem."

"I see."

On past experience Quinn was fully aware of the wider implications of such a euphemism.

"Did she go into a home?"

"Yes, there's a really good place here in Bangor and Dad managed to get her in there."

"Your dad looked after her a lot then?"

"He was there practically every day when she was still in the big house. And afterwards too." Another thought struck him. "Mum wasn't too happy about him being away so much when he was supposed to be off work. It was difficult."

Quinn gazed out through the kitchen window. It wasn't hard to imagine Linda feeling neglected. She was one of those women who require a lot of attention.

The sky hung dark and heavy above the garden. Already there were a few raindrops trickling down the window. Beyond a crumpled privet hedge the naked fingers of an apple tree gesticulated at the sky.

"Didn't your uncle lend a helping hand?"

Max puffed out a short breath through closed lips. "He was never here. He'd taken over the business, Grandad's company, and he was always at work or away on business trips."

"What sort of business are we talking about?"

"Pharmaceuticals. 'Groundbreaking research and innovation worldwide,' that's the slogan. The company's called Norstream."

"Yes, I've heard of it."

Yeah, Quinn recalled, it's featured in the local news now and again, and the coverage hasn't always been complimentary. The usual tales of bribery and corruption. And lately there was a story about some drug for diabetes that proved to be ineffective as well as having certain injurious side-effects.

"So when your gran was moving into a home, she decided to give the big house to your dad as a sort of compensation for all he had done for her."

"Something like that. Uncle Doug wasn't the favourite. I don't think she even liked him. She once told me he was just like Grandad. 'A chip off the old block,' she said."

"Your grandparents didn't get on."

It was both a question and a statement.

He shrugged his shoulders again and looked out of the window. A sudden gust of wind shook the frame and raindrops splashed spasmodically on the glass.

"Grandad didn't have time for the family, for her. She told me herself. He was all business. She never said a good thing about him. Just the opposite."

"So she gifted the big house to your father."

"Yeah. It's been rented out and the money has gone to pay for Gran being looked after in the home."

"So when your gran dies, I suppose the house will be sold and your dad will get the money."

Max looked up from the table, his eyes as big as saucers.

"That's just it. Gran died two months ago. The problem is that Dad promised Uncle Doug that he would give him half of what the house was sold for, when the time came."

"When did he make that promise?"

"Years ago, when Gran signed the house over to him."

"But why did he do that? Why did he make such a promise?"

The boy's forefinger had now graduated from the table to his chin. It circulated round a cluster of small pimples, as if surprised that they were still there, nestling among the fluff of his pubescent beard.

"I think he felt pressured into it. Dad's a bit soft. Uncle Doug was on at him all the time about how it was unfair and how Grandad had always wanted everything to be split evenly between them, fifty-fifty. And, like, Doug is Dad's elder brother and Dad has always looked up to him. There was a lot of pressure. I think, in the end, Uncle Doug more or less pushed him into making that promise."

"So what's happening now that your gran has died? I mean, I assume she inherited a lot after your grandfather."

"She did, yes. Dad says it's a whole bloody mess. There are stocks and shares and funds and I don't know what not. The solicitors are trying to sort it all out, but it looks like Gran left most of the estate to Dad."

"What about his promise to your uncle, his brother?"

"That's the problem. Mum's been on at him, told him that Doug has taken over Grandad's company and is already very well off and doesn't need the money from the house sale, all of which is true. Dad has been tiptoeing around it, but in the end he plucked up the courage to tell Doug he isn't going to pay him."

The boy looked up almost apologetically before he continued, feeling a need to explain, to justify his father's actions.

"He was the one who looked after Gran and he has every right to be compensated for that. And it was Gran's wish that he should have it. But the big house is worth a lot of money and Doug says that not keeping his promise is a betrayal of the worst kind. I mean, it's not as if Doug really needs the money – he's very well off as it is – but he says it's the principle that counts, that he trusted Dad and now Dad has betrayed that trust."

Your father isn't a perfect man, Quinn thought, and of course you idealise him. But he makes his mistakes just like the rest of us. And Quinn's heard that line before, people saying it's not really about the money, it's the principle. But in Quinn's experience, it's always about the money. Always. As for trust …

"Yeah, well, trust is often something unspoken, something you just take for granted, especially between brothers. I don't suppose anything was ever put in writing about the promise?"

"No, it was just something Dad promised when the gift deed had been registered and he told Doug about it."

"Why didn't he tell him before it was registered? I mean, it must have felt like he was going behind your uncle's back."

"I know. Doug asked him the same question."

"What did your father say?"

"He said it was because he was afraid of Doug's reaction."

"He was afraid…?"

"Yes. Apparently Doug has a violent temper. He literally explodes, you know, goes bananas. I've never seen it but I think Dad is a bit afraid of him."

This rings a bell with Quinn and he thinks: another prospective customer for the late Dr Benjamin Musgrave. What was it he had said? 'Your rage often springs from hatred, and if you hate a person, you hate something in him that is a part of yourself.'

They sat silently with each other looking down at the table before Quinn spoke again.

"Then your dad must have been pretty nervous when he told your uncle he wasn't going to honour his promise and pay him the money."

"Well, he did that on the phone. I doubt if he would have dared do it face to face."

Quinn realised he was seeing another side of Arthur Williams, a personal side, a side that contrasted sharply with his picture of a man of integrity who was enterprising and courageous in his professional life.

"How do you know all this, I mean, about the gift deed and the bad feeling it's caused between your father and your uncle?"

"Dad told me. I came home late one night and he was

sitting up, waiting for me. I could see he'd had a couple of whiskies – the bottle was half empty. There was just the two of us."

"Had your mother already gone to bed?"

The boy seemed perplexed by the question, distracted from what he had planned to say.

"Mum was away at a sales meeting, at a hotel, some money-making project she had. She was away overnight."

"Did that happen a lot?"

"What do you mean?"

"That she was away overnight, like you said."

"A few times, I suppose. She gets involved in these money-making schemes."

"She's enterprising."

"Yeah, I guess so. Anyway, Dad and I got talking and it all came out. He told me Grandad used to quote a line from some poem: 'A promise made is a debt unpaid,' and he'd been thinking about that and how he'd gone back on his word."

"He felt guilty, did he?"

"Well, maybe up to a point. But then he said, everything changes in time, even that. I think he just needed someone he could confide in. Like, he was trying to justify himself in some way at the same time."

"But you don't actually think your uncle would harm him, do you?"

The boy examined the top of the kitchen table, as if searching for more coffee stains; then he looked up at Quinn with an accusatory look in his eyes.

"You asked if there was anyone else who might have a grudge against him, and I'd say that's a definite grudge."

"Yes, it is. But to have him abducted, to go to all that trouble and break the law? I mean, that's big-time stuff. That's serious crime."

"I don't know." Max shook his head. "Dad says he's a

pretty unscrupulous guy, in business anyway – told me he's cut a few corners to get what he wants."

Quinn smiled at this. Cut a few corners? Business is all about cutting corners. Niceness is hardly a characteristic quality among successful businessmen.

"What do you think of him yourself? What's he been like as an uncle?"

"Haven't seen much of him. He's divorced, no kids. I think he's become a bit of a loner. Then there was the gift deed, so he didn't come here at all after that. Well, not much before either, really. He was always working, travelling, building up the business."

Quinn looked round the kitchen. Beyond the window he saw the early afternoon sky already darkening, scowling down through the naked trees in the back garden.

"Have you got his address, phone number?"

"Sure."

The boy got up, went over to the bookrack on the wall and picked up a floral-backed address book. "It's all here," he said, flicking through the pages and handing it over. "It's in a new estate in Helen's Bay, very up-market. Dad calls them neo-Georgian egg boxes."

He chuckled at this, then seemed to think better of it. Quinn jotted the details down and got up to leave.

"That's a long phone call," he commented, nodding towards the kitchen door.

"It always is," the boy said with a dejected smile.

He followed Quinn towards the hall. As they passed the closed panel door to the living room, they heard Linda Williams' voice rising in strident volume.

"Never. I never said that!"

Out in the hall Quinn retrieved his overcoat from the gnarled arm of an antique hall-stand and pulled it on. Glimpsing himself in the dusty mirror somehow added a sombre touch to his departure. The information he had received revealed a complexity to the case that he had not anticipated.

"Tell your mother I'll be in touch," he said, "soon as I know anything."

The boy was instantly jolted by his words, reminding him of what had happened. His shoulders slumped and his eyes teared up.

"Find my dad, Mr Quinn," he said. "Please find him."

"I will," Quinn said, "I will. Don't worry, I'll find him."

That's probably another lie, he thought as he edged away, like your father's promise, but he liked the boy; he was smart and vulnerable and he felt for him. The memory of losing a father was still with him. He knew it would always be there.

He walked out into the grey light, through the sleeting rain and along the gravel path to the newly painted gate in the middle of the hedge. When he glanced back, the boy was still standing there in the porch with his hands jammed in his jacket pockets, watching him intently, an orphan looking for his father.

TEN

The flight from Stansted was an hour late. A technical difficulty, they said. So much for Aran Air, he thought. They couldn't organise a good shit in a public lavatory. He watched the cabin staff moving around in their cheesy blue uniforms. For Christ's sake, he swore to himself, they look as if they've been picked up off the street ten minutes ago. From behind the counter at Burger King direct into the fuselage of a Boeing 737. Not a native English speaker among them. Safety drill in Latvian English. He forbade himself to even think about the pilot.

His attitude to air travel was ingrained and constant: he hated it. From the moment he sat down in what he regarded as a somewhat bloated sardine can, he felt vulnerable, insecure and utterly defenceless. He was no longer in charge of his life. Up in the air the occasional gulping drops in altitude caused by turbulence – that unspeakable word – could provoke cataclysmic bowel movements over which he had no control. There had been several close calls.

He had no sooner sat down than he tongued in the buckle of his safety belt. Even while still on the ground, you couldn't be too careful. As usual he had chosen an aisle seat. He couldn't really explain it, but it somehow felt marginally safer. He certainly had no wish to look out through the porthole window. And as for the business of a bulky sardine can that weighed over 60 tons actually being able to rise off the ground and ascend into the sky – well, it defied all logic. He decided to banish such thoughts from his mind and examine the other sardines as they came on board. It was a habit, almost a reflex action, acquired over the years.

On average he travelled two or three days a week. Often, while his father was still alive, it had been more. And, despite his better judgement, he invariably expected on these travels to catch sight of someone from the past, a far-removed face from school, university, rugby-playing days on muddy fields of yore. As usual he recognised no one. All gone, he surmised yet again. All long gone. He was surrounded by the faces of strangers – pale, tense, unapproachable – totally engrossed in the heedless routines of their own quite separate lives.

Since his divorce he had experienced a series of social and semi-social snubs: people he knew and used to stop to speak to who now pretended they didn't see him and walked in the other direction; people who were about to enter the newsagent's but changed their minds when they saw he was already in there; next-door neighbours who jumped in their cars and drove off as soon as he came out of the house. And then he realised that all their friends, except for his business associates and commercial toadies, had been his wife's friends, people he had got to know because she had been friendly with the wives. The men had just been along for the ride. They had no real interest in him, nor – if he were honest – he in them. The one social event he looked forward to was the annual rugby club dinner, which – by common consent – always turned out to be a monumental piss-up. But he could relax there, let his guard down, be himself. No doubt the alcohol had a lot to do with it. When was the next one? It was usually this time of the year. He fumbled in his briefcase on the floor and found his leather-bound Filofax.

"Excuse me, can I…?"

A man in a rumpled dark grey suit stencilled with a faint checked pattern was indicating that he wished to gain access to the inside seat. He had dark, lifeless hair that lay flat on his head, a limp, careless quiff falling down over his forehead. Short and stocky in stature he leaned forward and directed a pair of sharp blue eyes at the Filofax, then at the man holding it.

"Doug Williams, isn't it?"

It took a moment before Doug recognised him. The round, midlife-crinkled face was certainly familiar, the hairstyle reminded him of Bill Haley in rock-around-the-clock mode, but it was the twinkling eyes and little button nose that jogged his memory in a matter of seconds.

"Joe? Joe Stewart?" It was a question that was simultaneously a confirmation of identity. Awkwardly Doug toed his briefcase under the seat in front, retracted the tongue of his seat belt and rose to allow Joe Stewart to ease past him. As he sat down the aircraft began to move. Jeez, he was cutting it fine, Doug thought, and swiftly refastened his belt.

"You know," Joe Stewart said as he slumped into his seat, "if God had meant for us to fly, he would have made it easier to get to the airport. Bloody train from Liverpool Street was half an hour late."

He squeezed a portly briefcase under the seat in front, withdrew the seat-belt buckle from under his left buttock and snapped it shut round his thickening waist. "Last time?" he said, turning to his neighbour.

"Last time?" Doug echoed.

"Yeah. Do you remember the last time we met?"

Doug rummaged through the clutter of memories in the back room of his brain as they taxied out to the runway.

"Rugby dinner, 'bout six years ago?"

Joe Stewart slipped him a congratulatory smile.

"More like ten. It's always further back than you think. Have you noticed that?"

"Yeah. Part of the ageing process, I guess. Everything speeds up. But you stopped coming, didn't you?"

"Don't get me wrong. I mean, no offence. But it was the

same people and the same conversations time after time. And even if there was a year in between, the constant re-enactment of scenes of glory on the rugby field – real or imagined – began to wear a bit thin. Even with drink taken. And there was a lot of that."

Yes, the macho machinery of their athletic exploits had been well oiled by a torrential flow of liquid refreshment courtesy of Arthur Guinness and the Bushmills Distillery. But Doug had partaken with such enthusiasm that even if the broad outline of most of the stories was vaguely familiar, the inherently juicy details were often completely lost to him and consequently he never failed to rejoice in the yearly retelling. However, at this point he decided a change of subject was necessary to ensure a smooth continuation of their renewed acquaintanceship.

"Over on business?"

"Yes. Actually something that links up with your line of work. You're still in pharmaceuticals, aren't you?"

"I am. Even more so since I took over at Norstream."

Joe Stewart seemed to waver before he continued. "Have you heard of Simon Vega?"

"The investment banker? Yes, of course. What about him?"

Joe paused again before replying.

"He seems to be interested in establishing something in our neck of the woods."

"I'd have thought he was more than satisfied with his business operations here in Britain. He's big time now. I know my father had some dealings with him, but it never really got off the ground."

"Yeah, he doesn't exactly rush into things, but he does seem interested in Norstream. He has a daughter working in Belfast. That could be a part of it too."

Joe Stewart broke off abruptly and turned away to look out of the window, as if afraid that he might have divulged too much. When he turned back, he had decided it was his turn to change the subject.

"What about your brother, Arthur? Took a lot of guts to go after the Newry bombers like he did. In the States he'd have won the Pulitzer prize. I've never met him but he seems to be quite a guy."

The aircraft jerked to a halt, poised for the final, frantic rush down the runway. Doug felt closed in, trapped in the oily air bubble of the fuselage. He reached up and swivelled the ventilation switch to feel its welcome breeze. This is the point of no return, he thought. For all of us.

"My brother?" he said. "He's a cunt."

* * *

The plane charged mindlessly down the asphalt ribbon, lifting off the ground and swinging into the air at what seemed like the last possible second. The feeling for Doug was always the same. The take-off seemed to go on and on, lasting an eternity, thundering ever faster down the strip but not rising into the air, screaming to him that the aircraft was too heavy, that it would not get off the ground, that it would soon reach the end of the runway and … . He knew it was crazy, idiotic, that he was being childish, but the chill of fear in his heart made him quiver. It would not go away. Until at last he felt the slight lurch as the plane raised a defiant nose and soared up, up into the sky. And he could relax. Well, up to a point. Unless there was … turbulence.

At the same time he was angry with himself and confused. Why couldn't he, who flew so often, both near and far, why couldn't he get used to the experience so that he felt comfortable sitting up there, so that he didn't get that icy chill of fear in his heart? And yet at the same time as he asked himself, he already knew the answer. That shrink he had gone to years ago in his fancy top-floor office on the Malone Road in Belfast, he had hit the nail on its psychoanalytical head: "Mr Williams, you have an enormous need to control – to control both the people and the things around you."

Hearing this, Doug had almost slid off the slippery Chesterfield sofa onto the floor. His wife had been telling him the same thing for years, pointing it out to him at regular intervals when the evidence was so abundantly plain to see; but this time it was someone he had to listen to, someone he respected, someone with a string of letters after his name – he was a doctor for Chrissakes – someone with professional competence and experience who was telling him the unadulterated truth. He knew then as now that it was something he would have to learn to live with.

He observed Joe Stewart glancing at him as his hands clenched tightly together in his lap. Abruptly Doug released them and pressed the metal button in the side of the armrest to recline the seatback into the ultimate resting position.

"Busy day," he mumbled sideways to Joe. He closed his eyes and pretended to doze. A minute later he could hear Joe shuffling through papers he had gathered from his briefcase. He kept his eyes closed, determined to drowse for the next sixty minutes until they landed at Belfast Airport. With any luck he might even relax for a time. All things considered, it was a smooth flight. He almost succeeded.

ELEVEN

Quinn had come away from the house on Carnalea Road feeling somewhat disgruntled. There was an uneasy sensation in the back of his head, a nagging suspicion that he was missing something, that there was a clue there somewhere to Williams' disappearance and he was probably looking at it, staring it straight in the face, but he just wasn't seeing it. The conversation he'd had with the boy was somehow unsettling. He began to realise that there was more to the Williams' home situation than met the eye. Much more. Christ, he thought, I need to concentrate. It was vital to remain vigilant, to fight off the creeping lassitude he often experienced after an interview, the confusion he sometimes felt in sorting out his impressions.

Under a darkening sky he followed the road back down to the station instead of the woodland path on which he had come. Rain dripped lethargically in the garden hedgerows. Commuters from Belfast were trailing up the hill from the railway station; some shot him an indifferent glance as they passed, briefcases swinging with homebound alacrity.

Half-way down Station Road he came to a shop, the Mini-Market. Some kind of professional intuition made him push the door and go in. At the back, beyond a seemingly haphazard array of stalls and racks cluttered with chocolate bars and snacks, greeting cards, paperbacks, notebooks, pens and stationery, a man was standing behind the counter. The sugared scent of past-its-sell-by-date milk chocolate struggled helplessly with the impregnated odour of antiseptic disinfectant.

"That's a brave day."

The man behind the counter looked familiar. In his late forties, he was of medium height with an incipient paunch and dark, greyish streaked hair topping a puffy, floury face that seemed ready for baking. But it was his broken nose that rang a bell somewhere.

"Looks like it's clearing up," he added with a smile.

It was mid-afternoon in December and the wan sunshine Quinn had seen earlier walking up the woodland path had long since gone, replaced by a sleety shower and the creeping shadows of dusk. The light was already fading, retreating into quiet evening. In an hour it would be dark.

"Tomorrow is another day," Quinn told him.

The shopkeeper seemed a little baffled by this response. His eyebrows arched in wonder.

"Aye, that's for sure," he agreed.

Quinn dipped into his inside pocket and unveiled his warrant card. The man's eyes widened like a deer caught in headlights on a busy road.

"I expect you've heard about the abduction this morning at Carnalea Station," Quinn said. The man nodded, his bafflement replaced by avid curiosity.

"Sure I know him, the big fellow, Arthur Williams. Stops in here every morning. Well, almost every morning."

"Really? Was he here this morning?"

"He was, yes."

Now it was Quinn's turn to show interest. Eyebrows raised, he took out his notebook and began scribbling.

"Could I have your name, please?"

"Simpson. Billy Simpson."

The bell rang again. This time the clapper struck Quinn's memory. "You're Billy Simpson, the welterweight."

The man's face radiated immediate pleasure, the doughy features kneading themselves with ductile delight.

"That's me," he said. "But my welterweight days are over," he added, tapping his midriff tyre.

"I saw you box once," Quinn told him, "at the King's Hall."

"You did? Who against?"

"Eamonn Boyle."

"Yeah, that's right." He looked wistful. The battered features of Billy Simpson's face sank, a puffed-up cake suddenly deflated. "I lost on points."

Quinn launched a consoling smile.

"Well, he was just starting out and you were close to retirement. Anyway, as I recall, it was a close decision. You took him all the way."

"He was a southpaw. I always had trouble with southpaws."

"They say Boyle could've been a champion."

"Yeah, that's for sure. He had the talent."

"But maybe not the dedication."

"No, there's that too. And then he got into trouble with the Provos." He looked at Quinn uncertainly before elaborating. "One of them punishment squads shot him in the leg."

The mention of the Provos steered Quinn back on track. The counter between them was littered with residual copies of the Belfast Telegraph and the News Letter. Tomorrow they would report the abduction of one of the country's leading journalists.

"Arthur Williams came in here this morning, you say. "

"Yeah, he came in for his paper."

"His paper?"

"He usually gets the Guardian."

"What time would that have been?"

"About ... half past eight."

The double chime of the doorbell behind him told Quinn someone had entered the Mini-Market. He nodded to Billy Simpson to go ahead and serve the customer, and stood to the side while an elderly man made his way to the counter. Muffled up in a thick overcoat the customer bought a tin of pipe tobacco. The former welterweight's standard comment on the weather was ignored as the man fumbled in the overcoat for his wallet. Looking around, Quinn could see no sign of foodstuffs to justify the 'Market' in the name of the shop. He waited until the man had left before resuming the interview.

"Did Arthur Williams talk to anyone when he was here?"

"Talk to anyone? Well, he said a few words to me, about the weather or something. Then he left and … wait a minute, there was someone he met on the way out. A woman."

"Someone he knew?"

"I don't think so," Billy Simpson said. He screwed his eyes up as he tried to remember. "But I can't be sure."

"But they spoke to each other?"

"Yeah, they did."

"Did you hear anything they said, any part of their conversation?"

"No. I had the radio on."

He jerked a pudgy thumb at an ancient transistor radio on a shelf behind him, wedged between tottering stockpiles of Benson and Hedges and Gallagher's Blues.

"And I'm a bit deaf anyway." He touched the lobe of a cauliflower ear.

"What did she look like? I mean, how old?"

"Hard to say. I didn't pay much heed to her."

"Not a looker then?" Quinn said.

Billy smiled back. "No, I s'pose not." He screwed his eyes together again. "I think she had a head scarf on. Quite young, about 30 maybe."

He paused, and the pale pastry features of his face reassembled themselves in a dumpling expression of grave uncertainty.

"She could have been older," he added. "I didn't really get a good look at her. Couldn't see much of her behind the stands."

"She didn't buy anything?"

"No, she walked out of the shop again and he followed her."

"They went out together?"

"That's right."

"Did anyone else see them? Was there anyone else in the shop?"

"There was a couple of schoolboys. I was, like, keeping an eye on them to make sure they didn't take anything. There's quite a lot of shoplifting, y'know, even in a district like this."

"I'm sure there is," Quinn said. "You've no camera in here, CCTV?"

"Naw, can't afford it."

Quinn flicked back a page in his notebook and asked, "Regency Avenue, is that far from here?"

"It's in Helen's Bay. Out past Crawfordsburn. Swanky area."

"Bit of a walk from here then."

"Yeah, it'll take you the guts of half an hour, at least. No wheels?"

"No, it's Shank's mare today. I came on the train from Belfast."

Billy Simpson looked out towards the street. It was almost dark outside. The shop was an oasis of warmth and light in the enveloping gloom of the evening. He rubbed the broken bridge of his nose between forefinger and thumb as if endeavouring to reshape it, abruptly gave up and said: "If you can be back here by six, you can borrow my car. It's a red Vauxhall Vectra parked a wee bit down the road on this side."

Quinn was quite taken aback by this offer. He mumbled his thanks as Billy Simpson handed him the key and gave him directions.

"Not everyone who remembers seeing me fight," he said

by way of explanation. "I shut up here at six. Can you be back by then?"

Quinn consulted his wrist watch. It was ten past four. "You can count on it," he said.

* * *

He drove out to Helen's Bay in the subsiding rain and found Regency Avenue one wrong turning later. He parked outside the address given him by the Williams boy. There was no car in the driveway. He got out and walked to the two-storeyed house with its pillared entrance. The garage door was down and locked, and there was no response when he knocked at the front door. He walked back to the Vauxhall and lowered himself into the sunken driver's seat to wait. It was almost the end of the week and he felt sure Doug Williams would be appearing before long. He decided to give him half an hour. Ten minutes later he arrived.

As Doug Williams swung his Mercedes off the Crawfordsburn Road and whisked along the maple tree-lined fairway of Regency Avenue, he noticed a maroon Vauxhall Vectra parked by the kerb outside his house. In the late-afternoon gloom the streetlamps glowed along the street, amber islands of illumination. He swept into the drive, switched off the engine and opened the door. The downpour that had pursued him from the airport had ceased, rivulets of rainwater gurgled through the avenue gratings and the thick, leafy scent of wet privet hedges hung in the air. He heaved himself off the leather seat and out into the puddled driveway. In the avenue he heard a car door clunk.

"Mr Williams? Douglas Williams?"

The man coming towards him walked with a measured tread on the wet paving stones. He was about medium height or a little above. He wore a dark blue overcoat that hung open and he was bare headed. His black hair was thick and wiry. It had begun to recede slightly at the temples where it was greying with the inevitable collateral of middle age.

"Yes. Who are you?"

"My name's Quinn. I'm a police officer."

Williams did not ask for proof of identification; Quinn did not offer any. Douglas Williams was standing beside a sapphire-blue S-Klasse Mercedes saloon. Watching him, reading his body language, Quinn's initial impression was that he was keyed up and tense, his posture already on the defensive. In short, Quinn thought, a first-class tightass in a made-to-measure suit. A couple of inches over six feet tall, he looked a lot like his brother, though more heavily built and sporting a dark toothbrush moustache that made him look like an overgrown Charlie Chaplin. Or, Quinn thought, Adolf Hitler.

"I've already given you people a statement in the diabetes drug case and I don't see…"

"It's not about that," Quinn interrupted. "It's about your brother."

"My brother? Arthur? What about him?"

Doug Williams turned away to open the rear door of the Mercedes and retrieve his cabin bag from the back seat.

"He was abducted early this morning on his way to work. You haven't heard?"

Williams whirled round. "Abducted? This morning?"

The surprise he evinced was either genuine or worthy of an Oscar nomination.

"You haven't heard?" Quinn repeated.

"I've been in London since Tuesday. How could I have heard?"

He glared at Quinn, his tone instantly aggressive.

"Someone in the family perhaps?"

"I've no contact with his family. What do you mean he's been abducted? Where? Who did it?" His head snapped back slightly as he posed each question, as if he were demanding answers of a subordinate.

"Witnesses say there were three people involved, two men and a woman. They lifted him outside Carnalea Station, on his way to work this morning. We don't really know why – not yet anyway."

Williams shut the doors of the car, locked them with a click of the key and stood still in the driveway, puzzlement rippling across the millpond of his face. "Is it political, some story he's working on?"

An Audi cabriolet pulled up in the neighbouring driveway, a silver saloon with a funereal black canvas top. A garage door security light illuminated its arrival in the gathering gloom. The driver, a tall, elegant woman in her thirties with honey-blond hair and a tight-fitting charcoal trouser suit, climbed out and glanced over at them. Doug Williams stared at her. She did not speak. She moved to the boot, opened it and began to extract several well-filled plastic shopping bags and a tan leather shoulder bag.

"Perhaps we could take this indoors?" Quinn suggested.

Williams nodded assent and they walked up to the pedimental porch with its slim white columns. Built with a rusty red brick, the house façade was set off with ground-floor windows that were tall and narrow, the white paint contrasting attractively with the chestnut brickwork. So this is neo-Georgian, Quinn thought as he stepped inside. The columns were a bit pathetic, but the rest was doing its best.

The hall was surprisingly spacious, bright and uncluttered. Williams flicked an electric switch and the cut-glass ceiling light sparkled to life in a wide rectangular mirror. Quinn followed him into what Linda most definitely would have called the lounge, a large living room dominated by a sectional sofa in a plush beige fabric that resembled the coat of a golden retriever about to moult. A glass-topped coffee table squatted on a multi-coloured Kashmir rug with an intricate geometric pattern that Quinn could not quite decipher. The room exuded an odourless, shut-in atmosphere that cried out for an open window.

Williams made straight for a modern credenza sideboard long enough to accommodate a buffet for a dozen people. On the white plastered wall above the sideboard hung a series of gilt-framed hunting motifs, prints with scarlet-frocked people on horseback gallivanting across the countryside alongside an array of excited gun dogs. Quinn was reminded of a line from a televised comedy series: 'Pretentious, *moi*?'

"Drink?" Williams said, uncorking a bottle of Jameson's Single Malt that was half full. Or half empty as he suspected Williams chose to see it.

"A small one," Quinn decided after a brief deliberation. Doug Williams might not be the sort of man who would be comfortable drinking alone. He might even hold it against you. Quinn had come across such oddballs before. And the drink was likely to put him in a more expansive frame of mind, more inclined to talk about his brother and what might have happened to him.

"I can't believe that Arthur's been abducted," Williams said, handing over a heavy crystal tumbler with a diamond-cut pattern round the base. The measure of whiskey was decidedly shallow, Quinn noted. Or did the fancy glass distort the quantity? No matter. A small measure was perfect in the circumstances, even if it was Single Malt.

"What does Linda say about it?" Williams asked, as he reached for another glass in the sideboard.

"Linda?"

"Yes, his wife. Has she any idea why he's been lifted?"

Quinn decided to play his cards close to his chest. "Not really," he said and watched as Doug filled his tumbler almost to the halfway mark.

"Want anything in yours? Water? Ice? Ginger?"

"No, no. It's fine," Quinn said, glancing down at the whiskey as he swirled it slowly in the glass. He looked up again. "Do you think Linda might know what's behind it?"

"Well, she's behind most of the things that happen there, and not all of them are good," Williams said with a careless shrug of his shoulders.

"Why do you say that?" Quinn asked. He was beginning to suspect that the members of the Williams family might have even more problems than the combined countries of the Middle East. Doug raised his hand, swivelled his wrist and emptied almost half the contents of his glass before replying.

"Listen, Mr Quinn – or should I say Inspector?"

"Inspector hits the mark," Quinn said with a bland smile.

"Well, the fact is, I never had any trouble with my brother until he met her."

"There's trouble now?" Quinn suggested, looking his angelic best. "You and your brother don't get on?"

Williams paused to sigh before having another swig from his glass.

"He's become another person since he married her. She calls all the shots and she shoots from the hip. He just goes along with it."

"That's probably true of a lot of marriages."

"Well, it wasn't true of mine."

"And how did that end up?" Quinn said the words without thinking where they might lead. He quickly appended a conciliatory smile to show he meant no harm. But there was something about Doug Williams that antagonised him, something in the superior way he spoke and behaved that made him want to shock him, to knock him out of his stride, to shut him up – which was the exact opposite of his initial intention.

About to move over to the sofa, Doug froze in his tracks and stared at him. He was tall, an inch or two shorter than his rangy brother but more heavily built.

"I see you've been talking to Linda. That bitch." He said the final two words with such vehemence that Quinn was taken aback. There was no mistaking the aversion in his voice.

"You don't like her," Quinn stated. It wasn't a question, but it begged a lot of answers.

Williams swung his head to the left, then to the right, as if inviting the attention of an unseen audience to confront them with an obvious truth.

"I'm not alone, believe me, not by any means. My father sure as hell didn't like her. What was it he said? 'She's been round a few corners, that one.' Yeah, he had her taped from the start. Just out for the main chance, he said. Then she had a fling with some guy, an estate agent, Arthur told me, but he didn't have the guts to pull the plug. She reeled him in again, like a herring on a hook. And of course my mother couldn't stand her – that bitch, taking her wee darling boy away from her. Linda was her worst rival So no, based on what I've seen and heard, I certainly don't like her. And I mean, let's face it – we can't all be wrong."

He drained his glass and stepped back to the marble-topped credenza for a refill. Quinn sipped his whiskey and waited. Give him enough rope, he thought. They sat down in the middle of the sectional sofa, turning slightly sideways to face each other on either side of the join.

"Okay, I get it. You don't like her," Quinn said again. "But why are you not on good terms with your brother? What exactly has happened between you?"

Doug sniffed and placed his tumbler on the coffee table, glass upon glass. "Didn't Linda tell you about that too?"

When Quinn shook his head he added, "Maybe not something she wants to talk about."

He surveyed the hunting scenes above the credenza as if seeking inspiration from the hunters who sought the fox, a tallyho explanation that would perfectly describe the nature of the conflict. He turned back to Quinn, making up his mind.

"My brother let me down," he confided. "He made me a promise about our inheritance, and then he chose not to keep it. He promised me a half share in the family home. Then he changed his mind."

"Why would he change his mind?"

"Money." He spat the word out. "That's what motivates people – money. It's what they care about most of all."

His face became flushed as he wound himself up, the colour of his cheeks beginning to imitate the scarlet hue of the hunters on the wall.

"Don't kid yourself," he snarled, "everything else takes second place: trust, loyalty, yeah, even brotherly love."

He paused for a slurp of whiskey before he went on. "But one day he will discover that money is not all in this life. It just begets greed. Envy and greed. It makes people weak."

Quinn thought of the sleek Mercedes saloon parked in the driveway, the alabaster pillars he had passed on his way into Doug's neo-Georgian residence, all the attributes of wealth he saw posturing in the room around him.

"And he's weak?"

Doug's eyes jumped like bubbles in a pot of vitriol coming to the boil.

"He went behind my back, saw a solicitor and had the house signed over in his name. Didn't tell me anything about it until afterwards and even then he couldn't say it to my face. Rang me up and told me. Let me put it in plain English so you'll understand: he's a sleekit fucker."

Quinn noted that the tone of Doug's English was dropping with the level of whiskey in his glass. He pressed on.

"What about your mother? Didn't she say anything?"

"Arthur could do no wrong by her. She thought the sun rose out of his arse. He was there every day, pandering to her – Mummy's little boy. It was sick really, the relationship they had."

"So when he told you about it, you protested."

"You're fucking right I did. Dad was already gone and I had only a minority quota of shares in the company. But I knew that when my mother went she would give all her shares to Arthur. So it was only right that I should get an even share in the house."

Quinn watched him working himself up into a rage, recognising the symptoms, anticipating what would come next, waiting for the explosion. It was like winding up an old clock, tighter and tighter, until the spring snapped.

"What did Arthur say then?"

"He agreed. When I met him and spoke to him, he actually seemed to see the light. Or he was too fucking scared to do anything else. I don't know. Like I said, he's spineless. He took the easy way out. No conflict."

"Until now."

"Right, until now."

"But didn't you have anything in writing?"

"No. I trusted him, trusted his word. The word of a brother."

Doug Williams snorted and took another gulp at his glass.

"Yeah. When Mum died he changed his mind. Or had it changed for him. Maybe he had never intended sharing with me anyway. I don't know. But I do know for a fact that Linda, that bitch, had more than just a say in it. She writes his fucking agenda for him."

Quinn stared at the pattern in the Kashmir rug, trying to fathom the decorative design. Perhaps it was some sort of semi-floral arrangement, a geometric representation of botanical colours. However, it would be inappropriate to ask Doug Williams for elucidation at this juncture. There were other puzzles to be solved. He looked up again.

"One thing baffles me. How come your mother was so much in favour of your brother, and so dead set against you? Had something special happened between you to make her feel that way?"

Williams smiled a sad smile and nodded briefly, almost as if welcoming the question. "That's something it took me years to understand." He hefted the crystal tumbler to his lips and drank again. He was slurring his words now with woozy confidentiality, his eyes gleaming with alcoholic assurance. "Then I started thinking back to when I was a boy at home, things that happened and things she said to me."

"Like what?"

The interview was moving faster than Quinn had expected. He knew he just had to keep asking the easy questions, press the right buttons, help him along the path he was taking.

"Well, like I say, I was just a kid. But I remember one time my mother was giving off about Dad – she did that a lot – what a shit he was, always away on business, no time for her, that sort of thing. 'He's a cold person,' she would say, 'a cold fish.' Then, almost in the next breath she says to me, 'You're just like him, Doug. You should never get married.'"

"How old would you have been then?"

"Maybe twelve or thirteen." He shrugged and drained his glass. "She was probably drunk at the time, I don't know. I wasn't really aware of her drinking then. That came later. Like I say, it took a long time for me to work it out, but I finally realised my mother didn't really like me. I mean, I suppose she loved me – you know, dutifully – as a mother. But as a person, she simply didn't like me. And if I could choose, if anyone had ever asked me, I'd rather be liked as a person than loved out of duty."

Quinn was taken aback by this baring of the soul. Then again, he realised, alcohol can be a wonderful truth serum. And, despite himself, he couldn't help feeling a slight twinge of sympathy for the dutifully loved but nonetheless personally disliked son of Mrs Williams. The legacy left by parents was always much more than monetary. Words uttered without reflection could leave brand marks forever on the soul of an unsuspecting child.

Doug Williams heaved himself up from the sofa and, taking exaggerated care to bypass the coffee table without stumbling into it, made his way over to the sideboard again. Quinn had rarely seen someone shift so much alcohol in such a short time. He may not have liked his mother but he sure as hell liked her habit. And, Quinn thought, he may not like his brother and the bitter fact that he had reneged on his promise, but could he really have had anything to do with his abduction? Watching him refill his glass, knowing how a seriously bad drinking habit could affect people, Quinn realised that anything was possible. He decided to go for the investigative jugular.

"Mr Williams, it's been suggested to me that this conflict may have triggered an unwise decision on your part and that you might have had something to do with your brother's disappearance ...."

Doug Williams was raising his tumbler to his already parted lips. Now they parted even more. Quinn watched the expression of surprise on his face transform almost magically through indignation, annoyance and anger into full-blown fury. He had read reports on how alcohol impaired normal brain function in certain men when they felt threatened or provoked, leading them to think they were being unfairly victimised and discriminated. Without fail they reacted by becoming aggressive and violent.

"Listen, you fuckpig," Williams hissed. "I don't know what you've heard from that whore – for all I know she's probably fucked you too – but if you want to find out what's happened to my brother, you better start with her."

"What do you mean by that?"

"If you weren't so fucking stupid you'd realise she's got a hidden agenda. She's a player, you dumb shit, haven't you realised that? You come here and accuse me and you don't know your ass from your elbow. Who are you anyway? Piss off! Get the fuck out of my house!"

They had risen to their feet. Quinn was leaning forward, putting his drink down on the coffee table, when he glimpsed the crystal tumbler rising in Doug's hand, the contents whirling into the air as he swung his arm back, eyes rampant with rage, until Quinn slammed his fist into Doug's midriff and followed up with his knee to the groin. The taller man wheezed, doubled up and went down on his knees. His unbroken glass rolled in a half circle over the Kashmir rug, across the parquet and under the sideboard. Quinn automatically drew his right foot back, prepared to deliver the coup de grâce when, out of nowhere, the words of Benjamin Musgrave came to him: 'Your rage often springs from hatred, and if you hate a person, you hate something in him that is part of yourself.' He straightened up and drew back.

Doug Williams emitted short staccato gasps, desperately trying to get his breath back. As his respiration improved he began to groan, both hands clasped reverentially between his legs.

"Thanks for the whiskey," Quinn said. "You should see someone about that temper of yours." he added, and walked swiftly out of the house.

* * *

As he drove back to the Mini-Market on Station Road, Quinn thought about what had happened, how he had somehow managed to take command of himself and pull back from the edge. It felt like a triumph, a victory he had won over himself. Dear Mother of God, he had gained control of himself at last.

He was still congratulating himself when he swung into a service station in Crawfordsburn and filled up with petrol. Good men are hard to find, he thought, especially when you need them. The heavy homebound traffic crawled through the village and the fumes hung like a grey net curtain over the street. With a full tank he slipped back into the endless procession and continued along the road to Bangor West.

In his shop Billy Simpson was still busy with commuters returning by train from Belfast, buying cigarettes, chocolates and sweets for the evening's entertainment. Quinn nipped in swiftly to hand over the key and say thanks.

"You take care," Billy said with a quick, ready-baked smile on his mashed-potato face and turned to serve an impatient customer who thought Quinn was trying to jump the queue. Quinn hurried out and made his way down to Carnalea Station. The abduction site was no longer taped off. The technician, the sergeant and his constables were gone. There was no sign that anything untoward had happened here just a few hours ago. Arthur Williams and his abductors had simply vanished off the face of the Earth.

He caught the first train back to Belfast Central. There were only two other people in the carriage. It smelt of dusty upholstery and engine oil. He sat as far away from them as possible, at the very front of the train. Some people would use any excuse to strike up a conversation.

As the train passed Holywood and the City Airport, he went through in his mind the events of the day and pondered the possible involvement of Douglas Williams in his brother's abduction. All things considered, he thought it highly unlikely. On the other hand, drink can affect some people in unexpected ways, impairing normal brain function and driving them – especially those with a paranoid bent – to acts of unpredictable violence.

Of course he'd check up that Williams actually had been in London since Tuesday as he maintained, but of course that wouldn't exclude him from having planned the whole thing. Quinn's gut feeling though, was that he wasn't involved. His reaction to the news had been too convincing. The train was approaching Bridge End Station when his phone rang.

He didn't recognise the chief inspector's voice straight away, but by the time he got to his second sentence the braying baritone was readily identifiable. "If I can speak off the record," Joe Stewart had once confided, "the man sounds like a constipated donkey." Quinn described as briefly as possible his interviews with the Williams family, omitting the final scene of his visit to the dipsomaniac brother, but Chief Philip Hall seemed eager to graduate to another subject.

"Yes yes, Quinn," he said. "Make sure you put it all in your report. But there's been a new development in the case. We've got reliable intelligence that Michael McCann could now be in the village of Ballyfoil in the Mournes – you've heard of it, I take it?"

Quinn mumbled assent.

"Well, it's something of an IRA nest, as you know. The South Down Brigade are well established in the area and I doubt that they've even heard of the Good Friday Agreement down there."

"They probably think it's a prenuptial you sign at Easter," Quinn suggested.

"What?"

The chief inspector wasn't known for his partiality to banter.

"Nothing, sir."

Quinn made a fresh start. "Yes, even with the Peace Process underway, it's still something of a breeding ground for terrorism. The South Downers are known to have worked closely with the South Armagh Brigade, and they were bloody lethal. Remember Eamon Collins? He was unrecognisable when they'd finished with him. Looked like a steamroller had run over him."

"Yes, we all know what butchery they're capable of. Don't forget Francis O'Reilly, a Catholic officer like yourself, Quinn. They murdered him in Portadown just a year ago."

Quinn wasn't sure how to take this. Yes, he had a Fenian name, but he hadn't been brought up a Catholic, hadn't gone to mass, celebrated the sacraments, taken holy communion, gone to confession. With his Protestant-born mother a devout atheist, the onus had been on his father to give him a religious education. But when it came to lapsed Catholics, his father had lapsed to the point of extinction.

"Well," he said slowly, "topping a Catholic copper is generally seen as a real bounty, the cherry on the killing cake."

"So watch your back, Quinn," Hall cautioned. "Now, as I say, there seems to be a strong possibility that Williams may have been taken to Ballyfoil. Nothing definite, you understand, no hard and fast evidence, but we have to follow it up. I want you to get down there first thing in the morning and check it out. And if there's any sign, any sign whatsoever, that he's actually being held captive there we can have back-up with you in a jiffy."

"In a jiffy, sir?" On past observation and in comparison with his previous work experience in England, Quinn realised that an Irish jiffy could be anything from five minutes to five hours.

"We have access to an army chopper stationed at Newry, a CH-47 Chinook," Hall elaborated. "It can be at Ballyfoil within ten minutes."

"Good to know, sir. If they are holding Williams there, things could easily get out of hand."

"Yes, and that's why I'm allocating you a driver. This is not a job for the Lone Ranger."

This caught him by surprise and he thought immediately of the implications.

"So you're assigning me a Tonto?" Quinn said.

As the chief went on to explain, a cartoon picture of him at his desk in HQ flashed across Quinn's mind: a donkey sitting upright at a desk braying into a telephone.

"Correct. You've lost your licence to drive a police vehicle anyway, after that incident in the Ardoyne when you used your car as a bloody bulldozer. It's a wonder no one was killed."

Quinn cringed inwardly as he recalled that time when he had snapped and used the Land Rover Simba as the closest thing to a lethal weapon he could find in pursuit of a sniper on the roof of a block of flats. The chief inspector had not finished.

"I'm giving you a highly skilled driver and you'll do well to work together with her without any hassle. You follow?"

He paused for Quinn to digest this information, anticipating the query that would follow.

"Her?"

"Sergeant Gillian Rice is a first-rate police officer. She's also SAS-trained and can handle herself in a difficult situation, believe you me. You're lucky to have her."

"Yessir."

"Just be here at 9 o'clock tomorrow morning and ready to go. She'll meet you here at the reception desk."

"What about the car?"

"She'll fix that. Just be ready to leave here at nine."

He hung up and Quinn suddenly realised the train had already passed through Belfast Central and was coming into Botanic Station. He jumped up, got off and walked over to University Road, up past Queen's University amid the petrochemical haze of stagnant traffic, then into Eglantine Avenue and home.

As he collapsed into his easy chair and looked around his 'studio apartment,' he sensed Renée's presence everywhere in the room. The feeling filled him with unease, a presentiment that he had somehow entered an emotional no-man's land, an underworld abounding with soaring, ragged peaks and bottomless canyons. In a way he didn't understand, he felt a sort of grief, a sorrow for what he had lost as well as regret for what he knew he would never have. In his heart he understood what he had known for some time now, though he was loath to admit it, to meet it head on in the same way he faced predicaments and perplexities in his working life. Life with Renée would always be an emotional roller coaster with the dips becoming ever deeper. It would never have worked out anyway. The truth will set you free, he thought, but he wasn't quite there yet.

He had just hauled himself and his empty belly to his feet, on his way to explore the contents of the fridge, when the telephone rang. He turned back to the dresser and lifted the receiver.

"Hello."

"Hello Quinn, is that you?"

"Yes. Where are you?"

"I'm in London, like I said. Listen, I'm just calling to

say I miss you. Sorry about the Stevie Wonder lyrics. Bit corny, I know, but there it is. Sometimes I just talk in song titles."

Her precise enunciation and choice of words indicated that she wasn't entirely sober. In some respects he knew her so well.

"I tried ringing before but you've been out and I don't have your mobile number. You've got a new police phone."

"It's been a busy day."

"Well, I know I left a bit… well, abruptly."

"You didn't say goodbye. That's as abrupt as it gets."

When she didn't say anything he added, "In fact, that's more than abrupt."

She hesitated for a second or two before replying.

"Well, I had a flight to catch. I was late, really bloody late – after what happened, between us."

She was waiting for him to say something, to put a verbal plaster on the sore, but he was silent.

"I just had to get away," she said at last, "and you were on the phone."

"Renée, you can say goodbye in a moment."

There was a tightrope pause. He listened to the hum on the line.

"Quinn, I know you think I'm a bit … well, impetuous is maybe the word."

"*Le mot juste*," he said.

She half-chuckled. "Yes, *le mot juste*. I… I don't mean to be. I just feel I have to do my own thing, go my own way. It's not something I can really … control. It just happens."

"Yeah, well, I've seen that movie."

"What?"

"I've had the same feeling. Things you can't control. A sort of déjà vu."

There was another short silence, then an intake of breath.

"The fact is, I have to have a life of my own, Quinn, a working life. I can't just sit around in the hope that you or some contact of yours will pass on a morsel of news now and again that I can write up and maybe flog to one of the dailies. I need something more substantial, something that gives me real security, something I know will also be there tomorrow."

She might have been talking about her working life, her career, but Quinn had the feeling she was also describing her life with him, the way she felt about living with him. It's all about you, he thought, just as he realised that it was also all about him.

"I'm seeing about the job tomorrow."

"On Saturday?"

"It's the newspaper world, Quinn. Saturday's just another workday."

He thought about the choice she had made and wondered once again why she was ringing. What was the point?

"Well, good luck with all that."

He felt his words rebound from the receiver back into the room. They sounded flat and dry and empty of meaning.

In the background he heard another voice, a man's voice saying her name.

"I have to go now," she gasped, as if she was short of breath. "Goodbye."

And the line went dead.

TWELVE

Ballyfoil, Mountains of Mourne

Michael McCann crossed the back fields from his mother's cottage in the early morning mist. In the filmy darkness before him he sensed rather than saw the shapes of the village houses. Above him he could just make out a patchy sky. The thin winter grass ran wet with dew. He cursed as he stumbled over a tussock and felt the Ruger dig into his thigh. The night had been cold but there was no frost and the ground was still springy. He drew a deep breath and walked on. The air carried a peaty tang, the beckoning light of dawn seemed to shimmer through the mist and the way forward filled him with fear.

Treading awkwardly on stones and dodging small rocks he made his way to a ragged hedgerow running behind the row of terrace houses that formed one side of Ballyfoil's main street. Through a gap in the hedge he cut across to a narrow alley that provided access from the back fields to the street. From the end of the alley he had a clear view diagonally over the street to O'Leary's pub on the other side. A light shone in an upstairs window. A shadow moved across the roller blind, then moved back again. He couldn't discern if it was a man or a woman.

Michael stood rigid in the alley, becalmed in the raw stillness of the morning. He pulled his quilted jacket tighter around him. Liam had said that Gerry Savage often drove into Newry in the early morning to organise deliveries and bank the pub takings from the night before. Not every morning but near enough. Michael looked over again at the upstairs window above the pub. He glanced up and down the street. There was no sign of life, no movement in the half-light. The morning was hushed, looming, about to take shape.

He knew the street so well. He thought of the Caledonian Café where he had spent so many hours in his teens. It was gone now, replaced with a tobacconist's shop that also sold computer games. But the memories were still there. The nostalgia of his old haunts hit him, alternately filling him with nourishment and dismay. In some way he fed off the bygone places that had not changed, their images similarly unaltered and burnished in his mind. And he shuddered with incomprehension at the venues that had vanished, for with them had gone the distant happenings of his youth so that sometimes he wondered if they had ever happened at all.

A sudden sound at his back made him whirl round. A mongrel dog with a mangy, brindled coat sauntered past him and urinated contentedly against the foundation wall of the alley building before disappearing down the street.

Michael sighed and looked up again at O'Leary's as the upstairs light went out and the blind ruffled as if someone had just left the room closing the door behind them. Backing into the shadows, Michael clenched the Ruger in his pocket and ordered himself to be ready. His eyes were watering in the damp air and he wiped them with an unsteady hand. He thought of his arrival home yesterday, of his mother's tears when she had opened the door and seen him standing there holding his bag like a peace offering between them. Her sorrow at what had happened, what she thought he had done, and, ultimately, what he had done, only intensified his feeling of guilt. It was inevitable that he should become the target of blame. Too much had still been left unfinished, too many words left unsaid.

The pub door with its thumb-latch handle suddenly swung open and Gerry Savage stepped out onto the pavement. The light of day was straining through the cloud, through the mist, filtering down to the despondent street. Savage was wearing a coffee-coloured leather pilot jacket and light brown corduroy trousers. As he zipped up the jacket, his breath billowed momentarily in the morning air. All dolled up like a steaming dunghill, thought Michael, he's dressed like the pretentious turd he is. In his hand he carried a thick canvas bag.

Gripping the Ruger in his pocket, Michael started to go forward. All at once Savage paused and turned back to the door, to Mary suddenly standing there in the entrance. He went to her, put a hand on her shoulder and they kissed lightly. She said something and he laughed. Michael clutched the Ruger. There was a tightness in his chest. He tried to take a deep breath but felt something like heartburn in his stomach, in his throat. O'Leary's is the hub in the social wheel of Ballyfoil, he thought. Savage sees and hears everything that's going on: he must know something. He slipped back into the alley.

Gerry Savage sauntered over to a black BMW saloon, looked back at Mary and waved before he climbed in. As the car drove off up the road and into the hazy morning mist, Mary backed into the pub entrance and the door closed behind her. Michael had intended to use some pretext to ask him for a lift into Newry, to be alone with him, to sort things out in the car, but Mary's appearance had unnerved him. It was too late for that now, but it was not too late to get answers. He crossed the street, walked up to the pub door and pushed down the latch. The door was unlocked. He nudged it open and walked in.

There was a decayed, musty smell in the airless damp of the porch. Michael stepped onto a ceramic chess board, the floor tiled with black and white squares. Double swing doors on the right afforded entry to the public bar. Through the red and yellow stained-glass windows a light shone faintly. Further in, at the end of the porch, Michael saw a russet-brown panelled door that he knew led into the living quarters. He walked towards it in the shadowy half-light, his brogues leaving wet imprints on the tiles.

He stood listening at the door for a few moments before he turned the handle and went in. The oblong hall was flanked by an assortment of coats and jerkins hanging from a rack on the gable wall to the left, and a large, oval, gilt-framed mirror on a hardboard wall to the right. Under the mirror a collection of keys cluttered in a square china dish on a chest of drawers. With a start Michael glimpsed his shadowy reflection in the mirror as he moved towards the half-open door and the artificial light of the kitchen and dining area. He saw the doubt in his face and the fear in his eyes, and he knew they were feeding off one another.

The kitchen was immaculate. The machines gleamed white and bright in an atmosphere of culinary efficiency. It struck him that this was where the pub grub was prepared, where Mary had cut the sandwiches he had eaten yesterday. In fact, everything might have been installed yesterday. Mary Devlin swung round from the stainless steel sink with a frying pan in her hand. She was wearing a cream-coloured maternity dress and grey suede mules. For a moment she looked almost frightened. Michael suddenly saw her again as she had been that day when they came back from Castle Ward and he had finally told her that the end justified the means. He blinked and looked at her again. He saw her brown hair tied up in a ponytail, the open expression in her face, the pale blue eyes that stared hard at him and then abruptly softened.

"Born in a field?" she said.

"What?"

"You didn't close the door," she said. "And you didn't knock."

He turned back to the door and shut it. When he came back into the room Mary had placed the frying pan on the draining board.

"I was afraid you were going to use that on me," he said.

"It's a bit late for that." She smiled a little as she spoke, but he still felt tense and uncomfortable.

"Yes, I suppose it is."

He watched her standing pregnant in her maternity dress as she wiped off the sink.

He was uncertain why he still felt so drawn to her. Being there in the room with her, he was beset by his vulnerability. He felt bereft of resolve, spent, quite powerless. An inner voice told him to get a grip on himself. It was all too late anyway. She was Mrs Savage now. He had had his chance and he had chosen not to take it. He had made other priorities. 'We are our choices,' he thought. Seeing her now, moving about in her home and apparently content with her life, he sensed a strange, alien quality come over him, as if he were a displaced person in a foreign land. He was an outsider in her presence and he did not belong.

"Are you married now?" he asked her, wanting to be sure.

"Yes." She hung the dish cloth over the outer rim of the sink. "We got married when I became pregnant."

He wasn't sure how to take this. "It doesn't matter," he said at last.

She looked at him with her clear blue eyes. "No," she said, "it doesn't matter." Abruptly she walked over and stood before him, looking up at him with that soft, open expression on her face, almost smiling but not quite. "What is it you want, Michael?" she asked him.

At once he felt uneasy. He didn't like the question. It was too direct. He felt exposed and confused. He wasn't sure exactly what he wanted. Then he thought about Gerry Savage, about how he had somehow come into money, a legacy from some distant relative in America. The suspicion swelled in him like a metastic tumour. Now he had taken over O'Leary's, and he had also taken Mary.

Jesus Christ, now he had Mary too!

"I want to know where the money came from to buy this pub," he blurted out. Mary took a step back. Her eyes narrowed in sudden apprehension. She placed her hands flat across her stomach, protectively, like a shield.

"So that's what this is about," she said softly. "And I thought you had come to ask my forgiveness."

"Forgiveness?"

"Yes, forgiveness."

"What for?"

"You turned me into the Blue Lady, remember? I asked you not to that day we went to Castle Ward. You didn't listen. You had other plans, a bigger agenda."

She seemed to think about this before she added, "No, not bigger. Different."

Michael started to speak, to try to explain, but the words sat like a dry cloth balled up and stuffed down his throat. There was nothing he could say that would exonerate him. He would only be acting, playing a role, indulging in make-believe. And she would see through that, for she knew him for what he was, she saw through him to the bone. He didn't want to look at her, but there was nowhere else to turn. He met her gaze. She was looking at him, her eyes moist with sadness.

"Did you really think it was more important not to betray a cause than to betray a friend?"

"It wasn't as simple as that," he said gruffly.

"Wasn't it? Really?" she asked, not without irony. "Michael, a cause like nationalism is nothing more than an abstraction. It will still be here when you and I are dead and gone." She kept looking at him. "A friend is a person with a life, a limited time, a human being with a heart."

He recalled the creed he once had followed, the words recited in the unison of faith.

"And that heart is partly pumped by the blood of national

identity – otherwise it's just an empty shell," he said, uttering the words like the automatic response in a catechism.

Mary looked at him and sighed. "Jesus, spare me the party line."

They stared at each other until Michael glanced away. 'We are our choices,' he thought again. All at once he knew he had to get away, out of this house, away from Mary. It was too much to be confronted like this with his past, with the future that might have been. It confused and bewildered him. And in the core of his being he sensed a sickening feeling of loss that made him nauseous. He thought swiftly about the best way to resolve his reason for being there, the best way to ask her.

"Listen, I've heard that Gerry inherited a small fortune from some relative in the States. Is that right?"

She gazed at him as if he were a portrait in an art gallery. All expression seemed to have left her face.

"Near enough," she said, after some deliberation. "Near enough."

"Well, there must be some papers, some documentation which verifies that."

Mary looked him up and down, from his harried brow to the wet brogues that had left their mark on the kitchen floor. "And why would you be interested in that? What's it got to do with you?"

Michael sighed, a long exhalation of weary resignation. Did he really have to spell everything out? Surely she understood why he had to know.

"It might have nothing to do with me, nothing at all. On the other hand it might have everything to do with me. It might explain why I've spent the last five years in the Maze."

"Jesus, Michael, you can't be serious." She almost laughed as she said it. "You went to prison because of what you did in Newry with those bombs. You think Gerry might have informed on you, is that it? For Christ's sake he didn't know anything! He wasn't involved in that in any shape, manner or form!"

Mary Savage backed away to the kitchen table to lean assertively against it, the heels of her hands supporting her on the top. Michael felt instantly more comfortable with the distance between them. It was unnerving how her nearness seemed to weaken him.

"Gerry stood close enough to the movement to have heard something," he asserted. "He was well known as a sympathiser even if he wasn't a member. He probably knew that something was under way, and it wouldn't have been too difficult to put one and one together. Isn't that what you did at the time? And maybe you told him what you suspected."

"Jesus Christ!" Mary cried. "So now I'm the informer, or at best an accomplice. Michael, even if I had known what you were planning, I would never have betrayed you. Never. I would have done everything I could to stop you, but I would never have betrayed you. You're just whistling in the dark. I had no idea what was going on. I hardly even knew Gerry Savage in those days, at the time of the bombings. I knew who he was, of course, that he played Gaelic for Down, but I'd never met him, never spoken to him."

"Well, there's one very easy way to sort this out." Michael felt a dryness in his throat but he continued, his voice growing hoarse.

"Just show me the letter from America or the paper from the solicitor, or whatever. You must have some kind of documentation that will verify that Gerry got an inheritance from some relative in America."

"You want to see a piece of paper that, in your eyes, will prove that Gerry Savage wasn't an informer. Because, as far as you're concerned, if I can't produce that piece of paper, then Gerry must have got the money from the Belfast Telegraph or the British government in exchange for naming names. Is that it?"

"Dear God in heaven, where else would he have got the money from if it's not from some rich uncle in America?"

"I don't know, Michael." Mary's voice had grown quieter, but there was a dangerous edge to it, a subdued sharpness that Michael had not heard before. "Maybe he won it on the horses. Or on the football pools. Or the Lottery. There's lots of ways to win money nowadays."

"It doesn't matter a damn how he got it, as long as there's documentation to prove it. Just show me the papers," he demanded, his tone rising with the tension.

"So if I don't show you a piece of paper," she said in the same quiet voice, "you're going to destroy my life, the life I've built up after you dumped me, after you went off and murdered 23 innocent people to liberate Ireland from the British oppressor, or whatever the fuck you thought you were doing. And what are you going to do now? Shoot Gerry, my husband, the father of the child I'm carrying? Will you shoot me too then, as an accomplice, as another bloody informer?"

It had gone so far now that Michael wanted to believe that there was a letter, a document of some description, which would let Gerry Savage off the hook and thereby also exonerate Mary.

"Will you for the love of Jesus just get me the paper and I'll be gone?" he begged, his voice harsh and congested. "What is it, a solicitor's letter? Just show it to me and I'll get out of your life."

Mary looked him straight in the face, her pale eyes seeming even paler, still pools of acid blue.

"All right, all right. If it'll put your mind at rest, I'll get it. I'll get it."

She said it so quietly it frightened him. The calm placidity of her speech was somehow more threatening than if she had started screaming at him. She spoke to him in softly murmured words that were little more than a whisper. A deadly whisper.

"I was so wrong about you all along, Michael, but I never thought you would come here and treat me like this, that I would mean so little to you. You're beneath contempt."

She hissed the last words, turned on her heel and swept out of the room, waddling slightly with her swollen torso as she went. Michael followed her into a short, stone-floored corridor, past a door he guessed led into the bar and on to another door diagonally opposite which she wrenched open and stepped inside, switching on an over-bright, pillbox ceiling light. Michael walked in behind her and looked tentatively around. It was a small, windowless office room with a portable computer on a wooden roll-top desk, a swivel chair, a metal filing cabinet in a corner and a floor-to-ceiling bookcase along one wall. A framed photograph of Mary smiling in a summer dress stood at one end of the desk, an old-fashioned black Bakelite telephone at the other.

Seemingly undecided at first, Mary crossed to the filing cabinet and pulled the top drawer open. She flipped spasmodically through the folders before closing the drawer and proceeding to the one immediately below. Michael observed her with growing disquiet. She continued to flick her way through the contents of the second drawer, occasionally stopping as if to examine a heading, then going on.

"Don't you know what you're looking for?"

Mary fired him a look brimming with ill-suppressed rage. "I know what I'm looking for."

"Well, don't you know where it is?"

She did not answer. With one hand in the filing cabinet and the other on her stomach, she seemed to be making up her mind. Abruptly she slammed the drawer shut and turned towards the bookcase. Made of wood and lacquered in white gloss, half-filled with files, books and photo albums, the bookcase rose to a crown moulding just under the beige plaster of the ceiling. Mary grabbed hold of a chair with a woven wicker seat and nodded at the bookcase.

"I need to get up there," she said, placing the chair in the corner of the room beside the bookcase.

"I can do that," Michael told her. "In your condition you shouldn't …"

"No, I'll do it."

"But you shouldn't be climbing up there. What if the bookcase…?"

"It's bracketed to the wall." She looked up at the top shelf. "I'll do it." she repeated adamantly.

Putting her slippered left foot on the seat, she took hold of a shelf and heaved herself up onto the chair. As she swung her right leg up, Michael moved in to take hold of her other elbow, to support her. She recoiled instantly.

"Don't touch me!" She spat the words out.

Michael froze, stung by the venom in her voice. Holding onto a higher shelf with both hands she stood still and gazed up at the crown moulding.

"Where is it?" Michael asked.

But she did not speak, did not say anything more. She stood motionless on the chair, looking up at the top of the bookcase. Michael did not know how to interpret her silence, the sudden stillness around them. Somehow everything seemed to depend on it. He was about to speak again when she reached up and stretched her hand and wrist over the edge of the crown. When she withdrew her hand again it was holding a Webley .38, a large top-break service revolver at least twenty years old. She swung round to him.

"Get the fuck out of my house!"

Michael stared up at her, at her face, at the gun.

"Do you hear me? Get the fuck out of my house." she hissed.

He wondered if the Webley revolver had a safety catch. He wondered if it was on. "I'll shoot you. I'll say you attacked me."

Mary's eyes were wild with intent. Michael suddenly realised he was threatening everything she had built up, all that she held dear. There was no doubt in his mind that she meant it.

"I won't say it again. Get the fuck out of here!"

Slowly he began to back away past the desk, towards the door, while Mary clenched the gun in her right hand and started to descend from the chair holding onto a shelf with her left hand. All at once her slipper seemed to catch in the wickerwork and she stumbled forward, lost her balance with a wordless cry and fell tumbling headlong to the carpeted floor flailing with her arms before her.

Michael heard her cry and the shot that came almost simultaneously, propelling him backwards against the desk. He clutched frantically at the phone cable, pulling the Bakelite case with him as he fell to the floor and collapsed on his side where he lay listening to Mary whimpering behind him out of sight. And somehow he managed to pull the phone to him and ring for the ambulance and then the whimpering abated and finally stopped and he just lay there looking up at the ceiling light getting brighter and brighter and then darker and darker until all he felt was the blood dripping softly onto the carpet and softly dripping like a leaky tap as he drifted towards the welcome satisfaction of nowhere.

THIRTEEN

Police Headquarters, Belfast
Saturday morning, 4th December 1999

Gillian Rice sat cross-legged in the outer office of Police Headquarters in east Belfast waiting for Chief Inspector Philip Hall. The atmosphere in the room felt stifling, almost suffocating. The ventilation isn't switched on, she concluded. She opened her black fleece jacket, swivelled her head briefly from side to side and expelled air through rounded lips as if blowing out an unseen candle.

The round Quartz clock on the wall above the reception desk told her it was twenty minutes past eight. She glanced at the tinted watercolour hanging on the wall. Its languid rendition of the building in which she sat, the dripping touches of a nonchalant brush endeavouring to build a redbrick structure with what looked like runny cement, captured her frame of mind to perfection. She no longer felt like a police sergeant in the Royal Ulster Constabulary. She did not belong in its wishy-washy womb. No, her present inclination was to become a Carmelite nun. She crossed her cotton denim legs more tightly as she recalled the events of the previous evening. There had been no warning, no indication that anything untoward was afoot. Indeed it had all come about quite by chance. As these things often do, she thought with world-weary resignation.

She had been out in the kitchen, feeding the dishwasher and hand-washing the frying pan and saucepan after their evening meal. Usually they only ran the dishwasher at the weekend, preferring to wash up by hand during the week. But what the hell, Gillian thought, it's almost the weekend anyway.

Alex was sitting in his recliner, a leather armchair by the living-room window, but he was not in a reclining mood.

He was wielding his red marker pen over a bundle of third-form tests in his lap, occasionally slashing quite mercilessly and scribbling supposedly pertinent comments in the margin. Out in the hall the telephone rang.

"Alex, can you take that?" she had asked him from the kitchen sink.

As Alex sat up, the pile of papers slid down onto his knees, preparatory to spilling all over the floor. He groaned.

"I'm up to my eyeballs in test papers – can't you?"

"And I'm up to my elbows in dirty dishes," Gillian said, but she added, "All right, I'll get it."

Wiping her hands with the kitchen towel and quick-stepping out of the kitchen and into the hall, she felt her anger grow – not for the first time – realising she was bowing to his will, yet again, failing to make a stand in the never-ending battleground that was their marriage. Yes, it was just a small concession, admittedly, but they did tend to accumulate until she ended up feeling like a hopelessly harassed housemaid in her own bloody home.

How had it come to this, she wondered for the umpteenth time? Was it to avoid the incessant bickering she remembered from her own parents' marriage, which had marked her childhood and adolescence and which never failed to taint her mood with sadness. Yes, that was probably a large part of it, that and an inherent fear of conflict. The one was born of the other, she realised.

Out in the hall she lifted the phone and recited the number. When she heard the woman's voice, she experienced that sudden sinking feeling that always came with the incipient dread of defeat. She listened numbly and replied, listened some more and without another word slipped the receiver back into its cradle.

Alex didn't look up when she came into the living room. He kept his head down, his red pen hacking intermittently at the pages. She imagined the biting little remark he was making in the margin: 'A preposition is a bad word to end a sentence with.'

For perhaps half a minute Gillian stood watching him, observing his posture of absolute concentration, wondering how much was veritable focus, how much practised simulation. It was as if there was a window between them. He was on the outside, in another place, completely shut off from her. She used to want to smash the glass, shatter that glazed pane, just get through to him. But over time her exasperation had abated, had gradually receded, subsiding almost imperceptibly into a state of bland indifference. Alex stabbed at a split infinitive and jotted a reprimand in the margin. He looked up at last.

"Was it your mother?"

"No," Gillian said. She paused involuntarily before telling him. "It was that teacher at school, the one who keeps ringing you up."

She saw the fear spread like a vagrant rash across his face. "Pamela Boal?"

"If that's her name. She's never introduced herself."

Alex hesitated before apologising for Pamela Boal. "She's a bit shy."

Gillian's face took on a slow, sceptical expression. It might have been a smile. "Shyness is a fatal handicap in the classroom," she told him. "You used to say that, remember, when you were telling me what it takes to be a good teacher?"

Alex shuffled the papers together in his lap and looked up at her. A strained look flitted across his features. He was like a poor poker player with a bad hand. Finally he had to ask: "What did she want?"

Gillian looked down at him as if he were the victim of a bad car crash, someone too horrifically injured to invite immediate help.

"You," she said at last.

"Me?"

"Yes, she wanted to speak to you."

For a moment he looked relieved. "What did you tell her?"

"That you were out… at a meeting. That's what you wanted, isn't it? That's what you told me to say the last time."

For a second Alex believed he'd been let off the hook.

"Gill," he blustered, "I've told you before – she's always bothering me about something. If it's not problem pupils, it's what exam questions to set, or what grade to give, or —."

"It wasn't anything about school." Gillian's voice was taut and pointed, a drawn bowstring about to be released.

Alex gripped the papers tightly as though he was afraid they would blow away. He looked at Gillian, expecting a gale-force wind. He waited for her to continue. When she didn't, he finally asked her.

"What was it?"

"It was about how she couldn't go on."

"Couldn't go on?"

"How she couldn't stand it anymore."

"What?"

"How you're breaking her heart."

"I'm what?"

They stared at each other, eyes locked together: Alex looking desperately for salvation, Gillian seeing only damnation; until the silence in the room became almost tangible, a calm of such fragility that they knew the next sound would splinter it, irreversibly, beyond all repair. And in the deafening stillness Gillian whispered to herself, 'This is the end of our life together.' So, finally, she asked him, the triteness of the question surprising her with its utter banality.

"How long has it been going on?"

He seemed to jerk to attention, trying to sit up straight without losing the papers in his lap.

"Going on? It hasn't been going on, as you say," he said. He swallowed as if something was stuck in his throat. "Nothing has been going on."

Gillian smiled at him. It was strange. She felt different somehow. It was out in the open. She was another person. Her smile was a shallow, humourless grin of disbelief. It was the smile of the enemy.

"Are you seriously trying to tell me that you and – what's her name? – Pamela, Pamela Boal, aren't having an affair? Now, wait a minute. Maybe she was just reciting her lines for the Christmas play. What is it this year? Twelfth Night? Othello? No, no, it must be Romeo and –?"

"Listen, Gill, please listen."

She watched his face falter, contorting itself as he was energised into speech, into explaining the inexplicable, defending the indefensible. He glanced down at the test papers. The split infinitive glared back at him: 'To always be true.' There was no escaping his failure, no avoiding his transgression. At last the words emerged limply, slipped out, like dry faecal droppings from the orifice of his mouth: "It was a … one-off thing … it didn't … mean anything … really, it didn't … mean anything."

For a moment she looked stunned. Then she thought she was going to laugh. Laugh hysterically.

"Christ no. A one-night stand. I don't believe it. When was it? Last night? No, you were home last night. Last Saturday? No, you were out with me –."

He said, "It was after the Hallowe'en party at school. I dropped her off. She…invited me in for a drink."

"For a screw, you mean."

She snapped it out and wished she hadn't. Alex sat gazing numbly at the papers in his lap.

"I should never have gone. It was stupid. It… it just happened."

Gillian somehow resisted the urge to scream. She kept her voice tight and low, the tone nonetheless rising steadily as she soared to the end of each sentence.

"Oh don't be so bloody naïve. And don't insult my intelligence. These things don't just happen, as if you had nothing to do with it. You wanted it to happen. You instigated it. Be honest with yourself – just for once! You made it happen!"

He couldn't meet her wild-eyed glare. He looked down at the test papers again. The red-ink marks were shaking, a neon blur in his hands. Fearfully, he placed the papers on the floor.

"Gill, I didn't go looking for it, please believe me."

"No," she said, "your dick went looking for it, and do you realise what that makes you? That makes you a mutant. You know what a mutant is, Mr Teacher? No? A mutant is a malformed human being, a freak, a weirdo. And why are you a mutant? Because a man who has his brains in his dick and not in his head can't be anything else. He must be a mutant. And, Alex, here's the bottom line: I don't want to be married to a mutant."

"Gill, I've told you, it wasn't like that at all." Once more he tried desperately to explain, his brain fumbling around for the words. "She's … emotionally involved. I hadn't realised. It wasn't something I planned. I wanted to tell you, but … well…"

He hesitated, tapered off and was silent. She stared back at him, granite-faced, implacable, merciless. Without fully realising it, he had stripped off layer after layer of her conviction until even the last sliver of resolve was gone. Her mind had snapped ajar and it was out in the open. No more Mrs Nice.

"Our life together is over, Alex," she declared. "Pamela

bloody Boal isn't the first. There was that PE teacher at Lagan College too. Remember her? And God knows who else. Christ, I could write a book about living with you – 'Life with a Mutant,' a sci-fi tale of married life. It's over. I want you out of here. Now!"

In case he might have misunderstood, she tore the gold wedding ring off her finger and hurled it at him. Appropriately, it struck him in the crotch before falling to nestle in the deep pile of the rug.

A constable approached her bearing a cup of tea. The universal remedy for all ills, she thought, as if he knows the pathetic, soap-opera memories that have been running round in my head. The chief inspector was momentarily tied up in a meeting with the chief superintendent, but he would only be another five minutes or so. The constable was sandy-haired and pale with orange-peel contours marking the acned terrain of his face. A custard cream biscuit was perched somewhat precariously on the edge of the saucer.

A five-minute time frame was an elastic concept in Ireland, even in the Royal Ulster Constabulary, but the tea was scorchingly hot and welcome. Gillian settled as best she could in the cushionless wooden chair and nibbled at the biscuit.

Of course it wasn't only Alex's infidelity that had caused their marriage to founder. She recalled with melancholy all the tests she had endured to determine why she was unable to conceive. Alex had refused to be tested. "Let's do you first," he'd argued. "It's probably something in the piping that can be easily fixed."

"Yeah, it's sure to be all my fault," she'd said. "Why don't you just call a fucking plumber?"

But it was with her the fault lay, the attack of acute salpingitis she'd suffered in her teens, infecting and inflaming her fallopian tubes, leaving her with only a 10 to 15 percent chance of conceiving even if everything else was all right, which it seldom was. And it was her misbegotten feelings of guilt, she realised, that led her to take a back seat, to let Alex take the upper hand in their marriage. Alex didn't even appear to notice her anguish. Wrapped up in himself and his self-imposed martyrdom, half the time he didn't even seem to know she was in the same room.

And after a while they avoided the subject, didn't talk about it, swept it under the threadbare carpet of their withering existence. She grabbed the teacup, blew ripples across the steaming tea, and drank. It was a blessing she had this special job coming up, whatever it was, giving her something else to think about. Focus, she said to herself, focus now on the meeting with Chief Inspector Hall.

"He's just come in."

The sandy-haired constable stood before her. He reached forward to take the cup and saucer. The remains of the nibbled biscuit were awash in tea she had somehow spilt in her marital reverie. She glanced apologetically at him and rose to her feet. He led her down a corridor windowed with smoked glass and steel to a covered walkway that ended in an annex. Outside she saw that it had started raining again, a grey gauze shrouding the urban landscape, filtering the winter light. She followed the constable to a door at the far end of the annex, her rubber heels making no sound on the tiled floor. The constable knocked lightly and opened the door.

"It's Sergeant Rice, sir."

She walked past him and into the room.

Unsure as to protocol, Gillian stood uncertainly as the door closed behind her. CI Hall was hunched over an oversized desk, peering at a copy of the Financial Times.

"Medicine," he said, "I think I need some medicine."

Gillian kept a straight face. "I hope you're not unwell, sir," she said.

He looked up. "No no, my portfolio. Pharmaceuticals. perhaps Norstream."

The chief inspector pushed himself up from a high leather-backed chair using his desk as leverage, and came round smiling and extending his hand. As she shook it, Gillian gazed up into round goldfish eyes set wide apart in a broad, slightly buck-toothed visage that somehow reminded her of a Hallowe'en turnip. His shorn head resembled a field of straw stubble, nodding down at her as he released her hand and moved back to his chair.

"Good of you to come," he intoned in the smooth Campbell College vowels of east Belfast. "Please take a seat."

Gillian sat down in the wooden armchair thinking she had been summoned here and had no choice in the matter and that Chief Inspector Hall thanking her for coming meant something out of the ordinary was going on. It was also weird that she had been told to come in outdoor civvies. The room was overheated and stuffy, which explained why the chief inspector was sitting there in a short-sleeved white shirt complete with black epaulettes and a black tie. He beamed his professional smile at her again.

"Would you like a coffee?" he said. "I've got a cappuccino maker."

He gesticulated proudly at a shiny silver machine with black plastic handles that stood on a small table in the corner. He might have been exhibiting a pedigree dog or a prize bull.

"No thanks," Gillian said, "I'm not long after breakfast."

CI Hall rounded his desk and sat down. The social smile had vanished as he switched into serious police-business mode.

"Sergeant Rice," he began, "I have a meeting in 20 minutes so I'll come straight to the point. You've probably heard about the abduction of Arthur Williams, the journalist…"

Gillian nodded. The chief inspector rapped the knuckles of his left hand lightly on the desk, an ossiferous rattle of drums to announce the matter at hand.

"Well, it seems we may have got a lead in the case," he confided, leaning his Hallowe'en head forward to convey the gravity of the matter. "As you know, we have a number of dissident republicans who are not happy with the direction the peace process is taking. It's early days yet, but several things are pointing to the Newry bombers being behind Williams' disappearance. As I've no doubt you are aware, they've just been released under the terms of the Good Friday Agreement. The officer in charge of the case is Inspector Quinn, who you perhaps know…?"

He paused for Gillian to respond.

"No sir," she obliged. "I know *of* him, but I've never met him."

The chief inspector seemed surprised at this. Briefly he raked the stubbled field on his scalp with a ham-like hand as if savouring the thought.

"No? Well, he was deeply involved when Williams got inside information that led to the culprits being eventually brought to trial and convicted."

"And now," Gillian ventured, "they've all been let loose – according to the Good Friday Agreement."

"Precisely. So it seems not unlikely that they may be trying to ferret out the identity of the person who informed on them in order to exact some sort of revenge."

"Which is why they may have lifted Arthur Williams," Gillian said, feeling a need to help the chief inspector on his expository way.

"Yes. He never revealed his source, of course. As a

journalist, and a highly respected journalist at that, it would have been completely taboo. However, at the time I believe Quinn built up quite a close relationship with Arthur Williams, respected him for his courage and integrity, that sort of thing. I think you might say, to some extent, he's personally involved here."

CI Hall paused, as if to let this information sink in. He glanced sideways at a gilt-framed photograph standing upright on his desk. Gillian assumed it portrayed members of his family. Momentarily she wondered if they resembled the father of the family.

She decided to focus on the task in hand, whatever that might be. "Excuse me, sir, but where do I come into this?"

The chief inspector's face took on a slightly pained expression, as if he was somewhat averse to being reminded of Sergeant Rice's reason for being there. Watching his features tighten, Gillian asked herself if he was also trying to suppress an outbreak of wind.

"Well, one of the leaders of the Newry bombing was Michael McCann. He was released yesterday and we have good reason to believe that he may be involved, that the whole thing had been planned beforehand and they were just waiting for him to get out. Now, McCann comes from Ballyfoil in the Mournes, a well-known nest of IRA sympathisers. There's a chance they may have taken Williams there, at least temporarily, maybe before taking him across the border."

CI Hall paused again, his pescatorial eyes fixed rigidly on Gillian, as if to ascertain that she was still listening, still paying attention to the information he was divulging. Gillian was relieved to note that the possible attack of flatulence seemed to have passed.

"I'm sorry, sir, but I still don't see…"

"We're sending Quinn down there to see what's what, and we want you to go with him, ostensibly as his driver."

He transmitted his professional smile once again, a somewhat toned-down, abbreviated version, before he added, "I understand you've done some rallying."

"Some," Gillian admitted, realising he had obviously done his homework. "I've done a few hill climbs too," she added lamely, and immediately regretted saying anything at all. There was something of an aura about CI Hall that made her feel like a little schoolgirl – a little schoolgirl in the presence of an imperious headmaster.

"Excellent."

He sat back in the pliant leather of his high-backed chair and Gillian assumed that the interview was over.

"That's it then. You want me to go along as his driver?"

"Yes, but that's not all. I understand that you have recently undergone a specialist training course with the SAS."

"I was selected to go on a two-week intensive course earlier this year."

"I imagine it was pretty rigorous…"

"Well sir, it wasn't for girl guides. The physical was tough, really tough. And there was advanced weapons training and a series of practical Aikido exercises."

"Aikido?"

"It's a Japanese martial art, but without the Zen bollocks."

The chief inspector looked taken aback.

"That was how they described it, sir," Gillian hastened to add. "Not my words."

"Yes, quite."

He paused as if undecided as to how much more he should say, how he should proceed. His dental configuration seemed to necessitate a slight lisp when tackling sibilant sounds.

"There's something else you should be aware of."

He paused again.

"Yes?"

"Well, Quinn, as I said, has been in on this case from the beginning, which makes him eminently suitable to follow it up now. But he's a member of a special group of officers who have hitherto been allowed to use somewhat unorthodox methods to achieve results in their work."

"The D-Specials?"

The chief inspector's jaw dropped, his mouth revealing a need for radical dental alignment.

"Well, that may be their unofficial title," he said, his bushy eyebrows sprouting with surprise. "They're a covert undercover force."

"Yes, sir, word does get around."

"In this case, it's not supposed to."

He looked affronted and glared at her accusingly.

"However," he continued after a short silence, "and I tell you this in strictest confidence, they are being disbanded even as I speak, at this very moment. It's all part of the peace process. In fact, it's as if they never existed."

Gillian decided she had never heard a better example of wishful thinking.

"But what I'm trying to tell you about Quinn," he continued, "is that he's something of a loose cannon, if you know the expression."

"I know the expression," Gillian said, wishing he would stop trying to make her feel like a schoolgirl.

"Yes, well, he can be rather … unpredictable at times. I mean, he has a tendency to go out on a limb. Some might even say, off the rails."

"In what way, if I may ask?" Gillian asked, feeling somewhat confused by the chief's choice of metaphors.

Chief Inspector Philip Hall stared at her for a moment, making up his mind. Then he reached down, pulled out a drawer and withdrew a portable CD player which he placed on the desk.

"You'll hear part of an interview here with a man who was attacked recently on the top of a double decker bus. He and his friend were on their way home when there was some sort of altercation with another man about smoking. Apparently the two friends lit cigarettes and the other man objected – violently. We have good reason to believe that the other man was Inspector Quinn. He had apparently been out for a night on the town. We have CCTV footage that shows him getting on the bus at the City Hall with a woman."

"Were the men badly hurt?"

"One of them is still in hospital. He's on the mend. The other one gave us this interview. Broken nose and cheekbone, pretty smashed up. He says the attacker seemed to go berserk. Came at them with a fire extinguisher."

The chief inspector stretched out a hairy, short-sleeved arm and pressed the green button.

What was he like, the man who attacked you?
Sneaked right up on us. Sleekit piece of shit. Caught us by surprise.
I mean, how old is he? How big is he? What's he look like?
(PAUSE) Hard to say. Happened so fast. Like, he could be forty, forty-five. Could be more. Could be less. Dunno.
Had he long hair, short hair? What colour? Was he bald?
Dark hair, short. Maybe a bit grey at the sides. Maybe.
Big man? Short, tall, stocky, thin?
Big? He's no giant, but he's big when he comes at you. You don't see it till he's there. Like, he moves careful, almost slow, but acts fast. Sleekit cunt.

Philip Hall half-rose and leant over the desk to stop the recording. As he bent forward Gillian almost expected his bulging eyeballs to roll out of their sockets and splat down onto the desk. He slumped back in his chair and looked up at her, waiting for a reaction.

"He took on two of them?"

"It would appear so."

"And they both ended up in hospital?"

"Yes. He … he can be a bit of a handful."

"Got a short fuse?"

"At times, Sergeant Rice, he's got no fuse at all."

"And it was Quinn, was it?" Gillian said.

"I'd say that's a fairly accurate assumption."

"Not a smoker then. Good. He won't stink up the car."

"Well, we've buried the case. The fact is, they probably got what they deserved. They have form, both of them, serious form. Couple of scumbags, actually. We're not pursuing it."

"Lucky for Quinn, I suppose."

The chief inspector nodded. "The fact is," he said, "he's got away with a lot of highly debatable actions simply because of the times we live in."

"Let me get this straight, sir. You're saying Quinn is something of a maverick."

"Well, for various reasons, he prefers to work alone."

"Let me guess. Because there's no one there to check his behaviour."

"Something like that."

He put his elbows on the desk and placed his open hands together as if in prayer. "Sergeant Rice, I'm counting on you to see that things don't get out of hand down there in Ballyfoil. You call for back-up at the first sign of trouble. You follow?"

"I see what you mean. The man's got a quick temper."

"Understatement of the year. There have been other

incidents too, but I think you've got the picture. He's not allowed to drive a police vehicle, which is another reason for your input here."

Input? What did he think she was? Something to be fed into a computer? With Quinn as the hard drive? What was she then, the software? Screw that. What next?

CI Hall glanced at his watch, a CD-sized, glittering timepiece inset with several small dials and anchored to his wrist with a massive gold-leafed bracelet.

"Look, I've got to run now. Inspector Quinn will be here within the hour. He'll meet you at reception. You can sign out now for a car at the depot. It's been cleared. Unmarked, of course. And no Land Rover, nothing too armoured-car like. They'll be sensitive to that in the Mournes."

He heaved himself up and came round to shake her hand, a little unnecessarily, she thought, almost as if she were leaving the service, never to return.

"Good luck," he said, his Halloween-turnip head lighting up with an encouraging smile. "Quinn's a damn good policeman, but keep an eye on him."

Gillian walked out of the room. At the same time CI Hall snatched a wrinkled leather briefcase from under the table grandstanding the Cappuccino machine and followed her out into the corridor, sweeping past on his way to the main exit. Gillian tagged along behind him, listening to his heels clicking on the corridor tiles, wondering what the hell she was letting herself in for. Swinging the briefcase like a trophy, he clip-clopped along the walkway, turned a corner at the far end, and was gone.

At the depot she wandered around, examining what they had. There wasn't a lot to choose from. If she was going to be driving in the country lanes and byways of the muddy Mournes, she definitely wanted something with four-wheel drive. She settled for a Mitsubishi Shogun with a five-speed manual gearbox and around 200 horsepower. A car with automatic transmission always left her feeling somewhat insecure, as if the car in some way had an independent life of its own over which she did not have full control. She checked the headlights, indicators and fuel gauge. Full tank. With the key in her jacket pocket, she made her way back to reception. She looked around the almost empty entrance hall.

There was a man sitting in the far corner watching her. As she walked over to him, he rose slowly to his feet. Gillian realised that the depiction of him that she had just heard was pretty accurate. In physical appearance he belonged in a no-man's land of human identification.

He was wearing an olive-green hunting jacket with deep zip-topped pockets, beige-coloured hiking trousers, no headgear. His hands hung at his sides as if he was wondering what to do with them. The thin scars on his face made him look menacing, yet slightly vulnerable at the same time. He stood with his legs apart trying to look more confident than he was. He didn't extend his hand. Gillian decided she didn't much like him.

"You're Rice," he said, "Gillian Rice?"

"Inspector Quinn, I presume," she said. She had no wish to know his first name. It was never going to be that sort of relationship. To mask her initial reaction to him she flashed him a professional smile, the one she'd just learned from the chief inspector. He looked her up and down, a cursory appraisal, from urchin-cut blonde head to police-booted feet. No make-up, no spectacles, no attempt at allure. He probably thinks I'm butch, she thought.

"Have you got the car?" he wanted to know, all business and no charm.

"It's just outside," she told him. "All tanked up and rarin' to go."

"Bit like yourself then," he said, picking up a duffel bag at his feet and turning to the exit.

FOURTEEN

Ballyfoil, Mountains of Mourne

"Bloody hell!"

Dominic Fairon clenched the words through rigid jaws as he took in the scene in the small, windowless room. He sniffed in the sickeningly dry, metallic scent of blood. The sharp ceiling light glared down on the carpet and the figures lying redundant upon it. The woman was sprawled on her side across the bloodied floor, her pregnant belly bulging ominously against the distended maternity dress. The man, spread-eagled at right angles beside her, groaned briefly and lapsed once more into silence. A gun lay on the floor between them like a grey metal signpost, pointing the way to calamity. A wicker-seated chair reclined on its back in the corner, its front legs horizontal stumps in the fusty air.

EMS kitbag in hand, Fairon swept into the room to kneel over the woman. He checked her breathing and pulse, the ragged gash on her temple, the area between her legs for signs of bleeding. The driver, Jimmy Kerr, on his first emergency, had bent over the other casualty, crouched like a sprinter in his blocks.

"Dom, this fellah's in a bad way. Looks like he's taken a bullet in the stomach." Fairon glanced over. "Christ, Jimmy, you're supposed to be a fuckin' care-support worker. Do you even have a first aid certificate? Do your best to staunch the bleeding."

"But Dom, we can't go in here. This is a crime scene. The peelers have first shot at this."

"No they don't. Saving lives has priority. Where the fuck are they anyway? These people'll be dead by the time they get here. Got your gloves on?"

"Course I bloody have."

"Put a bandage on the hole and press it down with the palm of your hand."

"I have, for God's sake, but the blood's seeping through already."

"So put another bandage on top."

The clump of ponderous footsteps came from the stone floor of the corridor. Both ambulance men turned to see a heavy-set man of about sixty appear in the doorway. He stood gaping for a moment, ran a calloused hand through a haystack of white hair and breathed out: "Aw Jesus."

Dominic Fairon glanced up at him. "And who the hell are you?"

"Liam Hogan," he gasped. "Live just down the street."

"Then you know who these people are."

Liam swallowed hard and opened his mouth to answer when the high-pitched wail of a police siren provided a welcome distraction.

"That'll be the ice cream van from Newry," he said.

Jimmy Kerr gaped at him: "Ice cream van?"

"The meat wagon," Fairon explained. "The peelers."

A minute later the siren was doused, doors slammed and heavy footsteps came charging into the building. From the corridor a voice called out:

"Where's the fellah who said he'd been shot?"

Dominic Fairon recognised the grim nasal whine of Bill Pollock's investigative diction. Sergeant Pollock elbowed Hogan to the side and hoofed into the room like a bull in a farmyard of cows in heat.

"For Christ's sake, Fairon, this is a fuckin' crime scene."

Dominic Fairon took a quick look at the sergeant standing there, hands on hips and nostrils flaring.

"If you don't let me do my job, Sergeant, it's going to look more like a bloody morgue."

Pollock snorted and seemed about to stomp a foot on the floor.

"Jeez, you've already contaminated all the evidence."

"All what evidence? What you see is what you get."

The sergeant glared round the room and groaned. "What the hell's happened anyway?"

"Hard to say, until these two start talking," Fairon said in a fast mutter, working with a sterile gauze pad and trauma dressings. "If they ever do. He's been shot in the gut. She seems to have taken a fall. Why don't you take your photos double quick so's I can get them out of here?"

"Get the tech in here! I need a camera," Pollock called over his shoulder. Moving back into the corridor he turned to Liam Hogan and jabbed a nail-bitten finger in his face. "And you are?"

"Liam Hogan. I'm a neighbour. Live just down the street," he repeated as if praying the Rosary.

"So you know these people?"

"Yes, I know them. The woman's Mary Savage. She and her husband run this place."

"And the man's her husband?"

"No, her husband's Gerry Savage."

Sergeant Pollock tilted his head knowingly backwards as the penny dropped. "Gerry Savage, the Gaelic player?"

"That's him."

"So where's he?"

"Dunno. Didn't see his car outside."

"Well, who's this fellah then?"

Hogan glanced down at his feet, as if he might see the name scrawled in the dust-lined toecaps of his boots. He looked up again, into the sergeant's rheumy grey eyes.

"That's Mickey McCann."

"Does he live here too?"

"In Ballyfoil?"

"In Ballyfoil."

"He used to." Hogan hesitated. "He's just got out of prison."

"Prison?"

"The Maze." He faltered again. "He was one of the Newry bombers."

Pollock's broad head jerked forward.

"Jesus, *that* Mickey McCann."

"Yeah."

"When did he get out?"

"Just the other day."

"But why would he come here?"

"He comes from here. He grew up in Ballyfoil."

"And what's his connection to the woman, this Mary Savage?"

"I'm not sure."

"You're not sure?" Sergeant Pollock's face registered blatant disbelief. "Come on, this is a small community. Everybody knows everybody else here. Word gets around. You must know something."

Hogan shuffled his feet on the thinly carpeted floor. "Well, I heard just yesterday that they used to go out, y'know, before he ended up in the Maze. But that would have been five, six years ago. I mean, that's ancient news. It's just a rumour anyway," he added lamely.

Pollock leered at him.

"Have you got Gerry Savage's phone number?"

"No, I hardly know the man."

The sergeant swung back to the crime scene. "Is there a phone in here somewhere?"

Jimmy Kerr nodded at the Bakelite on the floor beside him. The receiver lay a couple of feet away, the electric cord winding its way along the carpet between them.

"I mean a mobile," the policeman snarled.

"Think I saw one on the kitchen table on the way in," Fairon said.

Sergeant Pollock turned towards the kitchen and almost collided with another policeman coming in.

"Bag that gun, Terry, first thing you do when you've done the camera work," he barked and tramped on into the kitchen. A stretcher trolley was parked alongside the table. He pushed it out of his way and found a Nokia mobile phone beside a wooden napkin holder at the far end of the table. He dug in his pocket for a pair of latex gloves and put them on. His thick stubby fingers fumbled momentarily with the keys until he located and pressed the connection to Gerry Savage.

"Yeah?"

"Gerry Savage?"

"Yeah. Who's this?"

"Sergeant Pollock, RUC."

The sergeant wheezed impatiently as Gerry Savage digested this information. He damned the head cold that had gone into his chest.

"RUC?"

"I'm ringing from your home in Ballyfoil. There's been an accident. Where are you at the moment?"

"I'm at the Quays in Newry."

"The shopping centre?"

"Yes. What's this about an accident?"

"It's your wife. She seems to have suffered a fall."

"A fall? Jesus Christ! What's happened? How is she?"

"She'll be leaving here double quick in the ambulance. I suggest you make your way to the Daisy Hill Hospital. She'll be coming to A&E there in a very short time."

"But the baby? What about the baby? Is it all right?"

"I don't know any more than you do. You'll find out more at the hospital."

"Daisy Hill, A&E." He seemed to need to memorise this before he added, "Right, I'm on my way."

As the sergeant replaced the mobile on the kitchen table, Dominic Fairon scurried in to grab the stretcher trolley. He backed out again, pulling the trolley with him and calling to the driver to come and help him with the woman. Sergeant Pollock looked thoughtfully at the Nokia mobile before picking it up again. He had just placed it in a breast pocket under his flak jacket when Jimmy Kerr trundled the trolley bearing Mary Savage into the kitchen and past the sergeant on his way out to the ambulance.

"Send someone in with the other stretcher," Fairon shouted after him. "And get the maternity pack out. We might need it."

The sergeant walked out into the street and over to the police vehicle where he talked in a low, forceful voice on the radio for several minutes while Michael McCann was borne out on a stretcher with Liam Hogan in close attendance. People had come out of their homes: men, women, children, some dogs. They stood in the street in couples and small groups, whispering and talking in subdued voices. They did not approach the police. Minutes later Liam Hogan watched the Land Rover ambulance accelerate up the slight gradient out of the village and follow the rutted asphalt ribbon that led steeply up the hill, over the ridge and down through the valley beyond to Daisy Hill Hospital in Newry.

FIFTEEN

Belfast to Ballyfoil

Gillian Rice drove with mute determination westwards on the A55 ring road through south Belfast. In the persistent morning traffic they skirted the Castlereagh Hills rising on their left, passing through the city wards of Knock, Castlereagh and Newtownbreda, motoring along the dual carriageway in legal tempo over to Stockman's Lane and the M1 motorway. As the Mitsubishi Shogun chugged steadily along Balmoral Avenue, Quinn sat sullenly beside her, glancing occasionally to the side as he feigned interest in the residential emblems of middle-class suburbia. The silence between them ballooned like a suppurating boil, until the temptation to puncture it became too great to resist. As Sergeant Rice changed down on the slip road to accelerate neatly into heavy traffic on the three-lane motorway going south, Quinn found it necessary to speak.

"You drive purty good for a gal," he said with a phoney mid-Atlantic accent. He'd no sooner said it than he thought, Christ, what a pathetically sexist line. Did I actually say that?

Gillian Rice kept her eyes on the road and sighed.

"You talk pretty dumb for a guy," she told him with her own American twang.

Quinn glanced at her, then looked ahead again as she swerved out to overtake a slow-moving brewery lorry.

"Yeah, sorry 'bout that," he said. The corners of his mouth twitched fleetingly with self-reproach. Safely back in the inside lane, he tried again.

"Well, actually I thought, you being such an expert driver, I thought you'd be wearing driving gloves, y'know, those shiny black leather ones with pinprick holes in the back."

"I left them on the grand piano," she said. "Next to my carbon-fibre Ray-Bans."

"Listen you—," he began, with an involuntary chuckle.

"You can call me Sergeant Rice," she interrupted him, "or if that's too long for you, Gillian will do."

"Okay, Gillian. Since we're going to be working together, I'm simply trying to make some polite conversation here, make sure we get off on the right foot."

"No left-footers, then?"

Quinn was tempted but decided to ignore the remark. "In his infinite wisdom Chief Inspector Philip bloody Hall has sent us on a search-and-rescue mission to Ballyfoil in the Mourne Mountains and..."

"Is it search and rescue or search and destroy?"

"Well, there's always the chance that one could lead to the other."

Gillian glanced at him to see if he was smiling. He wasn't.

She said, "Ballyfoil? That's just a wee village, isn't it?"

"It's a one-horse town."

"So what's the problem?"

"The problem could be that everyone there thinks they're the jockey."

"Wow," Gillian said. "And the race is the United Ireland Derby."

"Something like that. It could turn into a regular shitstorm," Quinn said and leant a little closer. "And just so we know where we stand with each other, I was surprised when Hall told me you were coming. Did he point out the danger? Nothing personal, but the fact is, things could get pretty rough. And I usually work alone."

The deliberately measured tone of his voice possessed its own portent, she noted, as if he was trying to charge the words with the current of his underlying authority, his superior experience in the field. Well, fuck that, she thought. Fuck him and his male chauvinist condescension.

"Don't tell me," she said, sounding surprised. "You're the lone stranger. Or is it Lone Ranger? The Man with no Name. The Equaliser. The man that every man would love to be. If they only knew who he was."

Quinn's mouth widened into a humourless grin. He peeked across at her gloveless hands on the steering wheel: the pale skin, the fingers without rings, the nails neatly trimmed and unbitten.

"Gillian, you know me so well."

"Believe me, I wish I didn't."

As she raised her left hand to grip the wheel higher up, he noticed the thin band of lighter skin on her ring finger.

"Maybe we need a little music," he said, "to further improve the atmosphere in here." Abruptly he reached over and jabbed at the radio button, stabbing it so hard that it seemed unlikely it would ever retract again. The dial lit up and they heard Van Morrison serenading his brown-eyed girl with a low-volume rendition of Sha la la la la la la la. Gillian Rice wrinkled her nose; Quinn creased his features into an attenuated smile, diluted like watered-down whiskey in the frosted glass of his face.

* * *

I remember that song, he thought, I remember it so well. It had that semi-calypso rhythm to it, the nostalgic lyric and a great arrangement with the lead guitar sparking it off. It was his last year at school. They could have been in Trinidad, in Jamaica, in New Orleans. But they were at the Maritime Hotel in College Square North in the sixties when rhythm and blues was born in Belfast. The song came a little later, of course, but it always made him think of those nights at the Maritime, and the warm, smoke-hazy memory of watching Marian Patterson with the hot-chocolate eyes flecked with honey, and the tantalising way she swung round and twirled her trim little figure in the jive. Of course I fucked that up too, he recalled, but that was long before I came under the auspices of Dr Benjamin Musgrave.

* * *

"Your kind of music?"

Quinn was surprised at the question. She glanced over at him.

"Yeah," he said, and thought about it. "Brings back memories."

"Good memories?"

"Some good, some not so good."

"Your misspent youth?"

Quinn thought about it. "Misspent? Missed chances."

"Ah, now I think you must be talking romance."

Quinn shook his head and cleared his throat. "Gillian, you're a very perceptive woman."

"Well, Inspector Quinn," she told him, "it goes with the territory."

Casually she flipped down the indicator as they approached the turn-off for Lisburn and the A1 dual carriageway to Newry. The rain was slithering in fits and starts down the windscreen, the worn wipers straining grudgingly against the glass. The morning lay grey and damp around them, the sky a recumbent canvas of plum-purple clouds hanging low over the land.

There was a complicated roundabout just after the turn-off where Quinn realised – had he been driving – he would have taken a wrong turn. Fortunately he kept his mouth shut and let his driver steer the SUV onto the road south to Newry and Dublin. He settled back but they hadn't driven for more than five minutes when she suddenly swung off the A1 and into the village of Hillsborough. Quinn turned to her with eyebrows raised.

"I need a pee," she informed him. "There's absolutely nowhere you can stop on this bloody road, and it's the main road to Dublin. It's ridiculous."

"Sergeant Rice," he intoned with mock authority, "we're in a hurry."

"So's my bladder."

As she sped past the Hillsborough war memorial with its monumental Celtic cross, Quinn glimpsed a few relics of Georgian architecture and a couple of antique shops before she jammed on the brakes and dashed into a tea room across the road. Four minutes later they were on their way again.

The dual carriageway continued south, winding its way through bleakly nondescript countryside past the country towns of Dromore, Banbridge and Loughbrickland. And as they proceeded south to Newry, so the glowering Mournes increasingly dominated the landscape like a sleeping herd of cattle, gently drowsing in the distance, but showing sharp, jagged outlines as the Shogun drew closer, as if they were rising in trepidation at the approach of the law.

"So what's the plan when we get to Ballyfoil?"

Gillian Rice popped this question as the sun emerged to shine in a remarkably large section of blue sky bordered by a wispy trail of grey cloud. Quinn looked up at the sky. With a bit of luck the day would stay dry.

"The plan?" he said.

"Yes," Gillian said, "the plan of action. Surely you have a plan. You're the Man with no Name, remember? The Pale Rider. The High Plains Drifter."

"Yeah, right. So you're a Clint Eastwood fan. Don't tell me we've actually got something in common. Well then, maybe I do have a name. And maybe it's Harry Callahan.

Which means that right now I'm packing a .44 Magnum, the most powerful handgun in the world. Certainly enough to scare the shite out of anyone in Ballyfoil. So you can relax on that count."

"Yeah, right, make my day."

Gillian took a deep breath, removed her right hand from the steering wheel and rested her elbow on the window ledge.

"Listen Quinn," she said, "let's cut through the horse manure. I've just split up with my husband and I'm feeling pretty shitty. I'm not exactly in the mood for any of your getting-to-know-you conversational gambits. So you can skip the talk-show routines. You're used to just doing your own thing, on your own terms, in your own time. I get that. But there are two of us here, by papal decree if you like, and I expect to be fully involved in the way we play this. And I mean, fully involved. So you can stop just thinking of yourself. "

"That's the way most people think," he said. "That's the way they are."

"Listen to yourself, Quinn. That's the way a cynic thinks."

"Gillian, what you see and what you do in this job doesn't exactly bolster your belief in the goodness of Man."

"Well, it just so happens I've had some experience in the goodness-of-Man arena, so I'd be inclined to agree with you. Men are generally steered by the cock. Know what that is? It's a sort of sexual GPS that leads them around."

Quinn stole a glance at the pale band on her ring finger.

"Okay, I understand you're going through a hard time at the moment. But we've got to stay focussed on the job in hand. When we get to Ballyfoil we need to be totally concentrated. The people there won't exactly be rolling out the red carpet."

"You mean because they're not all devout Presbyterians," Gillian said and took a deep breath.

"Christ, this country's just the same as it's always been. In spite of the Good Friday Agreement, it's the same old war of attrition between the Micks and the Prods. One group against the other, one army against the other, one church against the other."

"Ah, the church," Quinn said with a sigh. "I don't have much time for organised religion, Gillian."

"No, how come?"

"Well, look what it's done for us these past three decades."

"You can go back a lot further than that. Try three centuries. But is that religion or politics?"

Quinn shrugged. "In this country I don't know that there's a difference."

"Really?" she retorted with heavy irony.

"Well, let's look at it another way," he said, turning his head to look at her. "For example, how many Catholics do you know, I mean, go out with, y'know, meet socially?

"Quinn, you realise you're assuming – on the basis of no evidence whatsoever – that I'm a Prod."

"I know. I'm living on the edge here, I know."

"Yeah, like 90 percent of the RUC," Gillian said, suddenly reaching up to pull down the sun visor. "Quinn, if I'm a Protestant, it's only in the sense that I protest."

"Okay, protest away. But answer my question first."

"Well, as you've probably worked out for yourself, the answer is: just about zero."

"And why is that?"

"I've just never met any."

"Why not?"

"Jesus Christ, where are you going with this? We just don't mix in the same circles, y'know, the Rotary Club, the Freemasons, the Rosicrucians."

Quinn felt a strong, corroborating conviction spread within him, strengthening him, filling him with a sense of certainty about what he knew to be the root cause of the country's continuing ills.

"The fact is, Gillian, you didn't meet when it was most important to meet – when you went to school."

"Well, no, I didn't go to St Dominic's Grammar School for girls, any more than you did. What school did you go to anyway?"

"Inst."

"Inst?"

"The Royal Belfast Academical Institution. For boys."

"Boys only?"

"Yes."

"You must have been the only Catholic there."

"Gillian, now *you're* taking something for granted."

"And an all-boys school. That explains a lot."

Quinn's lips squirmed briefly as he fought a smile.

"The point I'm so laboriously making," he continued, "is that if we'd all gone to the same school, Micks and Prods, you and I might not be sitting here right now on our way to God-knows-what in Ballyfoil."

"I'm not so sure about that," she said, "but I see where you're heading."

The sun had slipped behind a fleecy cloud bank on the horizon, darkening the bright promise of the day. Gillian Rice braked behind a mud-splattered cattle lorry to allow a Ford Scorpio to pass before changing down and pulling into the outside lane to surge ahead with the acceleration provided by the elastic torque of the diesel engine.

As she drove on, Gillian lapsed into an unsettling reverie about what she would find when she returned home again. Would Alex really have left? Would he have packed up and taken his belongings with him? All his clothes in the bedroom, his books and files in the living room, his towels and shaving tackle in the bathroom? Would he have taken the Volkswagen Passat that they had bought together? And where would she stand judicially on the house when it came to divorce proceedings? With a sinking feeling she realised she had absolutely no experience and very little knowledge of what was involved. She had a sudden black-and-white vision of their wedding reception four years ago and the smiling faces of the guests: all the friends, all the relatives, all the eye-witnesses. God almighty, why had she insisted on having such a bloody monumental wedding with all the trimmings? How could she have been so stupid, so sentimental, so totally blind – a credulous victim of romantic glaucoma?

"You look worried, Gillian. Was it something I said?" He was staring at her, an amiable twinkle in his dark eyes.

"Don't flatter yourself."

She sat further back in the driving seat, arms stretched almost straight on the steering wheel, eyes focussed intently on the road ahead. Quinn cleared his throat and began again.

"Look – us working together, our partnership on this mission, maybe you can try to see it as a sort of marriage of convenience."

"And we're holding the wedding in Ballyfoil, is that it?"

"Well, something like that, yes."

"Quinn, you should know that on past experience I despise weddings. I hate them."

"Been to many?"

"Yeah, quite a few. And I think they're perverse and degrading. Every time I go to one I see another good woman go down the drain."

"What about the poor bugger who's married her?"

"That's just it. It's generally the poor bugger who's married her that is the drain."

Quinn smiled. "That's clever."

"Not only that, it's usually true as well."

"Speaking from personal experience, are we?"

"We? You including yourself in the equation?"

"I think we're all in that equation, Gillian, even me."

Just then, almost miraculously, the December sun eased itself above the cloud bank on the horizon, beaming yellow shafts of light through the windscreen to momentarily illuminate them. As she turned to look at him, she saw the solitariness of winter in his face.

"There's more to you, Quinn, than meets the eye, though I hate to admit it."

The dual carriageway meandered its uninspiring way through the disarray of the County Down countryside. As the sun skirted yet another downy continent of cloud, Quinn glimpsed a signpost that declared the distance to Newry to be five miles.

"Okay," he said, "we'll soon be in Aberfoil. We turn off just before we get to Newry and I reckon it's about another twenty minutes or half an hour's drive from there. McCann's mother still lives there – I've got the address – so we can pay her a visit first. If he's there, she'll most likely know where."

"If she'll tell us," Gillian said, looking dubious.

"Well, Aberfoil isn't exactly a vast metropolis. If he is there, there can't be so many places for him to hide."

"Hide? Maybe he's not hiding. Maybe he's just visiting his mother after five years in prison. Maybe he's got nothing at all to do with the Williams abduction."

Quinn realised abruptly that he hadn't really given these possibilities a thought, so convinced was he that the trail to Arthur Williams was leading to Ballyfoil. Now Sergeant Rice was outlining a completely different scenario that might alter the whole course of the operation, and it wasn't on his agenda. The thought unsettled and confused him.

"You've got a lot of opinions, haven't you?

"I know," she said. "Frightening, isn't it? Think you can cope?"

Quinn demonstratively shook his head. "I'm beginning to wonder."

He glanced at her and caught the smile on her face.

She said, "And what if Williams *is* being held there?"

Quinn suddenly thought of CI Hall and his exhortation to call for backup if the situation warranted it. And inevitably he was reminded of Joe Stewart's reference to a constipated donkey. The image in his head was quite vivid.

"Our orders are to call in backup immediately as soon as we know," he said.

"But, suppose things happen quickly, unexpectedly. I mean, suppose we don't have time?"

"If there's a meltdown, if things really get out of hand, just follow my lead. You understand. Don't do anything off your own bat."

"For Christ's sake, Quinn, if someone pulls a weapon, goes to attack me, you can be bloody sure I'm not going to wait for you to tell me how to react."

"Keep your hair on. I'm just saying, don't be doing anything impulsive. Don't be jumping the gun."

"Gun being the operative word."

"Oh for God's sake. All I mean is: Keep a low profile until we know what we're up against."

"The same goes for you, does it?"

"Yes, of course."

"Okay." Sergeant Rice ducked her head, assuming a subservient, lower-rank profile, and added,

"Whatever you say, Inspector."

"And Gillian…"

"Yes?"

"Just remember we're fighting the same enemy."

"Yeah," she said, and looked at him. "Each other."

They had just taken the gorse-hedged side road leading into the Mournes when they met an ambulance with beacons flashing on its breakneck way down the hill to Newry. Though quite unaware of its significance, Quinn felt a quivering rush of adrenalin as it careered past them and Gillian Rice pushed the Mitsubishi Shogun steadily uphill on the road towards Ballyfoil.

SIXTEEN

Newry

Gerry Savage's black BMW swerved through the main
entrance to Daisy Hill Hospital, swung ninety degrees right
and accelerated down to the 'pay-parking' car park just
beyond the A&E block. Savage scrambled out, slammed
the door and left the M5 saloon without paying. Racing
back to the A&E entrance, he dashed past the automatic
sliding doors and in through a side-door, almost colliding
with a porter wheeling a trolley.

"Has my wife come in?" he panted. "From Ballyfoil,
Mary Savage. She's pregnant."

"Ask the nurse," he was told.

The man in his short-sleeved, green, V-necked hospital
uniform walked on, pushing the empty trolley before him.
He moved with a slight limp.

"She's in the first examination room," he called back,
turning his head.

Unsure if the porter meant the nurse or his wife, Savage
hurried across the uneven concrete floor, worn with the
traffic of the sick, the injured, the indiscriminate casualties
of life in Newry and Mourne. Ahead of him a nurse darted
out of the room to his left. Savage moved in front of her,
blocking her path.

"Is my wife here? Mary Savage from Ballyfoil?"

"They've just rung. She's on her way."

"Is she all right? Did they say?"

"We won't know anything until they get here and the
triage nurse sees her. Take a seat. She'll be here shortly."

Gerry Savage retreated to the grey plastic chairs in the
hallway. Strip lighting cast its lugubrious glare over the
casualty area. A swollen-faced young woman with a black
eye and a sniffling child was sitting at the end of the row.

She looked as if she had been crying. An indeterminate, slightly caustic odour of new paint mixed with bleach infused the still air. Gerry sat down beside a middle-aged man with a blood-stained, bandaged hand, a self-defeating comb-over haircut and the smell of burnt tobacco in his workman's clothes. He glanced over at the packet of Benson & Hedges protruding from the breast pocket of the man's oily overalls. All at once he wanted a smoke. The urge hit him like a slap in the face. God, he wanted a smoke so bad.

Catch yourself on, he muttered to himself, it's ten years since you stopped. Are you going to start all that shit again? Remember the hell you had then? Waking up in the middle of the night in a cold sweat, dreaming you'd been smoking another fag. The overpowering, sickening guilt and then the joyous relief when you realised it had just been a dream. A bloody nightmare, more like. It was all for the game, of course. Paddy Mullan, the trainer, never let up. 'Kick that bloody habit, Gerry, before it kicks you.' Paddy was right. He smoked himself, non-stop, and he knew. The cancer took him last year. Gerry sat on the plastic chair thinking of Paddy Mullan, then wondering about the condition of his wife in the ambulance. Poor Mary, what had happened to her? Dear God, what the hell was keeping them?

The ambulance arrived ten minutes later. The sliding doors opened and the Land Rover backed in. Knowing he'd just get in the way, Gerry somehow held himself back. Then, as the porter wheeled the trolley in, he moved swiftly over. It was the same porter Gerry had spoken to earlier. He could see Mary's face. Her eyes were open. He saw her eyelids flicker. She was conscious.

"Mary," he called in an alien voice he didn't know, a voice that seemed to come from a faraway place. "Mary, I'm here."

"Stay back," the porter told him. "Let me through."

He limped past and Gerry watched as he manoeuvred the trolley through the nearest doorway and into the examination room. As Gerry made to follow, he heard someone call out.

"Mind out there. Let me past."

He swung round at the voice behind him and gaped confounded when he saw a second stretcher coming towards him. Michael McCann seemed to look up at him as he passed, his face inscrutable behind the oxygen mask, his eyes blank with incomprehension. Gerry stared in bewilderment as McCann was pushed into another room. What the hell was going on? Where did he come from? What was wrong with him? He was standing there, his mind searching futilely for answers, when he was startled by another question.

"Are you Gerry Savage?"

Gerry whirled round once more to look into the watery grey eyes of Sergeant Bill Pollock. He felt an instant and annoying sense of anxiety as he gazed into the ruddy breeze-block face of the man in uniform.

"Yes," he said.

"I rang you from Ballyfoil, from the pub – O'Leary's. Your pub, I believe."

"That's right."

"Well, as you may or may not have heard," the sergeant said slowly, "there was a shooting incident there earlier this morning."

"Shooting? A shooting?" He repeated himself like a child learning a new word.

"Yes. A man's been shot."

"McCann? Mickey McCann?"

"You know him?"

"I know who he is. We went to the same school when we were kids." Savage screwed his face up in disbelief.

"He's been shot?"

"He's been shot in your pub."

Gerry Savage stared blankly at the policeman, trying to get his head around this final statement.

"I don't understand. What was he doing there in the first place? It wasn't open. I was here, in Newry. I wasn't going to open till I got back."

Sergeant Pollock shifted slightly on his feet and raised his shoulders. It might have been a shrug.

"Maybe your wife let him in," he suggested.

"Mary? Why would she do that?"

"I don't know. You tell me."

"She wouldn't let him in. There's no reason."

"Was the front door locked when you left?"

"Locked? Well, no, I don't think so. We don't usually lock the door during the day, once we've opened it."

"So maybe he tried the door and just walked in."

"But why would he do that? What would he want from us? From Mary?"

"Mr Savage," Sergeant Pollock took a deep breath and exhaled. "Not to put too fine a point on it, but weren't they old sweethearts?"

"Who said that?" Savage demanded, forehead puckering, eyes hardening with instant resentment.

"It's common knowledge in the village."

"That was years ago."

Bill Pollock made a vain effort to shackle his impatience, but his anger gained the upper hand.

"Well, as I understand it, it was shortly before he pulled off that mindless atrocity here in Newry. Then he sat for five years in the Maze. Now he's out again, free as a fuckin' bird, and maybe he just wants to take up where he left off. Why else would he call round to see your wife?"

"I don't know."

"Can you think of any other reason?"

Gerry Savage seemed to give this some thought. The cogwheels of his beleaguered brain rotated briefly and shuddered to a halt.

"No, I can't."

"Mr Savage?"

In marine-coloured scrubs the triage nurse swooped on them like a bluebird in flight. She hesitated before speaking in front of the sergeant, then went ahead anyway.

"We're still doing preliminary tests, the most important of which is the ultra sound to make sure the baby is all right. Otherwise your wife is suffering from a head wound, concussion and a sprained wrist from the fall."

"Fall? What fall?"

Gerry Savage looked around him like a man who has excreted in a public lavatory only to find there is no paper.

"Well, at this point we're not quite sure. Perhaps the sergeant can clarify the situation there."

The sergeant was given no chance to elaborate, even had he wished to do so, as Gerry Savage broke in to ask: "Can I see her now?"

"Just give us a quarter of an hour to carry out our tests. The emergency nurse will let you know."

She turned on her heel and marched back to the examination room with a brisk, no-nonsense stride. Gerry Savage shook his shock of blond hair in hirsute exasperation.

"But what exactly happened in the pub? Were they in the bar? Was anyone else there?" He raised both hands from his sides and shook them, fingers splayed wide. "I want to know what the fuck is going on!"

Sergeant Bill Pollock withdrew his notebook from an invisible pocket inside his flak jacket and flipped it open. He glared at the page before him and seemed for a moment to be hypnotised by what he saw. Then he glared at Gerry Savage.

"The shooting took place in what looked like an office room. It was reached through a door beyond the kitchen on the left-hand side of a corridor."

"Jesus, my study."

"Okay, your study."

"But why would they go in there?"

The sergeant pasted a theatrically patient smile across his face. "I was hoping you could provide an answer to that question."

"I've no idea. Really." He added the adverb when Pollock hoisted his sceptical eyebrows in bushy reproach.

"Anyway, they were in your… study." Sergeant Pollock sniffed in the slightly antiseptic air of the hospital as he pronounced the final word. "That was where the shit hit the proverbial fan. Now," and here he hunched his shoulders, a rugby forward about to scrum down, "what I need to know is the exact nature of the laxative."

"Laxative?" Again Savage looked bewildered. Failing to follow the sergeant's train of thought, his mind had shunted into a siding. "What the hell do you mean, laxative?"

Sergeant Pollock breathed deeply and exhaled in what was indubitably a sigh. "I mean, what the fuck were they fighting about?"

"Fighting? What makes you think they were fighting?" He looked all around him, his blond locks flopping about like an upended mop. "Maybe the whole thing was just an accident."

"An accident involving a Webley revolver?"

For a moment Gerry Savage looked like a man on the edge of a cliff. Then the ice-blue eyes narrowed and his features reformed in a posture of divine revelation.

"So McCann had a gun with him," he said. His face lit up as if the truth had set him free.

"There was a gun in the room," Pollock stated equably.

"An old 455 Webley revolver. But it was McCann who was shot."

"Couldn't he have shot himself by accident?"

"Well, even if he did, why would he pull a gun on your wife in the first place?"

"I don't fuckin' know – unless he thought she had dumped him while he was in prison."

"Dumped him? While he was in the Maze?"

"Yes, something like that. I mean he must've been completely off his fuckin' head to even think something like that. After five years. I mean, it must've been like a sick obsession with him."

"So he took the Webley with him just to hammer the point home?"

"Yeah, or because he thought I would be there. What else could it be?"

Sergeant Pollock seemed to freeze, as if startled by a sudden thought. He tilted his head back and looked Gerry Savage in the eye.

"You sure the Webley wasn't your gun?"

"My gun? You must be joking. I don't have a gun."

"You don't have a gun?"

"No, I bloody don't." He acted surprised, trying to think of a better defence, racking his brain for a more plausible response. "I have a baseball bat behind the bar in case there's any trouble. That's all."

"And your wife doesn't have a gun of her own?"

"Course not. Why would she?"

"So, if the Webley isn't yours or your wife's, it must be McCann's. Is that what you're saying?"

Gerry Savage seemed to think he was home and dry, the good sergeant helping him out by eliminating the possibilities.

"Listen Sergeant, this is not some choir boy we're talking about here," he said. "This is the fellah who was behind the Newry bombing. He's hardly going to be walking around with a water pistol in his pocket, is he?"

Sergeant Pollock's face dipped into the semblance of a smile, a hard smile. "Maybe not. But why would he be carrying two big revolvers? Wouldn't one be enough?"

"Two revolvers?"

"Yes. We found a Ruger on him, a 357 Magnum, the big one. Now the Webley's a big gun too. Two big guns like that sounds like a clear case of overkill. And that's overkill in the literal sense of the word."

Gerry Savage stood with his mouth slightly ajar. He seemed to fully comprehend the improbability of the situation. Pollock eyed him carefully and decided to move on, to unveil another discovery.

"It was pretty obvious to us that your wife had suffered a fall of some kind, and that a chair in the room had played a part in that because it was lying on its side on the floor.

It also seemed highly unlikely that she had just fallen off the chair from a sitting position. Then we noticed that the wickerwork in the seat of the chair was ripped in one corner and the thought struck me that she might have climbed up on the chair and then lost her balance when her foot got caught in the tear. So we asked ourselves why she might have wanted to get up on the chair in the first place."

Gerry Savage stood as if listening to a judge who had just donned the black cap. Sergeant Pollock shifted his weight from one foot to the other and continued.

"We decided to take a close look at the files and books on the top shelf of the bookcase. The technician climbed up but couldn't see anything of any special interest. Then he examined the top of the bookcase, behind the crown moulding, just under the ceiling. Guess what he found?"

The expression on Gerry Savage's face showed clearly that he didn't need to guess, but the sergeant enlightened him anyway.

"A box of cartridges specifically manufactured for the 455 Webley – bullets that are known for their lethal stopping power." He presented Savage with a bleak smile and added, "I dare say Michael McCann can attest to that."

Sergeant Bill Pollock took a step closer to Gerry Savage and stood with his weight evenly distributed between his size-12 feet. The rheumy grey eyes focussed in a penetrating stare. Savage was the taller by several inches but his body language bespoke a man of significantly smaller stature. He shuffled uncomfortably and looked up the corridor.

"Suppose you stop lying and give me some answers," Pollock suggested. "Your wife's in enough trouble as it is," he added cleverly.

Savage looked back at him, then down at the floor.

"You hear what I say?" the sergeant said.

Savage uttered a monosyllabic grunt.

"Is that a yes?"

He looked up and nodded. "Is the Webley yours?"

"Yes."

"Have you got a licence for it?"

Gerry Savage looked like a man who's been in too much of a hurry to zip up his trousers in the urinal.

"No."

They were interrupted by the reappearance of the triage nurse, scuttling along the corridor with a thin sheaf of papers in one hand.

"Mr Savage, you can come now. I'll need you to confirm that your wife has no allergies to drugs or foods and to fill me in on her medical history, and the pregnancy in particular. She's suffering from concussion and is somewhat confused at the moment."

Gerry Savage bent his head forward in eager supplication. "And the baby – is it all right?"

"As far as we can see," the nurse told him, "there is no

evidence of perforation of the womb and there doesn't appear to be any laceration of the placenta. Judging from her external injuries, your wife seems to have fallen on her side, which is a blessing. So, unless there is some unforeseen development, the prognosis for the pregnancy looks fairly good."

They were about to move off when Sergeant Pollock cleared his throat and asked: "What about McCann, the man with the gunshot wound?"

The triage nurse shot him a testy look.

"Dr Kickham is moving him into the main hospital for operation now."

"Dr Kickham?"

"He's been assessed by Dr Kickham. I haven't seen him."

"Will he survive?"

"You need to speak to the doctor about that."

And she swirled round and sailed off down the corridor with Gerry Savage in tow.

"I'll see you later, Savage," the sergeant growled after him. "We're not finished here."

SEVENTEEN

Ballyfoil, Mourne Mountains

Inspector Quinn clanged the cast iron knocker with insistent force but the whitewashed half-door cottage with its sash windows and grey slate roof rang empty and hollow. Sergeant Rice peered through a window and shrugged her fleece-jacketed shoulders. The small house stood at the end of a row of almost identical buildings at the far end of the village. Beyond this terrace, a narrow macadam road meandered out into the mountains under a gunmetal grey sky.

"Lookin' for Mrs McCann?"

The top half of the door to the adjoining cottage swung open and they stared at the rosy-cheeked face of a woman in her fifties with short-cut chestnut hair and eyes that surveyed them with blatant curiosity.

"Yes," said Gillian Rice, standing nearer to her. "Any idea where she might be?"

The sharp eyes scanned her from head to toe, then switched to Quinn. Seemingly satisfied, she nodded her head in the direction they had come, back through the village.

"My neighbour took her to the hospital in Newry, 'bout ten minutes ago. You've just missed her."

"In an ambulance?"

They had met just three vehicles on their drive up to the village: first an ambulance, then a police car and shortly afterwards a battered van that had seen better days.

"No, an old van. Liam Hogan's pride and joy. The only thing holding it together is the rust."

"Mrs McCann – she's not been taken ill, has she?"

"No, she's gone in to be with her son. He was in the ambulance."

"Michael McCann?"

"Yes. Do you know Mickey?"

Quinn didn't hesitate.

"Old friend. We go way back. What's wrong with him?"

"He's been shot."

The police officers exchanged uncertain glances.

"Shot? Who by?"

"Don't know really. It might be some sort of accident. Mary Savage was injured too."

"Who's Mary Savage?"

"She runs the pub, she and her husband."

"Is Mickey badly hurt?"

"Don't know. The police were here. They didn't say."

"But he's alive?"

"Far as I know," she told them. She paused, then decided to tell them some more. "He came out on a stretcher. He wasn't covered or anything. His face, I mean."

"Came out? Came out of where?"

"O'Leary's."

"The pub?"

"That's right. There's only one," she said and sniffed, as if this was a major defect, a disgrace on the community.

"We better get down there and see," said Quinn.

"Thank you for your help," Gillian added as she walked back to the Shogun. Quinn climbed in, whistled a short blast of surprise and followed it with an exasperated "Holy fuck." Gillian started the engine, did a neat three-point turn and drove back through the village.

"What the hell's going on?" she said.

"I guess someone thought five years in the Maze wasn't enough," Quinn replied. It took less than a minute following the almost deserted main street of Ballyfoil before they slowed down coming round a slight bend in the approach to O'Leary's public house. Quinn sat gripping the edge of his seat, urging them on through the village to the open road where they could get up more speed when, without warning, Gillian suddenly swung the Shogun in behind a dark-blue Ford Mondeo and switched off the engine.

"What are you doing?" Quinn said. "We're going to the hospital."

"Interesting car," Gillian said, pointing a forefinger pistol-like at the car in front of them.

"A Ford Mondeo?"

"With a Belfast registration," Gillian told him and pondered briefly on how best to further justify her parking. "Maybe we should find out who's driving it, what they're doing here. Maybe there's a connection. And ...." She gave him a pitying look. "... you probably need a drink anyway."

"They?"

"Just a feeling I have."

Quinn looked out at the pub, then back at his driver. "Your female intuition?"

"Call it what you like," Gillian said.

He made up his mind. "Okay, let's go."

With his fingers on the outside of his hunting jacket Quinn checked the contents of the right-hand pocket and unzipped the top. He climbed out of the Shogun and inspected the front of O'Leary's pub. Not only was the attention of a window cleaner sorely needed, but the moss-green paint on the façade was flaking off like a bad sunburn. Sergeant Rice pushed the car door gently shut as if fearful of excessive noise and walked over to the pub entrance to look in. The rain-splattered grime encrusted on the pub windows rendered the frosted glass quite superfluous. She shrugged and moved towards the entrance.

The outer entry door had been pushed to the side. Quinn stepped into the vaguely fusty smell of a porch with a black and white tiled floor that stretched to a dark brown panelled door some fifteen feet away. Almost halfway there, on his right, he came to a pair of swing doors with red and yellow stained-glass windows in a checked pattern of small oblong panes: the entrance to the public bar.

Pushing his way in, Quinn took note of a window seat on his right and across the room in the gable wall opposite him a large Mourne-stone fireplace prepared with a turf fire that was still unlit. Almost simultaneously, to the left of the fireplace, he saw a couple of customers standing at the far end of the wood-panelled bar. As he turned to the near end of the bar, closely followed by Sergeant Rice, the conversation fizzled to a stop like spittle on a red-hot stove. The ensuing silence was intensified by the total absence of Muzak, television and fruit machines.

The barman greeted them with a broad smile. He wore a black shirt with white stitching and sported a bowl-cut hairstyle he'd probably shaped himself. When Gerry Savage had rung him up to "look after" the pub till he got back, he hadn't hesitated.

It wasn't the first time. A local potter with flexible working hours and little employment, he took to his task with the enthusiasm of a man simply happy to have a job that involved meeting other people.

"Morning, what can I get you?"

Quinn and Gillian Rice looked askance at each other until Gillian took the plunge. "Can you do us a couple of coffees? White no sugar."

"Same here," Quinn said quickly.

For an instant the buoyant barman seemed somewhat flummoxed. He gazed around until reassured by the high-speed kettle, adjacent jar of instant coffee and box of assorted tea bags beside the service hatch on a narrow hot-drinks shelf behind him.

"No sweat," he affirmed in the local patois that paid no

heed to the niceties of service-oriented intercourse.

As the barman busied himself with the kettle and arrangement of cups and saucers, Quinn took casual but detailed note of the two men standing beside a globe-shaped brass lamp at the far end of the bar counter. Both attired in wrinkled trench coats and cloth caps, they were engaged in low-volume dialogue interrupted only by the intermittent hoisting of tankards of the local Whitewater beer. They stood leaning lightly against the bar, facing each other, so that – to those at the other end of the counter – their faces were for the most part obscured. Quinn watched as they drained their tankards.

Pouring the coffees, the substitute barman decided to make customer-friendly conversation.

"Just passing through?"

"On our honeymoon," Quinn said with a shy smile. "We're fond of hiking."

He was about to place his hand over Gillian's on the bar when she anticipated the move and whipped her arm away. Just at that moment one of the men at the end of the bar turned round and called to the barman. The barman placed the coffees on the counter and walked down to them.

Gillian's eyes were narrowed, cold, flintstone hard. She said. "Watch your step, Quinn."

But Quinn was staring at the other end of the bar. He seemed a little agitated. "Got to go," he said in a flat voice. "Toilet."

He turned on his heel and stepped quickly over to the double doors and out into the porch, leaving the stained-glass windows swinging, casting coloured reflections that darted to and fro in the mid-morning haze of the bar-room. With his departure Gillian heard the name Mickey McCann being mentioned in broad Belfast vowels and turned her attention to the three men at the far end of the bar.

"He's in the hospital," the barman was explaining in subdued tones. "In Newry."

"Hospital? What's wrong with him?"

It was the taller of the two men who asked, his unkempt sandy beard wagging up and down as he spoke. Gillian thought of a much-used toilet brush and suspected it might smell similarly.

"He was shot."

"Mickey? Shot?"

There was an incredulous lull as they took this in. The shorter, stockier man broke it. His voice was soft and husky, fine sandpaper on an oily surface.

"Who the fuck shot him?"

"I don't know," the barman said uncertainly. "It might have been an accident."

"Weren't the peelers here?"

"Yes, they were here. And the ambulance."

"Didn't they catch anyone?"

"No, they just took them to the hospital."

The shorter man had taken over the interrogation. He kept his voice low. Gillian could see his face now, the bloodless pallor and the black, sunken eyes.

"Them?" he said. "Who's them?"

"McCann and Mary Savage."

"And who's Mary Savage when she's at home?"

"Well, she's at home right here. She runs this pub, she and her husband."

"Did the shooting happen here in the pub?"

"In the pub, yes, but not in here. In another room at the back."

There was a short silence while they thought about this.

"So, what was Mickey McCann doing in there with this woman?"

"I don't know," the barman said again.

When the two men seemed dissatisfied with this answer,

he added, "Nobody seems to know."

"Where was the husband."

"He'd gone in to Newry on business."

"And then Mickey had come in here?"

"Looks like that."

"But what was the connection? Did they know each other?"

"Well," the barman said, and hesitated, "there's a rumour they used to go out together."

"He was screwing her," the tall customer said, drawing his inevitable conclusion. The barman became uneasy. He looked from one to the other and said, "I don't know about that."

The shorter man constricted his sallow face, tightening his features, as he once again assumed control.

"You say they used to go out?" he said.

"Yeah, five years ago or more. Before he …."

"Before he ended up in the Maze."

"I suppose so."

The taller man leaned over the counter and stared at the barman. "You know why he ended up in the Maze?"

The barman looked nervous now. "Well, I'm not really… sure."

"Somebody ratted on him. Somebody said that he was behind the Newry bombings. Somebody that probably comes from here. From Ballyfoil. Did you know that?"

"No, not really."

The barman wanted to tell them 'Jesus Christ, it wasn't me' – it was on the tip of his tongue – but he just stood there looking from the one man to the other, wondering where this was heading.

"The Savage woman – was she shot too?"

"No. They said she'd had a fall or something. She was unconscious."

"And McCann was shot?"

"Yes, there was a shot. Maybe the gun went off by accident, I don't know."

"What was a gun doing there in the first place? Whose was it?"

"I don't know."

"You know fuck all," declared the tall, bearded one, determined to make an eloquent contribution to the conversation. His companion sighed and glanced over at Gillian Rice, who immediately decided to sip her lukewarm coffee.

"We need to go," he rasped.

He slapped a £5 note on the counter and started along the bar towards Gillian. The other man began to button up his raincoat and followed him. Coffee cup in hand, Gillian faced forward and watched them pass in the wide-screen Guinness Extra Stout mirror behind the bar. When the double doors were swinging behind them, she paid for the coffees and walked out after them.

The potter-barman looked after her as she went. He had thought of wishing her a nice day, but changed his mind when he saw the look in her eyes. The day had already lost its niceness.

There was no sign of Quinn in the porch. Gillian eyed the door with the male-female graphics and decided he can't still be in there – if he ever was – unless he's got the runs. Unlikely, but not impossible.

She stepped out through the main doorway to see the blue Mondeo disappearing up the street in the direction of Newry. The early afternoon had become hesitantly bright and a mountain breeze was breathing through the village. An elderly man on a bicycle pedalled slowly past with a smile and a "Brave day." Gillian smiled back and scoured the street in both directions. The smile soon vanished. Where the hell was he? They had to burn rubber to the hospital in Newry. She had just reached into her pocket for the key to the Shogun when a familiar figure emerged from an alleyway diagonally opposite.

Quinn crossed the street with his steady, resolute stride. Gillian Rice placed her hands on the bonnet of the car and riveted him with steely eyes.

"Did you have a nice shit?"

"I've had better," said Quinn, playing along.

"What's going on?"

"I had to get out."

"That was pretty obvious."

"I recognised one of the men, John Cooney. He was one of the Newry bombers. I met him a couple of times when they were arrested. He'd put on weight, or muscles, but I'm sure it was him."

"So he would have recognised you too?"

"Yeah, probably, though I'm not sure he got a good look at me. But if he saw me properly there's a fair chance he would."

"Which might have frightened him off…"

"Well, he's not exactly the kind that gets frightened. But we're close now, Gillian, I can feel it. Arthur Williams is locked up here somewhere, and Michael McCann is the key."

"So let's go see him."

They climbed into the Shogun and drove out of Ballyfoil. Quinn felt a debilitating sense of urgency surge through him as they chased down the endlessly winding road to Newry in the early-afternoon sunshine. The sand in Arthur Williams' hourglass was spilling down like soil being shovelled into a grave.

EIGHTEEN

Quinn leant back in the soiled grey cloth of the Shogun's passenger seat and glanced somewhat furtively at his driver. At first he had assumed Sergeant Gillian Rice had an attitude problem. Then the insight had dawned on him that it might just be a bad time of the month. Finally he had thought, perhaps it was a bit of both. There was also something in her feisty nature that reminded him of Renée, but he didn't want to think about that.

Yes, conversation had been a trifle strained at the outset. And it hadn't improved when she'd pulled off the A1 and driven into Hillsborough just because she needed a leak. Stopping for a pee when they were already 24 hours late hadn't exactly improved their on-the-road camaraderie. Chief Inspector Philip fucking Hall had probably plied her with oodles of coffee from that automatic cappuccino machine of his when he was soft-talking her into the job.

Quinn thought again about her demand to be treated as a fully fledged partner in the operation and not just some second-class appendage in what he was convinced was essentially a search-and-rescue mission. With the knowledge of her recent marital break-up he felt sure there was some sort of therapeutic payoff behind her wanting to be totally involved in every aspect of their assignment. Despite himself, he couldn't help but admire her resilience.

As they raced out of Ballyfoil Quinn felt a heart-pumping adrenaline rush as he recalled the sudden sight of a high-ranking member of the Real IRA in O'Leary's pub. It was well known among the D-specials that John Cooney had organised active service units of covert cells in an attempt to forestall the danger of being compromised by informers. He was also one of the Newry bombers incarcerated in the Maze together with Michael McCann

– thanks to an informer. So much for the efficacy of his covert cells.

"Cooney – did you hear any of the conversation, what he said to the barman?" Quinn asked.

"He wanted to know about McCann."

"How he came to be shot?"

"Yes. It seems there was some sort of romantic attachment between McCann and the Savage woman before the Newry bombing," Gillian said as she braked sharply to negotiate a 90-degree bend.

"Really? That's going back a bit. I was wondering what the link-up was."

"So were our two friends." Gillian Rice paused to accelerate out of the bend. "They started pumping the barman and he said he'd heard a rumour there'd been some kind of romance five years ago."

"Then the shooting could have been some sort of *crime passionnel*."

Quinn wasn't too sure about his pronunciation. "Pardon my French," he added.

Gillian said, "In that case it's one with a helluva slow-burning fuse."

"Can't wait to hear what McCann has to say."

"Don't forget Cooney and his Taliban boyfriend will also be doing their damnedest to see McCann, so you're going to have to find another alley to hide in," Gillian said as they drove out of the valley.

"Yeah, I'll have to stay out of sight. You could maybe pretend to be a friend of Mary Savage's. The best plan would be if you could go in on your own and suss the place out – without anyone knowing who you actually are."

"Quinn, sometimes I don't know who I actually am."

Quinn wasn't sure how to take this. Marital problems, he knew, can weigh heavy as lead in the conjugal head.

"Gillian, I appreciate you have a lot going on at the

moment, but–."

"Jesus Quinn, I was just being glib. Forget it. And don't worry, I'm on it. There's nothing like fear to focus the mind."

"Fear? Really? You feel afraid?"

"Not yet. But let's be honest. These guys aren't exactly on a Sunday-school outing. Anything can happen."

"Yes, you're right," Quinn said. All at once he realised he was beginning to worry about her. Gillian, he thought, is a hard-boiled sweet with a soft centre.

"We definitely need to treat this situation with the greatest respect," he said. "Those two cowboys haven't turned up here without a reason. And I'm pretty sure that reason's Arthur Williams."

"What about back-up? Chief Hall said we shouldn't hesitate if things were getting out of hand." Gillian recalled the serious look in those goldfish eyes when he stressed this.

Quinn pondered the question for a moment. The idea of already calling in help was anathema to him. Indeed, if he were honest, requesting any form of assistance had always gone against the grain. He always felt it contained an element of defeat, and he had long ago decided he had enough defeat in his life.

"I don't think we're quite there yet," he reassured her, "but we can bear it in mind."

They sat thinking about this for a minute. The Shogun was dropping on the gradual descent down to the A1 and the main road into Newry. Quinn watched the gorse hedges straining against the breeze as they skimmed past. The day was as yet fairly mild and dry, but the sky had now broken out in a rash of purple-black rain clouds that seemed to be issuing a flood warning of biblical proportions.

Gillian was nodding her head in contemplation, mulling over the imminent scenario at Daisy Hill.

"Looking at it realistically," she said, "it's very likely that our Mr McCann is being operated on at this very moment. And we've no idea how serious his injuries are, but in all probability – as far as we're concerned – he's going to be out of the running for the rest of the day. At least."

"Yeah," Quinn agreed. "So, at the very earliest – depending on his condition – he might be available for talkies some time tomorrow morning."

"Which is also when the dynamic duo will be wanting to chat to him."

"The dynamic duo? Gillian, I thought that was us?"

"Really? Are you counting me in, Quinn? Are we working together now? What happened to the lone stranger? The Man with no Name?"

"I guess he's gone through a change of life. He's become something of an alley cat."

"You're shitting me. Still, the way things are going, you might need all those lives."

Gillian Rice drove onto the A1 and they continued a short distance before turning off again onto the old Belfast Road into Newry. She took a right and crossed the Newry River and then the canal. After a couple of side-street manoeuvres they arrived at the entrance to Daisy Hill Hospital, an oblong, brick-bound block of a building that dominated the hill. Gillian followed the sign for Accident and Emergency and parked the Shogun in a far corner of the parking lot, half full with an assortment of saloons, hatchbacks and estate cars.

"You'll be less conspicuous here," she said.

"There's no sign of the Mondeo," he pointed out. "They've been and gone."

"Or parked somewhere else."

"Yeah, maybe."

"No point in taking chances. I'll go in on my own and

see what the situation is with McCann."

"Check up on the Savage woman too while you're at it."

"Her husband will probably be there. Difficult to quiz him unless I flash my warrant card."

"The need for discretion depends on whether our two boyos are there. Tell you what – give me a ring when you know one way or the other and we'll take it from there."

"Right."

She opened the door, sidled off her seat and took off at a canter for A&E. Quinn watched her go. She moved with a lilt to her walk, he thought, like a cheerful little tune. While she was gone, he sat thinking about the pros and cons of keeping a low profile in the case and realised he hadn't even considered the role of the local police in the current investigation. The surprising news of the shooting, he realised, followed by the unexpected sighting of John Cooney in O'Leary's pub, had knocked him off balance. He needed to make immediate contact with the local constabulary, find out who was in charge of the case and take it from there. The thought had barely crossed his mind when he spotted Gillian Rice returning between the parked cars in the company of a uniformed policeman.

Sergeant Bill Pollock looked like the sort of copper any semi-sane criminal would want to steer well clear of. He was about Quinn's height but heavier, stockier, with a redbrick, pockmark-indented face and watery grey eyes that stared straight into you. As he came up to Quinn he licked his lips as if in anticipation of something tasty. Bloody hell, thought Quinn, the man's a cross between a bulldog and Hannibal Lecter. He shook the sergeant's hand. The broad, stubby fingers had the texture of chainmail; the vice-like grip told its own story.

"This is Sergeant Bill Pollock," Gillian Rice said.

"So, is Belfast taking over here?" the sergeant asked in a voice that had a slight nasal drone. Wary of getting involved in the usual provincial neurosis suffered by country coppers, Quinn ignored the question.

"Has Sergeant Rice filled you in on the background?"

"She refused to say anything until you were in the loop." Quinn shot his sergeant a swift look of approval.

"Suppose you show me your warrant card before we go any further," Pollock continued. The request garnered Quinn's immediate respect: a man who took nothing for granted was usually a good copper.

Quinn dug deep inside his jacket and handed it over. The runny eyes zigzagged over the card.

"Okay," he conceded. "What exactly are you doing here?"

Anticipating the sensitivities of the local constabulary, Quinn pondered briefly how best to pitch it.

"You've heard about the abduction of the journalist, Arthur Williams, yesterday?"

"Yeah," Pollock said, his face instantly taking on an aggrieved expression, "we can read the smoke signals all the way from Belfast to Newry."

"Well, Belfast HQ has intelligence that he may have been brought down here."

"Intelligence? I'm not sure how intelligent that is. Why would whoever took him bring him to Newry?"

"Williams was the journalist who exposed the Newry bombers."

Sergeant Pollock cast his grey eyes between Quinn and Rice, as if searching for the answer to a prayer. His chin seemed to jut out unwittingly. He said nothing.

"In the outrage at the mass murder of so many innocent people," Quinn elaborated, "his paper offered a sizeable reward for information leading to the capture of the bombers. A local businessman put up the lion's share. It didn't take long before somebody squealed and got the money."

Pollock nodded. "So that somebody will be at the top of the bombers' death list."

"And with the Good Friday Agreement being put into practice, the Newry bombers are all out on the street again," Gillian Rice interjected.

"And probably hunting down whoever it was informed on them."

"Yeah," said Pollock. "It must feel good for the families of the victims that those fuckin' murderers are set free to help move the peace process along." His nascent smile was stillborn.

"Michael McCann was one of the leading Newry bombers," Quinn reminded them. "He comes from Ballyfoil, near here. John Cooney was another. They doubtless believe that Arthur Williams can identify their informer."

"Which is why it seems likely that they are the ones who have abducted Williams," Gillian complemented.

"And why we believe he's being held somewhere in this vicinity, since both McCann and Cooney have turned up here," Quinn said.

Sergeant Pollock glanced at them in turn as they spoke, his eyes tearing up like a pair of bubbling water springs.

"Well, McCann's in here now with a bullet in the gut. It's possible he was shot in the pub in Ballyfoil by the landlady, Mary Savage."

"Yeah, we've just come from there," Quinn told him. "What exactly happened –?"

"This John Cooney," Pollock interrupted. "I remember his name from the trial – is he here too?"

"He was in the A&E just ten minutes ago," Gillian told him. "His chum with the Gerry Adams beard was with him. One of the nurses told them McCann was in the operating theatre."

"I must've been having a cuppa tea," Pollock said.

"You spoke to the nurse?" Quinn asked Gillian Rice.

"Yes. She said there's no chance of seeing him today. He's out for the count. Come back tomorrow."

"Something to look forward to," Quinn said, and his eyes hardened. "We need to post a man here overnight. Keep an eye on things."

"I'll attend to that, don't worry. These dissident republicans think they rule the roost down here. But we'll be ready for the bastards."

Pollock's florid complexion flared up as he spoke – a harbinger of things to come. Quinn was a little taken aback to recognise the possible elements of future fury.

"Steady, Sergeant, steady," he said. "Our first priority is to locate Williams. Rescue him. Just get him out. Then we can have a go at them."

"I hate to pee on your bonfire," Gillian Rice said, "but if Arthur Williams has already revealed the name of the informer there's a good chance that he's no longer with us."

Quinn could see what Gillian was getting at. It was all a bit iffy. If Williams had seen the faces of his captors – and it was pretty certain that he had – then they had little reason to let him live once they had extracted the information they wanted. So his only chance of survival was to hold out for as long as he could. If he could withstand whatever methods of inducement they were using, perhaps he would make it. The other big 'if' was whether he actually knew the identity of the informer. If he didn't, if there had been no face-to-face meetings, if their contact had been exclusively non-visual, there was a good chance he was still in the land of the living and they would simply use him to glean whatever information they could in order to locate and identify the informer.

"It's possible Williams doesn't even know the informer's name," Quinn said. "And it's even possible that he never met him, or if he did, that he didn't see his face."

"You mean he was masked?"

"Yes, possibly. When I interviewed Williams, the only thing he revealed was that it was a man. Otherwise he didn't give anything away. Tight as a duck's arse."

"And you think McCann knows where Williams is?" Pollock pursued.

"I'm pretty sure of it. We need to speak to him as soon as he surfaces, so we should be here first thing in the morning."

"The surgeon who operated on him is a Dr Kickham," Gillian Rice told them. "The nurse said he's due in at 10 am and that's when he'll be doing his rounds, beginning with McCann. We can probably interview him after that."

"If he's conscious we can try to nip in earlier, before the doctor and before the Belfast boys arrive," Quinn said. "Whatever the case, we have to keep them out while we speak to McCann on our own. Can you have a couple of constables on guard outside tomorrow morning?"

"Sure," Pollock said. "So I come in with you and Sergeant Rice?"

"That'll be the best, I think. You know the people here and the territory and, if we can get him to talk, you can help us with the locals and the logistics, help us to find our way around."

Gillian noted how Quinn made a point of including the sergeant, of winning his approval and making him feel he was an integral part of the operation. He had nothing against involving others when it suited his purpose.

"You seem pretty sure they've got Williams here somewhere," Pollock said.

"It's our best bet at the moment," Quinn admitted.

Gillian Rice flashed the sergeant a nervous grin. "It's our only bet," she said.

They looked at each other for a few moments before

Sergeant Pollock spoke. "Supposing McCann doesn't talk?"

"Then we have to confront the other two, meet them head on," Quinn said. "Cooney's just come out after five years in the Maze. He can't be too keen on going straight back in again for murder. He may not have been actively involved in the kidnapping – I suspect McCann's the one behind that – and with a good lawyer Cooney could probably weasel his way out of it."

"A lot depends on their lust for revenge." Gillian said. "That might just outweigh everything else."

Ever since he had been told about the shooting incident at O'Leary's in Ballyfoil, the germ of a rather disturbing idea had been festering at the back of Quinn's head. He hadn't been able to formulate it in words; it had been more like a feeling of having missed something, almost of staring something in the face without being able to see it properly, without being able to focus clearly on its defining features. What if the gunshot fired in that back room in the pub had absolutely nothing to do with an eventual previous romance between Michael McCann and Mary Savage? What if, instead, it was in some way directly related to the disappearance of Arthur Williams?

"What do you know about the Savages?" Quinn asked the local policeman.

"Sweet FA. They run the pub in Ballyfoil, O'Leary's. That's about it."

"Could you check them out, see if they've got any form, ask around and get any gossip or background information that's going?"

"OK, I'll see what I can do."

Another thought suddenly struck him, an idea he felt he should have grasped earlier.

"One other thing, Bill. Are you able to get hold of a transponder?"

"You mean a tracking device?"

"Yes. If Williams is being held in Ballyfoil or thereabouts, and if we don't get any joy from McCann or Cooney tomorrow, it would be a godsend to know where that blue Mondeo goes when it leaves here."

Pollock looked doubtful. "I'll see what I can do," he said again. "Don't know offhand if we have one. Not something we have a lot of use for down here. And there'll be paperwork. Might take time."

Gillian Rice saw where Quinn was going with this. She switched on her professional smile, the special panoramic version she'd learned from Chief Inspector Philip Hall.

"If we're lucky, they'll both come into the hospital in the morning, leaving the car unattended, so we can fix it up without any bother," she said.

Pollock seemed to warm to the idea. "I'll see what we can do, but I think you need a warrant to attach it to a car."

"I'll pretend I didn't hear that," Quinn said.

The sergeant looked at him aghast. "Hear what?" he said.

Quinn smiled and looked from one to the other. "We're all set then," he said. They nodded in agreement. A sharp wind was now gusting across the parking lot.

Heavy clouds hung low in the sky. A few drops of rain splashed on the bonnet of the Shogun. They exchanged phone numbers and agreed to meet in the same corner of the parking lot at 8 o'clock the next morning. There was no saying when Cooney & Co would turn up. Bill Pollock stomped off to the A&E department. Rice and Quinn got back in the Shogun to keep dry and stop shivering.

"What's the situation with Mary Savage? How badly is she hurt?"

"She's suffered a pretty severe concussion," Gillian told him. "Husband's with her. She's semi-conscious. No one else is allowed in. Maybe tomorrow."

"Well, fuck that," Quinn said, steaming up. "We're going

in there tomorrow. There's no maybe about it. I'm pissed off with these doctors and their medical prerogatives. We need access."

Gillian Rice restrained an amused smile at this outburst and pulled on the door handle.

"I'll go over and check up again – see if there's any change in McCann's condition, when he's likely to be compos mentis again."

Quinn fired her a critically appraising look. "You mean you're going in for another five-minute pee."

Gillian paused on her way out of the car and looked him straight in the eye. "For want of something better to do," she said, "why don't you just go fuck yourself?" She made ready to shut the door.

"Excuse my French," she added with a tight smile. Then she closed the door and quickstepped away with her gently lilting gait in the direction of the A&E.

Quinn rang Chief Inspector Hall, thinking he'd probably be in some bloody meeting or other. By a minor miracle he answered the phone. Quinn gave him a rundown of the day's events and outlined the plan of action for the next day.

"This feels very uncertain, Quinn," Chief Hall demurred. "It's all up in the air."

"Well, we could hardly have foreseen the shooting, sir."

"True, true. But I don't like it." The line buzzed for a moment while he pondered the possibilities. "Listen Quinn, I want you to stay down there – don't be coming back to Belfast."

"Stay here overnight?"

"Yes, I know it's only thirty-odd miles away, but it feels safer to have you both on the spot. Anything can happen where those bloody hallions are involved. And it's absolutely vital that you're at the hospital first thing in the morning. Be there at 7. There must be a hotel or guest house in Newry. You can put it on expenses."

'Put it on expenses,' Quinn thought. 'Haven't heard that one before.'

"All right, sir. I'll be in touch as soon as we know any more."

Quinn pocketed his mobile and looked out across the parking lot. A woman was making her way towards a small red hatchback, hauling a young child behind her. Her face seemed swollen and as she turned towards him, Quinn saw that she had a black eye. She had just driven off when he saw Gillian's head bobbing among the other parked vehicles.

Gillian Rice looked dubious when he explained their orders. Quinn realised she was probably thinking about her home situation. After staring out the side window for a while, she seemed to make up her mind.

"OK. It's probably not a bad thing."

He was still wondering what she meant by this when she leant forward, jammed the key in the ignition and started the engine. As the heavens opened and the wipers strained to cope with the deluge, they drove out of the hospital grounds and down Monaghan Row towards the canal. Before they got there she swung off right and followed the street until she came to a roundabout, where she turned left and drove down to Merchants Quay and the canal.

"You seem to know your way around here," Quinn commented.

"I was here last summer and stayed at the best hotel in town, and that's where we're going," she told him. "A romantic weekend with my husband," she added.

He stared at her with question mark written all over his face.

"Don't say anything," she snapped. "Not a word."

He didn't. They turned left onto Merchants Quay and followed the road along by the canal. A line of leafless trees punctuated the broad pavement running beside the waterway. Volleys of raindrops were detonating on the grey paving stones. The Canal Court Hotel faced the canal and looked elegant, inviting and forbiddingly expensive. The Shogun slewed to a stop.

"This'll suit me," Gillian Rice declared.

Quinn looked across the street at the black marble-slab ground-floor façade of the four-storey hotel, knowing it was way beyond the reach of the normal RUC expense account.

"You're damn right," he said.

NINETEEN

The lobby of the Canal Court Hotel leads to a long, slightly curved and highly polished reception counter sculpted out of a sleek dark wood that looks like mahogany. Quinn sees himself approach it in a high oblong mirror placed between two glass showcases of crystal that adorn the wall behind the receptionist, standing there waiting in grey waistcoat, white shirt and striped tie. He finds himself gawping at leafy mosaics of the same inlaid dark wood on either side of two matching mirrors that bookend the backdrop to the reception area. To his mind, it's all in elegant good taste.

"Good afternoon, sir. Can I help you?"

The receptionist was a pink-cheeked young man with an auburn fringe dropping carelessly over the top of his forehead. He smiled his bright, deferential smile and moved forward to the counter, freckled hands pressing lightly on the dark wood.

"Have you a booking?" he inquired as Quinn continued to gaze at the surroundings.

"No, no booking,"

"Ah, that might be difficult," the receptionist confided, openly surveying Quinn's attire, assessing his status. "We have a wedding. A big wedding."

Gillian Rice appeared abruptly at Quinn's shoulder. "Is there a problem?"

"I'm afraid we don't have a deluxe double left," the receptionist told her. "The wedding guests have already taken them."

"You asked for a double? A deluxe double?"

She glared at Quinn as if he had just defecated on the lobby floor.

"Well, the bridal suite was taken," he said. "It was the next best thing."

She gave him a long, murderous look, trying in vain to divine the truth, then turned to the receptionist.

"We want two single rooms," she commanded. "Quite separate. At opposite ends of the building if possible."

The young man's eyes ricocheted between them, realising he had perhaps jumped the gun, belatedly attempting to establish the dynamic; then his fringe drooped in submission and he scanned the screen before him.

"There are a few standard rooms available on the fourth floor," he said, looking at Gillian. "I can give you two at opposite ends of the corridor."

"That'll be fine," Quinn said, eager to get on.

Reprieved, the receptionist nodded and played a lively mazurka on his keyboard. "We offer a package deal," he chirruped, "if you'd like to include a three-course dinner in the Old Mill Restaurant."

The police officers exchanged glances.

"We have to eat," Quinn stated. "We haven't had anything all day."

"The Old Mill," Gillian asked, "is that the hotel restaurant?"

"It is. The food is very good," he added dutifully. "We're having a French evening."

"When do you start serving?" Gillian wanted to know.

"Six o'clock."

"We'll take it," Quinn said.

They took the lift up to the fourth floor. He had his old duffel bag; Gillian had a brown leather shoulder bag with a multitude of zips and pockets. Who knew what a woman carried in her handbag? Or shoulder bag? But in Gillian's case he was counting on her also having some form of lethal weaponry. He wondered what sort of hardware she had brought and where she was carrying it, but decided it was not an opportune moment to ask. They didn't talk until they exited the lift on the fourth floor.

"Okay," Quinn said, "six o'clock in the restaurant."

"The Old Mill," Gillian confirmed, and they went separately to their rooms at opposite ends of the corridor. Quinn dumped his bag on the three-quarter size bed, had a pee, washed his hands after a wrestling match to extract the mini bar of soap from its wrapper, and went out to buy a toothbrush and toothpaste.

He walked out of the lobby and turned left onto Merchants Quay, then left again to Monaghan Row. The buildings were mostly commercial, a hopscotch of architectural oddities, all in need of refurbishment. The sky still resembled an upturned pot of damson jam, but the torrential rain had passed over to the Irish Sea.

Just round the corner on Monaghan Row he found a small, densely crowded supermarket. Half the population of Newry seemed to have realised they needed to make various last-minute purchases to be able to enjoy the weekend. Most of the customers were teenagers and people in the twenty-to-forty bracket. There was a buzz of Friday-night anticipation in the air.

Quinn scouted round, searching for the dental department. The supermarket had obviously been converted from a former convenience store; with its high shelving sections cramped into limited space it was an Eldorado for shoplifters. The only camera he spotted was at the checkout counter.

At the far end of a narrow shopping alley he discovered the shelf to satisfy his dental needs and, on the way to the check-out, he added a half bottle of whiskey to his plastic basket. Curious, he reflected, how the booze was always the easiest thing to find in a supermarket. Confectionery was also a dead giveaway. Looking around, it struck him that designing today's supermarket must take a lot of calculated planning and expertise in order to create the most tempting consumer-friendly experience. It's all about the money, he thought, recalling the lyric of a recent pop song.

Standing at the cash desk picking up his change, he was distracted by a commotion in the queue behind him. A tall, gangling black man with Rasta locks and John Lennon spectacles was engaged in a heated exchange with another customer, a thickset individual in wrinkled raincoat.

"I was here before. I left my basket here," the black man said. He was complaining, but his voice was mellow, with a deep, euphonious tone.

"You left the queue."

"Just for a second. I forgot something. I left my basket here."

"Back o' the queue, Sambo. You lost yer place."

As the white man turned to face forward in the queue, Quinn recognised the stocky figure of John Cooney, the murky sunken eyes in the sallow face staring with merciless determination. Abruptly the black man moved forward and bent to retrieve his shopping basket, there was a scuffle and Cooney slammed his forehead into the tall man's nose as he tried to straighten up. With an audible crunch the headbutt disgorged blood that spouted down over the man's upper lip. He cried out, gave an oesophageal gulp and backed away with tears in his eyes and an expression of sad surprise on his face.

"What's going on there?" The checkout assistant bent her head forward like a startled gargoyle over the cash register, an uncertain quaver in her voice.

Cooney turned to meet the challenge, caught sight of Quinn about to pocket his change, and held his eyes for several seconds while his brain worked overtime.

"Don't I know you from somewhere?"

"I don't know," Quinn said. "Where have you been?"

He grabbed his bag of purchases, swung round and

walked swiftly out of the shop. All the time, until he reached the street, he could feel Cooney's eyes drilling into the back of his head.

He returned to the hotel just as the first drops of a new downpour landed and burst ferociously on the pavement. As he dashed into the lobby he caught sight of Gillian Rice entering the lift with a brown paper shopping bag clutched in her hand. He deliberated on whether to brief her on the new situation, but decided to keep it for later.

He waited and took the next lift up. Going into his room he noticed for the first time that it had a skylight. The rain chattered on the pane of glass. He had another wrestling match with the toothbrush package, popped the brush in a Duralex glass together with a tube of herbal toothpaste, had a rethink and emptied the glass again, gave it a wipe with the hand towel and poured in two fingers of John Powers Gold Label. Thus provisioned, he moved into the bedroom and over to the mullioned window to look down on the rain lashing the water of the canal below.

As the Gold Label warmed his insides, he heard John Cooney's husky tones echo in his head: 'Don't I know you from somewhere?' Well, he sure as hell did, and it wasn't a memory he would relish. But it was five years ago and it wasn't absolutely certain he would be able to place him even if he'd glimpsed the ghost of a recollection. However, there was no point in entertaining the vain hope that he hadn't. What Quinn had to consider now was the eventual consequences for the case if Cooney had recognised him. He recalled the man's nickname from five years ago: Cutthroat Cooney. There were unsettling stories of his mindless violence. Cooney at his worst was capable of anything. He rang Bill Pollock and explained what had happened.

"I'll see if I can get an extra man in to keep watch tonight at Daisy Hill," Pollock said. "Fuckin' bad luck he should be in the same shop as you."

"I know. Worst possible. Like I say, there's a slight chance he won't be able to put me in the picture, but we can't play this as if it's going to have a Hollywood ending."

"No, you're right. Worst-case scenario is more like it."

"So we definitely need two men at the hospital."

"I'll see to it."

He hung up. The more he thought about it, the more convinced he became that Michael McCann was the key to the whereabouts of Arthur Williams, and Cooney would have to speak to him to find out his location. Which made it utterly imperative to be first to interview McCann in the morning. And get him to talk.

* * *

They sat on the carmine-red leather seats in the Old Mill Restaurant trying to decipher the menu. Gillian Rice had brushed her hair and applied some makeup. There was a new look about her that had Quinn sneaking surreptitious glances. She also seemed to be unusually animated. For some reason that he couldn't quite comprehend himself, he had decided not to divulge the events of his shopping expedition straight away, which would have been the natural thing to do. Perhaps it was the bare, starkly unreal atmosphere of the hotel restaurant where they were hitherto the only guests. Perhaps it was the hunger – he felt light-headed from lack of food and didn't want to go down that road on an empty stomach. Perhaps it was the gut-knotting tension he felt after seeing John Cooney in the supermarket.

He glanced down at the floor as he pondered his motives. The carpet underfoot took up the same deep shade of red as the chairs and was superimposed with a gold-patterned design that spoke of the orient. Gillian Rice decided it was time to speak of the food.

"You having a starter?"

"It's included in the package."

"That doesn't mean you have to have it."

"I'm having it," Quinn said.

"All right," said Gillian Rice in her best BBC voice. "I'm rather torn between the *moules à la crème Normande* and the *escargots de Bourgogne*. What about you?"

Quinn was impressed by her imitation of an upper-class English accent and the sound of her convincing French. She was quite a mimic, he realised. He glanced again at the menu.

"Haven't they just got a prawn cocktail? Or a bit of smoked salmon?"

"*Absolument pas!*" Gillian said, switching to nasalised vowels. "*C'est seulement la cuisine française.*"

"Don't think I can pardon your French this time," Quinn said. "Have you done a tour in the French Foreign Legion or something?"

He was beginning to suspect that his dinner companion had had a snort or two from something stronger than the bottle of Ballygowan Still Water that came with the room. There was a glitter in her eyes he hadn't seen before.

"Something," she replied. "It was my favourite subject at school, thanks to the teacher."

Quinn recollected his own French teacher at school; he couldn't recall ever saying anything in the language – it was all about reading and writing. When Gillian had helped him choose the food he pretended a superficial knowledge of wine and selected a bottle of *Crozes Hermitage La Guiraude* – without looking at the price.

"Jesus, Quinn, did you see what that cost?" Gillian said, when the waiter had retreated.

"Chief Inspector Hall is footing the bill," he bluffed,

"and I have it on good authority that he's an extremely generous man."

"Generous my arse. The man's so mean he steams the stamps off letters that haven't been postmarked."

"Says who?"

"It's common knowledge at HQ," Gillian told him. "The RUC economy is an absolute obsession with him."

When they had simultaneously sipped the *Crozes Hermitage*, peering somewhat cautiously at each other over their glasses, Quinn finally got round to telling Gillian about the incident at the supermarket and the likelihood that Cooney had recognised him. Her reaction was understandable.

"Bloody hell, Quinn." Gillian's brow drew together, her eyebrows dipped uneasily and her eyes seemed to cloud over with disquiet. "That's going to screw things up."

"Not necessarily. I mean, it's not absolutely definite that he remembers where we've met before." Quinn knew he was grasping at straws. "It could've been at the pub in Ballyfoil. He might have noticed me there."

"Come on, get real. We know he can't google you to make the connection. But you can be pretty certain he has a bloody good idea."

"Okay, okay." Quinn opened his hands and spread his fingers on the tablecloth in submission. "So he knows I've spotted him and we know he's spotted me."

"Yes, in all probability."

"And knowing he's got us on his tail now is also going to change the game plan. In all probability," Quinn said, finally acknowledging to himself the reality that lay ahead.

"In what way?"

"There'll be no more pussyfooting, no more tiptoeing around. He's not called Cutthroat Cooney for nothing. The man is known to have a hair-trigger temper. He's totally unpredictable. We have to be ready for him."

"And how do we do that?"

As she asked the question, Gillian leaned forward, placed an elbow on the table and supported her jaw with an open hand.

"We have to anticipate him and act before he does," Quinn said. "We have to make the first move."

"A pre-emptive strike?"

"Yes."

"Meaning exactly what?"

"Well, for one thing we have to get in and see McCann before he does. Otherwise…"

"Otherwise what?"

"Arthur Williams is a dead man."

The meal proceeded at a leisurely pace. They made periodic forays into the main course while their brains worked at full throttle. Intermittently they analysed the events of the day, but simultaneously they were both walking a highwire thinking about the day to come. Although the food was good and the wine had a deep, smoky taste, Quinn couldn't shake his apprehensive mood and enjoy it.

Later, in a half-hearted attempt to raise their spirits, Gillian gave a low whistle when the dessert came and designated it '*un objet d'art.*' The chef had applied a few artistic touches to its arrangement on the plate so that, as Quinn said, it resembled a still life by some 16th century Dutch painter.

"Now you're showing off," Gillian said.

"What?"

"Your knowledge of Dutch painting."

"Ah Gillian, sure I'm a man of many talents. Hadn't you noticed?"

"Not yet," Gillian said. "Not yet."

As they approached the bottom of the *Crozes Hermitage*, Gillian tended to drift off into her own world, observing the other diners in the room, staring at the flame flickering sporadically from the candle on their table.

Ultimately, they seemed to have run out of conversation and sat there preoccupied with their own thoughts. Gillian was uninterested in coffee this late in the day so Quinn called for the bill, then decided just to have it added to the room, and they walked out past various groups of wedding guests celebrating what Gillian paraphrased as 'another union made in heaven.'

The sedentary lassitude and enclosed atmosphere of the Old Mill Restaurant made them decide to sample the night air of Newry town. The rain had ceased and a salty breeze was wafting in from Carlingford Lough. They crossed Merchants Quay onto the broad greystone pavement bordering the canal and looked down the waterway towards the sea. The high pavement lamps cast sharp, brittle splashes of light at intervals along the street.

"This Cooney character," Gillian said. "If he's such a mad bugger, isn't it about time we called in for back-up?"

"I'll call CI Hall and put him in the picture," Quinn said. "But don't forget we already have Sergeant Pollock and the local force behind us. Pollock's putting two men on guard at the hospital tonight."

Gillian sighed and looked out along the canal. "I'm not sure that a couple of provincial peelers will make an effective task force in an emergency situation."

"Well, what are we up against?" Quinn said, feeling his customary reluctance to call for assistance. "So far it's just two men, two head-the-balls with shit for brains."

"We've seen two, but we've really no idea of their numbers. For all we know, there could be half a dozen of them."

"Okay, okay," Quinn assented. "I'll give him a ring."

The canal was swollen with the heavy rain, the water swirling black and impenetrable. The sky was beginning to break up, the winter moon straining to emerge completely from the fragmenting cloudbank. There was a dampness in the air that made Quinn rub his hands together and shiver.

"I need to take a walk," Gillian said. "On my own," she added, so there should be no mistake.

"I'll book a six-thirty wake-up call for the morning," he told her.

She nodded and set off in the direction of the sea. He watched her as she made her way swiftly between the lampposts. He thought again there was something captivating about her light, buoyant way of moving, her boyish, blond head bobbing slightly with each step.

Quinn turned to gaze down at the shadowy darkness of the canal water and thought about McCann and Mary Savage and wondered once more about the real nature of their relationship. He kept feeling he was missing something, that there was a connection staring him in the face that he just couldn't see. His hope was that Bill Pollock would dig something up that would provide the missing link. There was a wealth of information to be gleaned if you had local knowledge and contacts.

He turned away from the canal, walked back across the street and into the hotel. There was a new receptionist at the counter, a woman of about his age with the look of a pharmaceutical laboratory technician. She wore thick-lensed, horn-rimmed glasses showcasing an expression of terminal boredom. Quinn asked for a six-thirty wake-up call for himself and Gillian Rice. The woman seemed puzzled at first by the double booking, but slotted it in and bade him 'Good night.'

He went over to the lift and pressed the button. The door opened immediately and he smelt before he saw that a person or persons unknown had vomited in the corner. It looked as if someone had sprayed a pale yellow sauce haphazardly round a small mound of diced carrots. The smell was nauseating. Wedding debris. Quinn wheeled round and made for the stairs.

TWENTY

He was dreaming, and he knew he was dreaming. He was quite aware of it. And it was not a dream he liked. Wilfully, he tried to focus his mind away from it, to wriggle out of it, to shake it off. But it's too strong, he thought, it's happening again. He finds himself moving sluggishly down a dark, shadowy tunnel. Even in his reverie he knows he has been here before. The air is damp and heavy with the rusty smell of mildew. He gropes his way along in the muffled gloom. His eyes are blurred with perspiration. He feels suspended in a void, adrift in the wastes of consciousness.

All at once the tunnel gives way to a smoky, cavernous chamber. In the middle is a low, shrouded altar and on it a flickering candle casts a vacillating, dust-spilt pool of light. He looks around, searching for a presence, the priest of this subterranean chapel. But there is only the pressing darkness, the shadows of the night.

The flame draws him forward. An evil fascination swells in this breathing orb of light. The white flame quivers wildly, a punctured lung seeking air. For a second he sees his reflection in its spastic gleam. It is the face of a maleficent stranger. Frantically he leans forward and blows, blows with all his might. The candle shudders and goes out. His mind starts to slide, to slip away down the glaciers of space. There is someone beyond, calling to him in a shrill, sing-song voice.

The double jangle of the Nokia 3210 ripped Quinn from the cocoon of deep sleep and propelled him into a state of wired-up wakefulness. He rolled over towards the bedside table and scrabbled briefly for the phone, knocking the Duralex glass of water to the floor where it rolled onto its side and failed to break. In the engulfing darkness of the room he somehow managed to press the right button.

"Quinn?"

He grunted an affirmative.

"Quinn, you better get down here double quick. It's a fuckin' bloodbath." Sergeant Pollock spat the words out as if he was chewing a brick.

His head clearing, Quinn sat up. "What?"

"I'm at the hospital," Pollock said. "Cooney's beaten us to it."

Quinn was on his feet, the wetness of the carpet reminding him of the water glass. He bent over and lit the bedside lamp. He snatched up his wrist watch. It was half past four.

"I'm on my way," he said. His thumb bobbed up and down as he rang off and located Gillian's number. The signal chimed five or six times before she answered.

"It's not bloody six-thirty yet," she snarled. Ah, not an early-morning person, he thought.

As he explained in urgent telegraphese she rapidly awakened.

"Looney fuckin' Cooney," she croaked.

"At the lift in five minutes," Quinn said and gouged the button.

Toeing the water glass out of his way, he stumbled into the bathroom, splashed some water on his face, the back of his neck, the top of his head, ran his fingers through his hair and brushed his teeth for five seconds. Back in the bedroom he tossed toothbrush and toothpaste into his duffel bag, threw his clothes on and dashed out of the room.

Gillian Rice was waiting by the lift with her finger jabbing the button. He couldn't believe she was there before him. The door opened as Quinn arrived and they both stepped in. The Shogun was parked at the back of the Canal Court in the hotel's parking lot. As they rushed out into the gauzy morning darkness, Quinn smelt the distant salt tang of the sea. Racing across to the car he breathed in the air swiftly and deeply. Gillian wrenched the door open and leapt into the driver's seat. She's like a ferret up a drainpipe, Quinn thought as he hurried round to the passenger side.

The parking lot was deathly still. There was an almost tangible dampness in the air. Gillian had the engine started and was letting out the clutch almost before he had climbed into his seat. The car shot out through the gates, swung right and in a matter of seconds they were on Monaghan Row, accelerating up the slope to the hospital.

As they climbed the hill, Quinn transferred the Walther PP from the duffel bag to the right-hand pocket of his hunting jacket.

This time they did not drive as far as the A&E Department but turned abruptly left to stop behind a police car parked in front of the main entrance. Quinn hopped out in front of the red-brick portal and looked up at the white-lettered sign announcing Daisy Hill Hospital. The lofty brown-brick block of the hospital building loomed above. Almost all the windows were still in darkness. There was no sign of Sergeant Bill Pollock.

They dashed forward, the doors slid open and they ran in. Without staff and patients the entrance hall felt desolate, abandoned. The sergeant was standing by the reception desk, his police jacket unbuttoned, speaking rapidly into a mobile.

"Dr Kickham and other staff are on their way," he panted as they reached him. "But it looks like the Savage woman has lost her baby." He paused, looking thunderstruck. "And I've lost my best man, Jack Callen. Shot dead. Fuckin' murdered."

Before they could ask for details, he snapped, "Follow me," and led them along the main passageway and up a flight of stairs. Quinn had seldom seen a man of his bulk move so fast. They turned into a long corridor at the top of the stairway and stopped.

The corridor was a tunnel of beige walls and subdued lighting. A small red lamp glowed like a beacon at the far end. The faint odour of antiseptic liquid in the air may have killed off certain bacteria but it provided no protection against gunfire. About twenty yards away a man in police uniform lay sprawled across the vinyl floor. Jack Callen's hands rested near his cheeks, as if raised in shock at the neat hole in his forehead, the dark red rivulet of blood trickling down past his nose to coagulate at the corner of his mouth.

"Jack Callen, my best man," Pollock repeated. "And he's gone." He stared at the corpse and swallowed hard. "All he ever was and hoped to be is gone."

It was clear to both Quinn and Sergeant Rice that something more than collegial duty prompted this comment.

"You knew him well?" Gillian said.

Pollock cleared his throat, trying to hold the emotion in check, and looked her straight in the face.

"My son-in-law," he rasped. "Two young kids." He glanced back at the dead man lying in the corridor. "How am I going to tell my daughter?"

Quinn looked from Sergeant Pollock to Sergeant Rice, then back to Pollock again. "Jesus, Bill, I'm sorry," he breathed. "What the fuck happened here?"

Bill Pollock took a deep breath, his grey eyes watering more than ever. "I'm still piecing it together from what Mona has told me."

"Mona?"

"The night nurse. Apparently there were three of them. They just marched in and took hold of Mona, made her take them to McCann. My other officer, Terry Anderson, he was on a chair outside the room, probably half asleep. They took him by surprise. Mona says they just clubbed him over the head with a revolver. Laid him out. Then they dragged him into a store room just down the corridor."

Quinn half-raised his hand. "Where was Jack Callen?"

"Seems he had gone to the toilet. Mona says he'd had an Indian takeaway with him when he came on duty. He'd joked with her about what it would do to his stomach." Pollock exhaled a sigh that became a low, heavy moan. "For fuck's sake, I was the one who'd asked him to be the extra man, like we agreed."

"I know. I know."

"For God's sake, don't blame yourself," Gillian whispered. "You didn't do this." The sergeant shrugged with exasperation and buttoned up his jacket.

"Anyway," he continued, "one of them demanded to see Mary Savage. She was in a room further down the corridor, near the toilet that Jack had gone to. He took Mona with him. The other two went into McCann's room."

"Cooney and the Taliban?"

"Mona's description is a bit confused – she's in a state – but it more or less fits."

Quinn shifted uncomfortably on his feet. He was painfully aware that he had never made the back-up call to Chief Inspector Hall. He was assailed by self-reproach and remorse. He listened in silence and shame, the words he was hearing all bearing testimony to his culpability. His mind was an empty room, his feelings of guilt and blame like squatters who had settled there and would never leave.

"Is she all right?" Gillian asked. "Mona, I mean – she's not been hurt?"

"No, just a few bruise marks on her arms where they grabbed her. But she's in shock. It all happened so fast. She's originally from Aberfoil, by the way. She knows Mary Savage."

Gillian looked at Quinn, waiting for him to speak, but he was silent.

"What happened there, in the room where she was?" she said.

"Yer man was rantin' and ravin' at the Savage woman, working himself into a proper rage. Had she shot Mickey McCann? Why the hell had she shot him? Said he knew all about her and what she had done. And then suddenly she flared up and told him to get the fuck out of her room. You fuckin' scumbag, she called him and pressed her alarm button. Next thing was he had a gun in one hand and grabbed her by the hair with the other and began to pull her out of the bed. Mona said she seemed to twist round to get away from him and fell onto the floor. Stomach first."

Quinn noticed Gillian Rice clenching her fists, her whole body tensing like a spiral spring.

"Did he even know she was pregnant?" she asked.

Bill Pollock's shoulders moved resignedly before he replied.

"It's not certain. Mona said there were several blankets lumped up on the bed when they went in, as if she'd been tossing and turning, and she seemed to be lying a bit to the one side, so maybe it wouldn't have been immediately obvious."

"Jesus, where is she now?"

"She's been moved to the operating theatre at the end of the corridor and we're waiting for the senior gynaecologist to arrive. Mona's with her, doing the best she can."

"But where was Jack Callen while all this was going on?" Gillian said.

Bill Pollock took a deep breath before he answered. He blinked from glassy eyes and tears began to trickle down his cheeks.

"Well, he would have heard the shouting – he was just

across the corridor – and he must have slipped out because he suddenly came charging into the room, gun in hand. Yer man swung round, raising his gun, and Jack shot him in the face. Mona said he just stood there, like he couldn't believe what was happening, and Jack shot him again."

Quinn seemed to wake up. "Holy fuck!" he gasped.

A middle-aged woman in jeans and a suede jacket hurried past them, tiptoed past the corpse of Jack Callen, and hastened on to the small red lamp at the far end of the corridor. They watched her until she disappeared into the operating theatre.

"Mona said he must have hit the carotid artery because there's a basinful of blood on the floor all around him. He would have died within a minute, just bled to death. There was another, much smaller pool of blood closer to the bed, I suppose from Mary Savage."

"A regular bloodbath, like you said," Quinn mumbled.

"Yeah. Mona witnessed all this, of course. I just came afterwards. She rang the station and they rang me. I don't know how much Mary Savage saw because she was in a bad way lying there on the floor. According to Mona, Jack said, 'Take care of her,' wheeled round and went out into the corridor again."

Bill Pollock paused, gathered himself and said: "There was an immediate shot and Mona saw him fall to the floor – where he's lying now."

They stared for a moment at the young man's body before moving closer. He lay in the optimal foetal position, as if he were closer to birth than to death, but in Quinn's mind he would never be born again except perhaps from time to time in the memory of his family and friends.

"The man he shot, did he have any ID on him?" Quinn asked.

"Driving licence says he's Francis Brady. Ring any bells?"

"No, can't say it does. Francis Campbell rings a big bell – he was one of the Newry bombers – but not Francis Brady. You?"

"Never heard of him."

"Let's have a look at him," Quinn said. "I might recognise him."

Tentatively they approached the prone figure of Jack Callen, circled around him and edged into the room where Mary Savage had been. The man who had been Francis Brady was lying on his back staring at the ceiling with sightless eyes. His arms were stretched out straight down by his sides, as if he had been standing to attention when he'd been shot and toppled over with instant rigor mortis. A semi-automatic Glock 31 had somehow angled itself to rest diagonally against the skirting board. The bedclothes were partly bloodied and gathered in a frowzy heap at the foot of the bed. Out in the corridor Dr Kickham hurried past followed by a nurse. They stood inside the doorway and surveyed the body on the floor.

"No, I don't know him," Quinn confirmed. "What about your other man, Terry Anderson?"

"He's recovering in a room down near the operating theatre. Severe concussion. We can only hope it's nothing worse."

"And McCann?" Gillian Rice asked. "Is he in one piece?"

"He is. He'd been heavily sedated but they woke him up. He's pretty weak, but strong enough to nod and shake his head."

"Have you spoken to him?"

"Yeah, I have. He's saying nothing. Seems to have difficulty breathing. He did try to ask about Mary Savage though."

"Still carrying a torch, is he?" Quinn said.

"I don't know about that. Actually Mona did mention

something that could be useful. She still lived in Ballyfoil four or five years ago. She says there was some talk then about Gerry Savage taking over O'Leary's pub."

"Talk? What sort of talk?" Quinn asked, leaning forward.

"About where the money came from," Bill Pollock said. "Savage said it was from some well-heeled relative who'd passed away in the States, y'know, an unexpected legacy. But not everyone was buying that. He'd never mentioned any rich American relative before. And he hadn't really had a proper job. Mostly he was known as a pretty useful Gaelic player. He played centre half back for Down. But there wasn't much money in that."

"It's not exactly the Premier League," Gillian said.

But Quinn wasn't listening to her. All of a sudden his eyes took on an animated gleam. He seemed to realise he was about to have an epiphany.

"Wait a minute," he said. "You mean he actually bought the pub? He owned it?"

"That's right," Bill Pollock said. "That's what Mona told me."

"Jesus Christ, I thought it was just some sort of lease or franchise, that they were more or less just renting the place, the way you usually do if you take over a pub. But that's it. That's it! Holy shit, it was staring me in the face all the time. Gerry Savage is the informer. He picked up the reward and used it to buy the pub. That's who they're looking for now. That's why Mickey McCann was shot."

Gillian saw the pieces of the puzzle slotting into place. Good God, why hadn't they seen it before? She picked up where Quinn had left off.

"So he went to see Mary Savage to find out if she was involved, to get proof of the legacy. And when she couldn't provide any she pulled the gun in order to get rid of him."

"Yeah, that's probably how it went down," Quinn said. "She maybe just wanted to scare him off, to get him out of the house. But the gun was up on top of the bookcase and that meant she had to get up on that chair. In her condition that was absolute bloody madness. McCann might have tried to take the gun off her, or she simply tripped on the chair. When it comes down to it, the whole thing might just have been an accidental shooting."

Sergeant Pollock's broad head nodded in agreement.

"I suggest we have a serious chat with Mr McCann, the three of us, and get the bugger to tell us exactly what happened between him and Mary Savage, and why. We need to get this confirmed."

They moved away from the two corpses and made their way along the corridor to McCann's room. Quinn was reaching out for the handle when the door suddenly opened and Dr Kickham stepped out in crisply starched white coat with name badge in clear view. Realising their intention, the doctor raised an admonitory hand.

"I don't want Mr McCann disturbed any more this morning. He's suffered enough already. Bloody thugs."

"They've injured him?" Gillian said.

"It looks very much as if they were trying to drag him out of bed, to get him out of the room. That certainly didn't do his other injuries any good."

"But he was back in bed when I saw him," Bill Pollock protested.

"Yes," the doctor said. "I suspect they were interrupted by the shooting further up the corridor. Luckily for McCann."

"So, how is he now?" Quinn said.

"His condition is still critical but not, at this moment, life-threatening."

"You reckon he'll pull through then?"

Dr Kickham wrinkled his brow and licked his lips. He was a man who chose his words carefully.

"Well, he's lost an awful lot of blood and he's had

surgery, but we've stabilised him, at least for the time being. I think he'll live, but at a cost."

"At a cost?"

The doctor placed his hands carefully in the pockets of his white coat before he spoke.

"The bullet perforated the small bowel and transected the tenth thoracic vertebra, damaging his spinal cord."

Gillian Rice glanced with foreboding at Quinn, who appeared to be none the wiser, and turned back to the doctor.

"What does that mean?"

Dr Kickham seemed mildly surprised that she hadn't understood the physiological consequence of such an injury.

"He's paralysed from the waist down."

TWENTY-ONE

Gerry Savage thought it was the wind at first: a low, unsettling creak somewhere in the house, a draught-induced movement symptomatic of buildings erected more than a century ago. And yet at the same time it was as if an inner voice was whispering to him, murmuring softly that something unnatural had disturbed the winter stillness. He rolled over once more, shrugging it off, coaxing on the sleep that had eluded him for most of the night. The hours of darkness hung over him like a diaphanous veil on his consciousness.

He lay rigid, rewinding the mental film in his head, endeavouring to make sense of it all. He had been shocked by the sight of Mary lying pregnant and helpless in the hospital bed, frightened by the sudden realisation of how much he felt for her, how much she and the new life within her meant to him. He thought of the difficulty he always had in showing his feelings, if they weren't of vexation or downright anger. He saw again the dubious look she often gave him when he tried to express his affection for her, as if she couldn't really believe it.

You think you can protect your wife, your unborn child, shield them from all evil. But you are so fragile, so defenceless – you are no shield. When all is said and done, you are only a bystander, a witness observing life's futile struggle for love and survival. More than anything he sought to be close to her, to give himself to her in all his vulnerability, but it was as if she too was afraid of the emotional proximity, the danger of exposing the naked heart.

"Plenty of time for the lassies, Gerry, when you've hung up your boots." Out of nowhere Paddy Mullan's words came ringing back to him, spoken one morning when

Gerry had arrived late for training. Well, Jesus, Paddy was nothing if not fanatical. It was the same with the smoking. All was to be sacrificed for the game. The crazy thing was he had gone along with it.

In his day, Paddy Mullan had been such a brilliant player himself. He had a way of talking you into things. It was not so much hook, line and sinker as knee, balls and jock strap. You took him seriously because you knew he'd made all the big mistakes himself. Now he wanted you to learn from them. The Georgie Best of Gaelic, they called him, though in the end he had managed to stay on the wagon.

Gerry thought of the good years when he was in his prime on the field. They were the days of blood and glory as he moved up from centre half to full forward. And, that first match, when he had picked up a knock-down, burst through and scored the winning goal for Down in the All-Ireland Championship. He was lying on his back, sleepily savouring this memory, when he detected another noise somewhere down below in the house, a cold metallic sound that sent an apprehensive quiver slithering along his spine. He sat up in bed like a drawn-back bow string. The sound came again.

He slid out of bed and tiptoed to the sash window overlooking the back yard. The moon was up, and with the firm westerly breeze it cast shadows across the fields and hillside slopes from downy grey clouds ambling across the heavens. There was a muted lightening in the sky to the east, towards the Irish Sea. He looked out over the softly undulating landscape.

In the moonlight he could make out the barbed-wire fence and the iron-bar gate leading to the next field three hundred yards away. He could see no one in the yard below, though the projecting shed under the window partially blocked his view. In the summer he had replaced the rotting roof boards and a couple of the supporting rafters. He padded softly across the room, past the bed, over to the bedroom door and listened. Faintly he could hear the harsh rasping sound of metal on metal, then a hushed clinking noise. Gerry wheeled to the hardback chair where his clothes hung as he made up his mind.

Pulling on a pair of cords over his pyjama shorts he snatched up his shirt, jammed his arms in, ignoring the buttons, wrenched a sleeveless pullover over his head and jabbed his sockless feet into a pair of suede loafers. In seconds he was at the window drawing up the bottom sash, flinching at the squeaky yelping noise it made. As he heard movement in the kitchen, footsteps in the hall below, a steady tread approaching the staircase, he climbed feet first out of the window and dropped onto the felt roof of the lean-to shed, knowing it would hold. Briefly he listened for any sign of movement in the shadows beneath him. It was quiet. The only sound he could hear was the thumping of his heart.

He trod carefully to the end of the pitched roof, peered fleetingly into the gloom before he dropped to the ground, bending his knees as he landed to cushion the impact. The night air rushed into his lungs as he fell, smelling of damp soil and wet grass. In front of him the field stretched to an irregular fence of rusting barbed wire that skirted an iron farmyard gate leading into a grass meadow. Beyond that a copse of firs and a gorse hedge crossed the distant fields as they swept up to the rounded, lower hills of the highland range. And on the far side of the firs lay the last farmhouse before the mountain slopes took over and you climbed up high into the bracken lands of the upper Mournes. So many times he had gazed out in daylight at that rising landscape. Now, in his flight, it took on an aspect that was darker, bleaker, almost surreal.

Gerry looked out into the night and thought hard and fast. He knew Brendan Forde and his wife, Monina. Not well, but he knew them. Brendan had played some football in his younger days, before he took over his parents' farm. They were normal, straightforward, middle-aged people who kept themselves pretty much to themselves. They weren't regular chapel-goers, but neither was Gerry. Brendan had been in the pub a few times and they had talked, mostly about the game. But could he ask him such a favour? Would he lend him his car? Well, yes, considering Gerry was running for his bloody life, of course he would.

But then he thought about his own car, parked unlocked in the street outside the pub. With the key as usual lodged in the overhead compartment intended for his Ray Bans. After all, he always maintained, who would steal a car in the little village of Ballyfoil? Abruptly he made his decision.

Turning back towards the house, he walked with short, swift steps along the far side of the shed to the narrow side-entry beside the pub. Within seconds he had reached the street. The black BMW 535 saloon was parked under the streetlamp just past the pub entrance with the driver's door nearest the narrow, flagstoned pavement. He looked up and down the street. It was empty, silent, deserted. As he slipped past the outer pub door he noticed it was slightly ajar. He hurried on.

The car door opened with a muffled click and he slid onto the leather seat, reaching up frantically to douse the courtesy light. In the darkness he gulped with relief.

Sitting there in his own car that he knew so well, smelling the soft leather seats, he experienced a momentary feeling of comfort and security. As he reached up to release the lid of the compartment where he had placed the key, he caught sight of a pair of diagonal cutting pliers lying on the passenger seat. He noted at once that the jaws were unusually long. At the same moment as he also noticed the severed wiring hanging down under the dashboard, he felt the hard coldness of a metal pipe being pressed into the opening of his right ear. And he knew immediately what it was.

"Gerry Savage," a voice behind him breathed, "you fuckin' traitor. I've been waitin' for you."

'I'm a dead man', Gerry whispered to himself. 'It's just a matter of seconds. I'm a dead man. It's all caught up with me. I'm a goner'.

"He's here, John," the man's voice grunted into a mouthpiece. "I've got the fucker here in the car."

Gerry glanced over at the passenger seat beside him. Quick, quick, quick! All at once in his mind he was back on the football field and he saw the opening, the handles of the pliers beckoning like goal posts. He felt his breath coming short and fast as his heart pounded and the voice in his head screamed over and over again:

'Just do it! Just do it! Just do it!'

He felt the man shift position in the rear seat.

"Don't worry," he chuckled, moving the gun barrel to the back of Gerry's head, "it's a turkey shoot."

Gerry thrust down with his right hand to snap the seat-back lever and, driving his feet into the floor, propelled himself backwards to knock the gunman off balance. Bouncing against the back of the seat he jack-knifed forward to snatch up the pliers with his left hand, turn round and swing the pointed jaws with all his strength at the man's head. They could have just pierced his cheek, but they sank into his left temple. The momentum of the swing built up such force that the pliers entered the temple to half their length before Gerry twisted round to follow up with the heel of his right hand slamming into the handles so that they dug deeper into the man's skull.

Splayed against the window, the man gurgled and opened his mouth as if to say something, but the words remained clogged in his windpipe, never to be uttered. Blood trickled down over his cheekbone. Gerry was surprised there wasn't more. The pliers acted as a stopper, he surmised with unexpected rationality. The man slumped forward, his eyes petrified, staring down in demise. He was bearded. He looked tall, even collapsed on the rear seat with the pliers protruding from the side of his head like a satanic horn. The gun was still in his hand. Gerry disentangled it and slipped rapidly out of the car, leaving the door ajar.

He stood for a moment on the pavement, panting with exertion and relief, half expecting someone to appear at the entrance to the pub. When no one did, he ran back past the entrance and into the alley. Trotting along the side of the shed towards the back field, he stood on something squishy and slithered forward. He thought at once of the slanging match he'd had with his neighbour about her dog. He stopped at the end of the shed, wiped his suede loafers on a tussock of grass and peered out across the plot of land that extended to the fence with its iron-bar gate. They called it the 'boneyard', an abandoned area of weeds and stones and scuffed grass that had never been developed and probably never would be. At one time, before television, there had been talk of building a country dance hall there, close to the pub, but nowadays people went into Newry for their Saturday Night Fever entertainment.

It would take him fifteen or twenty minutes to make it to Brendan Forde's farm if he moved carefully, keeping low over the land. Whoever was in the house would be going to the car. To find him. To kill him. It was only a matter of seconds before they would be coming after him. Gerry grasped the gun tightly. He could smell the mushy dogshit still on his loafers. He wiped them again on another tussock and set off, lurching at times over the scrappy, uneven ground.

It was still dark, but the moonlight and the lightening sky in the east made him feel exposed, half naked as he moved forward in a defensive crouch with the gun held knee-high. He was halfway to the fence when he tripped on a stone and almost fell. He went down on one knee and lifted the gun to his face. He checked it for a safety catch. It was a modern revolver and the chambers were full. It didn't have a safety catch that he could find.

A cloud briefly obscured the moon and the land darkened. He pushed himself up and set off again. The shaggy grass increased as he neared the fence, thicker in patches and moist with early morning dew. He resisted the temptation to stop and look back, knowing how precious the seconds were. When he got to the iron gate he couldn't recall which side the latch bolt was on. He chose the wrong side. As he moved to the other side, he couldn't help risking a look back at the house.

His eyes were watering in the chill air. He felt himself shiver. His hand on the gun was cold and stiff. The pullover offered little warmth. The pub and the neighbouring house were in total darkness, but the light from the street partially illuminated the gap between the two buildings. He could see the entrance to the narrow alleyway. For a second there was no one there. He blinked his eyes to clear them and looked again. A man appeared in the alley, walking quickly towards the field. Then, suddenly, another man. He grabbed at the latch bolt and pulled. It didn't budge. He pulled again. No movement. He couldn't remember when it had last been opened. Jesus Christ! Corroded to hell. Rusted in place. Get over the gate, he said. Get over the fuckin' gate!

It was a six-bar gate. He wanted to glance back again to see where they were, but he didn't. He stuck a foot on the second bar up, clasped the top bar with his free hand and placed his forearm with the gun hand beside it for leverage.

As he heaved himself up he heard a dull clump-like thud resound across the boneyard and felt a hot ripping tear at the back of his leg. He thought of the words he'd heard just five minutes ago: It's a turkey shoot. Then he clambered over the top and collapsed on his side in the spiky grass below.

He felt no real pain, just a slight burning sensation. He put the revolver down beside him on the ground and used both hands to widen the hole in his corduroy trousers. The bullet seemed to have skimmed him, clawed through the outer flesh and passed on. His fingers explored the torn tissue. It was his left leg, above the knee, a wide laceration along the outside of the thigh, wet and thick with the sticky flowing blood. You're a lucky bastard, he said. Then he thought again: They're going to kill you. And he realised he had nothing to tie it up with, to staunch the flow of blood.

Anger shook him like a seizure. He took the gun and flattened himself in the grass behind the gate, scanning between the bars. Slowly he raised himself, rested his hands on the second bar and peered into the gloom. His eyes filled with tears, beads of frenzied desperation. There were shadows moving out there. Motherfuckers. He rested his wrist on the bar, pressed the trigger and fired off three, four shots in an arc. Then he turned and crawled away deeper into the field. When he had gone fifteen or twenty yards the field dipped and he stood up and ran down the slope until it panned out and began to rise again.

He could feel the wetness seeping down his thigh as he moved. He was surprised he could run so well, so smoothly, despite his wound. As the land began to slope upwards again, he slowed down and went into a crouch, fearful of becoming a silhouette on the skyline. Clumps of gorse loomed up ahead of him, misshapen phantoms in the grainy negative of the night. He stopped behind a bush and straightened up to get his bearings. In the distance he glimpsed the tops of the fir trees that marked the way to Brendan Forde's farm. Once he had reached the copse of firs, he knew the farmhouse was only another two or three hundred yards. He shuffled over to the far side of the bush and looked back. The moon was once again hidden behind cloud. From the area near the gate the light of a powerful torch suddenly pierced the night, seeking him out.

Gerry did not hesitate. He raised the revolver and fired two shots. The light went out. He pulled the trigger again. Nothing. He poked around the cylinder with his fingers. The chambers were empty. All of them. He tossed the gun into the gorse bush and took off for the firs, dragging his left leg slightly behind him as it began to stiffen. He both ran and walked at a trot, keeping his head down as much as possible as he went. He kept visualising a bullet shattering the back of his skull. He stopped several times and knelt down, listening. He staggered to a halt when he reached the safety of the fir trees. The air felt cold in his face but his shirt was running with sweat.

The trees stood as part of a gorse hedge that ran parallel to a barbed wire fence. He sat under them, resting against a trunk and sucking in air. The heavy, sticky smell of fir needles made him think of hair balsam. Then he thought of Christmas. The branches quivered in the morning breeze. He listened again for sounds of pursuit. It was darker among the trees but there was a manifest glimmer of twilight in the sky. Hurry, he said. You have to hurry.

He crawled under the fence and stumbled across a ploughed field. His leg was more painful now, burning with fire each time he put it down. When he had gone a couple of hundred yards, he spotted the outline of a building ahead. With renewed strength he pushed himself forward. You're nearly there, he told himself, nearly there.

He felt gravel underfoot as he met the lane leading to the

farm. He had never been there before. He came to an old stone barn on his left. At the far gable wall the lane turned left again and when he followed it he saw the house set back in a farmyard between the barn and another outhouse. He was surprised at the size of the farmhouse – it was a two-storey building – and the fact that there was a light on in the window nearest the lobby door. Then he realised five or six o'clock in the morning was not an unusual time for a farmer to be up. Working in the pub had accustomed him to late nights and late mornings. The two whitewashed storeys seemed to soar in the gloom, towering over the farmyard, a welcoming refuge that beckoned him.

As he stumbled to the door he passed a car, dark blue or black, standing alongside the barn wall on his left. He felt a stirring of hope. All was not lost. There was no knocker on the door. He banged it with his fist. Almost at once the door opened and Monina Forde appeared in the half-light, a tall, severe-looking woman in her fifties. It was almost as if she had been waiting there, he thought. She seemed startled to see him.

"Gerry Savage," she said, her voice distinct and low, beckoning him in. "Dear God in heaven, what's happened to you?"

He swallowed hard and tried to wipe the sweat off his forehead.

"I've men after me," he croaked, almost crying. "They're going to kill me."

"Kill you? Nonsense, nonsense," she said. "Come in, come in."

And she took hold of him with firm, strong arms, even as he protested, pulling him into the lobby,

"You're out of harm's way here, Gerry, never you mind."

She hurried him through the lobby, past the jamb wall with its spy window, and into the kitchen. Gently she sat him in a cushioned armchair by the hearth, regardless of his bloody leg. Gerry moaned briefly with the pain and shifted his weight to the other side.

"I have to get away," he begged and started to get up. "They'll find me here. Can I take your car? Please? Where's Brendan?"

"He went out to feed the pigs," she said. "I'll get him. Sit you there. I won't be a moment."

"I need to go now. I can't wait. They're coming!"

"Brendan's got the car key. I'll get him," she told him with a tight, reassuring frown.

She swept out of the room, out to the farmyard, and Gerry looked desperately around him, seeking some form of protection, something to defend himself with, something to stop him feeling so utterly, damnably vulnerable. Then he noticed the kitchen table, a low, much-scarred pine table with gilt-hinged drop leaves at either end. On the top sat four stained tea mugs, two on either side, a pot of home-made raspberry jam, a dish bearing traces of butter, and a breadboard in the middle with a serrated knife and a desultory scattering of crumbs. He thought of taking the bread knife, but all at once everything was standing still in his head. He stared at the items on the table as if transfixed. Fear filled him with dread.

As footsteps approached he looked up to see the lanky figure of Brendan Forde enter the room followed by another man, shorter and thickset. They were both carrying raised semi-automatic pistols.

"Ah, there you are, Gerry," Brendan said, panting, out of breath. "It's too bad it had to come to this." When he saw the expression on Gerry's face he said, "Don't worry, it won't take long now."

"You led us a merry fuckin' dance," his companion rasped. He was also breathing hard. His eyes were dark and hollowed. He lifted his head and sniffed. "You smell of shite," he said, his sallow face screwing up with distaste.

"Who are you?" Gerry asked, even though he knew.

The man stood in the doorway, an unreal, tenuous figure in the early morning light, almost ghostlike until he stepped forward into the kitchen and seized a handful of Gerry's mane of blond hair, pulling him roughly up out of the armchair.

"I'm John Cooney," he said, his voice now soft and husky. "You took five years of my life. Now there's just five minutes left of yours."

TWENTY-TWO

Gillian Rice had geared up to express mode as she pursued the twisting country road out to Ballyfoil. Quinn kept a firm grasp on the handle built into the mock-leather armrest beside him on the passenger door. He never felt comfortable moving at this speed in a vehicle not driven by himself. With the headlamps drilling into the morning murk, casting shiny reflections on the black asphalt, he imagined them hitting treacherous patches of black ice as they went into sudden bends or zigzags in the road, driving situations where he himself would always have slowed down. His driver, however, displayed no such vacillation.

Leaning slightly over towards this same driver, reeling his seat belt with him, Quinn managed to catch a glimpse in the wing mirror of Sergeant Pollock in the squad car behind them, desperately endeavouring to keep up.

"Trying to lose him, are you?" Quinn said.

Gillian Rice didn't take her eyes off the road. "Trying to get to Ballyfoil before Savage becomes mincemeat."

"How much of a head start can Cooncy have?"

"Too much. We'll be lucky to find Savage alive."

"Or to find him at all."

"Yeah," said Gillian, swerving to avoid an early morning rabbit. "Whatever."

Quinn sat back and attempted to relax, fingering the bulk of the semi-automatic Walther PP in his jacket pocket. He still hadn't found out what firepower his partner was carrying, but this wasn't the time to ask. Ahead, the sombre outlines of the first buildings on Ballyfoil's main street rose up in the gloom of early morning.

A black BMW stood parked just a few yards past the entrance to O'Leary's pub, facing them as they drove into the village. Gillian Rice pulled up nose-to-nose with the

German saloon. Quinn felt his pulse quicken as he noted that the driver's door was ajar.

"Careful," he muttered. "Door's open."

Gillian Rice extracted a Walther PP from her black fleece jacket and nodded. "Snap," Quinn murmured, withdrawing his own weapon from a side pocket.

As the squad car drew up behind the Shogun, Gillian stepped out into the dew-damp road. Quinn was already on the pavement, sidling gradually towards the BMW, clutching the Walther before him. Even with the streetlamp above, the tinted windows restricted his view, but he became swiftly aware that the front seats were empty. With Gillian advancing in the middle of the road to the passenger side, Quinn stuck his head in the door, reached up to click on the courtesy light and emitted a low whistle. Gillian opened the passenger door, surveyed the dangling electric leads and the corpse on the back seat.

"Christ," she said. "Somebody's unwired the Taliban." Sergeant Bill Pollock came bustling up behind her and peered in.

"Who the hell's that?

"That is, or was, John Cooney's Rottweiler," Quinn told him.

"Looks like his barking days are over," said Pollock. "What's that in the side of his head?"

"Some sort of tool. Looks like a pair of pliers," Gillian said. "Probably used first to cut the wiring. The dashboard's hanging loose."

"Check the glove compartment," Quinn said. "Who's the owner?"

Gillian released the lid and rifled through some invoices, delivery papers and service sheets, finally holding an official-looking document up to the light.

"Gerald Patrick Savage," she told them. "Car registration."

The three of them stood silent for a moment, looking around the inside of the vehicle. Quinn stepped back, glancing up and down the street. There was no movement, no sign of life. The place was deserted.

"Okay," he said. "Possible scenario: Savage gets wind that Cooney's coming. He gets in the car to make a getaway. But Beardie's already waiting for him in the back and gets the drop on him. Then Savage knocks him off balance and –."

"How do you know that?" Pollock asked.

"Look at the back of the driver's seat. It's bent over backwards almost in Beardie's lap. Savage knows his car, snaps the release lever and thrusts himself backwards."

"Yeah," Pollock said slowly. "Could have gone down like that."

They considered the likelihood of Quinn's scenario for several seconds until Sergeant Pollock took a step away from the car. "Okay, let's take a look in the pub. He might still be here."

"Or Cooney might be in there," Quinn said. He glanced at Gillian. "Take it easy."

"Let's go," Pollock grunted and began to stomp back towards the entrance to O'Leary's.

"Take it easy, Bill," Quinn said again. "They may be still in the building."

He wasn't sure exactly who he meant by 'they' but there was no sense charging in there like a wounded bull, though that was an accurate description of Bill Pollock in his present state. The sergeant was on an escalating trajectory fired off by the murder of his son-in-law. The loss was slashed across his face like an open sore.

"I'll go first," Pollock said. "I've been in here before. You stay here," he told the driver who was standing by the squad car. "Go up the side-entry," he said to the two uniforms standing in the middle of the street. "Take up positions at the back. Anyone comes out, stop them."

Anticipating a question which never came, he added, "Any way you have to." Quinn and Gillian Rice followed him into the porch. Sergeant Pollock clicked on a torch. The air smelt damp and musty. As they walked past the double swing doors that led to the public bar, their feet left moist imprints on the tiled floor. Treading lightly they moved on towards the panelled door at the end of the porch.

"Wait," Quinn said in a half-whisper. "We should check the bar too."

"I'll do it." Gillian turned before he could say anything and went back to the swing doors. They were unlocked. She pushed the brass pull handle and slipped in.

Quinn and Pollock turned back to the panelled door.

"They've forced the lock," Pollock muttered, directing the torchlight to the splintered woodwork before him. Keeping both hands free, he pushed the door open with his knee and stepped in. Walther at the ready, Quinn moved into the narrow hall behind him. He brushed past an assortment of jackets and coats hanging from a metal rack on his left. Momentarily spooked by his shadowy figure in a wall-hung mirror on his right, he moved forward into the kitchen.

Bill Pollock swept the room with his torch. Even in the limited battery-driven light, the bland whiteness of the walls, the cupboard doors and the household machines increased the visibility of the room. Nonetheless Quinn reached up behind him and switched on an array of ceiling spotlights. Pollock swung round on him.

"What the hell are you doin'?"

"They've gone," Quinn said. "I can feel it. They've gone. The house is empty." The sergeant glared at him. "What are you, a fuckin' clairvoyant?"

He had trouble getting his tongue round the final word,

but Quinn knew what he meant. A thin smile hurried across his face.

"We need to check it out anyway," he said.

"Too fuckin' right," Pollock snarled.

He wheeled round and bustled out into the stone-floored corridor. Quinn was halfway out of the kitchen in his wake when a door further down on the right suddenly opened just as Pollock reached it. Instantly the sergeant threw himself forward, past the opening door, and swung round, jerking his gun up to hip-level.

"Easy," said Gillian Rice, "easy."

There was a strained pause before she added, "The bar's clear, in case you were wondering."

"The whole bloody place is clear, according to Quinn," said Bill Pollock, lowering his gun.

Gillian looked at Quinn, then back at Sergeant Pollock, plumbing the dynamic between them.

"Yeah, well," she said, "it's common knowledge Inspector Quinn's got second sight."

They moved to the end of the corridor, ignoring the heavy-duty rear-exit door, and turned to climb the worn, wooden treads of the staircase. Bill Pollock led the way, Quinn followed and Gillian Rice brought up the rear. As they ascended, the boards groaned with plaintive squeaks and creaks.

At the head of the stairs Pollock swung round to the right, to the room at the back of the house. He had clearly come to the same conclusion as Quinn: the house was empty. The bedroom door was wide open. He tramped in and over to the up-drawn sash window on the far side of the room.

"Bird's flown," he growled, glancing down at the lean-to shed below.

Gillian looked round the abandoned bedroom, noting the old-style solid brass bed, the antique mahogany bedside tables and the hardback chair askew at the foot of the bed, hung with boxer shorts and a dark blue sock. The other sock lay crumpled on the carpeted floor. She gestured at the chair and stated the obvious.

"He left in a hurry."

Quinn stood at the window, looking out. The darkness was thinning fast. A clump of fir trees was outlining itself in the distance, solidifying in the swiftly fading gloom. The day was rising, bright and clear, the wind fresh. John Cooney was out there somewhere; so was Gerry Savage, running for his life.

"Hello! Anyone up there?"

The voice came from the corridor below. Gillian went smartly out of the bedroom and rattled down the stairs, Quinn and Pollock in hot pursuit. The bulky frame of Liam Hogan filled the doorway from the kitchen. His face was almost as pale as the white hair that jutted out in all directions from under his bedraggled cap. He jerked a thick thumb over his shoulder.

"I saw the police car outside."

Bill Pollock glared at him with rheumy eyes. "Hogan, isn't it?"

"Yes, Liam Hogan."

"You live just down the street?"

"I do."

"Any idea where Gerry Savage might be?"

Hogan seemed bemused by the question. "He's not here?"

"No, he's not here."

"Well, I've no idea, unless he's at the hospital."

He thought about this for a moment, his bushy eyebrows twitching with the effort, until he realised: "But he can't be. His car's still outside. Door's open too."

Leaning against the door jamb Liam Hogan screwed his face up in dyspeptic consternation.

"I don't know where he is," he said and belched mildly. Sergeant Pollock took a step towards him.

"Have you seen anything? Heard anything?"

"I just got up. I looked out the window and saw you driving past."

"So you came here."

"Yes."

"Why?"

"I thought I heard something."

"What? Just now?"

"No, earlier on."

"What sort of thing?"

"Sounded like gunshots."

"Gunshots?"

"Yeah."

"How many?"

"I'm not sure."

Bill Pollock expelled a long sigh.

"Christ Almighty, it's like trying to get blood out of a stone."

His exasperation was magnified by the man's seeming indifference. Hogan hastened to appease him.

"Four or five maybe. I don't know. I was asleep."

"You didn't get up? You didn't look outside?"

"Naw. I fell asleep again."

Quinn shot him a look of open reproach. "You were drunk."

"Drunk? Whaddya mean?"

"You're still half cut. I can smell it from here."

"The pub was closed last night."

"You've probably got a still at home."

Liam Hogan said nothing. Sergeant Pollock and Quinn glowered at him. Gillian looked at him framed in the doorway, his back to the illumined kitchen while they stood in the shadows of the corridor, seeking the light. She moved suddenly forward until she was standing face to face with Liam Hogan, smelling the stale alcohol on his breath.

"These gunshots," she said, "where did they come from?"

"I'm not sure," he said and shrugged.

"You must have some idea," Gillian persisted.

"I thought I heard a report, like a gunshot, and I dozed off again." He glanced uncertainly at Sergeant Pollock before he continued. "Then there were a few more shots, a bit later I guess, and I woke up again."

"But you didn't get up and go to see what was happening?"

"Thought it could've been someone out hunting."

"In the middle of the night?"

"I had no idea what time it was. I was knackered."

"Pissed, you mean," Quinn said.

"But you must have some idea what direction the shots were coming from," Gillian persevered. "I mean, what side of the street is your house on? This side, same as the pub?"

"Yeah."

"Well then, were the shots coming from the front of your house or from the rear?"

"I sleep at the front, on the street, and they were a bit muffled, y'know, like distant."

"So?"

"Well, yeah, I suppose they were probably coming from somewhere at the back."

"At the back?"

"Yeah."

"Thataway," Gillian said, pointing to the rear, just to be certain he knew the points of the village compass.

"Yeah," he repeated. "It must've been on that side."

"Well, the open window upstairs backs that up," Quinn said.

"But what about the corpse in the car?" Pollock asked.

"Corpse?" Hogan said. "What corpse?"

They ignored him.

"Savage hears somebody breaking in downstairs, nips out the window and heads up the side-entry to his car," said Quinn. "Getting away in his car must've been plan A."

"But he finds the electrics ripped out and the Taliban in the back seat," Gillian continued.

"Who must've been armed," Pollock added.

"Right," Quinn said. "So when Savage does a lobotomy on him, he takes his gun."

"Then what does he do?" Gillian asks. "Where can he go? His car's useless."

They deliberated on this in silence. Quinn listened to the wall clock in the kitchen tick-tocking the fugitive seconds.

"Well, what do you think, Liam?" he asked finally.

"Me?"

"Yes, you. What would be plan B? You know the village. You know the district. Where would he go? Who's he friends with? Who would help him?"

Liam Hogan looked doubtful. "I don't know that he's really friends with anyone."

"Jesus Christ, Hogan, he's the bloody pub owner here." Bill Pollock was frothing like a pitbull about to shake free of its leash. "He must know everyone in the village. And beyond."

"Yes, beyond." Gillian took up the thread. "What about outside the village? Is there anyone out there he might go to?"

"He isn't really a friendly sorta fellah," Liam said. "Keeps himself to himself. Maybe fancies himself a bit. Thinks he's a cut above the rest of us, big-time Gaelic player and all that."

Quinn had a sudden, determined gleam in his eyes, his

slightly aquiline features taking on the contours of a bird of prey.

He said, "What if he simply took off from here, from the shed out here at the back, and headed cross country? Where would he come to? Is there anyone out there that he knows?"

"No, I don't think so," Hogan said slowly. "Like I say, he's not the sorta fellah that invites friendship. On his guard most of the time, if you know what I mean."

But Quinn would not be diverted.

"Who lives out there? Is there a cottage? A farm?"

"Not really." He seemed to consider this for a moment before adding, "Well, there's the Fordes – Brendan and Monina Forde. They have a farmhouse about half a mile away, maybe a bit more. But I don't think he knows them at all."

"It doesn't matter a damn if he knows them or not," Bill Pollock rasped. "The bloody man's running for his life. And he's armed. If they won't give him help, he'll take it."

"How do we get there?" Quinn demanded. "What's the quickest way?"

Hogan seemed relieved to get a question he had an answer to.

"The shortest way is over the fields at the back, but the road's for sure the quickest."

"You better come with us," Pollock said harshly. "I'm not risking any fuckin' wrong turnings on these wee country roads."

Pushing Liam Hogan in front of him, he drove him through the kitchen and out into the street to the squad car. Gillian Rice and Quinn hurried after them.

"I'll drive," Quinn told her.

"In your dreams," Gillian replied, car key in hand.

TWENTY-THREE

Daylight had crept up over the mountains and eddied down through the hushed valleys to the lowland slopes of Mourne. It was as if it had sneaked into the village while they stood in the gloom of the corridor, so that the brightness of morning took them by surprise as they dashed out into the empty street. The peaty smell of damp soil had drifted in from the fields to mingle with the fresh morning air. The sole indication of life was a dog, a mongrel with a tawny coat, urinating at a lamppost. Perhaps, Quinn reasoned, it was the earlier sounds of gunfire that kept the people of the village indoors.

Wielding the steering wheel like a Vickers machine gun, Gillian Rice pursued the squad car out of Ballyfoil. Quinn sat sullenly beside her pondering their short, acerbic exchange when they had arrived at the Shogun outside O'Leary's pub.

"I'll drive," he had said again, reaching out to remove the ignition key from her grasp.

"I'm the driver," she told him, wrenching away, eyes burning with resolve. "I have my orders."

"You take your orders from me," he had replied, somewhat taken aback.

"My overriding order is from Chief Hall and it's to drive this vehicle," she said. "You know that!"

And she had pulled her trim, sturdy frame up into the driving seat and slammed the door. By which time Bill Pollock had already burnt enough rubber on the asphalt to make a dozen pairs of police gumboots and vanished round the one and only bend in the main street of Ballyfoil. Gillian Rice fired the engine, engaged gear and took off.

They drove out to the far end of the village and beyond, towards the rising hillsides and the mountains. Within a minute they had caught up with the squad car. Quinn watched the gorse and hawthorn hedges wing past, the small farms criss-crossed with drystone walls, the fields grazed by sparse flocks of dishevelled sheep. As they swung off onto a dirt road that twisted and turned through the fields, Gillian Rice ventured a conciliatory comment.

"Bloody doglegs."

Somewhat mollified, Quinn was ready to play along. "Must be nearly there now," he muttered.

They were silent again as the road narrowed to a single track. It was rutted and steep. Soon after it levelled off, the braking lights on the squad car suddenly lit up and the vehicle stopped. Gillian Rice stood on the brake and clutch pedals and brought the Shogun to a standstill, leaving a thirty-yard gap between the vehicles.

"He's missed the turn-off," said Quinn, indicating with a forefinger the gap in the hedge just ahead of them. Gillian immediately reversed to allow ample space for the police car to back up and turn into the opening. Following the squad car she steered the Shogun through the gap and drove on as the track swung round in an arc with a small wood of yew trees on one side and a sporadic hawthorn hedge on the other, until both dwindled away and there was only a gravelled path leading to an old stone barn. Then the lane veered round to the left and into a farmyard with another large outhouse on the right and a two-storey, whitewashed farmhouse straight ahead.

By the time Quinn and Gillian Rice had exited the Shogun, Sergeant Bill Pollock was already applying his fist to the front door. As they reached him, the solid iron-bound door swung open and Mrs Forde stood before them, a tall figure of dignified deportment and rural gentility.

"Dear mother in heaven," she said softly, seeming genuinely surprised by the burly uniformed presence before her. "What's wrong? Has something happened?"

"We hope not, but that remains to be seen," Bill Pollock said, somewhat disconcerted by her self-assured demeanour. "Have you seen Gerry Savage?"

"Gerry Savage, the publican?"

"The very same."

"Now? This morning?"

"Yes, this very morning."

"No. I hardly know the man. We've no business with him. What's happened? Has he broken the law?"

"He's disappeared. We're trying to find him. Can we come in?"

"Yes, yes of course."

They followed her in through the lobby and on through to the kitchen. Quinn took mental inventory of the room: the white enamelled two-piece cabinet, the worn, oak-veneered cupboards, the scratched, much-used pine table with its dropped leaves and the four wooden chairs neatly stationed around it. The table was completely bare. An old oak armchair draped with a woollen red-and-green check blanket stood by the hearth where a log fire burned with indifferent conflagration. The smouldering, ashy smell of the wood filled the room.

Quinn said, "Mrs Forde, are you quite sure Gerry Savage didn't come this way earlier this morning?

"Yes. Why would he come here? We don't even know him." She spoke in a quiet, controlled voice, as if reciting a liturgy.

"He's on the run." Gillian said. "His life may be in danger."

"My goodness," Monina Forde said. "What on earth's happened?"

Quinn didn't respond. He walked over to the doorway leading into the next room and scanned the contents. Before a chenille-curtained window a pair of chestnut-coloured, faux leather sofas faced each other across a sofa table with a smoked-glass top. The living room was empty.

"Where's your husband?" Quinn said.

For the first time Monina Forde seemed a trifle unsettled. She leant back against the kitchen worktop and folded her arms. Her eyes flickered round the room as if Mr Forde might suddenly pop out of a cupboard.

"He's out in the pigsty," she said finally.

"Strange that he didn't come out when we arrived," Gillian Rice pointed out. Mrs Forde shifted her weight from one foot to the other and took a paper handkerchief from the pocket of her cardigan to dab at her nose. "He's a bit hard of hearing," she said.

Sergeant Pollock decided to forego any semblance of rural gentility. "He'd need to be as deaf as that fuckin' doorpost," he said, gesturing at the jamb, "not to hear a couple of cars arriving on the gravel."

"Let's take a look outside," Quinn said. "Which building is it?"

Monina Forde hesitated before answering: "The pigsty's in the barn on the left as you go out."

They left her standing there and went out to cross the uneven, concrete-laid farmyard, prudently dodging the scattered patches of encrusted mud and porcine excrement. Quinn glanced briefly up at the sky. The sun lay hesitant beyond the hills, so low in the winter sky as to render its eventual appearance a matter of conjecture. He returned his gaze to the ground and walked on.

The stench assaulted them before they reached the barn. Sergeant Pollock marched in through the gateway and turned right past a planked stairway leading up to the loft, the rancid smell of pig manure guiding him to the sty that took up the whole of the far end of the barn. Brendan Forde turned towards them holding a pitchfork in both hands.

"I thought I heard a car," he said, a sheepish grin flitting across his face.

Bill Pollock said, "Two cars, actually."

Quinn stood looking around the barn.

"We're looking for Gerry Savage," he said. "Have you seen him?"

"Savage? Gerry Savage?"

"Yeah, the big-time Gaelic football star and pub owner with the long blond locks," said Bill Pollock, his face scrunched up in a sarcastic sneer. "Ring a bell?"

Brendan Forde shook his head. "Haven't seen him. Last time was a week ago, I think. Why, what's he done?"

As he said this, the farmer took a few steps towards them, the pitchfork held loosely in his right hand.

"We're not absolutely sure yet," Quinn said, eyeing the pitchfork. "You're certain he hasn't come this way?"

"You mean today? This morning?"

"Yes."

"No, I haven't seen him," Forde said, shaking his head. "Why would he come here?"

"He might have wanted to borrow your car," Quinn suggested.

Brendan Forde shook his head. "No, haven't seen him," he said again. "I've been in here for a while feeding the pigs."

He walked past them, over to the planked staircase leading to the loft, and placed the pitchfork against the roughly hewn wooden handrail. Then he turned to the open gateway and the yard.

"Where are you going?" Gillian asked.

"Well, I've finished here. Time for a spot of breakfast." He looked round at them. "Have you time for a cup of tea?"

Quinn stared at him, then looked back at the pigsty. The stench of the pigs was pervasive but he was also beginning to smell a rat.

"How many pigs have you got?"

Brendan Forde scratched the side of his head as if tackling a demanding mental calculation.

"I've a sow and three boars. And there's a dozen piglets, different sizes."

"Big animals," Quinn stated. "Not much room in there to move around."

"I know. I'm going to have to extend it."

"Christ," Pollock muttered, "they're really rolling about in all that pigshite."

Beyond a low brick wall with rough plastering there was a row of boxes along the outside wall, but all the pigs were in the main open area with a cement wallow in the middle where several of the smaller pigs were splashing around. The bigger pigs were sloshing about in a corner, trying to get in closer to the sow and the boars that were floundering and tumbling into one another, jostling to get at the mushy heaps of food.

Quinn said, "Looks like they haven't eaten in a week."

"What do you feed them?" Gillian asked.

"Oh, just slops, y'know, vegetables, grain, fruit, that sort of thing."

"It looks like swill feeding at the moment," Bill Pollock said.

"Well, yeah, they get household scraps too, leftovers from the kitchen."

"They'll eat just about anything, I suppose," said Quinn.

Brendan Forde just nodded and started once more for the yard. "Cuppa tea?" he said again.

"We've no time for tea," Sergeant Pollock said, his eyes puddling with tears. "How can you stand this fuckin' stink?"

Eager to reach fresh air, the two sergeants turned away and started to walk after the farmer. Quinn was about to follow when he noticed one of the biggest pigs seemed to have got hold of the leafy top of a large turnip. It took him a second or two to realise he was looking at the long, once-flaxen strands of Gerry Savage's hair.

TWENTY-FOUR

The discovery of Gerry Savage's body – certain parts of it – seemed to energise Sergeant Bill Pollock to such an extent he took full command of the investigation. After a moment's deliberation, Quinn went along with it. This was, after all, Pollock's home ground. In a discreet aside Gillian Rice decided the sergeant was high on the methane gas wafting up from the manure. Whatever, he was all go.

An immediate search of the neighbouring barn disclosed a high-powered circular saw, a 16-inch Makita that had recently been used for cutting more than logs. The evidence lay all around with little attempt at concealment or sanitation; there clearly hadn't been enough time. Pollock rang for help and the pigs were driven into their boxes so that a proper examination could begin. Other body parts were soon uncovered among the mass of slops and swill spread around the rest of the sty: pieces of a foot, an upper arm, a section of a thigh, both knees, part of the torso, a shoulder and various fingers – including one bearing Gerry Savage's wedding ring.

"They'd just tossed everything into the middle of the sty," Bill Pollock surmised. "The pigs don't usually eat there – they have a special manger – but they were in a hurry to dispose of the body and they wanted to have all the pigs in there fighting for the goodies."

"Regular feeding frenzy," Quinn said.

"Right. Another hour or two and you wouldn't see a fuckin' thing left."

"Really?" Gillian said. "I've heard they leave something – teeth or hair – something like that."

"Believe you me," the sergeant snorted, "they polish off even the biggest bones. In the end there's nothing, absolutely nothing left."

A disturbing thought crossed Quinn's mind: Were the dismembered remains of Gerry Savage all that lay here as pigsty fodder, or had Arthur Williams preceded him? And if so, what were the chances of finding forensic evidence if Bill Pollock's belief in the omnivorous prowess of swine proved to be correct?

When they took Brendan Forde out in handcuffs into the farmyard, his wife appeared at the lobby door. She was about to walk towards them but Sergeant Pollock raised his arm with open hand in warning, a traffic cop stopping the conjugal traffic. Brendan Forde was placed in a police car with two officers for company while they decided how and where to conduct the preliminary interviews.

Gillian Rice suggested they should interrogate the Fordes separately and that she should take the lead in questioning Monina Forde. Woman-to-woman stuff, she said; keep them apart and we eliminate the risk of them fabricating some story together. It made a lot of sense. She's a sharp cookie, Quinn recognised once again, if a bit uppity at times. All the same, there was a certain manner about her that he in some way found quite disconcerting. At times he caught her looking at him with something in her eyes he couldn't quite fathom

"Right then, we conduct separate interviews," Quinn said.

"As long as I get that piece of shit," Pollock growled.

Quinn agreed, thinking at the same time that he would make sure to sit in on it. With his murdered son-in-law weighing heavy on his mind, Bill Pollock's fuse was so short he made Quinn feel like Mahatma Gandhi on Prozac. It was also decided that it would be best to interview the pair of them straight away in the farmhouse rather than give them extra time to concoct their stories by taking them back to the barracks in Newry.

Sergeant Pollock marched over to the police car and

ordered Forde out. Unable to contain himself he began to bombard him there and then with a battery of questions: Who killed Savage? Who dismembered him? Did he know John Cooney? Had John Cooney been there? Had he been alone? Where was he now? But Forde ignored him, refused to answer, his gaze balefully fixed on his wife still standing in front of the farmhouse door.

They were standing there in the farmyard, still as an oil painting in the glazed morning light, when reinforcements arrived in a Land Rover Tangi and an unmarked white van. The first cursory search of the other barn had already uncovered the 16-inch circular saw. Now both barns were to be meticulously ransacked. While the crime-scene technicians set about their work, Quinn and the two sergeants took Brendan Forde into the farmhouse. Pollock and Quinn decided to interview Brendan Forde at the kitchen table; Gillian Rice and a policewoman ushered Monina Forde into the living room.

"I want that door hermetically sealed," Pollock called after them.

The heavy shellac-varnished door between the two rooms was firmly closed. They tested it by listening while Gillian Rice began her interview with Monina Forde, establishing her personal details. All that could be heard from the next room was a susurrus of indistinct dialogue. Pollock nodded approval and parked himself on one side of the table with Quinn beside him; Forde sat opposite them looking down at his handcuffed wrists.

The hearth was shirred with ash. Someone had added a couple of logs to the fire. Not quite dry, they sizzled intermittently in the temporary stillness of the room. Traces of blood were visible on Forde's flannel shirt, some of them smudged as if he had tried to wipe them off. The bouquet of his body sweat alternated with a tainted pigsty odour that drifted over the table in occasional fetid gusts.

He kept his eyes turned down as Bill Pollock riveted him with a homicidal glare and Quinn extracted his notebook from a breast pocket.

"Was it you or Cooney who killed Gerry Savage?" Pollock began, coming out punching, giving him the chance to put the other man in the dock.

Forde hawked up phlegm, seemed to deliberate on whether or not to swallow it, then swung his scrawny head to expectorate skilfully into the fire. It was clear that he had already acquired considerable practice in this manoeuvre.

"Well?"

There was an edge of menace to the sergeant's voice that boded no good. Brendan Forde looked up at last, flint-eyed and disdainful.

"Who's Cooney?" he said.

Bill Pollock sniffed in demonstrative disbelief.

"You mean you murdered and dismembered Gerry Savage all on your own? That's quite an achievement for a long drink of water like yourself, even with the help of a circular saw. Gerry Savage was a big, heavy man – all muscle too."

Brendan Forde was silent. He glanced at Quinn, as if expecting him to intervene, then looked down at his handcuffs again.

"Of course, I forgot," Pollock continued, a manufactured smile crossing his face. "You had your dear wife to assist you. I dare say it was much like slicing up one of your pigs for her. But how did you kill him? Bullet or knife? Was that you or Monina?"

Forde's head jerked up. His long, thin face lengthened even further. "Monina had no part in this. Leave her out of it."

"So," Pollock persisted, "was it you or Cooney who topped him?"

Brendan Forde seemed to squirm briefly on his chair. The lines in his narrow forehead deepened so that they appeared almost like gashes in the shadowy light of the kitchen.

"There was no Cooney. Just me."

"Really? All by yourself?"

"Yes,"

"And when the forensic boys have done their bit in here, we sure as hell won't find any prints of John Seamus Cooney, ringleader of the Newry bombers, the mad fucker who's spent five years in the Maze for murdering twenty-three innocent people before some halfwit politician let him out thinking we could all live in peace and harmony ever after? Till death us do part. Except that death has already parted us. Us and Gerald Savage."

It was the most Quinn had heard Bill Pollock say in one go. The sergeant sat with his fists clenched on the table. Quinn would not have been surprised to see smoke fuming from his nostrils.

"Savage was a traitorous bastard."

"Really? What had he done? Sold Ireland to the English?"

Following this exchange Brendan Forde became increasingly less communicative, finally refusing to answer any of Sergeant Pollock's questions and lapsing into a surly silence. Quinn chipped in himself then, thinking a little along the lines of good cop–bad cop, but Forde was having none of it. After a good five minutes of one-way communication he gave up. As the policemen exchanged frustrated looks, a flickering log crumbled and fell over in the hearth, sending a small cloud of wood smoke into the room. Brendan Forde lounged in his seat, almost provocatively, a defiant leer on his scraggy face, rocking to and fro on the rear legs of the chair.

The leer changed abruptly to panic when Bill Pollock

decided to get up, suddenly shoving the table forward and catching Forde in an upward tilt so that he crashed over backwards cracking his head like an egg on the sandstone-tiled floor.

"Lose yer balance?" Pollock grunted as he rose to his feet. He paused to look down at Brendan Forde spread-eagled on the tiles. "That's not all yer goin' to lose."

"I think that concludes our interview for the moment," Quinn said and closed his notebook.

TWENTY-FIVE

Gillian Rice regarded the woman sitting on the sofa opposite her with undisguised curiosity. Monina Forde had lapsed into her fifties, the promise of youth long gone, a well-kept woman far from the beginning but not yet near the end. Her brown hair was lightly streaked with grey and bunned up at the back with a plastic clasp. She had the look of an old-fashioned schoolmarm from a TV western: thin, somewhat austere, rigid in her outlook, strictly costumed in her cardigan and plaid woollen skirt. Gillian slid back on the cold plastic glacier of the sofa and wondered where to start and which strategy to employ.

"Ready?" she said to the uniformed policewoman sitting at the other end of the sofa. PC Hughes nodded and placed her notebook dutifully in her lap.

"Mrs Forde," Gillian began and paused. "Can I call you Monina?"

"You can call me whatever the hell you want," Mrs Forde replied.

Gillian saw how her face twisted with venom as she uttered the words. Monina Forde shattered her schoolmarm image with every word she spoke. This was an interview that would require communicative skills of the highest order. Gillian Rice adopted her professional smile, a tight-lipped economy version of the one she had learned from Chief Inspector Hall.

She said, "I don't think that would get us very far."

Mrs Forde sniffled disparagingly. "Depends how far you want to go."

"Well," Gillian said, "how about to the bottom of the butchery that has taken place here, in your home?"

Monina Forde did not respond. She sat with an elbow on the arm of the sofa and turned her sharp, brown eyes towards the door PC Hughes had carefully closed when they entered. Gillian looked round the room. The fading emerald-green wallpaper had lost contact with the walls in several corners. The walls were devoid of framed photographs. The room smelt of thick dusty curtains and dry vinyl floor polish. Gillian decided there was little point in making polite sitting-room conversation.

"Have you any idea where you are?" she said.

Monina Forde seemed to scrutinise the question for a hidden meaning before she replied.

"You mean apart from sitting here in my own home?"

"Yes, apart from that."

"Well, suppose you tell me."

The farmer's wife leaned back in the sofa and seemed to drift almost into a self-induced trance, secure in a defensive mindset of her own making.

"I will," Gillian said, enunciating the words with care and patience. "As I see it, you're up to your neck in blood and shit. You may be here in the living room right now, but in reality you belong out there in the pigsty. That's where you are in reality. You and your husband. Neck-high in blood and shit."

Gillian's voice, calm and modulated at first, had risen sharply as she outlined her view of the Fordes' situation. Monina Forde seemed a little taken aback by the change of tone, a reaction that Gillian noted as she pressed on.

"What about Arthur Williams?" she snapped. "Did he become pig fodder out there too?"

"Arthur Williams?" Mrs Forde said, startled from her self-engendered reverie. "Who's that?"

Gillian stared at her for a few seconds before asking: "You've no idea who that is?"

"No, never heard of him."

"The journalist abducted in Bangor two days ago?"

"I don't follow the news that closely. There's stuff like

that happening every day. You get tired listening to it."

Gillian deliberated on whether it was worthwhile to pursue this line of inquiry and decided against it.

"Okay, let's stick to Cooney."

Mrs Forde moved somewhat restlessly on the sofa as Gillian took a run along the springboard and dived into uncharted waters.

"If you want to have any chance of getting through this without spending the rest of your lives in prison," Gillian said, "you'd better give me some straight answers to my questions. And question number one is: Was it your husband or John Cooney who killed Gerry Savage?"

"Brendan didn't kill anyone."

"So it must've been Cooney. Or you."

"It bloody well wasn't me."

"So it wasn't Brendan and it wasn't you. Then it must've been John Cooney."

"John Cooney? There was no John Cooney here."

"That's what your husband said too. At first. Until he realised that it means it'll be him – or you – that'll take the rap for capital murder. And with a murder as horrific as this one, you'll get life. In fact, with the way things are going, you might never get out again."

"He didn't say that at all."

"So your husband's lying when he says it was Cooney?

"No." Monina Forde's cold, brown eyes narrowed as she recognised the trap. "He didn't say that Cooney was here. I know he didn't. Because Cooney wasn't here."

"That's right," Gillian said patiently. "He didn't admit it at first, but when he realised the full consequences of what has happened here, he owned up. He told us out in the car. He doesn't want you to spend the rest of your life in prison, Monina. That's what he said. He was thinking of you."

"Are you trying to tell me he said Cooney killed Gerry Savage?"

"Yes, but we can't just take his word for it. We need confirmation. That's why I'm asking you. Which one was it who killed Savage? Did you see what happened?"

Mrs Forde removed her elbow from the arm of the sofa and slowly massaged the back of her neck, as if the conflicting ideas in her head had rolled down towards her tongue and missed, taken a backward turn and stiffened instead in a cervical knot of indecision. Bloody hell, it was agony not knowing what to say or how much to say or how to say it. Their whole lives could depend upon it. She glanced from Gillian Rice to the kitchen door and back again, trying to unravel the strands of thought flittering about in her head.

At last she took a deep breath and made up her mind. She'd never liked John Cooney anyway. There was something callous and brutal about the way he looked at you with those pitiless dark eyes. And the way he'd done it out there in the farmyard. It was inhuman. Brendan had been forced to go along with it. And now they had landed in this sorry, bloody mess.

"Okay, he was here," she said at last. "Cooney was here. He came with another man, tall fellah with a beard. They slept in here on the sofas."

Gillian shifted uneasily over the plastic. She was about to probe for more information when Monina Forde resumed. Once she started talking, Gillian thought, it was like pressing a button.

"They came in a car. A Ford – Ford Mondeo, I think. Dark colour, blue or maybe black. Just arrived suddenly, no warning. They went out to the barn, the pigsty, with Brendan. Told me to stay here. I made a pot of tea. When they came back, Cooney told me not to feed the pigs. Wouldn't say why when I asked. Brendan told me to do as he said."

"When was this?" Gillian asked.

"Day before yesterday. Jesus, seems a week ago."

"Did Cooney bring Savage here?"

"Cooney?"

"Yes, John Cooney."

"Gerry Savage came here on his own. Cooney was after him. They'd followed him from Ballyfoil."

"Why did Savage come here?"

"He wanted to borrow our car, to get away. But Cooney caught up with him.

"You said they'd followed him. Who was 'they'?"

"It was the two of them. Cooney and … and the fellah with the beard."

"Wasn't Brendan one of them?"

"No, he was here. He was here with me."

"Really?" Gillian was silent for about ten seconds, just staring at Monina Forde, before she continued. "So it was Cooney and the bearded man who were hunting Savage, who chased him here, over the fields from Ballyfoil?"

"That's it, the pair of them."

"Well, that seems unlikely to me, Mrs Forde. Very unlikely."

Monina Forde looked at the uniformed policewoman taking notes, then back at Sergeant Rice. "Why?" she said.

"Because the bearded fellah was already lying dead in a car in Ballyfoil."

Mrs Forde glanced sideways at PC Hughes, then back at Sergeant Rice.

"I believe," Gillian continued, "it was your husband who was out there with Cooney hunting Gerry Savage across the fields, not some dead man with a beard and a pair of pliers sticking out of his head."

"Pair of pliers? What do you mean?" Her dark brown eyes fluttered round the room as if the tool might be lying there somewhere, a piece of evidence to fluster her even further. "You're trying to mix me up."

"You're mixing yourself up, Monina," Gillian said. "That's what happens when you tell lies."

Mrs Forde swayed almost imperceptibly from side to side on the sofa, as if physically struck by the news of another murder. Gillian watched her trying to compose herself, hoping to find a way out, seeking a satisfactory solution. It was time to give her what she wanted.

"I understand you just want to protect your husband," Gillian said, "but the shitstorm he's already in can hardly get any worse. The best thing you can do to help him is to tell me the truth. That way I might be able to make things easier for him. For both of you."

Monina Forde looked Gillian straight in the eye and was silent. Gillian stared right back and said nothing. Finally the farmer's wife glanced at the kitchen door, then back at Gillian and said: "Cooney had Brendan with him. He didn't have a choice – Brendan I mean. You don't say no to John Cooney."

"So they got here shortly after Gerry Savage?"

"Yes."

"Savage wasn't armed?"

"No."

"Was he injured?"

"He had a wound in the thigh. He was bleeding."

"Gunshot?"

"Don't know. He didn't say. He just wanted to borrow the car and get away. He was in a state."

"And then Cooney and your husband arrived."

"Yes."

"What happened next?"

"They took him outside."

"Both of them?"

"Yes. Brendan didn't want to go but Cooney made him, said he needed his help."

"So he went."

"Yeah. You don't argue with John Cooney." She paused and looked at Gillian with teary eyes. "Brendan was afraid of him. We both were."

"And you stayed in here, in the house?"

"Yes. Brendan told me to." Monina Forde caught her breath and exhaled, making a sound halfway between a sigh and a moan. "He knew what was going to happen."

Gillian bit her lip and said, "What did happen?"

"I went over to the kitchen window to see where they were going. Brendan was leading the way across the yard over to the pigsty. Cooney had Gerry Savage walking in front of him. Gerry half-turned his head, saying something, I dunno what. And suddenly Cooney pulled this long knife, or bayonet, from his trouser leg, grabbed Gerry with an arm round the head and just cut his throat. I couldn't believe it – it happened so fast. It didn't look like it was planned or anything, I mean, to do it just there and then. He seemed to blow a fuse or something. Maybe something Gerry said. It was like he went berserk, half-way across the yard. Then he just stood watching while Gerry lay there on the ground, the blood running out of him, like a burst pipe. He moved a couple of times, y'know, twitched a bit there on the ground. Then he was still."

Mrs Forde herself sat completely still, as if frozen in the memory. Her hands were clasped together in her lap, fastened in the fatal moment. She stared unseeing at a dish on the glass top of the table before her. Gillian recognised the blue-white Myott porcelain with its hand-engraved scene of the hunter coming home. Where had they picked that up? And she thought, John Cooney was the hunter, Gerry Savage was the hunted. He will not be coming home.

"What did Brendan do?" she asked.

"Cooney shouted something at him and he ran into the barn and got some rags to stop the blood spilling out all over the place. They hosed the yard off later. Then Brendan helped him to carry the body into the barn."

"To the circular saw."

Monina Forde simply nodded. The two women looked at each other without saying anything. All at once they heard a dull thud resound from the kitchen followed by a short, ominous silence and then raised voices that reverberated against the door between the two rooms.

"What the hell was that?" Mrs Forde said.

"Sounds like a difference of opinion," Gillian suggested.

Monina Forde began to get up but changed her mind and remained sitting. She fingered the wooden buttons of her cardigan and stared at Gillian as if expecting a further explanation. Gillian held her agitated gaze and leant forward over the cloudy glass table.

"Okay, Monina, let me tell you how this is going to play. As it stands, you and your husband are up shit creek without a paddle. In fact, it's far worse than that. You don't even have a boat. Now, what Sergeant Pollock and Inspector Quinn want above all else is John Cooney. Everything else takes second place. They want John Cooney by the bollocks. Full stop.

"If you can help us find him, you're still going to be up shit creek – I'm not going to lie to you about that – but I'm going to be in a position to give you both a boat and a paddle. We will then see Cooney as the mad-ass murderer who's forced Brendan to help him, thereby making your husband no more than an intimidated and unwilling accomplice. And you become even less, Monina, even less.

"But, if Cooney just disappears without a trace – if we can't get hold of him one way or another – then you and Brendan are all we've got and consequently you become the obvious perpetrators of the vicious capital murder of an outstanding Gaelic football star. You'll go down for that. Believe me, you'll go down all the way."

Monina Forde looked down at the porcelain dish on the table. Gillian followed her gaze. She could see the hunter walking with his dog towards an old timbered pub. The Swan, it said on the sign. A woman was standing outside with a basket, feeding some hens. There was a church spire across the fields in the distance, rising against a white sky. When Gillian looked up again, a strip of weak sunshine had filtered into the room between the window frame and the thick chenille curtain. Monina Forde was staring at her. Her bottom lip was trembling.

"I heard them talking in the kitchen," she said, nervously. "I'd been outside and was in the lobby. They didn't know I'd come in again. Cooney said he had to be going and Brendan asked him a question. I couldn't hear properly what it was, but then Cooney said something about a house. I think he said in Belfast."

"A safe house?"

"He didn't use that word, just said a house."

"Did he say where?"

"Not exactly, but I thought I heard him say Arboyne, something like that."

"Ardoyne? The Ardoyne?"

"Yes, that was maybe it."

"Anything else?"

"No. I closed the front door as if I'd just come in and they changed the subject, talked about how he was going to have to dump the car. Then he left just a couple of minutes later."

"What did you do then?"

"I had to tidy up in the kitchen. Brendan went out to the pigsty."

Gillian nodded at PC Hughes, who closed her notebook.

"Cooney was going to dump the car?"

"That's what he said."

"You were lucky," Gillian said to Mrs Forde.

"Lucky?"

Gillian looked at Monina Forde with a congratulatory smile, as if telling her she had won the National Lottery. "That he didn't decide to dump you too."

TWENTY-SIX

Officers Quinn and Rice drove back to Newry and the Canal Court Hotel in the early afternoon. The rear-entrance parking lot offered a wide choice of parking places, the previous night's wedding guests having crawled off elsewhere to lick their wounds. Sergeant Pollock with his technical and uniformed cohorts had repaired to the police station to accommodate Mr and Mrs Forde in surroundings considerably less congenial than the Canal Court Hotel. Inspector Quinn and Sergeant Rice checked out at reception and hurried to the in-house Granary Bar to get something to eat, drawn by the savoury odours emanating from the Carvery.

Quinn had rung Chief Hall on the drive back down from the Forde farm and Ballyfoil. He would have preferred to have had that conversation without Gillian Rice sitting beside him, but with all that had happened there was simply no way he could continue to put it off. With considerable foreboding and no little remorse he recalled that he had last spoken to CI Hall from the parking area at Daisy Hill Hospital the previous afternoon while his sergeant had gone into the A&E to check on Michael McCann's state of health. He had also promised Gillian after their dinner last night that he would ring Hall about back-up, and he had postponed it in the misguided belief that he had the situation under control. Christ, he of all people should have known what John Cooney was capable of. He wondered if the guilt showed as plainly on his face as it felt in his mind and in his heart.

As he listened to the phone ringing, he was hoping the CI would be tied up in one of his innumerable meetings. No such luck. CI Hall picked up on the first ring. His first reaction was: "I fuckin' well knew this would happen."

Quinn had never heard him use the F-word before. Gillian Rice heard it too. They swapped raised-eyebrow glances. These ocular exchanges were repeated on several occasions during the course of the somewhat unilateral telephone conversation that followed.

As Quinn attempted to give a coherent account of the morning's events, CI Hall's interruptions increased in volume and in length. Quinn knew better than anyone that he should have phoned his superior before they drove out to Ballyfoil rather than after, and the chief inspector wasn't going to let him forget it. Jesus Christ, Hall had even promised him helicopter back-up if necessary! As they pulled into the parking area at the Canal Court, Quinn managed to curtail the bombardment by saying they had just arrived at the hotel and were about to check out. CI Hall's final salvo was: "If Cooney's in some fuckin' so-called safe house here in Belfast, you better get up here double-quick and find him. Report to me here at HQ as soon as you arrive. I want this whole bloody shambles laid to rest. You follow?"

In the late lunch hour the Granary Bar was sparsely populated. Getting sandwiches to take away was an unusual service for the Granary, but not a problem. Arranging the same service with coffee was more complicated.

"You want coffee to go?" said the bright-eyed waitress, her rosy, dimpled cheeks shining in the artificial light.

Quinn seemed unacquainted with the term. "To go? Yes, we want to go out with it."

"Yes, coffee to go," Gillian, more fluent in the modern idiom, hastened to add. "No milk or sugar for me."

"Just milk in mine," Quinn snapped.

"I don't know if we've got Styrofoam cups," the waitress told them. "I'll just go and see." She came back almost immediately, cups in hand. "Problem solved," she said, dimpling as she smiled.

Quinn was extracting his credit card from a well-worn wallet when Gillian's phone jingled its trademark tone. She glanced at the screen, then at Quinn and back at the screen again. Quinn was expecting her to utter the standard, 'I have to take this,' but she just turned on her heel and left the room. When she returned she looked like a woman facing a menstrual cloudburst without a tampon.

"Are you all right?" Quinn asked.

Gillian Rice glared at him and at the credit card still clutched in his hand. Quinn looked back at her, waiting for a response. When it became clear that he was waiting in vain, he said, "We need to get moving."

Whipping out a £20 note, Gillian paid the bill. When Quinn protested, suggesting she keep the receipt to claim on expenses, she merely shrugged her shoulders and walked out to the parking lot. Quinn pocketed the receipt, grabbed the paper carrier bag with food and coffee, and followed her.

As they emerged from the hotel, church bells began ringing somewhere in the vicinity. Quinn remembered the cathedral was close by. He glanced at his wrist watch: two o'clock. The parking area was deserted. A breeze lifted a wrinkled poster across the puddled yard. The day was already fleeing to the west, the light easing its way rapidly out of the sky. Thin shadows were beginning to creep out from the tall, grey-faced buildings that surrounded them.

Thus provisioned with hot meat sandwiches and lidded polystyrene espresso mugs, they hurried across the parking lot, scrambled into the Shogun and set off. Quinn placed the carrier bag on the floor in front of him and glowered out the window at the pale afternoon, drumming his fingers lightly on the dashboard. Best to wait, he reasoned, until they were out on the dual carriageway before opening the food and drink. I'll have to serve her anyway, he realised, cheering up. She won't like that. He determined to let Gillian make the first conversational move and concentrated on the view out the window, his fingers now tapping in allegro tempo.

Until, out of the blue, as they stood still at traffic lights, she suddenly spoke:

"So, do you reckon Arthur Williams ended up in the pigsty with Gerry Savage?"

Quinn terminated his percussion performance on the dashboard and gave this some thought.

"Well, if there's a tuft of hair or a tooth that can still be found there, then maybe he did. But there's another possibility."

"What's that?"

"Williams might still be in Belfast."

"How do you figure that?"

Quinn leant back and bent his head upwards until it touched the head rest. Whether he was seeking inspiration from on high or simply exercising fatigued neck muscles was hard to say.

"Williams was lifted in Bangor," he said slowly, "which is just 10 miles from Belfast with all its IRA hideouts, many of them in the Ardoyne area. I think it's likely they took him there, at least to begin with. Suppose he buckled under to their subtle persuasive techniques and pointed the finger at Gerry Savage in Ballyfoil. That's what could have brought Cooney and co. down here."

"Wouldn't that also mean that Arthur Williams is no longer in the land of the living?"

"Not necessarily," Quinn countered. "They may have decided to keep him to see if the information pans out, in case he'd sent them on a wild-goose chase just to win time – a stay of execution."

Gillian Rice didn't seem to place much credence in that scenario but she remained silent, swearing instead at a pedestrian with an apparent death wish. The Shogun chugged out onto Monaghan Street, took a left at the lights and continued down Merchants Quay along by the canal until Gillian swung right and drove across Sugar Island.

"Quaint name," Quinn observed as they passed the street sign and headed north for Belfast Road.

"Yeah," said Gillian. "Considering this is bandit country."

"Speaking of which, I suspect the local sheriff will be giving Brendan Forde a rough time."

"You think so?"

"After what happened to his son-in-law, Bill Pollock will need to be strapped down to a chair. And there won't be any closed-circuit monitoring of the interview room like there is at the interrogation centre in Belfast."

Gillian gave him a knowing sideward glance.

"I think Brendan Forde has probably earned himself a rough time."

Quinn looked back at her. "You've been having a pretty rough time yourself," he said.

Ever since she'd received that phone call in the Granary Bar, Quinn had been wondering how to broach the subject that was obviously loitering at the back of her short-clipped head. She did not react. At first he thought she hadn't heard or hadn't understood what he was referring to. She stared straight ahead and seemed totally absorbed in her driving. Eventually though, she risked a swift glance in his direction.

"Quinn, you've been married, haven't you?"

"To my cost, Gillian, to my cost."

He attempted to keep a light air, but her posture and the look in her eyes remained thoughtful and serious.

"And you're divorced now?"

"Since three years back."

"A happy divorce?"

"There's no such thing."

"Any kids?"

"No."

"Well, that's something. I mean, in my case too."

"You've no children?"

"No."

"It probably makes it simpler, emotionally anyway. But it's still a bloody ordeal. Don't kid yourself it's going to be anything else."

"Thanks for those few encouraging words."

Her face was so serious he thought it might crack.

"Gillian, I wouldn't want to give you a false picture. You'd be surprised how many people think of divorce as a cure. But it's not, even if there are no children to consider."

"Listen Dr Phil, there's no way I'm going back on this," Gillian said in a quiet voice. "The marriage is over, kaput, finito. Maybe you think we can sort it out with a bit of soft-soap counselling, but it's gone way beyond that."

She said this with such finality that Quinn suspected she had reached the end of a long process of intense deliberation: the end of her marital tether.

He took a deep breath and said, "Well, I'm sorry to hear that. Everything changes, I suppose, and not always for the better. At the start you're both wearing rose-tinted glasses, and you think you see it all, but you're still blind. You want to believe there's something called happiness and you can attain that, you can get there. So you have a wonderful wedding and you go on holiday together and you buy a lovely home and you convince yourself you're happy. But it's all a myth, because happiness doesn't exist."

Gillian concentrated on the road ahead and said nothing.

"Sure," Quinn continued, "you can experience a happy evening, but then you maybe have a bad night and wake up to a depressing morning, and then maybe you have a nice lunch and a pleasant afternoon. Happiness, such as it is, is usually something remembered – a day, a minute, an hour in your past when you think: I was happy then. But there is no set state of mind or being called happiness. It just doesn't exist."

Gillian was somewhat taken aback by Quinn's flow of words. A quick glance told her he'd spoken his piece.

"I thought you were just the strong, silent type, Quinn."

"Yeah, sorry about the pseudo-philosophical babble."

"But you loved each other at the start, didn't you?" she said after a pause. "You saw something special in each other and the feeling was mutual."

"That's probably true," Quinn said. "But I realised afterwards I was just looking at the packaging. I hadn't stopped to read the list of contents."

"She would probably say the same about you."

"Yes, she probably would."

"You sound bitter," she told him. "Do you know that?"

He gave her a wry smile. "I'm working on it," he said.

She slotted the gear lever into top as they gained speed and looked across at him. "You know, Quinn, I think you miss her."

"I don't miss her," he told her. "I miss who I thought she was. They were two completely different people."

As they filtered out onto the A1 and the dual carriageway up to Belfast, Quinn retrieved the sandwiches from the paper bag at his feet and unpacked them, giving one to Gillian. Munching with a voracity that threatened to decapitate several fingers, she told him it was no longer a hot sandwich but still decidedly edible. Christ, she said, I haven't eaten since that fancy meal at the hotel last night. That explains the strange noises your stomach's been making, Quinn told her. Gillian thought of cracking a few ribs with her elbow, but decided against it in the interest of road safety.

They were quiet after that, content just to sit in the dimmed-light ambience of the dashboard as the countryside swept past. Out of the corner of his eye Quinn watched her while pretending to glance out of the window on her side. She possessed a sudden, unpredictable energy, a vitality that drew him to her. She changed gear as if reloading a gun. He thought for a moment about what might await them in Belfast, how the hunt for John Cooney could suddenly escalate into a murderous, bloody battle. Her pert manners and jaunty little walk were all very well, but how would she cope when push came to shove? She had no knowledge of that, no real experience of these people and their mindless brutality. Quinn recalled his interview with CI Hall when he'd been informed that he was being lumbered with a 'driver,' and that she'd been trained by the SAS.

"Weren't you on some sort of intensive training course with the SAS?" he asked as she gathered speed on the dual carriageway.

"So you know about that," she said. "Chief Hall's been shooting his mouth off."

"If you must know, he was selling you in as my driver."

"Gee, that must have been hard."

"Mission imposs."

There was a brief pause before he said, "Anyway, did you have to go to England to do it?"

"It was in Wales actually."

"England, Wales – same dog, different leg action," Quinn said, trying to sound smart.

Gillian snorted. "Try telling a Welshman he lives in England and see how popular you become."

"Okay, point taken. But what about self-defence training? Did they use Krav Maga?"

Gillian realised she was being tested.

"The Israeli self-defence system?" she said. "No, we did

a series of practical Aikido exercises."

"Japanese martial art. That's hard-nosed stuff."

"It was pretty basic. They just taught us how to handle ourselves, how to put an attacker out of action."

"Okay."

Quinn looked thoughtful, staring straight ahead at the traffic coming towards them. "So what do you do if a guy comes at you, say swinging a knife? Or a hammer?"

"A guy?"

"Yeah. A big guy, y'know, 200 pounds, muscle-bound, psycho type."

"Well," Gillian said without hesitation, "you have to derail his train of thought, which is primarily just to batter your brains out. So if it's a guy – any guy – you just kick him in the balls." She looked at him coolly for a moment before adding, "That's where *his* brains are."

"Really?" Quinn said, trying to mask his smile. "And that's true of all men?"

"I have yet to meet the exception. Instant brain damage. That's what puts them out of action."

And she has that hard-diamond glitter in her eyes that makes Quinn, with an inner onslaught of mixed emotions, want to grab her or just shake her or something. Until he recalls a moment out there in the barn, when they had Brendan Forde up against the wall and her face took on another expression, a look that made him think for an instant she was going to demonstrate a snap Aikido kick and inflict some of that instant brain damage there and then. There was no need for that, however. Forde had just stood there, passive and seemingly resigned to his fate – as Quinn suspected Gerry Savage had been a couple of hours earlier.

They drove past Banbridge, Dromore and Hillsborough under a darkening sky, the small country towns retreating, closing ranks against the gathering winter gloom. Gillian

Rice ignored the speed limits with increasing disregard. Quinn said nothing. Their instructions were to report to CI Hall at police headquarters in east Belfast. An appointment had not been specified but for Sergeant Rice ASAP was ASAP. The headlights speared a dual path through the darkness, cleaving a way forward into the December night and RUC Headquarters in Belfast.

Quinn felt himself swept up in her urgency. The life of Arthur Williams was trapped in a fragile hourglass and the sands were running out at breakneck speed. Out of nowhere the words of the Williams boy came to him, the last thing he had said: 'Find my dad, Mr Quinn. Please find him.' And that was what he had promised to do.

If Arthur Williams was in Belfast there was a chance, albeit a slim one, that he was still alive. Quinn thought of Cooney with his cold, black eyes and what he had done to Gerry Savage and Jack Callen and God-knows-who-else in his merciless, murderous way. And he felt the embers of rage flare within him, kindled and fanned by the warm wind of retribution. Soon, he knew, regardless of Dr Benjamin Musgrave, they would burst into flame.

TWENTY-SEVEN

In a blustery west wind the Shogun had just swirled round
the Lisburn roundabout and charged up the slip road onto
the M1 motorway to Belfast when Quinn's phone rang. He
grappled with his seat belt before extracting it. For some
reason he thought it might be Renée Vega. For another
reason, which surprised him, he realised he didn't want to
speak to her. Certainly not now, with Gillian sitting beside
him. Another unwelcome possibility was CI Hall, ringing
up to wonder what the hell was keeping them. With an
inward sigh of relief he saw that it was neither: it was his
solicitor, Joe Stewart.

"Joe, how's it going?"

"Busy, Quinn, busy."

His voice was a trifle tense, eager to get to the point.

"When was it ever anything else?"

Quinn had never met a man with so many irons in the
fire. He was a judicial juggler with the gift of keeping half
a dozen felonious balls in the air at one and the same time.

"Ah, you've got my number all right. Are you here in
town?"

"Almost, Joe, almost."

"Sounds like you're out driving."

The Shogun drew level with a tourist bus that began to
edge into the outside lane and Gillian leant on the horn.

"You're right there. Just passed Lisburn. We'll be in
Belfast in ten, fifteen minutes. What's on your mind, Joe?"

There was a short delay, a loaded pause before Joe
Stewart fired off the reason for his call.

"I've got a client here," he began. "He's in a bit of
trouble."

"Trouble?" Quinn said, unable to hide the resigned tone
of his voice. "What sort of trouble?"

Joe hesitated for an instant. He said, "Have you any idea who Kathleen Farrell is?"

"Kathleen Farrell?" Quinn paused to scan his memory bank. He recalled an old song, Sweet Kathleen Machree, but that was all. "Never heard of her."

"What about George Martin? Heard of him?"

"The fifth Beatle? Are we in the same golf club or something? Kathleen Farrell, George Martin – what is this? Come to the point, Joe."

"All right, all right. The thing is, Quinn, this George Martin may have information that could help you in the Arthur Williams case. Knowing your previous involvement with Williams, I suspect you're working on that… "

Quinn saw no reason not to enlighten him.

"You know more than is good for you, Joe. And not for the first time. Who is this George Martin?"

"Martin's an estate agent, has his own company, owns a bit of property here and there around the town. There've been rumours he's been involved with loyalist paramilitaries, the UVF maybe, and made some dodgy business moves with their backing. A lot of these cowboys are moving into organised crime, as you know, now that the peace process is well under way. Martin says himself that he's had a bit of a bad run lately. Money problems. That's the way he puts it."

Quinn sighed. "Is he there with you now?"

"He's in the next room."

Quinn wondered how thin-walled the room was before he asked: "So what sort of trouble is he in?"

"Apparently he's been trying to bribe a senior civil servant to give him planning permission for a new shopping centre in east Belfast."

"East Belfast?"

"Yes, out at Dundonald."

"Well, if he's down on his luck, as you say, how's he going to build a shopping centre? Where's the capital coming from?"

"He has certain connections in the building trade. Some say UVF connections."

"Whatever that means."

"It can mean quite a lot, Quinn, the way things work today."

Quinn lurched against the window as Gillian swerved out to overtake a large commercial van that had suddenly braked and pulled onto the hard shoulder.

"Silly bugger," she said, addressing the rear-view mirror.

"And this civil servant is accusing Martin of bribery?" Quinn said, picking up the thread.

"Yeah," said Joe Stewart, sounding just a little world-weary, "it's some over-conscientious PO in the hierarchy who doesn't realise that's how you do business in Belfast these days."

"Pardon my ignorance, but what's a PO?"

"A principal officer – your high-ranking, top-dog pen-pusher in the civil service."

"So you're saying your client has been wiping his arse with planning permission and the paper broke. Has the PO got proof?"

"Well, there's the rub. Because of previous hints dropped by Martin, he'd suspected what was coming and secretly recorded the interview when Martin offered the bribe."

Quinn rubbed his eyes briefly as the picture began to take shape.

"Joe, I get worried when you start quoting Shakespeare. And I'm not sure how a recording will stand up as evidence. There can be a problem with voice identification. Anyway, I assume this Martin character wants us to make the bribery charge go away?"

"He's looking for a bit of mutual back-scratching, yes."

"So where are we itching? What exactly is he selling?"

Joe Stewart made a point of clearing his throat before he spoke.

"He claims he may have vital information about the whereabouts of a certain John Cooney, you know, the Newry bomber."

Quinn froze in his seat. He glanced at Gillian but she was fully focussed on the motorway ahead.

"Did I hear you right, Joe? This fellah says he knows where John Cooney is?"

Gillian looked at him now with high, widescreen eyes.

"Well, I'm not sure I'd go as far as that," Stewart said, backtracking with courtroom aplomb. "He says he's got information that can at least point you in the right direction. He's been pretty vague about the details."

"So, if we can make the bribery charge go away," Quinn summarised, "he might be able to give us the location of John Cooney, which might in turn shed light on the disappearance of Arthur Williams – maybe lead us to him."

"Yes," Joe said and coughed. "That's more or less the shape of things."

Quinn narrowed his eyes as if searching his memory for something he had missed. He was struck by the highly unlikely likelihood that his solicitor should contact him at this very moment with information that could help them run John Cooney to ground, that might well provide an ultimate solution to the whole case. The utter serendipity of what was happening made him distinctly uneasy.

"And who's this Farrell woman? Where does she fit into all this?"

"Quinn, I was maybe a bit hasty in mentioning her," Joe said, apologetically. "The best thing is if you speak to Martin yourself."

"And he's there with you now?"

"Yes, like I said, he's waiting in the next room."

"Joe, this is important. Can you bring him to Police Headquarters on the Knock Road?"

The pause that followed would have been justified if Quinn had made a suggestion involving an unnatural sexual act, which was possibly how Joe Stewart interpreted it. "Aw, come on, Quinn. I have another meeting at four. Can't you come here? Or do it tomorrow?"

"For Christ's sake, Joe, this isn't some pissing-in-public indecency charge – a man's life may depend on it." Quinn's voice rose as he sensed the burgeoning urgency of the situation. "What the hell are you thinking?"

"Okay, okay. Keep your hair on."

"Joe, this information could be vital."

The thought of finally catching up with John Cooney and possibly rescuing Arthur Williams galvanised Quinn, charging through him like a massive electric current.

"And, if we're going to give Martin some leeway on the bribery charge," he said, dangling the obvious carrot, "I'll have to clear it first, right here with the chief. There's no other option – you need to come to HQ."

"All right, Quinn, all right. We'll be there in twenty minutes." There was a sharp intake of breath on the line before he added, "Make that half an hour."

He rang off.

"Is this the breakthrough we've been waiting for?" Gillian Rice said as she swung the Shogun onto the slip road to Stockman's Lane and the A55 ring road to police headquarters in south Belfast. "Someone who claims to actually know where Murphy might be holed up?"

"I smell a rat," Quinn said. "We've just lost track of Cooney in Ballyfoil and now, out of the blue, my solicitor rings me and says he has a client who knows where to find him. I don't like it."

Gillian shook her head. "No, you don't like it, but you love it."

"Damn right."

"What about CI Hall?"

"We'll be there in 10 minutes. We'll tell him then."

"We? Rather you than me."

"I don't like it," Quinn said again. "Too good to be true."

"I know," Gillian said. "Or maybe it's serendipity."

Quinn looked at her with eyebrows raised. "If I knew what that meant I'd probably agree with you."

They continued along the A55, skirting the gently sloping hills of Castlereagh, while Quinn filled in the details of Joe Stewart's phone call. Gillian Rice listened impassively as she slalomed her way through the mid-afternoon traffic like a Norwegian skier on speed.

TWENTY-EIGHT

Inspector Quinn and Sergeant Rice walked briskly down
the corridor with its slate-grey tiles and high, smoked-glass
windows. As they entered the covered walkway leading to
the annex, Quinn sensed the day dwindling around them,
the newly planted shrubs outside blurring in shadow, the
protective fence fading in the gathering darkness and the
intense yellow glaze of the streetlamps signalling the busy
road beyond. Looking up he could discern urgent, murky
clouds scuttling by in a low, windblown sky.

They continued to the far end of the annex, stopped and
glanced at each other pointedly before Quinn rapped twice
on the door. Inside the room Chief Inspector Hall's muffled
baritone drone was interrupted with a sharp 'Come in!' and
they entered to find him turning from the square casement
window where he had been standing with a mobile pressed
to his ear. Abruptly he switched the phone from one ear to
the other.

"What the fuck were you doing in the Ardoyne
anyway?"

He was silent for several seconds while static noises
emanated from the phone like the crackling of dry, waxed
paper. A muted voice attempted a response until Hall
interrupted: "I've heard all this before. Listen, it's over
now. Sort it out double quick and get the hell out of there.
No more bloodshed, you hear?"

CI Hall buttoned an end to the call and dumped the
mobile on the brown leather mousepad on his desk.

"Bloody Specials," he growled and looked up at them.

Gillian observed that he was clad in the same clothes as
the day before: black worsted trousers with a well-honed
crease, short-sleeved white shirt complete with black
epaulettes and black tie. Of his professional smile there

was no trace. Like yesterday, the central heating was on full blast and the room felt airless and muggy with the dusty smell of damp heat. Gillian was reminded of a long-ago visit to Scandinavia and a Finnish sauna.

"Now, what the hell have you two been playing at down there?" he said. "Are we really no closer to finding Arthur Williams?"

"Well," Quinn began, "we …"

But Chief Hall had not finished his hardline preamble.

"So far, all this case has produced is the decapitated body of the local publican in Ballyfoil."

Abruptly, he flung both hands in the air and seemed to lose all restraint.

"What the fuck is going on?" he snarled, swivelling his goldfish eyes between them before drilling them expressly at Quinn.

The inspector looked over at Sergeant Rice as if hoping she would furnish him with an acceptable answer, with any answer, but she was having none of it. Hall sat down suddenly in the leather-backed chair behind his desk and glared at them. Quinn and Rice remained standing, two sinners before an angry god.

"Well," Quinn ventured at last, "we've pretty much established that it was the local publican, Gerry Savage, who provided the information to Arthur Williams that resulted in the arrest and conviction of the Newry bombers five years ago."

"Are you saying that Arthur Williams revealed the identity of his informant, that he disclosed his source?"

"That's open to debate."

"This isn't a fuckin' debating society, Quinn." Chief Hall fixed him with his goldfish glare. "Did Williams disclose his informant's name or not?"

"It's possible. We simply don't know. But it's also possible that McCann's former girlfriend, Mary Devlin, got wind of what was going on. They were an item leading up to the bombing."

The chief inspector seemed to perk up at this news. "Pillow talk?"

"Yeah, maybe," Quinn said. "It probably wouldn't have been too difficult for her to work out later who was responsible. And McCann had five years in which to wonder if he had maybe said too much to Devlin when they were together. That's what brought him back to Ballyfoil."

"But what about Savage?" Chief Hall executed a drum-roll of impatience with his fingers on the desk.

"It seems likely that Mary Devlin could have mentioned her suspicions to Gerry Savage at some point soon after the bombing," Quinn said. "Savage saw his chance, contacted Arthur Williams and – when it turned out the suspicions were well founded – cashed in on the reward money."

"He had put out the story that some rich uncle in the States had left him an inheritance," Gillian said, "but that seems to have just been a scam."

"Then where does this leave Arthur Williams?" the chief inspector snorted. "Pushing up the shamrocks in some godforsaken bog?"

"Not necessarily," Quinn balked. "We're still hoping for a positive outcome."

CI Hall sighed, his piscine eyes rolling skywards in search of guidance.

"And where does John Cooney come into all this?"

"Well, as I said on the phone yesterday, he turned up out of the blue at Savages' pub in Ballyfoil," Quinn told him.

"He was already there with another fellah when we arrived," Gillian added.

"I know, I know." CI Hall nodded his broad, turnip-like head impatiently and raked a hand of dumpy fingers through a stubbled field of hair. "The question is whether Cooney was already tipped off about Ballyfoil and Savage as the possible informer, or whether he was there hoping that McCann had the answer to that."

"Well," Quinn said, "we still don't know whether or not Arthur Williams actually knew his informant by name – it's possible that he could only tell Cooney that the leak came from Ballyfoil. Our only hope now is that Cooney went to Ballyfoil to check it out and that Williams hasn't been liquidated yet."

"You really think that's a possibility – that Cooney's still holding Williams captive here in Belfast?"

Quinn said, "It's a fond hope, but it's the only one we've got."

Chief Hall scratched his head. "And how the hell do we find out where Cooney's hiding?"

Quinn looked over at Gillian Rice. She shrugged her shoulders with what-the-hell nonchalance. He turned back to CI Hall.

"We've got a possible lead, someone who thinks he might know how to locate him."

The chief inspector raised his spiny eyebrows. "Really?"

"Yes. My solicitor is bringing him here as we speak."

"Your solicitor? You don't mean Joseph Stewart, do you?"

"Yes, Joe Stewart," Quinn said hesitantly, well aware of the chief's view of certain elements in the legal profession.

"Jesus, Quinn, that shyster lawyer is up to all the tricks of the trade. We've talked about him before. He's not to be trusted. He uses the law like some cheap bartering tool. The man is never happy unless he's wheeling and dealing and …"

"Some would say that goes with the territory," Quinn said.

"Now just hold on there." The chief inspector paused as

it struck him that there would be an inevitable cost to be levied for the information on offer. "What is it he's asking in return for the possible whereabouts of John Cooney? Because I'm bloody sure he's not doing this out of the goodness of his heart. Right?"

Quinn hesitated again before replying. Gillian directed her gaze at the round mousepad on the chief inspector's desk, wondering if it was standard police issue.

"That we take a lenient view of a bribery charge in connection with an application for planning permission."

"How lenient?"

Quinn shifted uncomfortably on his feet. "Very lenient."

"Oh for Christ's sake!"

As CI Hall threw his pale, fluffy-haired arms up in exasperation, the mobile lying on his mousepad began to ring. He snatched it up and hissed, "Yes?"

The one-sided conversation that ensued had Quinn and Gillian Rice exchanging bewildered glances during the minute that followed.

"Yes, I've just been speaking to them.

"Yes, I know they've been disbanded.

"This was to have been a final raid.

"There were four of them.

"Yes, Ronnie, I'm aware of the political implications.

"Well, we've just got a lead in the Arthur Williams case.

"So the Ardoyne takes precedence?

"Right, I'll get down there straight away."

A pained expression on his face, Chief Hall replaced the phone on the desk and squirmed briefly in his chair as if suppressing a bilious attack.

Finally, turning to officers Quinn and Rice, he barked: "I have to deal with this. Quinn, get Cooney. Use whatever means you think necessary. Give Stewart what he wants.

Absolutely nothing in writing, nothing in writing! You follow? We can fix it later."

And, fired with near desperation, he rose and ushered them out of the room and into the corridor, closing the door with a jolt that echoed down the corridor.

"Jesus," Gillian breathed, "what was all that?"

"Politics." Quinn said. "The art of the impossible in this country."

"And Ronnie? Is that who I think it is?"

"Well, I don't think it's Ronald Reagan."

They walked to the end of the annex and out into the covered walkway.

"If I'm not mistaken you got *carte blanche* there," Sergeant Rice said.

"Gillian, you're showing off your French again." Quinn replied. "Where the hell has Joe Stewart got to?"

They found him at the desk in the outer office area. The receptionist was informing him firmly that CI Hall could not be disturbed – not under any circumstance. Standing slightly behind him was a tall, middle-aged man in a dark business suit. As they approached, Quinn took note of his gently burgeoning paunch, partly veiled by the buttoned jacket. His neatly combed black hair looked dyed at the sides to mask the senescent hint of greying temples. Up close he reminded Quinn of one of those improbably handsome doctors in an American hospital series he had once seen on television. Was it Dr. Kildare? Ben Casey?

"Where have you been hiding?" Joe said, always first to the verbal punch.

When Quinn merely nodded, Joe introduced George Martin who shook hands with both of them, reserving a strained smile for Sergeant Rice.

"We can't talk here," Joe said.

"There's an interview room along the corridor that may be free," Quinn told them. It was. Seated on the black vinyl upholstery of chromed metal chairs, they crouched over an oblong plastic-topped table and looked at one another. There was a faint smell of stale coffee in the room but no sign of an espresso dispenser.

"So, what is this information that Mr Martin has to offer?" Quinn began.

"First," Joe Stewart said, almost ruefully, "I need an assurance from you that this bribery charge against my client will be dropped. Is that forthcoming?"

George Martin leant back in his chair, lit a cigarette and slipped the lighter back in his pocket. No one spoke.

"An assurance?" he said. "That's not enough. I want something in writing."

He turned his sideways gaze from Joe Stewart to the policeman sitting opposite.

"A written document is out of the question," Quinn told him. "What we can do is our uttermost to significantly reduce the charge and, if there is a successful outcome to our case, at best, make it go away. And we're going to be really motivated to make that happen if you can disclose the present whereabouts of John Cooney."

"So all I can get is your … word," Martin said. He made the final word sound interchangeable with turd.

"That's right," Quinn said, "provided you can deliver the goods."

The pause that followed was charged with sudden tension, Martin and Quinn staring at each other without saying anything.

"The inspector's word is good enough for me," Joe Stewart interceded, "even if it goes against the grain as a solicitor not to have everything in writing. But I've known Inspector Quinn long enough to be confident that we can depend on his full cooperation on your behalf."

Joe's so full of shit, Quinn thought admiringly, he'll say anything to swing a deal. And it's usually the right thing.

George Martin deliberated on the solicitor's declaration of trust for several seconds before he nodded.

"All right," he said and smiled. Quinn noticed how his left eye blinked when he smiled, as if he was sharing some special secret with you that only he could divulge.

"So," Gillian Rice said, looking round at all of them as if she had just arrived at a crime scene, "where is John Cooney?"

"I don't claim to know exactly where he is," Martin said, flicking back a long lock of jet-black hair that had slipped down over his forehead. "But the information I have may well lead you to him."

"Why don't we cut the bullshit and you just tell us exactly what it is you know?" Quinn said, his patience and blood glucose running low.

George Martin slid back in his chair and folded his hands together on the table. "Well, just over a month ago I arranged a house rental over the phone for someone in the name of Kathleen Farrell."

"Kathleen Farrell?"

"Yes. Ring a bell?"

"Not even a tinkle."

Quinn glanced at Gillian who shook her head.

"She's John Cooney's sister," Martin told them. "Younger sister."

Both Quinn and Gillian Rice slid forward on the vinyl seats of their chairs. "Now you're talking," Quinn said. "Did you meet her?"

"No, just phone contact. I have an agent in Donaghadee, Dan Crawford, a local man. He met her and handed over the keys. She produced ID that confirmed who she was – Kathleen Farrell."

Quinn struggled visibly to curb his incredulity. "Donaghadee? She rented a house in Donaghadee?"

"That's right." Martin confirmed, acting as if it was

nothing out of the ordinary, just another commonplace property transaction.

"Supposing, just supposing that this is Cooney's safe house, why would he choose a small seaside town in the County Down?" Quinn wanted to know.

"Well, judging by your reaction, it's obviously the last place you'd go looking for him," Gillian pointed out after a brief pause. "It's also less than 20 miles to Belfast. Short distance to travel if and when the need arises."

"But it's a Protestant bastion," Quinn said. "Over 95 percent of the people there must be Prods."

Gillian spread her palms on the table and shrugged her shoulders. "What better place to hide than in the midst of the enemy?"

"She's got a point," Joe Stewart chipped in. "It's just about the last place you'd expect him to go. And in the middle of winter too. In many ways it's a smart choice."

Quinn stared intently at the estate agent. "Have we got a plan, a drawing of the house?"

"It's a substantial residence, a pre-war building on New Road, set back in its own grounds," George Martin said, delivering his customary sales pitch. "Number 59. I think I've got the plans at the office – the owner was considering selling at first, but then decided on a rental."

"We haven't got time for that," Quinn decided. "I'll try to get a couple of Specials to come with us."

"Specials?" Gillian queried.

Quinn stared at her, irritation tightening his forehead like a failed facelift.

"All right," he muttered, "former Specials. Come on, let's go. The sooner we get down there, the greater the chance of finding Arthur Williams alive."

"If he is still alive," Gillian said.

"We've got to believe that," Quinn said grimly, pushing back from the table.

"Hard to imagine John Cooney just strolling along the seaside promenade in Donaghadee," Joe Stewart remarked.

"Strolling?" said Quinn as he made for the door. "More like dead man walking."

TWENTY-NINE

Sergeant Gillian Rice had a determined Indy 500 look on her otherwise pixie face as she manoeuvred the Shogun out of police HQ and into the easy-going Sunday traffic on the A55. Illuminated by the late-afternoon streetlamps, exhaust fumes surged up between the vehicles in sudden flurries as the traffic edged forward towards the lights. In the growing darkness the road gleamed wet and shining under headlamps beaming homeward from the Christmas-in-the-City events in Belfast. Finally reaching the junction, Gillian filtered off to the right and onto the A20 to Newtownards and Donaghadee.

In the dense traffic they crawled past the Stormont Estate, the white Portland stone of the Parliament Buildings barely discernible at the end of the mile-long avenue of approach. Quinn watched as his driver became increasingly agitated by the hold-ups, frustrated by the lack of pace, until – passing the Ulster Hospital – he felt obliged to tell her to simmer down.

"For God's sake, Gillian, we don't want to end up in there."

As they drove through Dundonald on the outskirts of the city, Quinn recalled George Martin's shopping centre plans and his possible ties with the UVF. They picked up speed as the road widened to a dual carriageway on the long, gradual climb past the industrial estate and up into the farmland countryside that led on to Newtownards. The traffic thinned as Belfast retreated behind them and Quinn sat gazing ahead as the headlights pierced the blackness, illuminating the shiny wetness of the road, beaming a way forward through the December night.

"How many Specials did you get hold of?" Gillian wanted to know.

"Three of them are going to follow us from the Ardoyne."

"What's been happening there?"

"Shooting incident. One man down and several injured. They're coming as soon as they've sorted it out."

"But haven't the D-Specials been disbanded?"

"Strictly speaking, they've never existed – so there's nothing to disband."

"Jesus wept," Gillian muttered. "Ireland my country."

Quinn turned sideways to look at her. He didn't speak. He'd heard the three-word coronach before. There was nothing more to say. It said it all.

They reached a roundabout coming into Newtownards and followed the A20 round the outer limits of the town before veering onto the A48, the final stretch of road to Donaghadee. Before long they were approaching the Six-Road Ends. Quinn recalled the notorious junction of six rural roads from his youth, when he had ended up in a ditch after approaching too fast on a borrowed motorbike and failing to negotiate the turn-off. Now, as they neared the crossroads at speed, he felt himself tense up with apprehension.

"Keep your knickers on, Gillian," he urged. "Take it easy, slow down."

"Watch your language, Quinn," Gillian said, as she changed down and swung smoothly round the bend and onto the last stretch of the A48, "or I'll have you up for sexual harassment."

Five minutes later, just before they reached the Maxol filling station on the edge of Donaghadee, Gillian turned left onto New Road. A pavement with widely spaced streetlamps stretched down the left-hand side of the road towards the coast and the Irish Sea; a grass verge fringed the right-hand side. Though not a tree-lined avenue it gave the impression of one, bordered on both sides by high privet hedges and tall, denuded trees belonging to the front gardens of its large and lofty houses. Gillian drove a short distance along the road and parked beside the pavement.

The road was deserted. They got out of the Shogun and discovered almost immediately that the entrance to number 59 was partly illuminated by a streetlamp a short distance away on the same side of the road. The long, gravelled driveway resembled a country lane. It was bounded by bushes and swaying trees and curved as it approached the house, which was just as George Martin had described it: an elegant pre-war building set well back from the road. From the pavement, with moonlight from a gap in the drifting clouds, they could make out part of the house showing a wide bay window under its own pitched roof. The rest was hidden behind the trees and dense shrubbery. The house seemed to be in complete darkness. New Road itself was utterly silent, the streetlamps like lone sentinels standing in a line all the way down to the sea.

"If Murphy's not here at the moment and comes back, he may recognise the Shogun," Quinn said quietly. "Can you move it to the petrol station on the main road?"

Gillian gave the question some thought before she answered. "All right. What are you going to do?"

Quinn drew his right foot backwards on the gravel and looked up towards the house. It was as if he were about to take a penalty kick and the house was the goal.

"I'll just take a walk round the property," he said. "See if anyone's at home."

"Don't you think we should do that together?"

"The Shogun has to be moved," he said. "I won't be long. Just a quick reccy."

"You think Williams is in there?"

"It's a possibility."

"Jesus, Quinn, you want so much to believe he's still alive."

"Yes, I suppose I do." He looked at her with his steadfast eyes and nodded.

"Y'know, Quinn," she said with a defiant smile, "you're so determined to find Arthur Williams, but in some weird way I get the feeling you're also looking for yourself."

"Aren't we all, Gillian? Aren't we all?"

Gillian eyed him with misgiving. His infuriating self-sufficiency was a constant threat. "You'd better give me that contact number for the Specials," she said. "Just in case."

Quinn took her phone in his right hand, compared with his own in his left hand and thumbed in the number.

"His name's Tom Madigan," he said, returning her mobile. "He's a fellah you can depend on."

"Just like you then," Gillian said.

But he was already moving away, delving into the bushes, seeking a path through the unfettered vegetation, pursuing a wide arc towards the rear of the house, ever mindful of eventual tripwires as he trod through the undergrowth. Gillian turned back to the road and walked quickly along the pavement to the Shogun. She flung open the door and got in.

As he neared the house Quinn slowed down, placing his feet with care to manoeuvre his way through the thickets and underbrush. Until, finally arriving at a gap in the shrubbery, he saw the house in its entirety just twenty yards distant. He stood shielded by the waxy greenery of an outspread laurel bush, examining every aspect of the building before him. Moonlight illumined its pale, plaster façade; within there was only darkness.

Quinn scanned the walls, the gutters and the roof for security cameras or the tiny giveaway blink of a red lamp. Nothing. He felt oppressed by the thought of Arthur Williams, unprotected and defenceless, in the clutches of a merciless psychopath like John Cooney. The stress made him tense and frustrated. He looked up again at the building in darkness, imagining him in there, possibly just a few yards away, incarcerated somewhere in the house.

He thought of the SAS motto. What the hell, he muttered. He stepped out from the laurel and walked as if on eggs across the loose gravel and round a buttressed corner of the house to the entrance: a massive, panelled, rust-red door under a vaulted window with small leaded panes. No light shone in the hall. No light shone anywhere. He took a few tentative steps to the side to get a better view. A garage came into view. It stood apart. It had the same plaster façade and a saddle roof with eaves. As he approached, Quinn noticed a metal extension ladder hanging under the eaves.

He looked back at the side of the house and caught sight of a sash window upstairs with glazed panes. Treading closer over the gravel, he saw that the lower sash was slightly ajar. In a matter of seconds he had unhung the ladder from its wall brackets, extended and positioned it against the side of the house.

Two minutes later he was crouching on the linoleum floor of a bathroom that smelt faintly of mould and damp. Feeling his way around he brushed against a toilet bag balanced on the porcelain edge of the wash-hand basin. He snatched at it but it fell to the floor. The dull thud seemed to reverberate throughout the house. He froze, clenched his teeth and listened. He counted slowly to twenty. There was no other sound.

Holding his breath he squatted beside the toilet bag and checked its contents. He felt the bushy hair of a shaving brush and the T-shape of a plastic razor. His eyes grew accustomed to the gloom and he began to perceive the layout of the small room. The wash basin was beside a door in the wall opposite the window. A small acrylic bathtub and a toilet occupied the side walls. He took a step to the door and softly turned the handle.

Treading out and onto a runner carpet he stood rigid in the corridor and listened again. The house breathed reverently with the stillness of a church. Ash-grey light strained through a window at the end of the corridor. He scanned the walls and ceiling for a red-light sensor, but saw none. He thought about Cooney. If he had come here, he would have arrived sometime in the morning; after last night's activities he would be close to exhausted; he would want to rest; he might still be here, sleeping. He drew the Walther PP from his jacket pocket and released the safety catch.

Quinn moved along the corridor to the door nearest the bathroom. The door stood slightly open, as if to let the air in from the landing. He listened intently and pushed it. The room contained little more than a bed, a wooden chair and a freestanding, old-fashioned, mahogany wardrobe. The bed, near the window, had been slept in. Blankets and sheets lay in a rumpled pile to one side. A white shirt lay draped like a shroud over the back of the chair. Quinn opened the wardrobe. It was empty. Half a dozen metal coat hangers dangled in the empty middle space. The cloying, bleach-like smell of mothballs hung in the air. He pushed the door to and left the room. Moving methodically he checked the other upstairs rooms. They were sparsely furnished and empty.

He had padded half-way down the stairs when he heard it. Somewhere below he sensed a movement. Something had stirred. He stood ossified, one foot on the stair, the other in the air. Cautiously, gradually he placed his airborne foot on the wooden stair. It creaked. Step by step, in slow motion, he continued down the stairs.

At the bottom of the staircase he found himself facing the hall. Moonlight sifted in through the small leaded panes of glass above the front door. He veered to his left on the hardwood floor and approached the sitting room. The door was wide open. He stood on the threshold, Walther in hand, and looked round the room: a sofa, a coffee table, two armchairs, a mirrored sideboard and what seemed to be an oval dining table with attendant chairs beside a wide bay window. Nothing else. The pieces of furniture stood like varnished tombstones, polished and cold, obsolete memorials to people who once had lived there.

He heard it again, a crisp metallic sound from deeper in the house. He moved towards the door further down the inner hall. It was slightly ajar. His heart was thumping fiercely, a muffled alarm bell clanging in his breast. He raised the Walther before him and nudged the door. It swung noiselessly open into the kitchen, the moonlight from a window revealing an oblong, Formica-topped table, high-backed chairs, various wall cabinets, a Belfast sink, a cooktop stove and a dark corner cupboard – at the base of which a large Siberian cat slurped at a metal dish. It turned briefly to view the intruder before returning unperturbed to its meal.

Quinn felt the breath go out of him. He lowered the Walther, walked to the window and looked out. In the moonlight the house cast a long shadow out over the lawn.

The grass in places seemed to sheen with silky gossamer webs. The tips of a line of poplars at the end of the lawn bent lightly in the wind. The cat nuzzled the metal dish, ignoring him.

He left the kitchen and went rapidly through the rest of the house. It was deserted. There was no cellar. No trace of Arthur Williams. The house was empty. He had gone to the front door in the hall when he heard light footsteps outside crossing the gravel. Suddenly they stopped. With the Walther still in his hand, he reached up to the antiquated lock and twisted the brass knob. As he eased the door towards him, Gillian Rice appeared before him, feet spread wide apart, her own Walther raised and pointing at his chest.

"Bloody hell, Quinn! What are you playing at?"

"Open window. Too good a chance to miss," he said. Then, to distract her, "He's been here and gone."

Quinn sidled out, closed the door with a muted clunk and stepped onto the gravel. "Looks like he's had a nap," he continued. "Chances are he feels so safe here he's gone out for something to eat. I mean, who the hell's going to come looking for him in Donaghadee?"

All her qualms confirmed, Gillian wanted to bawl him out, to read him the unexpurgated version of the Gillian Rice riot act, to tell him what a stupid asshole he was to have gone in on his own, completely shutting her out, jeopardising the whole operation. Anger made her features stretch tight as piano wire. Somehow, exercising supreme self-control, she contented herself with a scowl.

"We are," she said. "So, where could he have gone?"

Quinn gave the question no more than a moment's thought.

"Grace Neill's is just down Moat Street, not far. It's not the only place in town, but it's the best."

"You seem to know your way around Donaghadee."

"We came here every summer when I was a boy," Quinn said.

Gillian thought he looked a trifle embarrassed with this disclosure, as if revealing a memory of his boyhood somehow demeaned him.

"Grace Neill's was here then?"

"It's been here since the 17th century."

"So you're about the same age."

"Give or take a century."

"Let's check it out then."

She set off with her easy lilting gait, her short-cut blond

head bobbing slightly with each step. Quinn pocketed the Walther and caught up with her. They saw no one on New Road or at the filling station. A single-decker bus swept by, heading west on the High Bangor Road. A black Porsche Carrera was glued to its tail, itching to get past.

They climbed into the Shogun and drove into town, down Moat Street, following the one-way system to the seafront until Gillian found a parking space in New Street, a short, wide thoroughfare linking High Street with the Parade and the harbour.

Quinn was struck by the fortuity of the name, but did not mention it. With recent events in mind, he phoned Madigan and updated him on their whereabouts.

They walked along New Street and crossed Donaghadee High Street to Grace Neill's Bar, a black-and-white, pebble-dashed building with mullioned period windows, sandwiched between two slightly larger buildings. By the entrance stood a thin, pinched-looking man in baggy clothes and a knitted bobble hat, holding out a Styrofoam cup in both hands.

"Is it just a bar?" Gillian asked.

"It's a pub and restaurant," Quinn said. "The bar's just a cubby under the stairs. There are a couple of snugs at the front and if he's here I'd guess he's likely sitting in one of them. But we'll be pretty exposed if we go in through the front door. The restaurant's at the back and there's a side entrance. We can slip in there fairly unnoticed and get our bearings."

Gillian nodded agreement and they walked through a passageway in the adjoining building that gave access to a half-filled parking lot beside the restaurant. Quinn walked swiftly past the parked cars with Gillian close behind him. At the restaurant entrance he touched his jacket pocket for hard-metal reassurance, opened the door and walked in.

The lobby had a couple of toilets on the right, an artificial Christmas tree with blinking lights directly opposite and, further in on the left, the entrance to the restaurant area. Quinn wheeled round abruptly as a toilet door opened and an elderly man came out. He gave Quinn an affable, surprised look, as if apologising for having startled him, and exited to the parking lot.

The inner door to the restaurant was partly open. Quinn prodded it with his elbow and stepped in. Frosted green-leafed garlands with red berries decorated the walls and hung from a crown-shaped metal chandelier in the centre of the ceiling. The oily aroma of frying onions had somehow percolated from the kitchen. Moving forward a couple of steps he stood still and scrutinised the people in the room.

There were a dozen rustic, walnut-brown tables and two of them were taken: an elderly couple at one table and two middle-aged women at another. It's early yet, he said to himself. He recognised no one sitting there. He was about to move further in, towards the pub area at the front, when he felt Gillian's hand on his arm. As he turned to her, he saw the Walther PPK gripped firmly in her other hand pointing into an alcove to the left of the doorway where they had just entered.

Sitting at a table in the alcove was a dark-haired woman in a blue denim jacket and grey blouse. Beside her, watching them with bitter, coal-black eyes, sat John Cooney.

THIRTY

Quinn and John Cooney stared at each other in bemused silence, the tension between them an electric storm about to break. Cooney was slouched in a thick, navy blue donkey jacket which he hadn't bothered to take off. Quinn almost expected him, in view of what he had done, to avoid eye contact. But his look was direct; his look was one of deadly defiance, eyes seething virulent animosity, a pair of black nails driven into a grey skull.

Quinn's gaze strayed to the table, taking note of the serrated steak knives and forks sprawled across empty white plates scored with gravy stains, and the pint glass in front of Cooney that contained no more than a final mouthful of the black stuff.

They sat there at the table, without design or distinction, at first sight commonplace, wondering – in the accidence of time – what was going to happen next. The woman, Quinn saw, bore a strong sibling resemblance to the man beside her. He turned back to Cooney and met his eyes, dark holes in the optic hollows of his head – at once brutal, bottomless, beyond redemption. In the background Quinn could hear Perry Como announcing Santa Claus is coming to Town. The irony of the title was not lost on him.

"Flynn, isn't it?" Cooney said, his voice soft and husky.
"Quinn."

Cooney slumped deeper into the hardwood dining chair, as if deriving comfort from its solidity, reaching under the table to scratch his thigh.

"Just keep your hands on the table," Gillian told him, raising the Walther. Cooney placed both hands alongside the gravy-streaked plate in an act of mock obeisance. Then, abruptly, he placed his elbows on the table, hands raised and fingertips touching to form an outline like some satanic church steeple behind which he stared at Quinn.

"I mind you from the trial," he said to Quinn. "Never forget a face."

"I guess we're two of a kind," Quinn told him. "You were instantly recognisable in Ballyfoil."

For a moment the murky, sunken eyes looked almost puzzled. "Ballyfoil? Don't think I've ever been there."

"No? Must've been your twin brother then."

A diluted smile flickered across his face. He glanced at his sister to share it. "Yeah, must've been."

The woman beside Cooney was not yet middle-aged, yet somehow far from the springtime of life. She had her brother's pallid complexion, no attempt at makeup, and dark, straggling hair that hung lankly on the collar of a wrinkled denim jacket. Abruptly she grasped her glass of red wine and said to Gillian with a sly grin, "Are you sittin' down?"

"I don't think so," Gillian said, shifting the direction of the Walther towards her. "This isn't exactly a social call."

"You'll be leaving soon then," Cooney said.

Quinn looked from brother to sister.

"We'll be leaving together," he told them.

Sensing the imminence of the moment of crisis, Quinn was filled with a grim foreboding. Glancing at Gillian he recognised the charged tension in her stance, the determination in her unblinking eyes. He took a deep breath.

"Look, Cooney, I have a question that needs to get a straight answer. The right answer might improve your chances of not spending the rest of your life in prison. You follow?"

John Cooney tilted his head slightly to the side, his expression sardonic, his face hardening like molten wax on a death mask.

"What have you done with Arthur Williams?" Quinn said. "Where is he?"

Cooney straightened up marginally in his chair.

"The journalist?" He looked genuinely surprised. "You think I took him?"

"You were out to get the informer, to exact your revenge," Gillian stated bluntly. "Williams was the one who knew, who could lead you to him."

Cooney laughed, a dry artificial guffaw. "Jesus, you got that wrong. We didn't need Williams. Mickey McCann already suspected who it was. He just had to get the proof. And he got it. He told me."

It was a second or two before he realised he had said too much.

"At Daisy Hill, in the hospital," Quinn continued, "where you murdered a policeman – Jack Callen, a married man with two young children."

"I don't know anything about Williams," Cooney countered. "He was never on our agenda."

Christ almighty, Quinn thought, he thinks this is some sort of homicidal board meeting. He took a step forward to charge him, rehearsing the words swiftly in his head: 'John Cooney, I'm arresting you for….' In the same second, as if from the bowels of the restaurant, a waiter suddenly materialised at his elbow, oblivious to the woman beside Quinn holding a gun.

"Are you joining this table, sir?"

The moment's distraction was enough. Cooney shoved the table forward, upending it, slamming it against Quinn, knocking him off balance. At the same time as he was falling backwards Quinn heard a shot, glimpsed John Cooney rising with an automatic pistol, heard a second shot before he cracked his skull on the iron radiator by the window and the light in his head went out momentarily until he felt rather than saw Kathleen Farrell rush past him and he tried desperately to get up but slipped down, down and away once more into the void.

* * *

When he surfaced again, Quinn found himself looking up into the frantic, furrowed face of Tom Madigan.

"Jesus Christ, Quinn, what happened?"

"Cooney and his sister… surprised us… where are they?"

"We've got the sister. The bouncer here managed to stop her. But Cooney's on the run."

"How long have I been out?"

"We got here just a few minutes after it happened," Madigan said, pulling up his jacket sleeve to look at a charcoal-black, military wristwatch. "That was five minutes ago."

Quinn groaned and endeavoured to sit up.

"Where's Sergeant Rice?" he said, fingering the back of his head, feeling the dewy stickiness of the seeping blood. "Where's Gillian?"

"She's lying on a bench at the front, in the pub. We're waiting for the ambulance from Bangor Hospital."

"Ambulance? What happened?"

"She's been shot. Said she hit him first. In the shoulder, she thinks. The waiter said she tried to get up, to go after them but … collapsed."

"Shot? Where?" Quinn was sitting up now.

"In the neck. There's a nurse with her – one of the customers. She's looking after her. Lotta blood."

"That fucker Cooney. Where'd he go?"

"He's out there somewhere. There's a local peeler outside organising a search with my two men."

"Let's get out of here," Quinn said, rolling over onto one knee and struggling to his feet. The burning pain in his head soared skyward with his upward progression, a white-hot flame from a cranial blowtorch that scorched him with every movement.

They walked through the empty restaurant to the pub, Quinn swaying to and fro on groggy legs. Kathleen Farrell stood handcuffed to a vertical wooden post that supported a timbered beam in the ceiling. She glared at Quinn but said nothing. Beside her on a bar stool sat a man in his mid-twenties. Under a close-cropped head he had the brawny hunched shoulders of a wrestler or a front-row forward from the local rugby club. Quinn deduced he was the bouncer.

Along the wainscot panelling in the snug ran a cushioned bench upon which lay the prone form of Gillian Rice. Quinn stopped short beside her.

"How is she?" he asked, bending over the woman sitting with a bar towel clutched to Gillian's neck. The nurse looked up at Quinn, perching her head at an angle, her slightly bulging eyes peering at him from behind brown-rimmed glasses.

"Not good," she said, a whiff of juniper wafting up towards him from crimson lips and rosy cheeks. "She's bleeding a lot." She nodded at several bloodied bar towels lying in an enamel basin on the tiled floor and added despairingly, "Where's the ambulance?"

Gillian seemed to be semi-conscious, drooling a little from the mouth, eyes half-closed. The towel at the front and left side of her neck was saturated with blood. More blood had pooled on the cushion beside her head.

"For God's sake, get me more towels," the nurse called out. A barmaid ducked under the bar top. The bouncer darted into a doorway behind the bar.

"Hang on, Gill," Quinn whispered before he hurried out of the snug, through the lobby and into the street with Madigan trotting behind him. As he emerged, a uniformed policeman climbed out of a squad car parked at the kerb.

"Where the fuck's the ambulance?" Quinn yelled.

The constable walked swiftly over to Quinn. He was a gawky six-footer in his thirties with bat-wing ears protruding from behind the shiny peak of his cap. "I've just spoken to them," he said. "They'll be here any minute."

"Where are your two men?" Quinn asked Tom Madigan. "I've been inside," Madigan said, "with you and Gillian." He turned to the constable for an explanation.

"They went up Moat Street," he said. "I've been on the phone getting the ambulance. There's been a serious road accident on the High Bangor Road. They've been busy with that. I couldn't get through at first."

The sporadic early-evening traffic was making its way home, a detritus of customers and pedestrians stood around the entrance to Grace Neill's Bar and Quinn felt a pulsating wave of desperation sweep over him at the thought of Cooney escaping, the distance between them increasing with every second that ticked by.

"Did anyone see which way he went?"

"I didn't get here until afterwards and I haven't had a chance to ask," the constable said, his face melting into defence and apology. "I've been busy with the hospital."

Quinn looked around in anguish. Cooney was further away with every second that passed. And he had been so close to nailing him. So close. But someone must have seen him run out, gun in hand. Someone must have.

Quinn walked over to the small group of people gathered round the pub entrance. He almost bumped into a man moving through the crowd with a Styrofoam cup in his hand, a bobble hat on his head. Quinn seized him by the arm.

"Did you see the man who ran out of the pub?"

The beggar just looked at him vacantly.

"He was wearing a donkey jacket, dark blue, probably had a gun in his hand."

The beggar held the cup a little higher in front of him. Quinn dug in his trouser pocket, fished out a couple of one-pound coins and tossed them in the mug. The man's face lit up like a Christmas tree.

"He took off up the street here, towards Millisle Road," he confided and paused, a revelatory gleam entering his eyes. "But I seen him turn left into Manor Street."

"You're sure?" Quinn said.

"Dead certain," the man confirmed.

Quinn ran to the squad car, calling to Madigan and the constable to get in. The constable got in the driving seat with Quinn beside him and Madigan in the back.

"He's gone up Manor Street," Quinn told the constable.

"Manor Street?" said the constable. "But that only leads to the harbour. It's a dead end. Unless he turns left and cuts back onto the Parade. How well does he know the town?"

"We don't know," Madigan said. He turned to Quinn. "Do we?"

"No. But if we're lucky, he hasn't a fuckin' clue where he is."

As they swung left into Manor Street Quinn told the constable to stop the car.

"The sergeant and I'll get out and walk. You take the right-hand side, Tom, and I'll take the left. Don't put the beacon on. Just cruise along beside us. Easy does it."

Just before he closed the car door Quinn leant in and said, "Get your revolver out, constable. Have it at the ready. This fellah kills coppers."

Manor Street stretches through the old quarter of the town towards the harbour, a narrow thoroughfare lined with rows of small, unassuming, one- and two-storeyed houses built around the middle of the nineteenth century. Eyes darting left and right, hardened in concentration,

Quinn and Madigan followed the pavements on either side of the street. It was a one-way system and the squad car was driving in the wrong direction; but there was no traffic.

They walked with careful, calculated steps, neither fast nor slow, past cars parked on both sides. Widely spaced, the Victorian lampposts provided intermittent pools of light. Quinn stopped for a moment to scour the street ahead; it seemed to be deserted. He moved on, making his way with caution from one amber island of light to the next. It was colder now, with the dampness of December in the sea air. Their breath clouded up before them. They walked as far as the Tivoli Bar on the corner of a crossroads.

They met no one.

Madigan crossed the street and he and Quinn went quickly through the pub. It was the twilight hour, between six and seven. The pub had two customers. People were at home, having their tea. They checked the toilets, one at a time. When they came out, the squad car had moved on up Manor Street.

"What the hell's he doing?" Quinn said. "I told him to take it easy."

"Which way?" Madigan asked, gesturing with a thumb at the crossroads.

Quinn looked up Bow Street to the left, then Meeting House Street to the right. If he knew the town, Cooney would go left here, back to New Street and the road to Belfast. Quinn prayed for intuition, a hunch, a gut feeling. The wind gusted and he smelt the salt tang of the sea ahead.

"Let's keep straight on," he said.

Madigan was about to cross back onto the right-hand side of Manor Street when his phone emitted a muted, buzzing tone. He answered it, all the while looking at

Quinn, standing under the streetlamp at the crossroads, attending the one-way dialogue.

"No luck on Moat Street?

"We went the other way – got a tip.

"We're in Manor Street.

"Go up High Street and take the first left.

"Has the ambulance come?"

There was a longer pause before Madigan spoke again. "Gone? Whaddya mean?"

He was silent then, listening intently, clenching his free hand into a fist. Quinn could hear the blur of words, saw Madigan's face change, transform into a dark mask he couldn't read.

"What is it?" Quinn asked. "What's happened?"

Madigan stuffed the phone back in his pocket before he replied. "Gillian's dead," he said.

THIRTY-ONE

"She had no pulse when they took her out of the pub," Tom Madigan panted as they jogged after the squad car down Manor Street towards the harbour. "There was a doctor in the ambulance. He said the bullet must have hit the jugular – the external jugular, he called it. You only last five to ten minutes after that. The nurse in the pub did what she could, but …."

Quinn trod forward saying nothing. He was moving in total darkness. A blackness enveloped him. He had failed her. The realisation appalled him. For pity's sake, there in the restaurant, he hadn't even drawn his gun. Sorrow surged through him like a massive tidal wave, enfeebling him, flooding him with a frightening sense of insecurity and dismay. He saw again her pale shorn head on the bench, the pool of blood beside it, and he was overcome with the weary futility of defeat. It was insufferable.

The brake lights of the police car up ahead flashed red and it came to a halt, snapping him into the immediacy of the moment. As the red spots dimmed to black he pictured the merciless look in Cooney's eyes as he shot Gillian Rice in the neck. The awful truth that he had lost the encounter with Cooney in the worst possible way, that he had lost Gillian, filled him with a searing, agonising pain for which, he knew, there was no antidote. Yet at the same time he realised that it was only a defeat if he allowed it, if he accepted it, if he let it win. She must not have died in vain. She must not. He said it to himself with every step he took.

He pictured Gillian in his mind's eye, he saw her as she was, and he knew with a terrible clarity what she had been for him, and what he had been for her. In an instant he was filled with the sense of his own identity, his living being, driving him on. As he quickened his pace down the street, he could feel the fury suppurating within him, swelling up in his breast, bursting in his head like a septic boil.

The squad car abruptly took off with the urgent squeal of rubber on asphalt, accelerating down Manor Street towards an SUV parked near the end of the street. Quinn and Madigan exchanged glances.

"What the fuck?" Tom Madigan exclaimed.

The squad car had closed the gap to fifty yards when a sharp rat-a-tat-tat burst of gunfire erupted between the whitewashed houses, four, five shots in rapid succession. In the squad car headlights Quinn caught sight of a figure leaning across the bonnet of the SUV. A second later the squad car slewed to one side, skidded up onto the pavement and crunched into a lamppost. When Quinn looked up the street again the figure had disappeared. He and Madigan raced to the crash.

The upper part of the windscreen was shattered. Quinn counted three bullet holes across the laminated glass; two were high, one was slightly lower. The driver's side window was also smashed, broken into a row of jagged shards. They pulled the constable out. Most of his left ear was missing. His forehead and cheeks showed traces of glass splinters. Blood was trickling from his left eye.

"I can't see," he gabbled, the shock making his voice harsh and rasping. "He was trying to break into the SUV. I had to stop him."

"You did that," Quinn told him gruffly. "You stopped him. Get an ambulance here," he rapped to Madigan.

They sat him on the edge of the pavement. Madigan used his phone, his tone hoarse with urgency. Quinn fetched the first aid kit from the car, thinking how lucky the man was that Murphy had aimed a little high, or that his sights were ill adjusted. "Look after him," he called as he climbed into the car, fired the engine and reversed back into the street, bodywork metal screeching against the asphalt.

"What the hell are you doing?" Madigan cried. "Wait for backup! They'll be here any minute."

But Quinn was already in second gear, the rev counter spinning up to the red band on the dial, the front bumper hanging loose and scraping up a spray of sparks as he tramped the accelerator to the floor. He eased off only when he got to the seafront. A woman with a dog was standing still on the Parade staring towards the pier. He braked abruptly beside her and called through the shattered window, "Man on the run?"

The young woman pulled her long sheepskin jacket closer to her and inspected him and the police car. The dog, a black-and-tan cocker spaniel, trotted forward to sniff the front tyre.

"He was running towards the market," the woman said a little uncertainly.

"Market?"

"The Christmas market. On the pier. Santa's arriving on the lifeboat."

"What?"

"We have it every year."

"Jesus."

She glanced at the buckled bonnet. "I think he had a gun," she said, as if she realised there might be a connection. Quinn shoved the gear stick forward and released the clutch too quickly. The engine stalled. He cursed and swivelled the ignition key. The car shot forward and he drove steadily in third gear to the end of the Parade, scanning the promenade as he went.

Outside the lifeboat station he spotted a space and parked. He pushed himself out and moved swiftly toward the shanty town of market stalls that filled the start of the pier and spread out along the quayside. A large group of parents and children thronged round an elongated stall that offered 'Lantern Making'. Opposite was an equally popular stall with an illuminated sign that said: Santa's Grotto.

At once Quinn understood why there had been so few people in the High Street. Other stalls lit with fairy lights were selling mince pies, mulled wine, wax candles, roasted nuts, toys, jewellery, hot chocolate, Christmas cards and gifts. Seasonal music was being piped through a series of stall-linked loudspeakers.

Hand clutching the Walther in his jacket pocket, Quinn made his way through the crowd, past the assembled stalls of gifts and goodies, the palpitating ache in his head resounding like a Lambeg drum. At one point he caught sight of a close-cropped female head bobbing in front of him and he thought with a sinking feeling of Gillian: she should have been here now. She would have wanted nothing else, would have accepted nothing else. He paused on the pale limestone surface of the quayside and looked at the flight of steps leading down to the Donaghadee lifeboat. There was no sign of Santa. Nor of John Cooney. Perhaps they'd both been and gone.

Quinn knew he was following a gut feeling: his investigative intuition. But who can divine the machinations of a murderous mind? He was aware that Cooney could have turned right at the harbour office, just before the pier, followed the coastal path down to Commons Park and then, soon, he would be on his way out of town, south to Millisle. But Quinn was banking on him not knowing the layout of the town, being drawn to the festive commotion generated by the local townspeople and deciding to lose himself in the bustle and confusion of the Christmas market on the pier. Also, if indeed Gillian had hit him, he was wounded and probably not thinking too straight. That would also affect his judgement. Quinn pressed on.

About half-way along the pier the Christmas stalls

suddenly petered out. The last stall was placed close to the high rampart that formed the pier's seaward wall. The sodium lamps normally in use along the pier had not been switched on in order to enhance the Christmas atmosphere generated by the garlands of fairy lights around and between the stalls. Except for the white light flashing twenty yards up in the lighthouse lantern, the final stretch of the pier out to the tapering cylindrical tower of the lighthouse was in darkness.

The young man attending the stall had just sold a box of Christmas crackers and a roll of wrapping paper to an elderly couple. As they moved off, Quinn caught his eye.

"Anyone gone past here – towards the lighthouse?"

The man turned his head and looked towards the silhouette on the circular bastion at the end of the pier.

"Yeah, there was a fellah, about five minutes ago. He'd had a few. I reckoned he was just going for a slash."

"He'd had a few?"

"Yeah. He was, like, stumblin' a bit, y'know, as if he'd had one too many. "

"Did he come back?"

"Naw, not that I saw."

"No?"

"Don't think so. Hard to say though. I've been busy with customers."

Quinn stepped warily out beyond the glow of the market illuminations, moving along the pier from the shelter of one stone capstan to the next until he reached the darker shadows offered by a small mobile crane. He hunkered down behind an iron stanchion and peered out towards the lighthouse, trying to focus on any sign of movement, any odd detail in the area ahead. Nothing.

A stepped stone wall ran along the top of the seaward rampart, sheltering the pier and the inner harbour. Some thirty yards from where he crouched, Quinn spotted a fixed iron ladder set in the limestone wall. It led up to a modern look-out post built up on the rampart. A position there would give him height and perspective.

As he set off again he tripped on the rings of a boat chain and almost fell. Recovering his balance he darted to the nearest capstan and knelt down. He felt the smooth, grainy texture of the limestone under his fingers. His breath was coming fast and even. He smelt the tarred fibre of shipping rope round the capstan. He could feel his heart beating with the rising tempo of his fear. He listened.

Behind him he could hear a distant choir singing a Christmas carol. Good tidings we bring, to you and your king. Somewhere ahead of him, quite abruptly, he thought he heard the sound of running feet. When he looked over the capstan he saw a shadowy movement down near the lighthouse. He blinked furiously and looked again but the murky shape had disappeared and he began to wonder if it had ever been there at all.

The ladder was now just ten yards away. Quinn extracted the Walther from his jacket, bent over from the waist up and scuffled swiftly over to the limestone steps. There were three of them up to the bottom of the ladder, each one some eighteen inches high. Quinn used his left hand to steady himself as he climbed. He had just reached up and grasped the ladder when the stone above him splintered and he heard the first shot. He felt the chips flake onto his head like plaster from an unseen ceiling.

The shock made him clutch wildly at the side-rail, losing his grip on the Walther, feeling it slip out of his right hand. It recoiled off the steps and clattered onto the ground below. His immediate instinct was to drop back down for the gun and flatten himself on the ground, but his body was already moving in an upward trajectory and he continued pulling himself frenetically from rung to rung until he clambered onto the level top of the wall just as a second shot echoed round the harbour and he felt something rip through his leg.

Dragging himself onto the rock-paved downward slope of the seaward rampart he lay still to examine the wound, only to discover that the bullet had passed through his trouser leg leaving a two-inch, burn-like furrow across the calf. Blood was oozing from the middle of the gash. He ignored it and rolled further down the slope towards the sea until he felt safe enough to rise to his feet.

He stood for a moment deciding what to do and cursing himself for dropping the Walther. His headache was like the worst hangover. As he set off again towards the lighthouse, scurrying along half-way down the rampart slope, he fought against his exploding, convulsing anger, telling himself to stay calm, to keep control. The words of the SAS instructor rang in his ears: 'Lose an arm, lose a leg, but never lose your head.'

Quinn recalled the direction of the pier, how it veered to the left just before the final stretch to the lighthouse and the harbour entrance. As he approached the turn on the rampart slope he saw the top of a ladder, identical to the one he had almost died on, leading back down to the pier. He stopped and stood still. The lantern high in the lighthouse was revolving like a wheel, the light flashing every so often as it came round, as if challenging the darkness. He counted the seconds.

Without his gun he no longer had the advantage afforded by the superior height of the rampart wall. As he considered his options, he made two assumptions: Cooney had seen him climb up onto the top of the rampart and would be expecting him to attack from the higher position of the rampart wall; and Cooney wouldn't know for sure that he no longer had a firearm. At the same time he realised he would need a close physical proximity to Cooney if he was to have any chance of taking him down.

With this in mind Quinn decided to drop down again onto the pier, using the ladder he saw ahead.

Edging his way on all fours up to the top of the wall he dislodged a couple of flat stones, pieces of the original harbour rock that had been used to build the rampart.

He slipped them into his empty jacket pocket and inched up to the brow of the slope. With the lighthouse lantern high above flashing every four seconds, he peeked over when the light was extinguished. In those few seconds he could make out a dark figure crouching in the shadows just to the left of the black-based plinth, so as to place the tower between him and the end of the rampart where he would expect Quinn to attack. Beside him was a spiked railing that ran shoulder-high in a circle round the lighthouse to restrain eventual intruders.

Quinn drew back from the brink, took out the smaller of the flat stones and threw it baseball-style to the end of the rampart just before the lantern flashed. It landed simultaneously with the flash. There was a twofold petrifying clatter. Quinn raised his head and watched as the murky figure disappeared behind the plinth. Instantly he slipped over the edge and down the ladder and steps, praying that Cooney's attention was now totally focussed on the location of the fallen stone. A couple of yards from where he landed, a large black rubbish bin was conveniently positioned between him and the lighthouse plinth. He sneaked in behind it and risked a peep.

Cooney was nowhere to be seen. He must have moved round the lighthouse to cover the end of the rampart. Abruptly a shadow moved out from the side of the plinth and its circular railing. Quinn ducked down and held his breath.

The sounds of the Christmas market seemed to have died. Quinn heard only the sea lapping insistently against the quayside, realising he was now close to the choppy swell at the mouth of the harbour. Slowly, carefully, he rolled up the trouser on his uninjured leg and unstrapped the Glock field knife with its six-inch, spring-steel blade from its sheath. Much nearer the lighthouse, by the quayside, was another stone capstan. He knew he had to make it that far to have a chance with the throw. It was the distance he needed. Christ, it was weeks since he had last practised. He heard again the words of his instructor: 'Don't clutch the blade. It has to slip easily from your fingers. The release has to be perfect. You have to know the line-up and when to let go.'

He took three deep breaths, as he'd been taught. He placed the knife on the ground and took the second flat stone from his pocket. Keeping low behind the capstan he swung his arm back, tensed and straight, and lobbed the stone high into the air across the quay to the end of the rampart. At the sound of it clattering down the slope, he picked up the Glock and rose to his feet. He saw no one. He sprinted towards the lighthouse. As he reached the capstan Cooney ran out from behind the plinth, round the circular railing, gun in hand, swinging to focus on Quinn as he came to a stop at the capstan.

Quinn stretched out his left arm, pointing it at Cooney, and spun sideways to raise and swing his right arm forward in a smooth arc releasing the knife in a flowing motion while Cooney snapped off a shot before the firing-pin mechanism jammed beyond recall and he stood yanking viciously, futilely on the trigger. With a sound like a short, indrawn sigh Cooney tottered back against the railing, blood seeping then spurting from the knife in his throat, and Quinn sprang forward with a roar, clamped Cooney's head vice-like in his hands and drove the back of his neck onto the top of the spiked railing behind. There was a bursting, crunching noise and John Cooney's black eyes bulged out to stare sightlessly up at the winter sky in a world that was no more. And as Quinn glared at him, savouring the requited bloodlust that pulsed through his being, he realised that his therapeutic sessions with Dr Musgrave had only been helpful up to a point.

THIRTY-TWO

Des parked the Ford Transit van down at the bottom of the drive and looked up at the elegant white house nestling in early summer sunshine just below the brow of the hill. Under a long, low roofline the wide overhanging eaves were supported by a pair of marmoreal pillars framing the double-doored grand entrance. Flanked with shutters, large panorama windows looked out over a recently manicured lawn that swept down towards the sea.

"He's had the gardener in," Des told them.

The man beside him grunted and gazed out the window. Flaring and crusted, his face was a relief map of pitted acne sores, in the middle of which a fleshy nose jutted out as if in flight from the encircling skin condition. A mantle of woolly grey hair drooped over his forehead like a knitted beanie cap without a peak.

"He's onto a good thing here, that's for sure," he said, nodding towards the property. Des shot him an irritated glance, but said nothing.

"It's not just about the money."

The woman in the back seat leant forward to press her point. The paleness of her thin face was accentuated by dark wiry hair cut short, lending her a gaunt, mannish appearance. "I think he's in love with her."

"In love with her money, y'mean." The man sniggered. "She's a rich woman. Get real, Bren, that's what this is all about."

He scratched a match, lit a cigarette and rolled down the window. The warm humid smell of freshly mown grass wafted into the van to mingle with the smoke.

"You haven't seen the way he looks at her," she said.

"That's called lust, Brenda. Lust." He laughed again, a throaty, gurgling noise that soon expired.

"For Christ's sake, Bobby, you must be blind. He's absolutely obsessed with her. Why else would he get us to do the things we've done? I never thought he would go that far. Never."

Abruptly Bobby spun round and told his sister to shut the fuck up. They sat in silence for a minute until Bobby turned to the driver. "You been here before, Des?"

Des glanced at him as if he smelt of vomit.

"No," he said, tapping his fingers lightly on the steering wheel.

"What is this place anyway?"

"It's where they're going to live."

"It's all been decided then?"

"Far as I know."

"So, what exactly are we doing here?"

"He'll tell us when he gets here."

"And when's that?"

Des consulted a chronograph pilot watch lashed round his wrist with a cracked leather strap. The morning had almost gone.

"Ten minutes ago," he said.

"He's always fuckin' late," Bobby said.

They sat in silence for another five minutes before the silver grey Jaguar coupé coasted past and parked twenty yards in front of them in the driveway.

"She's with him," Brenda said, uneasily.

Des turned to look at her. "So what?"

"Does she know anything?"

"She doesn't know shit."

"Are you sure?"

"Sure as hell I'm sure."

Brenda was dubious. She frowned as she thought about it. "Sometimes I think she knows, but pretends not to know."

"That's the opposite of you then," Bobby said.

"What?"

"You pretend to know but the fact is, you don't know a fuckin' thing."

The couple seemed in no hurry to get out of the car. When they eventually emerged, Bobby heard snatches of their conversation through the open window as they walked slowly towards the van: 'court order', 'death certificate', 'probate'. The woman appeared to be somewhat agitated; the man was doing his best to exert a calming influence.

Des climbed down from the van and went to meet them. "You remember Mrs Williams," the man said.

"Sure," Des said. "Hello."

"Hello," Linda Williams said, eying him through metal-rimmed aviator sunglasses. She was wearing a pair of tight-fitting sequinned pants under an avocado-green sweater. "I just need help moving some pieces of furniture out of the house."

Oversized hoop earrings dangled brightly in the sun as she spoke, swinging in time to the movement of her jaws.

"They'll be going up for auction," the man told him. "You can store them in the warehouse in the meantime."

"Right," Des said.

"Don't put them in that corner where the roof's leaking."

"Right," Des echoed.

"We'll just go up to the house and I'll tell you which pieces have to go," Linda said and turned to the man beside her with a sedulous smile.

"Have you got the key, George?"

"In my hand."

George Martin showed her the leather pouch, took her by the arm and started walking up the scimitar curve of the driveway to the pillared entrance of the house on the hill.

THIRTY-THREE

Quinn's Notebook, 3rd May 2000

I suppose I feel a sort of confessional need to be finally opening the notebook to write something after all this time, and after what has happened. Although it's probably because of what has happened that it has taken so long. Or perhaps, by putting pen to paper, I just want to express a wish for some kind of atonement. I don't know. Probably it's a bit of both. It does help, though, to put your thoughts down on paper, to try and crystallise your feelings in words, come to terms with them. Dr Benjamin Musgrave was right about that.

It's taken me a long time to get over the shock of what happened to Gillian, to finally accept it. In fact, I don't think I'm quite there yet. I still torment myself with the whiplash of 'what if?' As in: What if I had pulled out my own gun as soon as I saw Cooney sitting there in the alcove at Grace Neill's?

What if I hadn't relied on Gillian's drawn weapon to give us the upper hand? What if I hadn't been momentarily distracted by the arrival of the waiter? What if? What if? What if? Blame and guilt sit like squatters on my heart.

Joe Stewart says it's a complete waste of energy to have regrets, to dwell on the past in that way, and he's probably right about that.

You should never look back, he says; and that's how he lives his life, a man who's always working on plans for the future. But I've asked myself these questions countless times, ransacking my brain over and over again in an effort to find even the semblance of an answer. But there is no answer to such agonising hypotheses. They just eat your heart out.

There is no closure.

Of course the most important and incredible thing that happened after Gillian was shot and we got the message that she didn't make it was when I was walking back alone from the lighthouse to the Christmas market, leaving Cooney hanging there on the railing, and my phone rang, which made me angry with myself because I realised it had been on the whole time I'd been chasing Cooney along the pier and suppose it had started ringing when I was about to rush him or even earlier. At any rate I was in a daze after what I'd done and it took me a minute or two to get the phone out and it's Tom Madigan saying that he's on the pier now coming towards me and then suddenly he's there in front of me asking where's Cooney and what's happened to him. So I tell him and he grabs me and says that's great Quinn you got the bastard but I have even better news and I get a shock when he tells me Gillian is still alive, that they were able to revive her in the ambulance with a defibrillator and they could give her a lot of O-negative blood they didn't need for that traffic accident on the High Bangor Road, and the artery that was damaged wasn't the jugular but some smaller one, the vertebral I think he said, though it bled a hell of a lot too but she's alive, Quinn, she's alive!

When Tom told me this, it was a beautiful bolt from the blue that immediately propelled me out of the mental stupor I was in after what I'd just been through. The bombshell came the next day when we found out that Gillian had lapsed into a coma as a result of her injuries. The artery shattered by Cooney's bullet was one of several that supply blood to the brain and the damage done had rendered her comatose. And so she lies in a special ward at the Royal Victoria Hospital in west Belfast. For how long? They can't say. Or won't. They test her responsiveness every day. They check her for eye, motor and verbal responses. They say she can definitely get better, and then – when I push them – they disclose reluctantly that she can possibly get worse. In other words, her future is totally unpredictable. I wish, more than anything I've ever wished for before, that she would wake up again.

I only knew Gillian for a couple of days, so I didn't really know her at all, not really. But I think about her a lot. I'm up there at the Royal most days to see her, to see if there's any change. I've met her parents a few times in the ward. They wonder about me, I think, why I visit her so much. Do they see the guilt in my face? I make polite conversation and pretend I'm just a respectful colleague. Which, of course, I am, too.

Mostly, though, I'm sitting up there on my own, watching her, telling her occasionally about the day outside, the leaves coming green on the trees, the peonies blooming pink in the park, the sun a yellow rose in a bed of white clouds in the sky. I get carried away with the words, hoping a miracle will happen and she'll say something back.

I liked the sound of her voice, the way she rolled the words out, sharp and bright. You knew where you stood with her. And sometimes when I'm at home in the flat, my 'studio apartment', I see her in my mind's eye, sitting beside me in the Shogun, ordering French food in the restaurant, walking in front of me down the street with that jaunty little lilt to her step.

What makes it worse is that I now realise I was probably a bit sweet on her. Perhaps more than a little. She had this playful way of looking at me; you could see it in her eyes. And I admired, and eventually respected, her practical, no-nonsense attitude to us working together. As I got to know her, I came to see Gillian as a strong woman with an independent spirit. But she was still vulnerable, and I sensed that and wanted to do everything to protect her. And she made me feel, at times, that she would let me do that, that she would give me that trust. Jesus Christ, it makes me tear up even now, after all these months, just thinking about it. Sometimes I wonder what would happen if she were ever to wake up again. I imagine us talking together again. I even dream about it.

* * *

I had a meeting with Joe Stewart in his office last week. It took some time to work out a scheme to get George Martin off the hook on that bribery charge. CI Hall had managed to put the whole affair on hold for a couple of months, intimating one or two possible ways of resolving the situation – red herrings really, but they succeeded in keeping the whole sorry business under wraps. Now, finally, it seems that the top-ranking civil servant Martin attempted to bribe has been persuaded to drop proceedings with the promise of an MBE in the Queen's honours list. Nothing is in writing, of course – it never is in this game – but that's the way the greasy wheels of politics turn.

It also turns out that Joe is doing the legal groundwork on setting up a new property development scheme with two main investors. One of them is, surprisingly, the same George Martin who fed us Cooney. He appears to be in funds again though no one seems to quite know the source of his income. The other major investor is Simon Vega, Renée's little-loved father and a dark horse if ever there was one.

And, speaking of dark horses, Renée Vega is back in Belfast. Out of the blue she rang me the other day with the news. When I heard her voice I realised that it just wasn't there any more. It wasn't so much what she said, more something in the way she said it. What is it they say in the song – the magic has gone? It made me feel a bit sad in a way, but if I'm honest with myself, I mostly felt relieved.

The Spanish job didn't work out as she had hoped – she declined to go into detail – and she had decided to take on a new challenge. Apparently her father has opened an office here and given her a job – something to do with business information technology, whatever that is. She must have swallowed her pride to go to work for him after all she told me about their father-daughter relationship. I also suspect she was interested in rekindling old flames, but I put her off, said I was seeing someone.

And, in a special way, I am.

* * *

The whereabouts of Arthur Williams and what happened to him is still a mystery, and it grieves me that I haven't been able to get to the bottom of it. We found no forensic evidence in the pigsty or in the other farm buildings that he had ever been there. He was a good man and the truly good people I have met in the course of my work, or of my life, you can count on the fingers of one hand. His courage and integrity were unmistakeable, even to me.

That night in Donaghadee, last December, we drove back to the house on New Road and went through every room, every cupboard, every nook and cranny with the finest of fine-tooth combs. In my haste, in the half-light of the upstairs corridor, I had missed the access hatch to an attic. As we pulled down the folding ladder, we found ourselves suddenly and desperately hoping for a breakthrough. But it only took a minute groping around up there in the dust and grime to realise we had once again drawn a complete blank. Much of the garden was also dug up during the following days – with the same result.

It's a strange thing, but – despite all the setbacks, all the dead-ends – I've never completely given up hope on solving the mystery of what really happened to Arthur Williams, and of finding him. And since hope is a feeling that always seems to apply to the future, I sometimes think the answer may be just around the corner.

I ran into Arthur Williams' brother yesterday. It was in the late afternoon and I'd just had a beer with Tom Madigan at the Duke of York in Commercial Court. We were on our way out and Doug Williams was on his way in. He recognised me and – surprisingly, after our previous encounter – he stopped.

By the look of him, flabby features and blowzy complexion, he hadn't reduced his alcohol intake. Sometimes it's hard to keep an open mind about people. He appeared to hesitate, then gather himself before he decided to speak.

"So, my brother seems to have joined the ranks of the Disappeared."

"Looks that way," I said, somewhat on my guard.

He fired a sideways glance at Tom as if making up his mind whether to say anything more.

"You didn't follow my advice then," he said at last.

"What advice?"

"*Cherchez la femme*," he said with a half-smile. His French pronunciation sounded pretty good. With a sudden lurch I thought of Gillian. When I didn't respond, he amplified: "The lovely Linda, Mrs Williams, the multi-millionairess."

"Right," I said, moving away. "I'll bear it in mind."

At the time I didn't place too much importance on what he said, not yesterday afternoon and not last December. But the more I've thought about it since last night, the more it's aroused my interest. There was something going on there in that house, something that I sensed at the time but couldn't quite put my finger on. The boy – what was his name? Max – he said there was some guy always ringing up. He rang up when I was there. The boy didn't know who he was, but he thought it was weird. He seemed to suspect something. I guessed it was probably just another admirer – Linda Williams is an attractive woman – but you never know. There might be more to it than that. I'll look her up tomorrow, see what the situation is with her and the boy, maybe go out and see them again. I think it's worth following up. I've tried everything else.

I know – if I could only find out what actually happened to Arthur Williams – I know it would help me come to terms with Gillian's situation, to feel that she hasn't suffered for nothing. And I promised the boy I'd find his dad. I promised him that. Maybe it isn't too late. Which reminds me of something Dr Musgrave once said to me, something that has stayed with me since his death: 'It's never too late to be what you might have been'. I want to believe that.

About the author

Born and bred in Belfast, John McClintock worked for a short time as security guard at the Bank of England in London before becoming a teacher. He has taught English and German in Belfast as well as in England, Germany and Sweden. He suspects there must be a 'police gene' in his family. His father and grandfather were both in the force, and his son is also a policeman. A prolific writer of English schoolbooks, he now lives in Ystad, Sweden. *Finding Arthur* is his first crime novel.